MW01378529

Notorious

Notorious

James Wassick

Library of Congress Control Number:		2009914285
ISBN:	Hardcover	978-1-4500-2333-7
	Softcover	978-1-4500-2332-0

This is a work of fiction. Names, characters, places and incidents either are the product of the author's imagination or are used fictitiously, and any resemblance to any actual persons, living or dead, events, or locales is entirely coincidental.

This book was printed in the United States of America.

To order additional copies of this book, contact:
Xlibris Corporation
1-888-795-4274
www.Xlibris.com
Orders@Xlibris.com
69438

For Betty Wassick and Gloria Osbrey, two extraordinary women that are truly inspirational.

A special thanks to:

Tom Hyman, Dr. Robert Briston, Michael Mirolla, and John Gannon.

Also the XLIBRIS team which includes: Janine Kramer, Claire Miranda, Richard Peralta, Roy De La Cruz, Charliz Elle, Kathee Sanchez and Carolyn Gambito.

CONTENTS

PART III

PROLOGUE

A HERO'S WELCOME

May 1713, London, England

Jack McGinnty jumped off the ship and landed hard on the wharf, legs rubbery as a result of two months at sea. The stink of fish, tar, and dirty water filled the air; and the Thames River smelled like dockside. But it was the noise of the crowd that greeted McGinnty and his men that took them by surprise. It was deafening. Well-wishers screamed their approval. Peddlers looked to sell their goods; drums were struck outside alehouses to attract business.

Rumors swirled throughout London as to how much wealth McGinnty accumulated, and as a result, he and his crew were afforded a hero's welcome as they arrived. His men filtered into the streets to spend money. A woman grabbed one of the men and threw her arms around him, her left breast exposed. He returned her affections with a long embrace, hands clasped around her buttocks.

McGinnty shook his head and lurched from the wharf onto the street in a trancelike state. He was a tall, well-built gentleman, but the last few years at sea had taken a toll on his once-striking good looks. His previous smooth tanned skin was now leathery. His thick coarse brown hair acquired small streaks of gray down the sides. His eyes were drawn, the result of sleepless nights.

A large rat whisked across his path, but he hardly noticed it. Thoughts weighed on his mind of his latest mission, extracting plunder from enemy ships. And extract it he did. Eight years as a privateer captain had netted him vast amounts of gold, silver, silks, rum, and plunder, but nothing compared to this. His latest haul was the achievement of a lifetime, yet his mind could not escape the lives lost to obtain it.

Wheels rumbling on the cobblestone interrupted his daydream. McGinnty jumped out of the way of a wagon carting wool. He looked around as dockers yelled, ships and cranes creaked, rigging flapped. The city was alive with a vibration of five hundred thousand people. The war against France and Spain had just ended, and people celebrated. Beggars pawed at him.

"Sir, can you spare a few pence?"

McGinnty stared at an old man sitting on the edge of the street. He was wretched, with no teeth and torn clothing. He smelled of stale ale and feces. McGinnty reached into his pouch, pulled out six guineas, and threw them to the man as he continued to walk forward. Five other men seated on the street raced over and dove for the gold. Two women joined in the fracas, and a scrum ensued. Others saw what he had done and followed him, screaming for him to throw more. Beggars held out their hands while McGinnty noticed nobles wheeling past them in carriages, totally oblivious to the population that struggled on an annual income that was less than an aristocrat's wig.

He glanced at London Bridge to get his bearings. At the north end of the bridge was a phenomenal waterwheel pumping thousands of gallons of water throughout the city. No one drank it. Beer was the basic liquid of choice throughout the city. McGinnty's mouth watered for one. It was the elixir of life. But fatigue won out, and he wanted to get to a boardinghouse for a well-earned rest. Once rested, he would trek to Nottingham where his wife and four-year-old son were waiting.

The crowd thickened, but as McGinnty pushed his way forward, he was intercepted by a colonel and two soldiers.

"Jack McGinnty?" the colonel asked.

McGinnty stopped in the middle of the crowd and turned around. The colonel was tall and thin. He wore an immaculate red uniform, white gloves, and a powdered wig.

"Yes, I'm McGinnty."

"My name is Colonel Pitts. I have orders to escort you to see Lord Killingsworth. He is awaiting your arrival at the Custom House."

"Lord Killingsworth?" The name surprised him. "What business do I have with him?"

"I don't know, sir, but we do have our orders."

"Yes, of course." McGinnty held out his hand as if to say "after you." The two soldiers led him through the crowd. They shoved the beggars aside and threatened anyone coming close.

The Custom House was located east of London Bridge, overlooking the Thames River. It was a large two-story building made of brick and stone; it was fairly new, having been built in 1671 after the Great Fire.

McGinnty entered and noticed traders and merchants exchanging merchandise. A few rushed over to McGinnty to try and sell him items, but Pitts signaled them away.

"Keep close," he told McGinnty.

"Make way!" one of the soldiers yelled as McGinnty followed.

The soldiers quickly shoved away anyone at close quarters of McGinnty. Pitts led them through the crowd, up the stairs, to the customs room, which was guarded by two soldiers.

It was a magnificent fifteen-foot-high room, which ran across the entire building. McGinnty followed Pitts past officers and clerks into one of the doors of a side room. A man in a blue-powdered wig signed orders at his desk.

"Jack McGinnty, I've heard a lot about you," the man said without lifting his head. "Your reputation precedes you, congratulations on your latest haul."

"Thank you, sir. I also wish to congratulate you on your successful military career and election in the House of Commons."

Alexander Killingsworth slid his chair out and stood up shaking his head. He dismissed the colonel and clasped McGinnty's hand. He was a devilishly handsome man who had deep dark eyes, high cheekbones, and a strong chin. His clothes were sharp and fit snug, which accentuated his barrel chest and broad shoulders. A sword accompanied him at his side.

"Captain McGinnty, the burning question on everyone's mind is 'how successful were you.'"

"Yes, my lord, it was profitable in plunder but costly to the lives of my men."

"You sacked the *Lucinda*! Advance ships got word to us as far back as a month ago."

"We were lucky. We ran into them off the coast of Jamaica. There were two ships waving Spanish flags. They didn't appear to have full crews on board. We followed them, and after a couple of days, we attacked them early one morning using the fog as cover. We sank their warship, and the *Lucinda* lay crippled just outside of New Providence. I lost a sloop and half my men during the battle. Some of them are still in New Providence being treated for wounds."

"What was your total haul?" Killingsworth's tone was becoming impatient.

"My quartermaster has the final tally. He'll be reporting to the Custom House shortly. I paid shares to the men left behind, plus extras for the ones receiving wounds during the battle. I also took out shares for family members of the men that were killed. Of course, we are presenting England with the usual 20 percent."

"We know all about the cargo on board, and Spain wants it back. Of course, we're denying everything. Spain is up in arms, and we have to kiss their ass now because we are at peace with them. As far as I'm concerned, the *Lucinda* went down in a storm."

McGinnty watched Killingsworth pour two glasses of wine. He handed one to McGinnty and continued. "I could use a man like you working for me."

They tapped their glasses and drank. The wine went down smooth as McGinnty licked his lips.

"Regretfully, I must decline your offer. I'm retiring. I've accomplished everything I've set out to do as a ship's captain. It's time I settle down."

"You can't retire, it's in your blood. Anyway, just weigh my offer. I'm heavily involved with a new company, the South Sea Stock Company. Perhaps you've heard of it?"

McGinnty nodded. "Just bits and pieces."

"We bought the war debt in exchange for the trading rights with South America and its surrounding areas. You see why I'm interested in the *Lucinda*? A haul like that would go well with the company. A captain like you would be of valuable service."

"I need to clear a few things up. You say you diverted to New Providence on your way back."

"Yes, my ship took a beating during the battle, it needed repairs. Also, my men needed rest."

"Once again, how much treasure was on the *Lucinda* that we are not aware of and where is it?"

McGinnty felt surrounded. Pitts distanced himself from the two guards.

"We brought back everything, there was no magic fortune on that ship."

"Do you know the penalty for piracy? Where is the treasure?" Killingsworth slowly made his way to the window overlooking the wharf and signaled for McGinnty to join him. McGinnty approached cautiously and gazed at the pier, alarmed at what he saw. His men were being escorted by soldiers.

"They've done nothing to you. We served the queen and the country faithfully," McGinnty said, his adrenaline flowing.

"Of course, all this can be rectified if you stop being selfish and think this through. Where is the treasure?"

"I told you, it's all on the ship."

"Perhaps a few days at Newgate Prison will help restore your memory."

McGinnty started to rush toward Killingsworth but was stopped in his tracks by a sword from one of the guards.

"One more thing. We confiscated your ship and everything aboard. What's left of your crew will volunteer to join the Royal Navy or be tried accordingly."

Colonel Pitts grabbed McGinnty and pulled out shackles. McGinnty leaped up and drove the point of his elbow into his face. Pitts grunted and grabbed his nose. Blood spurted between his fingers. McGinnty grabbed the other guard and threw him into the one yielding the sword. McGinnty pulled out his cutlass and swung it at the arm of the guard, knocking the sword out of his hand. The sword landed at Killingsworth's feet.

Pitts, blinded by tears in his eyes and swelling of his nose, grabbed McGinnty from behind. McGinnty jerked his head back, catching Pitts squarely in the same spot his elbow landed moments ago. Pitts fell back and lost consciousness.

McGinnty let loose two thrusts into the arm and leg of the guard coming at him from the side. He turned and was greeted by a sharp pain on his cheek and forehead. In a split second, the floor pounded his body, and a sword was pointed at his throat. Blood eased down the shaft of the sword held by Killingsworth. McGinnty clutched his face. He could smell the blood as it seeped through his fingers.

Soldiers entered the room and reached for their swords. The two guards got up slowly. One had blood flowing from his leg and arm. Pitts was still unconscious in the corner.

"This isn't over. I'll be coming for you!"

"Oh, you will be back," Killingsworth said in a low tone. "You will be tried and found guilty for treason and piracy. You will be sentenced to hang until you are dead!"

McGinnty tried to reach for him but was losing consciousness. Killingsworth waved over the soldiers.

"Get him out of here!"

* * *

Newgate Prison

McGinnty was escorted by the prison marshal and six soldiers down the streets of London. His wrists and ankles were bound by shackles, which scraped the cobblestone. His face was caked with brownish dry scabs, left cheek colored in dark shades of purple as puss leaked from the wound. His white shirt was torn and splattered with dry blood all the way down to his waist.

Two of the soldiers taunted him with accusations of the whereabouts and size of the *Lucinda*'s treasure. McGinnty heard murmurs in the crowd questioning what was happening and his loyalty to England.

Newgate Prison greeted them on the corner of Newgate Street and Old Bailey. A five-story black hulking building, it was home mostly to debtors, prostitutes, and thieves. The prison itself was grim, almost no one escaped. If overcrowding became a problem, it was quickly resolved with hasty trials and sentences. The government had budgeted £1,000 for remodeling, but the money instead went to tidying up the outside and erecting life-size statues whose themes were liberty, justice, truth, and mercy.

McGinnty was led to an enormous thick wooded door with an exaggerated pair of shackles hanging over it for decoration. When the door opened, he was greeted by a stench of urine, feces, and other vile odors. The keeper, Henry Weese, smirked at McGinnty's reaction.

"You'll get use to it. They all do."

The marshal handed over Killingsworth's orders, followed by a fistful of coins. "I want you to welcome your new tenant, Jack McGinnty."

Weese shook his head, and the coins were quickly dispensed in his pouch, which lay against his waist.

He walked closer to McGinnty, looked him over, and smiled.

"We're going to do a lot of business, you and I."

The soldiers swapped the shackles on McGinnty's wrists and ankles with larger, heavier ones supplied by Weese. They shoved him inside, and the foul odors overwhelmed him.

McGinnty turned away, but two of the soldiers quickly shoved him forward and into the prison. They walked down the hall whose stone walls were lit with flaming torches. Once inside, he heard songs, shouts, and groans from the prisoners. The women were fouler than the men.

He was led to Condemned Hall and held in isolation. The marshal had earlier cleared out two prisoners to make sure no one had any contact with McGinnty while he was incarcerated.

The shackles were kept on him, and he was thrown to the floor of his new home. Once inside, the heavy door to his cell creaked shut. Keys fastened the lock as bolts slid across. The only light supplied was held by Weese's unsteady hand, which distorted the view to McGinnty's cell. The guards left while McGinnty's eyes roamed.

In the corner was a wooden cot with no mattress. The slop bucket was overflowing and provided a wretched smell.

Weese chuckled as he lurched toward the door, leading himself out of the isolation corridor. The door made a creaking sound as it closed. The light followed behind him, and now McGinnty found himself in total darkness, the only sound coming was from his breathing.

Weese returned later in the evening and tried to extort what he could from McGinnty.

"Ten guineas for a candle. Twenty guineas to release the shackles. Meals, women, rum, beer—we have it all."

McGinnty remained silent.

"What's money to you? You might as well be comfortable. I hear Killingsworth is going to hang you," Weese chuckled.

Weese tried to extort money for new clothes and linens. Even a mattress was offered. Since it was so dark on the inside, candles were his most popular item. Everything was for sale and at preposterous prices. He wanted to make his coin before McGinnty's trial.

The next day, Killingsworth paid a visit to McGinnty's cell. He excused the guards and looked into the room. A lit torch from the hallway provided a murky ray of light through the small window of the cell. It was now being covered by Killingsworth.

"Your men have been taken to Marshalsea in Southwark. Their time there will be a lot easier than yours, but don't misunderstand me. I will have them hanged if I don't get what I want."

"They've done nothing," McGinnty answered.

"We can salvage everything. Where is the rest of the treasure?"

McGinnty stayed quiet. Killingsworth let out a chuckle. Then he banged his fist on the cell door.

"Are you comprehending the overall situation here? I'm sure your wife will be here in the morning, begging for your life to be spared. I'm sure she will do anything I ask to save you. Anything!"

McGinnty stood up and approached the cell door. Killingsworth stepped back and continued talking. "Your boy? What about your boy? I may just cut out your tongue and send it to him as a trophy!"

McGinnty grabbed the slop bucket and threw it at the cell window, covering Killingsworth's face with piss and feces. He gasped and screamed for the guards.

"You're a dead man! The crows will be plucking out your eyeballs. Your limbs will be hung all around England, and God help your family!"

The guards entered, and Killingsworth ordered one of them to remove his shirt. After wiping his face with it, he handed it back and stormed out.

Later that night, Weese came by. He was gnawing on a chicken leg. Grease surrounded his lips.

"I bet you'd like to lick this."

He held up the lantern and chicken to the opening. After finishing it, he tossed the bone at McGinnty.

"Don't you want to taste some real food? What are twenty guineas to you? I can take those shackles off, give you a nice mattress."

He laughed as he banged his hand against the cell. McGinnty didn't budge, but the smell of chicken made his mouth water. He hadn't eaten anything but bread and water since he was arrested.

"Don't you want to go to the Tavern, the party hall for the damned? Women are waiting for you. You can have your pick."

McGinnty could sense Weese's frustration. McGinnty wasn't going to be held there for long, and he had yet to extract anything from him.

After ten days in isolation, McGinnty awoke as a gray light shone through the small window of the jail's cell door. He was eight pounds lighter and still wearing the same bloodstained clothes as when he arrived. Shackles still covered his wrists and ankles. He tried to avoid depressive thoughts and didn't count on any letters he wrote to reach his wife or any diplomatic connections he had.

There was no telling if it was night or day as the only glimmer of light was supplied from a torch down the hall. But something was different. McGinnty noticed gray light had entered the room from the outer edges of the door. He stood and tried to adjust his eyes. He walked over and slowly reached for the metal door, then paused. His chains scraped the stone floor slightly. He looked through the small opening and made sure the hallway was empty. He pushed the door, and it slithered forward as more gray light entered the cell. The door was unlocked.

He opened it slowly as a light creaking noise accompanied the opening. His head peered out of the cell as a torch lit up the hall. There was an eerie silence. McGinnty stepped out and looked around.

Nobody here.

He noticed a lump in the corner. He crept over as the man lay on his side, his back toward McGinnty who rolled him over.

"Weese."

A puddle of blood leaked from the side of his neck. McGinnty paused and stood motionless over the body, then looked around. He tried to listen for any type of noise, but the hall was silent. He proceeded toward the hallway door, gave it a shove, but it didn't budge.

The keys.

He stepped back to the fallen jailor and moved him about. He heard rattling coming from underneath the body. He reached around, grabbing the keys from his belt, and brought them closer to the light. He inserted the key into the shackles that bound his arms, and they fell to the floor. The shackles on his ankles followed, and he rushed over to the door. He twisted the lock, and the door snapped open.

Someone wants me free or killed.

The staircase was dim as he made his way up the stairs. He could see it was still dark outside. When he got to the top, he came upon a door with a large opening. He looked through. The bars were spread out farther apart and not as confined as the ones in his jail cell. He saw one guard slumped in a chair in the corner. Blood ran down the side of his face.

One door to go.

He inserted the key in the lock and twisted slowly. He pushed the door as the keys slipped and fell from his hand.

"Who's there?" a voice yelled from the corner. It was the guard who was moving slowly in his chair, clutching his head. He moaned and bent over, examining the blood on his hands, and reached for a lantern. McGinnty leaned back from the guard's view.

After a long silence, footsteps approached the door. There was a sound of a pistol hammer cocked open. McGinnty pressed himself against the wall, away from the light resonating from the lamp. The guard pressed his face against the door opening.

McGinnty sprung forward, reaching through the bars, and grabbed the guard's head with both hands and slammed his face forward into the bars. A gunshot went off, and the lantern fell to the ground, splattering at the guard's feet. His pants' leg went up in a blaze as he screamed out. McGinnty pushed the door open and kicked the guard out of the way. The guard's pants were completely on fire, and he was rolling on the ground, screaming in pain.

As he raced to the front door, McGinnty heard footsteps coming down the hall. Two shots were fired. The first one grazed his shoulder, and the second chipped stone above his head. He ran out the door and raced down the dimly lighted street. Two guards were joined in the distance by a third.

McGinnty ran down Newgate then south, past Fleet Street and Ludgate. He ran past the doorways of lodging houses, pubs, lampposts, dark alleys. The streets of London were short and narrow, faintly lit, twisting full of alleys and corners. As he ran down the road through vast stretches of darkness, his shirt came open and flapped behind him. He ran until he found darkness under an arch in one of the alleys. He hid there for a short time, catching his breath.

I need to get to the Thames!

He crept through a narrow passageway and saw windows of lodging houses. He was tempted to break in but kept moving forward. The distance between Newgate Prison and the Thames was short, but he had to take a more divergent route. He hid behind a dumpster and heard footsteps running past him and down the street. One yelled at the other, "Spread out. I'll check the alleyway."

McGinnty thought of the corpses that hung at Tilbury Fort when they first sailed into London. The bodies hung at the head of the Thames to discourage piracy. As the images came into his head, he briefly saw himself—his head tilted sideways and neck contorted and swollen. Rope was tied under his arms in the back, pinning his elbows together. Urine covered his crotch. His skin had a purplish tint, and his tongue was dangling from the corner of his mouth. His lifeless body hung limply, eyes wide open, staring back at him.

McGinnty wiped his eyes and continued on. He ran in full sprint as he passed Thames Street and was out in the open. The docks were crowded with boats. The larger ships were moored offshore in the distance. He heard voices behind him and footsteps closing in. The only way out was the water. He made his way to the end of the dock, flung his arms straight out, and dove as far as he could. He felt like he was in the air forever. The Thames smacked his chest, and the cold water squeezed the breath right out of him. He kicked along, staying underneath the water surface and strong currents. He struggled for breath but stayed under as long as he could, kicking and paddling. His chest felt like it was going to explode.

Finally, McGinnty's head slowly popped out of the water, and he sucked in air. Two of the soldiers were at the dock, searching frantically. One of them untied a dinghy and started rowing out toward the moored ships. McGinnty struggled with the currents and took cover against one of the bigger boats nearby.

He swam for one of the sloops that was dark, quiet, and appeared deserted. When he reached the ship's anchor chain, he grabbed it with both hands and shimmied his way up onto the edge of the deck.

Was anyone on here?

Exhausted, he struggled, flinging himself over, and flopped onto the deck. He needed a plan as the sun was starting to rise in the distance.

PART I

CHAPTER 1

HOME FROM SCHOOL

It was not like Edmund remembered it. Not at all! Bristol was growing. His eyes gazed at the new names of the streets being laid out. He rode by them—Prince Street, James Street, Orchard, Cornwallis Crescent, Windsor Terrace. They were all new. Even Queen Square, the ritzy area honoring Queen Anne's visit in 1702, was built up beyond recognition.

In the three years Edmund Drake had been away, Bristol expanded to become the second largest city in England. The slave trade was the number one industry. In one continuous triangle, manufactured goods such as woolen cloth, brass, and iron goods were sent to Africa in return for slaves who, in turn, were transported to North America and sold. The ships returned to Bristol with tobacco, sugar, and rum.

With the population growth, the city swelled in size, which resulted in the elite moving out to Clifton to enjoy the spoils of a booming economy. It was Clifton where Edmund returned to his father's home, and it was Clifton where he would avenge his father's death!

A welcome-home gathering was planned in his honor at the vicarage just outside the city lines in Radcliff. A part of him couldn't wait to see his old mates, but a larger part felt embarrassment over the fuss and wanted his return from school to be low-key. He wondered if his friends and relatives had changed as much as Bristol. How much had he changed?

Thirty to forty people had already arrived before Edmund dismounted from his horse. He was greeted by well-wishers, many he hadn't seen since he was a kid. Guests were laughing and chatting under the oaks that lined the lawn. Tables were filled with biscuits, chicken, potatoes, cakes, and other appetizers. Rum and wine were the drink of choice as they were lined up on the outskirts of the tables. The musicians were playing as couples danced on the deck overseeing the back lawn.

He noticed the vicar, Bartlett Graham, entertaining a small group of people. The way they were laughing, the vicar must have been telling his political jokes. Edmund chuckled, shook his head, and walked over to him.

Dr. Graham presided over the largest congregation in the outskirts of Bristol. He delivered long, winded sermons, led God-fearing hymns, and rounded off his service when the congregation gathered in small groups to bid him good night. He was responsible for organizing the welcome-home affair. As much as Edmund protested, no one refused the vicar.

"Sir, you've outdone yourself. I'm overwhelmed," Edmund said, extending his arms.

As they embraced, a small applause broke out from people around them.

"Edmund, glad you could make it. I was worried our guest of honor would be a no-show. How are you feeling?"

"I'm fine, sir, and my apologies for my moodiness the other day. I was a little overwhelmed coming home. It's been awhile."

The vicar grabbed his shoulders with both hands.

"It's all right. I wanted to get you out of the house. You haven't seen anyone since you've been home."

"Just trying to fit back in."

"Let me have a word with you before all the guests get a hold of you."

He pulled Edmund aside and excused themselves from the group. Edmund followed the vicar over to the gazebo near the rose bushes.

"We missed you, dear boy," the vicar said. "I hope you had a pleasant experience at Wescott. I pulled a lot of strings to get you in there."

"Sir, it was great, and thanks for getting me in there. Also, thank you for taking care of my father's estate while I was away. The place looks great!"

"Everyone in town chipped in, your father was very well respected here. You know that."

"I know. It was a bad time for all of us."

"Do you have any plans?"

The question caught Edmund off guard. Since he came back, he hadn't thought what his future might hold.

"I have some ideas I've been kicking around. I may even sell the estate. It's too large for me to take care of." He looked at the vicar, expecting a reaction. The vicar's demeanor stayed calm.

"Why would you do that?"

"As much as I have great memories of the place, I feel it's time to make a new start."

"Have you seen Sarah since you've been back?" Dr. Graham said.

A rush surged throughout Edmund's body. He knew he would have to deal with the subject of Sarah Bolden sooner or later. He just wanted it to be later.

"No, how is she?"

The vicar placed his hand on Edmund's shoulder.

"She's doing well. It's funny. I always thought you two would get married someday. Mrs. Edmund Drake!"

Edmund shrugged. "I'm no aristocrat. I would have never fit in with her father."

"Nonsense. Francis Bolden isn't like that."

"It was a confusing time. She probably thought I ran away from her!"

The vicar gave him a stern look. "We had to get you out of here. She understood that."

"I should have stayed!"

"No, you would have spent your time on vengeance. You needed time to clear your head. I just hope it was enough time." He looked at Edmund as if trying to read his mind.

"Perhaps. I thought about her a lot while I was away."

"Well, I hate to be the bearer of bad news, but she is to be betrothed to Lieutenant Governor Alexander Killingsworth."

Edmund thought for a moment, then his jaw dropped. "The war hero? Are you kidding me? How?"

"He and Francis are old friends. One might even say political allies."

"Isn't he married? Isn't he too old for her?"

"His wife passed away eight years ago. Apparently, he never remarried."

They walked back to the gathering. Edmund was in no hurry, fidgeting with his hands, unsure of what to say next. There was an uncomfortable silence.

"Is she happy?" Edmund finally blurted out.

"That you'll have to find out for yourself!"

She's probably better off, a lieutenant governor!

Before they reached the guests, the vicar stopped him.

"I need to know one more thing. This business with Cutler, it's over, right?"

Edmund stared into his eyes then turned away.

"Edmund, I need to know."

Edmund tried to look back, but his eyes wandered to the ground. He remained silent. The vicar shook his head.

"You have to let it go. You can't live your life seeking revenge. It was a fair fight. A fight both parties agreed to despite the outcome. I was as sickened as anyone about what happened. What's done is done. All I'm concerned about right now is your well-being."

Edmund could feel the disappointment in the vicar's voice, and no one ever wanted to disappoint the vicar. His mind was racing, and the memories were coming back to him. He wanted to walk away. Finally, he nodded in agreement, and they continued back.

"Come, my boy. A lot of people want to see you."

Edmund walked through the crowd and recognized many familiar faces. There was his old schoolteacher, Mr. Crain. Uncle Pete and Aunt Alice, who always argued, were in the corner, jabbering away at each other. When Edmund walked over, their argument ceased, and they were as pleasant as could be. They talked about growing old in Bristol, and hopefully, Edmund would find someone to grow old with in Bristol. They talked about the old days, the days when Edmund's father was alive!

Mrs. Graham was setting one of the tables. She stopped and gave him a quick hug but was too busy to talk.

"The plates have to be set, the food prepared, and I have to set up a few more decorations!" she said and then took a deep breath. "It's great having you home."

Many of his old mates from Clifton showed up. Mates he went to school with in his earlier years. He waved over to them, and they raised their mugs. They were in the middle of a card game but stopped to pay homage to their old friend.

Phillip Young gave a quick toast and rushed to his old friend.

"My god, Edmund, it's been three years. I thought you fell off the face of the earth."

Edmund smiled. "Sometimes, at Wescott, it felt like I did."

"Are you still an ace with the sword?" Phillip asked, eyes wide-open. "You were the best around."

The friends around Phillip listened keenly for a response.

"I practiced every day."

His friends roared their approval, clanged mugs, and chugged. He answered the same repeated questions, and his answers sounded rehearsed. They invited him to play, but Edmund politely declined. It was good seeing everyone again. Edmund knew he was lucky to have this much support around him. It was overwhelming.

The gathering increased in size, and the alcohol started kicking in. Many of the older gentlemen started singing seafaring songs from the old days. Songs imported by the merchant sailors from all over England. Men had their arms around each other, singing off-key. Edmund smiled. He knew the theme of the party was for him, but it did the community good to blow off steam. The times were in need of a celebration. The war with France and Spain had finally come to an end.

As Edmund poured a glass of wine, he received a pat on the back, which caught him off guard as he turned quickly.

"Sir, I didn't see you here. What a pleasant surprise!"

"Edmund, I wouldn't have missed it for the world. I always liked you and your fath—" Before he finished, Francis Bolden caught himself and looked down. "Anyway, it's good to see you. If you ever need anything, come see me."

“Thank you, sir.”

Although Francis Bolden came from vast wealth, he was very popular among the community. He had been a Bristol squire since Edmund could remember. He was also a principal landowner, justice of the peace, and donated a great deal of money to the church. An active member of the Whig party, he was very influential in Bristol politics and law.

“Look at them celebrating over there,” Bolden said, pointing to the men singing. “I mean, we fought for eleven years for what? Just to see who sits on the throne of Spain.”

“I think they're just glad it's over,” Edmund replied.

“They won't be singing when they realize their taxes are only covering the interest on our war debt. Between this war and the previous one, we've inherited quite a debt. Of course, the Tories will blame us for everything that is wrong in the world.”

Edmund felt uneasy and just nodded. He learned most wars were the result of religion or politics, and the War of Spanish Succession was both.

Bolden stared at Edmund. His face lightened up. “Enough about politics. Did you enjoy your time at Wescott?”

“Yes, sir. They kept me pretty busy,” Edmund answered. A strained look appeared on his face. There was one question he was dying to ask. A feeling of anxiousness came over him. Bolden gave him a strange look.

“Are you all right?”

“Is Sarah with you?” Edmund blurted.

Bolden's mouth curled at the corners. “She's around here somewhere.”

Edmund's heart raced, and he felt sweat running down his forehead.

“Good. I hope to see her—I mean, talk to her.”

“Don't worry, boy, she's been asking about you. I guess you heard she's about to be engaged to Lord Killingsworth. That dowry's going to cost me a fortune, but her future is secure with him. I'm a lucky man to have my daughter marry the likes of him.”

“I heard about Sarah and Alexander Killingsworth from the vicar. Congratulations are in order to you and her.”

He shook Bolden's hand, trying to hide his disappointment.

"Ah, the vicar. He does find out about everything in Bristol, doesn't he?" Bolden laughed and sipped his wine.

"Is Lord Killingsworth in town?" Edmund asked.

"No, his lordship has been held up in London. He has to deal with all that business with the escape of McGinnty. You were in London at the time. That must have caused quite a stir."

"It was the talk of London. People were afraid to leave their homes."

"Shame, he was a good privateer for England with quite the reputation. Why he turned into a rogue pirate is beyond me."

"I guess he was driven by greed."

"They all are, but to kill those two guards? He even set one on fire for God's sake." Bolden paused and shook his head. "Don't get me worked up with the likes of him. This should be a joyous occasion with you returning home and all."

Edmund smiled. "Thank you, sir."

"Let me get Sarah for you. She'll be so happy to see you again." He gave Edmund a pat and walked away.

Sarah Bolden stood in the corner of the dance floor with her best friend, Nell. She watched couples dancing and Nell flirting with the men. It reminded her of the balls she attended in Queen Square, where her father would tally prospects for her and secure introductions of those from the right pedigree.

Everyone knew her wealth and the considerable dowry granted to the man that captured her hand. Men used to line up in succession and present themselves under the watchful eye of her father. Faces eventually all looked the same. The men would bow, and she would curtsy graciously and go through her steps. Her face ached from forced smiles.

It was what women did.

Her father checked out all potential suitors but eventually would end up dismissing them. They were never good enough. It didn't bother Sarah. She was less than interested in them anyway.

All that changed once her father leaked out word that Lord Killingsworth was courting her. Now her once-prospective suitors were hesitant. In the game of courting, she was off-limits.

When she located Edmund, she tried to remain calm. He was taller than she remembered and his hair longer. She threw hidden glances his way until Nell caught her deep in reverie.

"Don't think I don't see you staring over at Edmund Drake."

Sarah blushed and turned her head. "I didn't know he was here yet. Where did you see him?"

Nell laughed. "Come on. I see you sneaking glances at him. Why don't you go over and say hello?"

Sarah regained her composure. "If Edmund Drake wants to see me, he'll find me."

"Well, if you feel indifferent to him, maybe I'll go over to him."

"I presume he's unattached."

"Well, if he is, it may not last by the end of the night."

Sarah shook her head. She didn't have to ask herself if Nell would go through with it. The last ball before Killingsworth entered the picture, Nell stroked Thomas Peary's ego, among other things, in the woods after he found Sarah was disinterested in him.

Would Edmund go through with it?

The party was in full bloom as Edmund sipped his wine. In the distance, his eyes came upon Sarah Bolden. She was wearing a white low-cut dress that complemented her slim figure and accentuated her curves. Her blond hair flowed, and she looked just the way he remembered her. In fact, she was even more stunning. In the three years while he was away, she truly filled out as a woman.

She was talking to Nell Blanton, her best friend and confidante. He snuck glances over at her, but she appeared to be oblivious to his very existence. Just as he decided to walk toward them, he was grabbed by Mrs. Kensington.

"Edmund, there's some people I'd like to introduce you to."

He barely heard her, his eyes transfixed on Sarah while he was being dragged away.

There's always something about when an old lady grabs you and wants to introduce you to someone.

Sure enough, it was her oldest daughter Anne. This was to be the first of many introductions to eligible women throughout the night. He was an eligible bachelor and very attractive to the ladies. He obliged her and took one more passing glimpse at Sarah. She glanced back at him then quickly turned her head.

As the party went to the wee hours of the night and guests started leaving one by one, Sarah and Edmund still had not spoken. Finally, Nell came over. She lowered her dress, exposing more of her developed breasts.

Although Nell was Sarah's best friend, Edmund didn't talk to her much while growing up. She was always a bit too forward for his liking.

"So, Edmund, you're looking good these days. Do you have a girl?" she asked.

She always had a way of speaking frankly and making him blush.

"No, haven't met the right one, I guess."

She giggled. "Well, you may have met the right one and not have known it. I mean, the right one could be staring you right in the face!"

He sipped his wine and smiled. "You may be right at that, Nell. You may be right indeed. By the way, where is your partner in crime?"

"She's over in the corner," Nell said, pointing over, which resulted in a look of shock on Sarah's face. She grimaced and started to walk toward them but was grabbed by her father.

"Aren't you going to ask a lady to dance?" Nell said, grabbing Edmund's hand.

Nell tugged at Edmund and led him to the dance floor. Edmund looked back at Sarah, who was talking to her dad, then turned back to Nell.

"I'm really not much of a dancer."

In fact, Edmund didn't much like dancing at all, especially in this situation with Nell. They walked out to the dance floor in the middle of a song, and Nell took his hand and placed it on her waist.

"Just relax and let yourself go."

Edmund distanced his hold on Nell who kept pulling him closer to her. Finally, the song ended and Edmund let go of his grip.

"That's good enough for me. Nell, it's time I let someone else have a chance."

Nell shrugged her shoulders and gave an expression of disbelief. Edmund quickly maneuvered and sidestepped through the crowd but was suddenly grabbed from behind.

"May I?"

Edmund began to refuse until he turned around. He was paralyzed. Sarah stared into his eyes and grabbed hold of his hand. They stared at each other, her blue eyes as expressive as ever, her mouth quirked at the corners. She turned and led him to the dance floor. The deck was large and, by this time, crowded with couples. Edmund knew most of them. Many nodded, smiled, or gave a brief greeting. The two stopped when they reached the middle of the deck. He bowed before her. She responded with a curtsy.

"It's been awhile, Sarah. How have you been?"

"Good, Edmund. I really missed you. I heard you were back. Actually, the vicar kept telling my father every time he saw him, so I thought I would stop by. You look great!"

She leaned over and kissed him on the cheek.

"Sarah, the years have been good to you!"

As they danced, the light of the lamps shone in her blond hair and sparkled in her eyes. She looked great in her white dress, which hugged her waist tightly and hung softly against her thighs.

Edmund felt a little uncomfortable. He wondered what their first meeting in three years would be like.

"We're catching a lot of stares from everyone," Edmund said, looking around nervously.

"Who cares?"

Sarah pulled him close and stepped forward until their bodies met. She took hold of Edmund's left hand and placed her own left hand on his shoulder. Edmund placed his right hand in the middle of her back.

They started dancing to a slow waltz. They held each other close as Sarah hardly moved at all, just swayed back and forth, taking small steps. Each step brought them closer together. Their faces inches away.

She smelled awfully good, a sort of perfume that filled Edmund's mind. It was a wonderful exotic aroma, but not nearly as wonderful or erotic as the feel of Sarah as they danced. Her face rested on his shoulder, her hair tickled the side of his face, her left hand caressed his shoulder while her right clasped his hand, her breasts pressed firmly but softly against his chest, her thighs rubbed against him in a subtle way, brushing his every step.

Edmund started to get aroused and bent forward slightly to break contact by his groin. Sarah's left hand went down and pulled at his rear until he was tight against her again.

He was in a trancelike state when a gentleman interrupted the mood.

"Um, Sarah, can I have a word with you?"

It was Sarah's father. He excused himself to Edmund and pulled her aside.

After a quick word, he left the dance floor. Sarah turned back to Edmund.

"My father says it's getting late. I wish we would have had a chance to talk."

"I wanted to," Edmund replied. "It's been so long. I hope to see you again. Soon."

She gave a quick smile and walked toward her father.

They left the party, shaking hands with guests along the way out. Other guests started to filter out as the musicians stopped playing.

Nell approached Edmund. "Looks like Sarah's leaving and I'm all alone. Do you think you can escort me home later? I'll make it worth your while."

She was grinning ear to ear.

"Nell, I won't be leaving for a while. You shouldn't walk alone, but I did promise to help with the clean-up." He looked around, trying to think fast.

"I can escort you home, Ms. Denton." The voice came from Phillip Young who was sitting at the table with a biscuit in one hand and a chicken leg in the other. Phillip was on the heavy side and carried a healthy appetite. He couldn't help overhearing Nell's concerns about getting home.

"There you go, Nell, I can't think of anyone I trust more than Phillip," Edmund said, relieved.

Phillip looked over at Edmund and almost knocked the table over as he tried to balance himself getting up. Nell had a shocked look on her face.

As Phillip made his way over, Edmund greeted him with a handshake and introduced him to Nell, who made a quick look away with her eyes.

"This young lady needs an escort home," he said, straining to hold back his smile.

"I thought, but look, I'm all right. I do have someone taking me home later." She gave Edmund a stern look.

"I won't stand to see a lady as beautiful as yourself go home unescorted," Phillip said, grabbing her hand to kiss it.

"I'm perfectly fine." She was repulsed.

"Nonsense. You're just saying that because you're too proud and shy to ask," Edmund said, and he turned to Phillip, noticing chicken grease on his upper lip. He smiled and thought of Nell's hand. "You take care of her and see she gets home safely."

"Ah, yeah, of course," he said, hardly able to contain himself.

Nell turned red and started stammering. "Edmund, I really appreciate you helping me out and having this nice young man escort me home, but really, I'm all right!" She was gritting her teeth.

"Phillip, make sure she gets all the way home. I'm sure Ms. Blanton will make it worth your while!" He looked at Nell. "Good night. Let me know how you made out tonight."

He walked back and found Dr. Graham sitting in the corner at one of the tables. His eyes were glassy, and he looked like he was feeling no pain. They shared a brandy and talked of days gone past as the place emptied out.

"Eight . . . nine . . . ten!"

Daniel Drake turned, aimed his pistol at Ben Cutler. As his finger squeezed the trigger, a bullet penetrated his chest. His gun went off as he was falling backward. As Drake hit the ground, he saw smoke being discharged from Cutler's pistol. Cutler's face wore a shocked look. As Drake struggled to breathe, he grabbed his chest with one hand and the crucifix he wore around his neck with the other.

Edmund Drake screamed!

Just a dream. Just a dream.

Edmund pulled the covers down. His shirt was soaked with sweat. He grabbed the sheets and wiped his face. He often had nightmares in London, and now they were back to haunt him in Clifton.

Although he never witnessed the duel, he remembered his father being brought home and treated, but the shot was embedded too deep into his chest. The doctor came out of the room shaking his head. There was nothing he could do.

"He's gone, son."

Daniel Drake died August 13, 1710, along with Edmund's childhood. He was buried at Cedarhurst, next to his wife, Cassandra. The days following the duel, Edmund somehow kept his head while men came to pay their respects and offer their condolences. They spoke in murmurs and shook his hand.

A soft knock came from the front door. Edmund tried to focus his eyes as the sunlight peered in from his windows. His breathing was slowing back to normal. Edmund rolled out of bed and looked out his window. He froze. A crooked smile appeared on his face.

"Sarah!"

He quickly grabbed a shirt and threw on some pants. He ran his hands through his wet hair, trying to straighten it out.

I'm a mess! What's she doing here?

There was a sense of excitement he hadn't anticipated.

The knocking continued. This time, it was harder and faster. He grabbed the door handle, paused, and swung it open.

Her hair was golden, her eyes glowed. Edmund felt his breath leave his body, and his heart was racing. She looked up at him and smiled.

"Hi, Edmund."

"Sarah, it's great to see you."

"I tried to speak with you last night, but when we finally got together, Father had to leave. Can I come in?"

He kept staring, then caught himself.

"Sure, I'm sorry. I'm just surprised you're here. Come on in."

She entered the house and looked around. "Looks like nothing has changed in three years."

"You can thank the vicar and friends for that."

They walked through the kitchen. He pulled out a couple of muffins left from the night before. He handed her one, his hand trembled, and she responded with a curious look.

"I didn't expect a gourmet breakfast!"

Embarrassed, he pulled it back. "I'm sorry. Can I get you anything?"

"No, I'm fine. So how does it feel to be back?" she asked.

"A little strange, I guess. Have you been all right?"

She stared into his eyes, and a corner of her mouth turned up.

"Why did you take off? I never heard from you . . . Three years!"

The words struck him like a blow to the stomach. He knew she would ask, but he wasn't ready for the question despite the countless number of times he rehearsed his answer.

"I had to go," he murmured.

"That's no explanation. Three years. Nothing!" Her eyes welled, voice was irate. "We've known each other for so long. We became so close. You left without even saying good-bye. I thought we had something between us. I guess I was wrong."

"I couldn't stay. The vicar was right. He made arrangements at Wescott to get me away before anything happened with Cutler. He was probably right in doing that. I'd only spend my life trying to end Ben Cutler's."

She shook her head, frowning. "What about me? If I meant something to you, the least you could have done is let me know. You never even wrote."

"I'm sorry, Sarah. If I could take it all back, believe me I would."

"All that time, I wondered why you left without so much as a good-bye. I thought you found a woman. I thought you may have gotten yourself in trouble."

"You'll never know how hard it was to leave. I was in love with you."

Sarah's face went red and looked bewildered. Her mouth hung open. "You were in love with me? You sure never did or say anything to . . . I mean, all the times we spent together, just the two of us and you never . . ."

"I thought about you every night. It's the only thing that kept me sane."

Sarah shook her head and started to walk out. Tears streamed down her cheeks.

"This was a mistake, coming here."

The words pierced Edmund's heart. She stopped short of the door and opened it. Edmund pushed it shut.

"Edmund, don't. I'm being courted by Alexander Killingsworth."

"Do you love him?" he stammered.

"When Alexander comes back from London, he wants to get engaged."

"But do you love him?"

She gave him a stern look. "Alexander is the kind of man a girl dreams of marrying. He's a war hero, wealthy, and one of the most powerful men in all of England."

"You haven't even admitted you love him."

"How do you even know what love is? Edmund, you can't just come back here after three years and think everything is how it was. I wish it could have been just you and I, but it's not."

"Sarah, why do you think I'm back here?" He reached over and gave her a hug. "It's never too late to start over."

Sarah pulled away. She gazed at him then to the floor. "Edmund, it's too late. My life is going in another direction."

CHAPTER 2

OLD FEELINGS

Weeks after his welcome-home gathering, Edmund rode to meet Dr. Graham for their weekly ritual at Knewt Gardens. It was an exquisite area with plush gardens and an empty lawn where many of the elite packed their lunches and spread out, relaxing and enjoying food and drinks. It was the vicar's favorite place to relax and chat. Anytime Edmund had something on his mind, the vicar was always helpful with advice or just lets him vent. He never asked advice about Sarah though he badly wanted to.

Edmund looked around as he dismounted but couldn't spot the vicar anywhere.

He's never late.

He wore a confused look until a familiar sight crossed his path, which explained everything. It wasn't the vicar.

"Hey, Sarah, over here!" he said shaking his head, wondering what the vicar was up to. He hadn't seen or heard from her since the morning she came to his house.

Sarah turned and looked at Edmund. A look of shock came across her face as she finally forced a smile at Edmund. There was an uncomfortable silence as the two stood there, looking at each other, before their heads turned away.

"So do you still have that old dog that used to attack me?" he said, breaking the ice.

She laughed. She must have remembered her old dog, Steed, taking a bite at Edmund's leg when he got too close to her. The dog usually ripped his pants in the process.

"No, he died. I have a new one, Major. He's even meaner," she answered with a crooked grin.

"You were always great with animals—dogs, horses, sheep. You always had a way about them."

"You didn't mention people."

"Well, ah, you were always a little bit harsher with us human folk."

A smile came across her face, and he felt some of his tension subside.

"What have you been doing since you've been home?" she asked.

"Just taking care of the house, trying to get the place in order. By the way, thank your father for me for trying to set me up with an apprenticeship in Bristol with the Baxter firm. I had to decline for now. I've got a few things I'm thinking about and want to see where they take me."

His answer surprised her. She was about to comment until an old friend showed up.

"I hope you accept my apologies. I seem to be running late this afternoon," Dr. Graham said with a smirk on his face.

"You late? There must have been quite an emergency to keep you from an appointment. You're never late for anything."

Dr. Graham chuckled. "You know what they say: a vicar's work is never done."

After some more small talk, the vicar again excused himself.

"Mr. Drake, would you mind escorting Ms. Bolden back to her home? I have unfinished business from this afternoon that requires my attention."

Edmund felt a rush go to his head. "For you, of course I don't mind."

"Ah, excellent." He hugged Sarah. "Sarah, I leave you in good hands." He turned toward Edmund, clasping his hand. "Please come by for dinner tomorrow night. The missus would love to have you."

He rode off. Edmund looked at Sarah.

"I'm sorry. This seems like such a setup."

"I don't mind at all. It's good seeing you again, as always." She grabbed his elbow, and they walked.

As they made their way back to Sarah's house, plans were made to go riding together the following afternoon.

Sarah loved to ride her horse out to the country. It was there she could unwind with a good book and relax. She loved the fresh air, gentle breeze, and freedom it offered. She also loved it when Edmund escorted her out there, which was becoming a more frequent occurrence as the days went by. They often talked of their future plans and past dreams they shared when growing up. They enjoyed reading to each other, talking about current events, or just sharing a quiet moment.

She loved the way he made her laugh or smile with his corny jokes. Edmund loved the way she made him feel special, and her smile made him forget about the tragedies of the past—one tragedy in particular.

"Edmund, Dr. Graham says you might sell your place and leave Bristol. Why would you want to do that?"

"I can't believe he told you that." He laughed. "I can't tell him anything."

"Come on, you know he just wants what's best for you."

"I know. I just think I have to make a fresh start somewhere else. I think I'll finish studying law in London and maybe get an apprenticeship there. I've made a few connections since going to Wescott."

"You'll hate London. It's too crowded. There is so much poverty and crime there."

"Crime is good for a lawyer, keeps us in business." They both laughed.

The walk through the fields was filled with silence, as if they were both trying to find things to say.

"Edmund, did you ever think of us? I mean, if you and I were the ones that would be together?"

He felt as though air left his stomach. A warm rush passed through his cheeks. He stopped, grabbed her shoulders, and stared into her eyes.

"Sarah, when I was in London, it's all I thought about." He couldn't believe what he just said. The words just flowed out of him.

She just turned to look at him, not knowing quite what to say.

"When we were growing up, we always hung out, and I never knew how you felt," she said, grabbing his arm.

"I always felt like your family would think I'm not good enough."

"That's not fair. I never treated you like that. My parents didn't either. As far as being good enough, they probably think the duke of Marlborough isn't good enough!"

"I didn't mean it like that. I guess I was just shy."

"You shy? Come on." She laughed and gave him a hug.

"What about Killingsworth?"

"Let's not talk about him now. How about a bite to eat?"

"Sounds good. So how did you meet him?"

"Edmund!" she answered as she hit his elbow. He laughed and wrapped his arm around her as they continued to walk the fields.

The next day, they rode their horses over Cascade Bridge to the old oak tree at Myers Plantation where they planned to set up a picnic. Sarah made sandwiches and brought some fruit. Edmund brought a couple of large blankets and a bottle of wine.

"Let's set up over there," Sarah said, pointing to a nice secluded spot.

As they rode forward, Sarah pointed to a large fox running ahead in the open field, heading for the woods. It was tan with a white stripe down the middle of its stomach. She turned to Edmund and started to speak.

A loud explosion coming from the woods blasted their ears and sent Sarah's horse into frenzy. Edmund looked into the woods and saw movement. Smoke dispersed from a rifle. He turned toward Sarah, but she was gone. He looked and saw her horse sprinting with Sarah hanging on for dear life. His jaw dropped, and he raced toward her. She was sidesaddled and had her arms wrapped around the horse's neck. She was falling backward off the horse. Edmund pushed his horse forward and kicked its side for more speed. He was gaining, but Sarah's horse was running awkwardly, as if trying to buck her off.

"Hang on, I'm almost there!"

He was close enough to hear her screaming and aimed his horse to parallel hers. Both horses were now in full sprint as Edmund pulled alongside. He first reached for her reins but realized quickly that was futile. She slipped some more, and one leg fell over the opposite side to him.

"I can't hold on!"

Her left arm was slipping off also. She was being held on by one arm and a leg. Edmund saw her foot going. He reached out and grabbed her dress and pulled. There was too much force against him. He crashed his horse into hers to slow it down. He jumped on Sarah's horse, grabbing her at the same time, but he couldn't hold on. They tumbled off and hit the ground with Sarah landing on top of him. The impact knocked the breath out of him, and they rolled over once and stopped. Sarah was on top and looked at Edmund. His eyes were shut.

"Edmund, you all right?"

She reached for his cheek. He didn't move. She shook him.

"Edmund, please be all right." Tears filled her eyes. She shook him

"Edmund, if anything happens to you, I swear!"

He laid there motionless. She looked around for help. Two men in the distance were running toward them. She grabbed him again and frantically shook him.

He opened his eyes. "What are you trying to do? Kill me?"

He started to laugh but coughed instead.

"Edmund, you were all right all along? I was dying over here, and you were all right. You were just fooling around?"

He tried to get up but just kept his weight on both elbows.

"I wouldn't say I'm all right. I feel like I rolled down a hill in a barrel."

"You should have let me know you were alive at least."

"I liked hearing what you had to say."

He slowly started to pick himself up but only made it to a knee. She shook her head and walked away. The horses had stopped running but were far down the fields. The two men with rifles came up. One was old with gray hair. The other was probably his son.

"We saw what happened. Are you two all right?"

"Apparently so," Sarah said, glancing at Edmund with a disgusted look.

"We didn't see you ride up. We've been after that fox for weeks. It's been having its way with our chickens," the older one said.

Sarah convinced them everything was fine and no harm done. The two men left. Edmund finally got to his feet and walked after Sarah who wanted no part of him.

"Sarah, what's wrong?"

She turned around quickly, and her eyes were filled with tears.

"You scared the hell out of me. I thought you were crippled or dead."

She started crying. He put his arms around her.

"When I saw that horse taking off, I didn't care about anything but saving you. If anything would have happened to you, I'd never forgive myself."

His eyes welled up. She looked into them. Her hands reached up and stroked his face.

"That was so brave."

Edmund's heart started racing. He stared straight ahead and nodded.

Sarah leaned against his arm. Edmund looked down at her. Their faces were drawn together, and he noticed her eyes darting up and down.

He reached down and pulled her toward him. He looked into her blue eyes. Their lips met. He wrapped his arms around her, kissing her passionately. His tongue found hers; and he squeezed her tight, not to let go, as her soft breasts rubbed against his chest.

"Edmund, we have to stop," she panted.

He continued kissing her neck.

"Edmund, please! I want to, but we shouldn't," she said as she pulled away.

"Are you sure?"

She smiled. "It'll only complicate things."

"They're not complicated already?"

Her smile faded. "You know I belong to someone else."

"I know, Sarah. I see that every time I see you wearing your bracelet or that gold necklace you have around your neck!"

She stared at him silently.

"Maybe it was a mistake for us to be together."

"I'm sorry, Sarah. I didn't mean that."

"Maybe we should take a break from seeing each other."

"Maybe so," he said grudgingly, agreeing to cool off for a while.

Maybe forever!

"Alexander's going to be visiting Bristol," she said, the words blurted out. "He's finishing up some business in London, and then he's going to stay in Queen Square while he's in town."

Edmund turned red when he heard it from her lips. He felt air struggle to get in and out of his lungs. She still belonged to Killingsworth no matter how much time they spent together.

"Now you tell me this?" he said, shaking his head.

"I didn't find out until yesterday. I wasn't sure what you'd say. I wanted everything to be like it's been the past few weeks."

"Are you looking forward to seeing him?" he asked, knowing the answer but hoping to hear something different.

"Edmund, I really appreciate the time we've had together. I don't know what else to say."

He looked at her, shook his head, and walked away.

"Let's get out of here."

He rode her back to her home, and on the way to his house, thoughts started creeping into his mind about Ben Cutler.

CHAPTER 3

AN IDYLLIC TRYST

The population of Bristol doubled in size since 1700 to fifty thousand people. The shipping industry carried industrial growth mostly due to slave trade with the British East India Company. Timber was imported from Scandinavia. Glass, shipbuilding, and tobacco flourished. With all the economic growth, brewing and public houses were located at every corner.

O'Shea's quickly became Edmund's favorite tavern. Since the ride in the country with Sarah, he blew off steam, drinking rum and ale with the locals or travelers passing through. He often asked seamen about their travels and the different countries they had visited. He questioned what dangers they experienced in foreign lands and treasures that lay beyond the sea.

Instead of the romanticized tales of heroism and treasure he had read about, the true accounts depicted were tales of brutal weather conditions, little sleep, little money, and taskmaster captains. There were also scurvy, starvation, plague, and a new growing fear that struck the chords of merchants everywhere—pirates.

The new breed of sea criminals included Captain Morgan, Captain Kidd, and England's newest menace, Scarface Jack McGinnty. It shocked Edmund to hear stories like this. He was always fascinated with William Dampier's *A New Voyage Round the World* and *Voyages and Descriptions.* They were books that educated him about excursions to the New World and islands of the Caribbean.

Other drinking buddies included traders and merchants that dealt with Daniel Drake. They told stories of the old days when privateering was one of the best jobs at sea and how they would buy and sell goods to his father. Edmund loved hearing the stories. They made his father seem real and alive once more.

"Ned, I'll take another ale," Edmund said as he threw a copper coin on the bar.

Ned was an older man who had been the barkeep at O'Shea's since it opened in 1702. He had often bragged of sailing with Kidd and Morgan though the tales were never substantiated.

"Edmund, take it easy. Maybe you should turn in for the night."

Edmund's eyes were glassy, and his speech slightly slurred. The ale was going down smoothly.

"One more," he said, pounding his hand on the bar.

Two men looked up at him and pointed over.

"Is there a problem, Ned?" the taller one said in a Scottish accent.

"Everything's fine," Ned responded quickly.

The door opened, and he heard a voice.

"Edmund!"

It wasn't a man's voice that screamed out his name. Edmund turned and came face-to-face with Sarah. He started feeling flush and rolled his eyes. He hadn't seen her in a week, and this was not the place for her to be meeting him. He sobered up quickly.

"What are you doing here?"

"I've been talking to the vicar. He's worried about your drinking, and frankly, so am I."

"He sent you here?"

"God no. If he knew I was here, he'd flip. Please, let's get out of here."

She walked toward him, eyes focused on Edmund and careful not to make eye contact with any seedy patrons.

"What do you care? You're going to marry royalty," he said, raising his glass to his lips.

The man with the Scottish accent screamed over as he was getting up.

"My lady, how much will it cost for a good time?"

Sarah turned toward him and had a look of shock. Edmund couldn't tell what he had just heard. She took hold of Edmund's arm and inched closer toward him.

"I said," he repeated, "how much for a good time? You don't look like the sort of girl that usually comes in here."

The Scot was getting closer. He was tall, lean, and slightly balding. His face was bony. Edmund turned and faced the man. He noticed the other man getting off his stool and walking over. He was portly with a stubbly beard and brown hair that had gray surrounding his ears.

Edmund turned to the Scot. "Leave her alone, she's with me."

The Scot approached Sarah, ignoring Edmund. She tried to look away.

"I can give you a better ride than he can," he said, throwing a silver coin on the bar next to her. "I'll give you a real good ride."

He smiled and touched her arm. Sarah ripped it away from her arm as Edmund rose off his stool but lost his balance and fell backward. The Scot finished him off by shoving him to the ground, then grabbed Sarah by her arm. The portly man came up from behind.

"How about two for the price of one?"

"Get your hands off her!" Edmund screamed.

The Scot laughed and pulled Sarah away. Edmund rushed to him but was grabbed from behind. Edmund shoved the man away but was quickly grabbed by the Scot who grabbed the front of Edmund's shirt and yanked him up. He rammed Edmund's back against the wall and then punched him in the stomach. Edmund's eyes bulged out. His mouth sprang open, and he bent over at the waist, gasping for air. The Scot grabbed him by the neck and thrust him back up against the wall. Edmund's face was twisted with pain as the other guy grabbed Sarah around the waist as she moved to help Edmund. The Scot had one arm around Edmund's neck and was about to strike when Edmund threw his arm up and around the man's wrist and twisted, freeing the man's clutch. He then lunged forward, throwing his head into the Scot's groin. Edmund hugged his legs and drove forward, driving himself backward as the Scot doubled over with his rump hitting the floor.

The portly man pulled a knife and threw Sarah to the ground. Edmund, still trying to catch his breath, quickly sprang to his feet. The man plunged the knife toward Edmund's midsection. Edmund jerked his body aside and grabbed the man's hand with the knife. He twisted it hard, causing the knife to fall. The man grabbed him around the neck, but Edmund kept hold of one of his fingers, snapping it backward. It popped like a twig. The man let out a high-pitched screech.

Edmund popped two more as the portly man's knees fell to the ground. Edmund turned and drove his right knee into the man's nose. He slammed down on his back as blood spurted everywhere.

The Scot staggered to his feet and moved toward Edmund as Sarah jumped on his back. They twirled around until Edmund drove his fist into the side of the man's face. The man fell backward, landing on Sarah.

"Get him off me!"

Edmund braced himself for the man to get up, but it didn't happen. He was out cold on the floor with Sarah writhing under him, trying to escape. Edmund reached down, threw him off, and helped her up.

They looked around and saw two patrons in shock at what just occurred.

"Why didn't you help us out?" he yelled over.

The two men turned away with a frightened look and chugged their beer. Ned, the barkeep, walked over.

"You better get out of here," he warned. "I don't want any more trouble, and when they get up, they may get their friends over here."

Edmund nodded, looking over at the passed-out Scot and his portly friend holding his head, agonizing in pain. He grabbed Sarah's hand and led her outside.

"You really took a chance back there," Edmund said as he dismounted. The brawl seemed to have sobered him up as he escorted Sarah back to her house.

"Edmund, look at you. What happened to you?"

He felt shame and looked to the ground as Sarah continued. "The vicar was getting worried about you, and I've been hearing stories about a rabble-rouser at O'Shea's that is getting a little too boisterous. It doesn't sound like you. It isn't you. What's happening?"

"I miss you. I just miss you."

Her stern look softened, and she rubbed her hand on his cheek.

When they arrived, she offered him tea, but he declined and rode off.

The next morning, on the bank of a small lake, Edmund worked off the alcohol and some frustration by flailing his sword on a six-foot stump that used to be an oak tree. It was now used for practice. He heard leaves rustling behind him and saw Dr. Graham riding slowly toward him.

Edmund continued. Each thrust and jab more aggressive than the previous. He took a wild swing and knocked off a large chunk that was dangling loosely. His face and body soaked in sweat.

"Getting better with the sword, I see," Dr. Graham said as snuck up from behind.

"I trained every day in London. It kept me sane," he replied, catching his breath.

The vicar watched Edmund's movements.

"I banged on your door, but there was no answer. Then I heard noises that sounded like logs being chopped up, so I knew you'd be back here. Look, Edmund, I know you had to grow up fast, but I did promise your father I'd look after you."

Edmund took aim at the tree again. He struck it with two jabs and then, with precision, swung through, knocking off more wood chips. With one more swing, he left his sword stuck in the oak and walked toward the vicar.

"You always said, 'If you're going to do something, be the best you can be.'"

"Well, I see that applies to your use of the sword."

Edmund grabbed his shirt and wrapped himself in it. The two of them walked toward the house. The topic of Sarah came up.

"Edmund, you know she's going to marry Killingsworth."

"I know that. Not much I can do about it."

"I always thought you two belonged together."

"Wait a minute. Didn't you warn me about Killingsworth and to be careful?"

"I've had a change of heart. I want what's best."

"Well, it's a two-way road. She has to want it too," Edmund said, throwing his hands in the air.

"She does. Why do you think I'm here?"

Edmund looked at him. "I can't compete with him. He's one of the highest officials in England."

"So you're just going to give up? That's not the Edmund I knew. You were always so stubborn. You never quit on anything. Or is it that you're so wrapped up on avenging your father's death you forgot what is important to you!"

Edmund wiped the sweat from his face, shaking his head.

"Their festivity is next Saturday."

"A piece of advice: Don't lack the courage to fulfill your destiny!"

Edmund smiled. "I thought you preach to make your dreams come true, you have to get out of bed."

"So you do listen to my sermons. I thought you slept through them."

"Every now and then, a few tidbits slip through the cracks."

Dr. Graham clutched Edmund's shoulders. Edmund looked up at him.

"Any advice on what to do?"

"Just follow your heart, son. You'll do just fine."

The vicar turned to walk away. Edmund stopped him.

"So you're saying I should talk to Sarah?"

"You better, she's up at the house."

Dr. Graham mounted his horse as Edmund grew nervous. He wiped the sweat off his face and chest. He looked around and buttoned his shirt and ran up toward the house.

Sarah was waiting with a smile on her face. Edmund was embarrassed for what had transpired the night before.

"How are you feeling?" she asked.

"Stomach is a little bruised and sore, but apart from that, all right." He opened the door and led her inside.

She shook her head and gave him a hug. He responded by holding her tight and running his hands down the arch of her back and buttocks. Their lips met. She pulled back and looked up at him. His eyes were lost in hers.

"Edmund, have you ever been with a woman?" she said, never taking her eyes from the sky above.

"Besides you?"

"You've never been with me. I mean, *been* with a woman."

He knew what she meant but just played dumb and shook his head no. Edmund had experienced brothels in London.

She grabbed his hand, and they walked slowly toward the bedroom.

She gazed into his eyes and turned toward the open door. He stopped.

"I've wanted you for so long," he said, caressing her shoulders.

She turned back toward him and whispered in his ear, "Me too."

She smiled and followed him inside. He led her toward the bed and slowly sat down. Still hanging on to her hand, he guided her down next to him. Edmund leaned over and kissed her cheek. Then his lips found hers, and she pushed her tongue into his mouth. His hands found the curves of her belly, and he could feel the warmth of her body through the soft fabric of her dress. She stopped him. She stood up and reached behind. In one motion, the dress fell to the ground, exposing her naked body.

Edmund gazed at her eyes and scanned her body. He had dreamed of this moment since he could remember. His breathing started to increase at a steady pace as oxygen raced through his lungs. His pants became tight. Her breasts were firm and accentuated by her thin waist and tight rear end.

"Very convenient, wearing no undergarments!" he stammered.

She sat down next to him and grabbed the band of his pants. She slipped her hand down his back and caressed his buttocks. She moaned when he felt her breast. He stroked its round smoothness, filling his hand, and then pressed his thumb against her rigid nipple. She squirmed and rolled over onto him, rubbing her against his thigh.

Edmund's erection felt trapped inside his pants until she reached around and freed it. She curled her fingers around the shaft and gently stroked its length forward and back. His mouth found her nipple, and he slowly stroked it with his tongue while she let out a soft moan. His breathing increased. She rolled onto her back while he kissed and sucked the other breast, tasting the salt from her skin. His hand reached down her belly into a fine patch of hair. Her legs parted as she was gasping for air. She felt warm and very wet as she clenched his hair with her other hand, forcing his mouth down harder against her breast. She raised her knees and squirmed against his fingers, which were now inside her. She moaned loudly.

He took his hand away, and she let go of his hair. He rolled aside and struggled to get out of his pants. She grabbed his shirt, and together they aggressively pulled it over his head. Edmund then rolled on top of Sarah, shoved his tongue down her mouth, grabbed her breast, and then thrust himself inside of her. She let out a shriek and gasped for air.

"You all right? Does it hurt?"

"Don't stop."

She dug her fingers into his buttocks and pulled. He penetrated deep inside her and was straining to get even deeper. Their rhythm increased, and he was now thrusting himself into her. She wrapped her legs around his thigh and bucked against his body—faster and faster, deeper and deeper—until he exploded and released inside of her, filling her up.

He stayed on top of her as they both strained to suck in oxygen. Beads of sweat rolled down Edmund's face onto Sarah's nose. They looked at each other and smiled. She rolled him onto his back and stroked his chest.

Life doesn't get any better than this!

He shut his eyes as Sarah rubbed his stomach. His breathing was easy, and his smile never went away from his face as he fell into a nice, relaxing state.

Sarah quickly dozed off. Her mouth was wide open. Her breath came soft and quick upon Edmund's neck. He stared at the ceiling with a slight grin then fell asleep.

Edmund jumped up.

Must have dozed off!

He looked around for Sarah. She was nowhere to be found.

"Hmm." He looked puzzled. He rolled onto his knees and reached for his clothes. They weren't there. Instead, a note lay next to the pillow. He read it and smiled.

> Edmund,
>
> You looked so peaceful. I didn't want to wake you. Come see me when you can.
>
> Sarah

He fell back onto the bed, staring at the ceiling. He wanted them to be together and spend the rest of their lives as one. He also felt life wasn't going to make it an easy transition.

CHAPTER 4

LORD KILLINGSWORTH

When Alexander Killingsworth arrived from London, a huge procession followed as he was marched down the streets of Bristol like a conquering hero. Queen Square was his final stop where he met with local politicians before following his extravagant parade. When it ended, the streets were alive with vendors and merchants. Alcohol flowed, and the day was treated as a holiday.

The next day, at his country estate, Bolden organized a tremendous gathering complete with food, entertainment, and hundreds of guests to honor one of the most influential people in England.

By the time Edmund arrived at the party for Killingsworth, most of the crowd was already there. Some of England's most elite had traveled all the way from London and Southampton. Edmund felt out of sorts being there until he spotted Dr. Graham and immediately felt better. The vicar returned the glance, grabbed a glass of wine, and walked over.

"These gatherings always bring out England's finest," he said with a smirk.

Before Edmund could get a word in, he was quickly grabbed by Francis Bolden.

"Edmund, I want you to have the pleasure of meeting one of our most influential men." He dragged him over to Lord Killingsworth, who was holding court with fellow Whig supporters from Bristol.

He was a tall, well-built man; his white wig was worn below the ears. He wore elegant and expensive clothes. The scars on his face from years of battle aged his handsome but reserved appearance.

"Alexander, I'd like you to meet Edmund Drake. His father was one of Bristol's most popular men."

Edmund went to shake his hand but received a strange glare instead. Killingsworth never offered his hand and turned away to continue his conversation with the politicians. Edmund withdrew his hand; and Bolden, embarrassed by the response, escorted him away.

"A man like that is very busy. He always has to entertain important people," Bolden said.

Edmund went to respond but looked up and saw Sarah walking over. She greeted him with a crooked smile.

Bolden looked strangely at him. Then his eyes lit up when he turned them toward Sarah. He kissed her on the cheek as pride filled his face. Edmund felt a rush of heat fill his veins and wanted to hug her tight. Bolden then excused the two of them and escorted her over to Killingsworth. Edmund felt a knot in his stomach as he watched Killingsworth promptly halt his conversation and grab her hand.

"Sarah, you still look radiant!" Killingsworth said as he stared at her. Everyone at the party eyed them. "Did you get the flowers and French chocolates I sent?"

"My dear Alexander, it is good to see you!" she responded, looking back at Edmund as if to apologize. "And yes, the gifts were lovely."

Killingsworth kissed her hand.

"I've missed you, my dear. I've thought about you a lot. We have been apart much too long. I'm going to make sure that doesn't happen again!"

She looked at him nervously with a trace of a smile. "What do you mean?"

Before he could answer, Bolden stood at the podium, waving to the crowd to get their attention.

The vicar walked up to Edmund with two mugs of ale. Edmund cordially took one off his hands as Bolden spoke.

"Gather round, everyone," he said with excitement and waited for the crowd to settle down. "We're here to honor a very special man. A man that needs no introduction. A man that has served England faithfully and is one of the queen's most important advisors. He fought bravely in the war. He was appointed to the staff of John Churchill, the duke of Marlborough, and led his troops to many victories. Who could forget his heroism at Malplaquet? A battle so bloody and vicious that this man led the charge after being wounded in the chest and leg."

The crowd applauded. Dr. Graham leaned over to Edmund and whispered, "Some say he was shot by his own men."

Bolden waved his hand for silence and then continued. "He led his men in the Battle of Blenheim. That was a huge victory for this country and just one of many held on his mantelpiece. The list goes on. His heroism has earned him election in the House of Commons. Ladies and gentlemen, I give you his lordship, Alexander Killingsworth."

The applause grew as Killingsworth walked over to Bolden, shook his hand, and waved to the crowd.

"Please, you're too kind. What have I done to deserve this honor?"

The crowd continued to roar. He waved his hands and waited for them to quiet down as he smiled and bowed to the crowd. Finally, when the applause died down, Killingsworth began to speak.

"Such an introduction. I have given my life to serve England and its countrymen. I will continue to do so with the same vigor as in the past. I have been asked by George Hamilton, the earl of Orkney, to run the Virginia colony for the next few years. After careful consideration, I have accepted his offer."

A large groan mixed with applause interrupted his speech. He waved to quiet them down.

"On a much happier note, I have another announcement that I am proud to share with you. I am proud to announce my engagement to one of your local women, Sarah Bolden."

With that said, he held out his arm, aiming it at her. Sarah was uncomfortable and in shock. She slowly walked up to the podium, unsure of what to do. The crowd applauded loudly, screaming their approval. She would marry one of England's most notable men. Francis Bolden looked on with the pride only a father could have. Edmund was paralyzed!

When she arrived at the podium, Killingsworth grabbed her hand and pulled her closer to him, smiling at the crowd. Sarah forced out a smile, but she could barely breathe.

Edmund felt a lump in his throat, and his legs went numb. He tried to walk away but was frozen.

Nell ran up to congratulate Sarah. She kissed her on the cheek and gave a seductive smile to Killingsworth. He acknowledged her with a sly grimace of his own.

"Nell, it is so good to see you again. It's been awhile."

Edmund needed to get out of there. He pushed and sidestepped his way through the crowd but was quickly intercepted by the vicar who grabbed him from behind.

"Where are you going?"

Edmund jerked his shoulder away and kept moving.

"I have to get out of here. Just let me go!"

"I'm going with you," the vicar said and followed him out.

The last thing Edmund wanted was company, but the vicar was not going to take no for an answer. They rode silently back to Edmund's home. Dr. Graham watched Edmund dismount and walk into his house. Once inside, Edmund slouched into his chair and stared at the ceiling. Moments later, he had a strange feeling the vicar hadn't left. That feeling was confirmed when he looked out the window.

"If you're just going to sit there, you may as well come in," he yelled.

The vicar dismounted and joined Edmund in the kitchen for a brandy. Edmund didn't say much. He just stewed and wanted to be alone.

When the procession ended, many of the locals offered Sarah and Killingsworth congratulations. Bolden loved the thought of having him for a son-in-law. He wanted the best for his daughter, and Killingsworth could provide a lifestyle she deserved.

It was a year ago that Killingsworth met Bolden on a trip to Bristol. Bolden was completely taken in by his politeness, charm, and humor. When Killingsworth met Sarah, he treated her the same way. Bolden was honored to have a gentleman of Killingsworth's stature to be courting his daughter and hinted he would bestow a healthy-size dowry to the man she married. Killingsworth was enamored by her beauty, but she initially declined his advances until mounting pressure from her father led to a lengthy courtship. It would take marriage before Killingsworth could officially put his hands on her.

One flaw that Killingsworth found in Sarah was her intelligence and her reluctance to conceal it. At the cocktail hour at the end of the night, she spoke of the Tories' influence in ending the war. Anything to do with the Tories usually angered Killingsworth. He mentioned he didn't anticipate her being as opinionated once they were married.

As the night came to an end and people started to filter out, Killingsworth took Sarah's hand and led her outside. She hesitated at first but finally followed him.

"I'd rather not, Alexander. I think I should just turn in for the night," she said nervously.

He leaned over and kissed her neck, but she instinctively jerked away.

"My dear, don't be nervous. It's quite all right if we're together."

She found it hard to catch her breath. She wanted so badly to be with Edmund. She couldn't get the image of seeing Edmund's disappointed look during the proposal announcement. Killingsworth leaned over and kissed her some more. The alcohol made him more aggressive, and he rubbed his hands on her backside and then to the front of her breasts. His breath smelled of whiskey and stale smoke. She tried to pull back, but he was forcing himself on her.

"Stop!"

The words just came out. She nervously awaited his reaction. He pulled back and wiped his hair back under his wig.

"All right, my dear. I see you want to wait." He was seething. "I can respect that."

"I think it's the news about Virginia. It's a little overwhelming to me," she said as her breathing quickened.

He opened the door and led her back in, where her father gave her a big hug.

That night, to relieve his sexual and mental frustration, Killingsworth turned to Nell, who was all too happy to accommodate one of England's most powerful men. She had been sleeping with Killingsworth since he started courting Sarah. Nell was jealous of Sarah's courtship, and by satisfying his lordship, she thought he may change his mind and court her.

She straddled him and rode him hard as Killingsworth impaled her. His hands were on her chest when he grabbed her and rolled her onto her back. He thrust inside her and let out a grunt. He paused, took a deep breath, and rolled off her. His body was covered in sweat. He looked up at the ceiling as his chest expanded up and down.

"It seems Sarah has been avoiding me lately. Is there something wrong that she's told you?"

Nell rolled on Killingsworth's side. Her fingers gently rubbed circles on his chest and stomach.

"Must we talk about Sarah?" She kissed his chest, working her way down.

"You're her friend, what's been troubling her? She seems distant."

She grabbed his penis and started stroking it. He grabbed her by the shoulders and pushed.

"Get off me. I'm done!" he yelled as he took her forearm and flung her off the bed. She crashed hard to the floor.

He got out of bed, grabbing his shirt and pants.

He looked down at Nell. She had curled up, covering her breasts and starting to weep. Killingsworth grabbed her dress and flung it down on her.

"Get dressed and get out of here. I don't want anyone seeing you leave either! Imagine, me having to explain what you're doing here."

She grabbed the dress and undergarments. Clutching them close to her body, she stood there until Killingsworth shoved her to the next room.

"Why are you treating me like this? You deserve what Sarah's doing to you!"

As soon as the words left her lips, she wanted to take them back. She felt flushed and scared. The words slipped out of her mouth.

"And what is Sarah doing?" He grabbed her cheeks with his fingers and squeezed. Nell had a frightened look about her, and now there was no telling what this man was capable of doing.

"Explain yourself, and you'd better tell the truth!"

His fingers still dug into her face, and she was beet red. She could barely get out the words.

"Edmund Drake—she's seeing Edmund Drake!"

Killingsworth let go of her face. His fingers left marks on Nell's cheeks. She was waiting for him to strike. The blow never came. He reached out his hand to her cheek. She flinched, but his hand rubbed her cheek as he let out a guffaw.

"So my little maiden has been keeping company with Drake." He looked Nell in the eyes. "My poor dear, do tell me the sordid details."

She filled him in on their fling, and just when she thought he was going to explode with rage, he just looked at her with a sickened smile. It scared her but excited her at the same time. She was in awe of Killingsworth's power. When she was done, he paced the room.

"I want Drake gone by week's end, but how? I'll get that scummer Pitts on it!"

Nell walked nervously to Killingsworth. "Are you going to want to see me again?"

Killingsworth looked at her as he tucked his shirt in. "When I want to see you again, I'll get a hold of you."

She wiped the tears from her face and forced a smile. Killingsworth forced one as well.

"Now go."

She finished dressing and left.

Near a clump of trees outside the Bolden estate, Edmund slowed his horse down. He proceeded cautiously. He pushed away the last overhanging branches. He heard branches crack but saw nothing. Underbrush stirred, and Sarah appeared from the small path to his left.

He jumped down, tied his mount, and ran to her. He grasped her shoulders, leaned forward, but she pulled back. She appeared tense. A look of panic flushed her face.

"Edmund, I'm so sorry about the engagement. I don't know what to do."

"I don't know either. You have to speak to your father. It's the only way out of this mess."

"It will crush him. He's wanted this for so long."

"No, he wants what's best for you. Eventually, he'll understand."

Her mouth softened, and the corners of her mouth lifted. "I wish that were true."

Edmund pulled her toward him and into his arms. "It's the only choice unless we run away."

"That would truly break my father's heart. I'll speak to him tomorrow."

Edmund pulled back. "You're not serious."

She smiled. "I will. I'll talk to him tomorrow."

They embraced, and Edmund covered her mouth with his. He felt her tongue with his as her lips opened. His hand covered her breast, and they eased down into a patch of grass. They rolled around until he hoisted her dress above her waist and proceeded to enter her. She wrapped her legs around him and dug her heels into his thighs. Her fingers gripped the nape of his neck. They increased to a frantic rhythm until she bit her lip to muffle the sounds of her moans. He climaxed into her and slowly rolled off.

She took a deep breath and folded her hands behind her head. The pale moonlight shone down on them. Edmund put his arm around her.

"You think your father will ever accept me?"

She placed her hand on his cheek and laughed. "No."

For the next hour, they spoke of Wescott, growing up, and their future plans.

Then Sarah looked deep in thought and smiled.

"What's on your mind?" Edmund asked.

"Just something Nell said. She thinks I should marry Killingsworth and keep you on the side."

Edmund shook his head. "I don't think Killingsworth would appreciate it."

Sarah's mouth opened. "How long have we been here? I have to leave."

Edmund smiled. "It's all right. No one knows about us."

"Just the same, when I talk to my father tomorrow, it might be best if we don't see each other for a while. At least until Alexander leaves and the smoke clears."

"That may be hard for me to do."

"Edmund, please. I have a feeling this is not going to go over well."

The next afternoon, Sarah waited outside her father's library. All morning, she paced nervously, rehearsing what she was going to say. She wouldn't mention Edmund's name but rather tell her father she just wasn't ready.

"But your mother was your age when she married," he'd say.

Could she dare tell him the truth? Earlier, one of the servants told her he was in the library doing work. She walked right up to the door but developed a change of heart and backed away.

Sarah stopped in the den and drank a glass of brandy. It burned going down and warmed her insides, but she felt a chill on the outside. Her eyes watered. It seemed to take the edge off. She placed the glass down and went back to the library to meet with her father.

She tapped on the door and listened for a response. Nothing. She slowly opened the door and peered inside. Killingsworth was staring back at her. He was holding works by Shakespeare.

"Do come in, my dear. I've been waiting to speak to you."

Sarah paused. She wanted to run. "I was looking for my father. I need urgently to speak to him."

"Well, he's detained at the moment." He held out his hand. "Please."

She proceeded cautiously and stopped at the doorway.

"Shut the door."

Sarah grabbed the doorknob with a shaking hand and closed it.

"What's this about?"

"You know, my dear, I've always loved Shakespeare. Such tragedy in his writing."

His tone was upsetting to her. She didn't want to be there.

"Love gone awry. Things aren't the way they seem."

"My lord?"

"*Hold your tongue!* I know you were with him. Are you trying to embarrass me? Are you?"

Sarah felt a rush of blood fill her head. "Let me explain."

"And who is this peon that has no idea who he's fucking with?"

"Please, it just happened."

"*Just happened!* We are engaged to be married."

"Alexander."

She hesitated, searching for the right words, but they escaped her. Finally she just blurted out what was on her mind since she met him.

"I don't love you!" She cringed and expected the worst. Killingsworth stared at her, then his face softened, and he started to laugh. She was confused as he turned and spoke in a calm manner.

"What makes you think I love you, my dear? I love your dowry. I admire your father's wealth."

"Then marry him," she interrupted.

He threw the book aside. "Sarah, you will marry me. You will bear my children."

Her eyes welled. She shook her head and walked away.

"I'm telling my father it's over!"

Killingsworth rushed over to her, grabbed her arm, and gave it a quick jerk. His face close to hers as tears rolled down her cheeks.

"You obviously haven't thought this through, my dear." He ran his fingers through her flowing blond hair and then rubbed his cheek against hers.

"Have you thought about your beloved? Cheating with a man's fiancée, I could take and challenge him to a duel to save my honor. I would then blow a hole in his head. Would you like that?"

He suddenly tightened his grip on her hair and yanked it. Sarah grimaced and squirmed to free herself from his grip, but it was too tight.

"Or maybe I can come up with something worse. Maybe Mr. Drake goes off the deep end and ends up on the wrong side of a rope. Have you ever been to a hanging, Sarah?" He chuckled. "It's not a pretty sight. The deformity it does to one's body, especially the neck!"

"Please let me go."

He pulled harder, his voice became angrier.

"Of course, your father would be involved. I'm sure I can dig deep enough to find, or create, skeletons in his closet."

"How could you? He respects you. He's done so much for you."

"I'm a man that gets what he wants. So you see, you are being very selfish, my dear," he said. The edges of his mouth curled up. "If you love this young scrapper, you will never see him again, or I promise you will both feel my wrath!"

He jerked her hair again and let go. Sarah took deep breaths. She tried to speak, but no words came out.

CHAPTER 5

BEN CUTLER

Edmund hardly slept. It had been two weeks since he heard from her. He had ridden by her house, Myers Plantation, Knewt Gardens. Nothing. He kept an ear out to hear of any announcement about a cancelled engagement. Instead, an announcement about Killingsworth marrying Sarah spread through Bristol. They set the date a week from Saturday.

The thought of not being with Sarah was overwhelming. She was the reason for his existence the last few months. He would not be able to hold her, and worse yet, she would be in the arms of Killingsworth. He had to get his mind off her, but how?

With Sarah out of the picture, thoughts quickly turned toward his father as the nightmares had come back to haunt him. It was time he paid a visit to Ben Cutler. It was time he made good on a promise to avenge his father's murder.

He pulled out his father's dueling pistol and held it. His father never used it, but Edmund had. He had fired many a shot with it and wanted to use it one more time. He planned on using it that night.

Just after dark, he rode his horse up to the Cutler estate just to the edge of the woods. Cutler had relocated here after the duel. He was ostracized from the Bristol community.

Staring at the house, he dismounted, trying to adjust his eyes through the dense fog and darkness of the night. It was to no avail, the fog was too thick. He tied his horse to a branch off an old oak tree and walked slowly up the passageway toward the house. The night was hauntingly quiet.

It was a good-size Victorian-style house with two white columns that surrounded the front porch. As he crept closer, the shape of the entire house appeared. He stopped, pulled out his pistol, and looked it over, inspecting it.

No going back now!

He held the gun in his right hand and searched around. The glow was coming from one of the windows upstairs.

Must be him!

He walked closer to the door, grabbed the knob, turned, and pulled.

Locked!

He checked the windows, tugging at each one, but none of them budged.

Take a deep breath!

He looked up and noticed one of the windows was slightly ajar. It appeared to be two rooms from the window with the glow. He tucked his gun into the front of his pants and grabbed one of the columns holding up the porch. He jerked himself up and shimmied his way to the top. Once there, Edmund gazed through the window and searched the room. It seemed empty, but it was too dark to be sure. He slowly pushed upward on the window and crawled through.

Looks like his bedroom.

The bed was empty and neatly made. It was a perfect spot for an ambush.

No, I want him to know it's me. I want to look in his eyes when I pull the trigger!

He searched in darkness, creeping along after stopping to listen to any slight noise. He continued his walk down the hall and came across a fluttering dim glow from the next room.

He walked carefully to the door and peeked around the corner into the hall. The lighting was better as the room with the glow was two doors down.

Grabbing his pistol, he crept slowly down the hall, trying not to let his feet touch the floor. He passed the first door and came upon the room with the flickering light.

At the edge of the door, he took a deep breath. His heart was racing. Holding the pistol up, he entered the room.

There was a man in a comfort chair with his back toward Edmund, reading a book. On the table next to him were a pipe and a glass of liquor.

Edmund stopped in his tracks. His pistol was shaking.

"You've come to avenge your father's death!"

The person in the chair never turned around or even flinched. He was still reading. Edmund slowly walked over until he was face-to-face with his father's murderer.

Cutler shut the book and turned his head in the direction of the young man holding a pistol to his face.

"I heard they sent you away, but I knew you would be back."

Edmund was still silent, looking curiously at Cutler. It was the first time he had seen him face-to-face. He knew of him and saw him on occasion from a distance, but face-to-face had a different feel.

Cutler grabbed his pipe and lit it. He sucked in a few puffs.

"I've pictured this moment a thousand times in my mind."

"So have I," Edmund responded.

"There was a time Daniel, your father, and I were inseparable. We ran trade with the privateers when they came to port. We acted as middlemen to cash in their plunder. We were well-known and respected. Our business flourished! We exchanged gold for rum, rum for gold, sugar—you name it. Whatever was on their vessels was fair game for trade."

He lit his pipe again, taking a few drags, and let out a cloud of smoke. Edmund stared at him transfixed, with a steady finger on the trigger.

"We took our fair share, and the money rolled in. That's why your father is so well-known in these parts."

"You killed him!"

"Our partnership," Cutler continued, "disintegrated when we both fell in love with Cassie, who would become the mother you never knew."

Edmund felt blood rush to his face.

What the hell is he talking about?

"We both courted her aggressively. It became like a competition. Who would outdo who. Our business started to suffer, so we made a deal. Whoever she chose to be with would be the one to run the business and buy the other one out. So you see, not only did I lose Cassie, but I lost my way of life as well."

He reached for his glass and took a swig.

"Brandy?"

Edmund shook his head.

"After choosing Daniel, your mother felt she made a mistake, and we started seeing each other again. It was very secretive. When she found out she was pregnant with you, she ended our relationship. I never saw her again."

"She died giving birth when I was born," Edmund said as tears welled up in his eyes.

"That crushed me as it did Daniel. We both held it against each other for the rest of our lives."

Edmund took a deep breath.

"And you think you are my father?"

"No. You're all Daniel Drake. You have his eyes, his chin, and from what I see tonight, his resolve."

Just shoot him!

"For ten years, we were at each other's throats. Finally, we couldn't even live in the same town. The duel was long coming. We set it up just outside Potter's farm. Your father, me, our seconds, and the squire. I could see when I arrived we both didn't want to go through with it, but our rivalry had gone too far."

Cutler just stared straight-ahead as he was talking. He didn't look at anything in particular, as if the duel had been taking place all over again.

"We kept staring at each other, not saying a word while our seconds loaded powder into the pistols. They stuffed the balls into the chambers and handed us our guns. The squire positioned us back-to-back."

I don't want to hear this!

"He started counting as we paced in opposite directions. When he reached ten, I turned and saw Daniel's pistol pointing at me. My gun fired, his never did!"

He paused and reached for his brandy.

"Why didn't he shoot me? He had me dead to rights. He never pulled the trigger."

Cutler started shaking his head.

"I can't get it out of my head. He had me dead to rights."

He looked up at Edmund and the pistol pointing at him. He had the look of a man wanting to die, to end his guilt of the whole situation.

Cutler then looked away, opened his book, and started to read. Never looking away from his page, he spoke up again. "It's hard to kill a man. It's even harder to live with it."

Tears flowed down Edmund's face. He wanted to kill this man so badly when he rode up, and now? Looking down, he lowered the pistol by his side and let it slip out of his hand, crashing to his feet. He paused and then slowly walked to the door and down the hall to the stairs. He walked out as quietly as he came in. He unlocked the door and walked toward his horse. His mind was venturing in every direction. It was all too confusing. Here was a chance to kill the very man that had done in his father, and he let it go. He shook his head and mounted. He stared at the house and started to ride back home. In the distance coming from the house, a gunshot went off.

CHAPTER 6

A NEW FUTURE

"Are you going to pick at your food or eat it?" Mrs. Graham asked Edmund.

"Evelyn, please," the vicar countered. He stared at her and made a head gesture for her to leave. She excused herself and grabbed the vicar's plate. She left Edmund's alone as it still had the eggs and biscuits on it.

Both men stood up as Mrs. Graham walked out of the room. The vicar watched her leave and gazed at Edmund. Dr. Graham had invited Edmund over for breakfast, having been worried about him since the gala honoring Killingsworth and the engagement announcement.

"What's troubling you, boy?" he said, sitting back at the table.

"I need to see Sarah. It's been weeks. I just can't let it end like this."

"What about Killingsworth? Do you know who you're dealing with?"

"I'll take my chances. She loves me, not him." Edmund's voice was firm.

"Killingsworth is a ruthless man. He's someone you don't challenge and certainly you don't mock. Another thing, word is out. If I know about you two, half of Bristol does. That also means Killingsworth will find out, if he hasn't already."

"I'm not afraid of him!"

"You should be afraid of Killingsworth. Quite frankly, I'm afraid for you."

"Don't be."

"There you go, that cocky arrogance that runs in your family. That arrogance killed your father."

"Don't say that!"

"You remember when Bolden brought up the Battle of Malplaquet at that hoopla for Killingsworth?"

Edmund nodded. "Didn't that change the momentum of the war? I heard it was the bloodiest battle of them all."

"Do you know who led the charge? He sacrificed many men to get recognition for that battle."

"Sounds like a real peach."

"When he left the army, he entered the political arena where he quickly rose through the ranks. He stepped on a lot of toes to get to where he is. In other words, don't get in his way. He'll do anything to get what he wants."

"Dr. Graham, I'm in love with Sarah and need to see her. You told me not to lack the courage to follow my destiny. It's Sarah. Can you help me?" Edmund's eyes were moist.

The vicar looked up to the heavens, expecting an answer to fall down on him. None came.

"Edmund, you're like a son to me. What do you need?"

Edmund took the fork and swirled his food around. He finally dropped the fork on the plate, wiped his mouth, and stood up. He reached in his vest.

"I need you to get this letter to Sarah."

The vicar gave him a concerned look as he grabbed the letter.

"She'll get it," he said, waving the letter. "But please be careful. He'll hang you from the gallows without thinking twice if he finds out about you two!"

Edmund started to leave but stopped. He placed his hands on his face and turned around.

"Dr. Graham, one other thing. I went to Ben Cutler's last night."

The vicar turned in horror. "You didn't. I thought we agreed on—"

"I had to do it, sir."

"And?"

"I couldn't kill him." Edmund turned away, unable to face him. "I wanted to so bad, but I just couldn't. He told me about the old days, the smuggling days. I wanted to shoot him so bad, but I just couldn't do it." Tears welled up in Edmund's eyes. The vicar walked toward him, grabbing his quaking shoulders.

"It's all right, son. It's all right." He hugged him and shut his eyes. "Hopefully, this whole ordeal with Ben Cutler is finally over."

"I don't know. While on my way home, I heard a gun go off. I didn't know what to do. I'm sorry."

"God almighty, I'd better stop by there. Don't tell anyone about this."

The vicar tapped Edmund's head and watched him leave. "Good luck, and may God go with you."

Later that afternoon, Dr. Graham rode up to Cutler's house. He had been detained by Mrs. Porridge's insistence he come check her three-week-old granddaughter. He finally pried himself away from the woman and on to the business at hand. The more he thought about Edmund visiting Cutler, the more anxious he was to see him. He knocked on the door, but there was no answer. He walked around the back and noticed the horses were still in the stable.

"Ben! It's me, Bartlett!" No answer. He walked back around and reached for the front door. He twisted it open.

Unlocked!

"Ben!"

No answer. He walked through the house and went upstairs. He almost walked by the reading room until he noticed the floor covered in red.

Ben! Oh my god.

The vicar looked down and saw the right side of Ben Cutler's head blown off. Next to his head on the floor was a dueling pistol. He picked it up, and the initials DD were inscribed on the handle.

Daniel Drake!

He picked up the gun and stuffed it in his vest. He ran down the stairs to get some help.

Please tell me Edmund had nothing to do with this.

After receiving Edmund's letter, she met him at the clearing outside Myers Plantation. It was not easy to rendezvous. Killingsworth watched her like a hawk. He had his men tail her and even paid servants extra to find out if she did anything out of the ordinary.

Killingsworth was going to make sure their wedding went off smoothly and get her out of England.

The wedding of Sarah Bolden and Alexander Killingsworth was scheduled a week from Saturday. It had to be rushed as Killingsworth's leadership in Virginia was needed. Tobacco became its leading export, and George Hamilton enacted the Tobacco Act of 1713, which required inspections of all tobacco products exported or bartered. C`haos ensued as the inspections were crooked, and often big payoffs were needed to pass the merchandise. Killingsworth was needed to restore order as even the wealthiest plantation owners were in an uproar. Hamilton received half of the profits on Virginia exports and made sure Killingsworth would get his share by working for him.

The thought of marrying Killingsworth sickened Sarah almost as much as leaving Bristol to live in Virginia. The place sounded so foreign to her. She would miss her friends and family. She tried to mention this to her father, but his attitude was more along the lines of "you do what your husband wants, you take care of his needs and raise a family."

Sarah had Nell create a diversion, and she slipped out through the back paths of the woods where she tied one of her mares. She was reluctant at first to meet with Edmund. She was worried about his safety and Killingsworth's threats to her family. Those thoughts were erased when she saw him waiting for her. They embraced and held each other, not letting go.

"I've thought about you all the time. Edmund, I'm so sorry about not seeing you. Killingsworth found out about us. He threatened my family if I didn't marry him." She cried, shaking her head.

"It's okay. I love you, Sarah!"

She looked up at him. She needed to hear those words from him.

"I love you too."

They hugged even tighter as Sarah buried her face in Edmund's chest.

"We need to run off. It's the only way," he said.

"My family. Killingsworth would hurt them. He'd stop at nothing to hunt you down."

"We have no choice."

"He'll cause so much trouble around here."

"He'll be gone in a few weeks. He has to go to Virginia. They need him there."

"You think he'll really leave?"

"Without a doubt. We'll meet tonight at twelve midnight right over there." He pointed to the edge of the woods. "Just pack enough clothes to travel light. We can ride all night and get to my uncle's estate in Kent. We'll be safe there until Killingsworth returns to Virginia."

"He won't let it go, Edmund. We'll be running for the rest of our lives."

"Do you trust me?"

She nodded and tried to smile. "You know I do."

"It's the only way we can be together."

"My father is going to be devastated. I'm his baby girl."

"He wants what's best for you, and Killingsworth is not it by any means!"

"Did you tell the vicar?"

"He would think I'm totally insane. I must be insane." He grabbed her shoulders and kissed her. "But I love being insane."

She gave him a quirky look, and they embraced. He kissed her cheek.

"Tonight starts a whole new future together!"

CHAPTER 7

THE PRESS-GANG

Edmund's mind was in a state of confusion all day. He gathered money and played out the day's scenario. Pack food, provisions, and clothing. Leave Dr. Graham a message. After that, he had to wait. He was anxious. Sarah and him finally together! He also knew it wouldn't sit well with Killingsworth or Bolden, and there would be a lot of explaining to do when they returned.

Time dragged slowly all day. Time especially dragged that night. He just sat around and waited. He lit a candle and started reading Dampier's novel about the sea. Then he would slam the book shut and pace about the room. After a while, he heard horses outside.

He got up and looked out the window. He recognized one of the riders from the Killingsworth gala. It was that colonel that was always a stone's throw from Killingsworth. Almost like his bodyguard. Four other riders accompanied him.

Edmund reached into his drawer and pulled out two pistols. He held one and tucked the other in his pants. He grabbed a sword and headed out the door.

The four men waited for the colonel to pass them as he led the way to the house. Edmund opened the door and greeted them at the head of the porch.

"That's far enough!" he said, drawing his sword and cocking his pistol.

Out of the corner of his eye, he saw a man coming at him. Edmund turned but was quickly jumped by a man off the porch ledge above him. They fell to the ground as Edmund's pistol fell out of his hand. Edmund escaped the man's grip but was jumped from behind by the other one who leaped on his back and hooked an arm around his throat. The other one got up and thrust his fist into Edmund's stomach. As his breath exploded out of him, the impact doubled him over, throwing his head down. His sword fell to the ground. The colonel rode up, screaming, "Enough! We don't want any trouble, boy. I'm Colonel Pitts. You need to come with us. Lord Killingsworth would like to have a word with you!"

Edmund looked up, trying to catch his breath and reaching in his pants for the other pistol.

"And if I refuse!"

Pitts laughed. "I hope you do, boy. I hope you do!"

The other men grabbed their pistols.

"Put them away, men. He's not stupid enough to shoot at us. Are you, boy? Besides, if we wanted to kill you, you'd be lying toes up!"

Edmund dropped his gun and walked past Pitts toward the barn to retrieve his horse. Pitts followed. He mounted it and waved his arm.

"After you!"

Pitts, looking disappointed that there was no resistance, led the group out.

Dr. Graham rode up to Edmund's house. It was late, but he had to confront him about Cutler and the pistol he found there. It was around eleven, but this was the earliest the vicar could arrive.

After finding Cutler's body earlier, he had sent a message to Constable Hughes to meet him. The constable was a very thorough man and grilled the vicar on every little detail and even as to why the vicar was there in the first place. The vicar answered all the questions and then dealt with consoling the few remaining relatives Cutler had.

He banged on the door, but no one answered. He saw a pistol and a sword on the porch. The silence reminded him when he first arrived at Cutler's house. He quickly barged through the door and screamed, "Edmund, where are you? Are you all right?"

He grabbed a candle and checked the rooms. When he arrived at Edmund's bedroom, he noticed it was empty. He walked back down to the living room, and on his way out, he noticed a stack in the corner. When he shone light on it, they were bags of clothes and other necessities packed tightly as if he was going on a trip. There was also a note on the windowsill. It was addressed to him.

> Dr. Graham,
>
> You told me to follow my heart and that's what I'm doing.
>
> I will find you soon!
>
> Edmund

The riders surrounded Edmund as they rode through Queen Square and to the house where Killingsworth was staying.

"Isn't it a bit unusual for a colonel to be doing this kind of legwork?" Edmund asked.

"If Killingsworth needs something done, he comes to me."

"I guess that makes for a quick rise up the ranks."

They pulled up to the rail, dismounted, and tied up the horses. Pitts led the group up the walkway. Edmund had two guards at his sides and the two others behind. The house was a minimansion, which was located off the main road. It was used to house royalty or important dignitaries during lengthy visits. Francis Bolden had arranged for Killingsworth to stay there from the time of his arrival until the marriage to his daughter.

Pitts arrived at the front door, which was lit by four lanterns, and banged the metal latch on the door. The door flew opened, and Edmund was face-to-face with Alexander Killingsworth.

"Come in." He extended his hand toward the hallway. He looked at Pitts and his crew.

"Good job, men."

Pitts and his soldiers waited outside while Edmund entered the guesthouse. Killingsworth gave Pitts a curious look and closed the door. He led Edmund to the library. Once inside, Killingsworth took a seat behind a large desk. There were books and folders scattered all over it, and he pointed for Edmund to take a seat across from him.

He declined.

"As you wish."

He opened one of the desk drawers and took out a small pouch.

"I asked you here to make an offer."

Edmund stared at the man, waiting for him to continue.

"Two hundred guineas are yours. You leave town and do not come back until my wife and I are in Virginia."

"Is that all she's worth to you?" Edmund said firmly.

"Obviously not, if you knew the dowry Bolden was paying me," Killingsworth replied.

"I'm really not interested in leaving. This is my home."

"How commendable, such honor. You know I'm a man that gets whatever he wants. We can do this profitably, or we can do this in an uglier fashion. You decide!"

"You can stick your money, I'm out of here!"

Edmund turned and walked toward the door.

"I wouldn't leave just yet." Killingsworth stood up and kicked back the chair. "It's a shame Ben Cutler was murdered." Edmund stopped in his tracks and turned back to Killingsworth, his mouth open. "Yeah, it was just discovered. Do you know anyone that would want to kill him?"

Edmund shook his head in disbelief. He remembered the shot.

Suicide?

"My history of this town is a little sketchy," Killingsworth continued. "Why were you sent away to school in London?"

"I didn't kill him."

Edmund felt heat rush to his face. He moved closer to Killingsworth.

"I know you didn't kill him. We actually followed you over there. When you chickened out, it was left to us to finish the job you didn't have the stomach for. Wouldn't you know, when my men broke in, Cutler already shot himself? The convenient part of the whole situation is that he used your gun! That doesn't bode well for you now, does it?" Killingsworth reached for a cutlass hanging on the wall and drew it toward Edmund. "I think we need to take you in. By the way, while I'm in this district, I am the law of the land." He smirked. "You should have taken the money!"

He walked closer to Edmund who looked around the room for an escape route.

"Don't worry, I'm fair!" Killingsworth said, smiling.

Edmund tried to get a sense of his surroundings.

Where were Killingsworth's henchmen?

There were a couple of smallswords hanging up on the mantle, which Edmund caught a glance of. Killingsworth smiled and pointed up to them.

"Go ahead, let's see what you've got. It'll be as though I killed an intruder breaking in. No, not an intruder, a murderer. A jealous, desperate boy!"

Edmund jumped onto a chair near the wall and grabbed a smallsword that was hanging there. He jumped down, swinging the sword wildly at Killingsworth who deflected it with ease. Killingsworth swung his heavier cutlass, and it ricocheted off Edmund's sword. He barely hung on. The next blow knocked the sword out of Edmund's hand.

Edmund grabbed a wooden chair and quickly held it up as a shield. Killingsworth quickly splintered one of its legs. The cutlass reached back and chopped off a second leg.

"Boy, you are trying my patience!"

As Killingsworth tried to reach around, Edmund shoved the splintered chair at him, knocking him off balance. With the other arm, he swung his fist, catching Killingsworth's jaw. Edmund dove for the sword and swung as Killingsworth drew back his cutlass. The smallsword caught Killingsworth's forearm.

Blood quickly spurted out around his sleeve, and then Edmund caught Killingsworth's wrist with another crisp swipe. A surprised Killingsworth dropped his weapon, and Edmund held his smallsword to his chest. He heard a noise in the hall and knew, in a matter of seconds, the soldiers from the hall would be on him.

Killingsworth backed up. Edmund heard someone at the door. He moved closer to Killingsworth and held the sword to his throat as the door busted open. Pitts and his men quickly stormed in and surrounded Edmund.

"Don't do it, matey," Pitts said nervously as he held a blunderbuss toward Edmund's head.

"You better back off or your governor is a dead man."

Everyone froze. The soldiers kept their weapons in check and watched Edmund. Sweat poured from his face as he looked around the room. There was no way out.

"Shoot him," Killingsworth ordered.

Edmund pointed the sword into Killingsworth's neck. It pierced the skin, and blood trickled down.

"I gave you an order!" he screamed.

Edmund's hand started to twitch as the soldiers waved their swords and inched closer. Pitts walked to Edmund and held the blunderbuss six inches away.

"Drop it now."

Edmund's sword fell to the ground. Killingsworth took the blunderbuss from Pitts and came down hard on the side of Edmund's head with the butt of his pistol. Edmund's legs went rubbery and went down with a thud as the soldiers looked on.

"Well, what should we do with him?" Pitts asked.

Killingsworth leaned down and clutched Edmund's blood-soaked scalp and lifted. He was barely conscious as the room spun around.

"Colonel Pitts, gather your men. You're to get a hold of Captain Morble first thing in the morning. I want him to take care of that business we discussed about McGinnty. He's to set sail by midday tomorrow. He has my orders. I want McGinnty caught and that treasure found."

"Yes, my lord. I thought he was to wait another week."

"The plans have changed. I want to make sure all goes well in capturing McGinnty. He's been on the loose too long. We're going to have Morble trail him to New Providence or wherever he's hiding."

"What should we do with him?" Pitts said, pointing to Edmund. "Haul his ass to jail? We left his gun by Cutler's body."

"No. A trial could take weeks. I want him gone now. We'll make it as though he killed Cutler and ran off. When they find the murder weapon, they'll look all over England for him."

"Yes, my lord, but shouldn't we take him in? He should be punished. He tried to murder you and—"

Killingsworth stared at Pitts, which silenced him immediately. He banged Edmund's head against the floor and stood up.

"Don't question me. Take him with you and give him to Morble. Tell him he's got a new recruit!"

"Yes, my lord."

He picked up the pistol and looked down at Edmund who was still groggy. "Make sure Morble knows where I stand concerning this new recruit and that he goes through hell. I want him to wish I had killed him tonight! Are we on the same page, Colonel?"

Pitts smirked. "I believe we are, my lord. Morble is a scummer. He'll know what to do."

"Now get him out of my sight!"

Sarah reached the Myers Plantation and dismounted. The light of the moon had shown bright as she walked to where she had met Edmund earlier that morning. She was torn between letting her father down and the excitement of a new beginning with Edmund. A smile settled in the edges of her mouth, and the anticipation of his arrival had her traipsing about the clearing.

Earlier in the evening, her father stayed up later than usual, and the two had a good conversation about her childhood. He told her how excited he was that she would soon be married and hopefully start a family of her own. He was happy she was marrying into wealth and prosperity, then toasted her future.

Sarah couldn't sleep for other reasons. The excitement of leaving with Edmund was filling her head. She was packed and ready. She had two small bags filled and left them down by the corner of the barn. She barely listened to her father speak but stared at him, wondering how disappointed he was going to be. When would she see him again, and would he understand? When she told him good night, she kissed him hard on the cheek and tried to keep the tears in check.

"My dear, what's the matter?"

She forced a smile. "Good night, Daddy. I love you."

"Why where did that come from? Are you all right? You don't seem yourself tonight. Must be nerves about the wedding."

She gave him a long look and walked up the stairs. Her legs were trembling. At the top step, she turned around and looked at her father in what would be the last time for a while.

I hope you forgive me.

In her room, she grabbed Shakespeare and opened it up. She always tried to read a few acts every night, and it usually put her into a deep sleep. Tonight, she read to hasten time. She moved over to the window to bring her lamp closer to her bed. Time moved slowly. She blew out the lamp and stared at the ceiling for an eternity.

Finally, it was time to go. She lit a candle in the corner of her room and quickly got dressed. Running down the stairs, she noticed her father was still awake and sipping a brandy by the fireplace. She dodged the study so as not to be seen and made her way to the door, which she carefully opened. She crept outside and then sprinted for the barn.

Once she made her way to Myers Plantation, thoughts raced through her head as she spread out a blanket and sat down. After a while, she laid back and rested her hands behind her head as she looked into the clear night. The stars were especially bright, and the night was quiet.

So we hide for a while. My father will forgive me . . . eventually.

She leaned up on her elbows and looked toward the path Edmund would be arriving on. A wide smile stretched across her face, and the wait was killing her.

"C'mon, Edmund."

The next afternoon, Sarah walked through the front door and was greeted by curious and worried looks. A number of unexpected guests were there including Killingsworth and Dr. Graham. Bolden looked aghast as his daughter's eyes were red and puffy. He walked over to her and put his arms around her.

"We've been looking for you all morning. Are you all right?"

She had a dazed and empty look about her as she shook her head. Dr. Graham walked over to her. Killingsworth followed.

"My dear, you put quite a scare into us. I have soldiers searching the countryside for you. Your father sent word that you'd been missing."

Sarah forced a smile and tried to speak, but words would not come out. Killingsworth rubbed her cheek and then gave it a pat. She stared straight-ahead.

"Let's get her inside," Bolden said.

Dr. Graham brought over a warm blanket and surrounded her shoulders with it.

"I'm all right," she muttered. "I just needed to take a walk last night. I couldn't sleep."

Killingsworth glared at her and then turned to Bolden.

"I think we can get back to the business at hand and look for this Drake fellow."

Sarah jerked her head toward him but kept her silence.

"What makes you think Edmund is involved with Cutler's murder?" the vicar asked.

"Come now. I know you were close to him, but who else could it be? He had every reason to do it, and he's nowhere to be found. Didn't they find the gun that killed Cutler?"

"The gun?" the vicar asked. He gave Killingsworth a curious look. "You mean the murder weapon was found?"

Killingsworth grimaced and turned toward Dr. Graham.

"I heard a gun was found by the body."

"I haven't heard anything of that nature," Bolden replied. "My lord, have you heard they found the weapon?"

Killingsworth looked at both men. "Maybe I heard wrong."

Sarah noticed the look in Killingsworth's eyes and became suspicious immediately.

"I'm going to get some rest," she said, and with a slow, almost languorous step, she walked toward the stairs. One of the servants stopped her and offered her tea. She declined.

"Yes, my dear, you do look tired," Killingsworth said and escorted her to the stairs.

"Please, I'll be all right." And in a trancelike state, she lurched up the stairs.

Dr. Graham turned toward Bolden. "Do you think they really did find a murder weapon?"

"Hughes would have mentioned it to me if they had. Does anyone need a drink besides me?"

Killingsworth and the vicar nodded in agreement as Bolden went to fetch some brandy.

"So you're sure the killer is Edmund," the vicar said to Killingsworth.

"I'm pretty sure. We have troops looking for him as we speak. We'll send word out to neighboring towns. We'll get him."

Sarah paused at the top of the steps.

Edmund, what's happened to you?

CHAPTER 8

THE FLOATING PRISON

Edmund woke up in a damp corner. The way everything swayed back and forth, it didn't take long to figure out he was on a ship of some sorts. His wrists and ankles were chained, and his head was aching fiercely. Gray sunlight pierced through the portholes of the narrow cabin. He was exhausted, hungry, and nervous. Men were moving about, giving him curious glances. He leaned against one of the sides and brought his knees up against his chest, trying to get comfortable. The sides of his face were caked in blood.

Sarah?

The thoughts of her wouldn't leave his head. He had to get word to Sarah what happened, but how? He didn't even know where he was.

Finally, three men in naval uniforms came down, lifted him by his elbows, and escorted him up to top deck. The sun pierced through Edmund's eyes and was especially bright as it reflected off the ocean. He lifted his arms to try and shield the glare, but it was no use. When his eyes finally focused, a large gathering of men had lined the deck, and one started addressing them. The voice came from above him and sounded coarse and harsh.

"A few of you are new to this ship. I welcome you aboard. My name is Captain Morble. Your names are not important. You are here to serve this ship. You screw up, and I will make sure you regret it every minute you are aboard."

Captain Morble stood on the deck directly above Edmund. His hair was dark, greasy, and scraggly. His nose was crooked and puffy.

His dark brown eyes were small and close together. He had a sunken chin, and his teeth stuck out. He wore sweat-stained clothes, and he didn't differ from the rest of the crew, with the exception that he was barking out orders.

Two of the crewmen unshackled Edmund's wrists and ankles. Edmund rubbed them, trying to get the circulation back.

Morble walked down the steps and walked past each of the men. When he came to Edmund, he stopped.

"You!" He lunged forward suddenly, grabbing Edmund by the hair. Edmund struggled to maintain his balance. Morble stepped back, his face stiff with anger. "Get down on your knees."

"What the hell!" Edmund grabbed Morble's arm to keep his balance.

"Chestus?" Morble gestured to a large man with a scraggly beard and most of his teeth missing.

He came over and slapped Edmund over the side of his head. Edmund staggered. He saw a second blow flying toward his face. He tried to jerk to the side, but his reactions were slowed by fatigue. The blow laid him on the deck. He lay on his side, barely conscious.

Morble smiled again. "I said on your knees."

Edmund rolled over, breathing loudly through his open mouth. Chestus's nails dug deep into Edmund's cheek, oozing blood as he straightened him up.

"Men, what you are about to witness are the results of disobedience! I'm told this man tried to steal something that wasn't his."

Morble signaled to Chestus who grabbed another crewman and some rope. They tied rope around Edmund's wrists and dragged him over to the stairs. They stretched his arms far apart and attached him facing the stairs. They did the same to his ankles and stretched him apart, back facing the crew. He was kept upright by two ropes over the crossbar at the top of the stairway and tied under his armpits. They stretched him out to the sides and latched them to upright bars. Morble walked slowly next to Edmund. He held out his hand, and one of the crew placed a cat-o'-nine-tails in it. Morble inspected it with a sly grin, noticing the miniature hooks tied to some of the loose ends of rope. He tapped his fingers along the sharp edges and nodded to the guards who proceeded to tear the shirt off Edmund's back. Morble addressed the crowd again.

"Disobedience will not be tolerated!"

He dipped the cat-o'-nine-tails in oil, turned, and quickly struck Edmund's lower back, leaving a red welt. The sound the whip made was not nearly as loud as the shriek Edmund made when it snapped against his back. Edmund barely caught his breath when a second strike hit him in the same spot. Skin ripped from his body. His back was burning.

He struck a third time, the whip cracked against his back, and the pain intensified, causing Edmund to almost lose consciousness. He cried out and twisted away. After the fourth strike, Morble stopped and took a sip of rum. Then he reached for a jar of pickle brine. Blood trickled down Edmund's back, soaking the bridge of his pants. The cool ocean breeze seemed to soothe the stinging pain, but that was short-lived. Morble poured the pickle brine down his back. Edmund shrieked. His back was on fire as his arms strained against the ropes, burning his wrists. Morble struck again. Crewmembers winced at what was transpiring.

Crack!

The leather smacked against his skin and sounded like a face being slapped. Edmund flinched again.

The whip snapped at his upper back, then lower and middle. It struck again and again and again. There was nothing but raw skin on Edmund's back side, and even a deep breath brought a sting to Edmund's back. Only the rope that tied him to the roped stairs held him up. Edmund heard crewmembers gasping in the crowd but couldn't make out what was said. Those were the last sounds he heard before passing out.

Edmund lay in a small hammock when he awoke. He was on his stomach, his back stinging and numb.

"You're quite popular with the captain. What did you do to feel his wrath?"

The voice came from the hammock next to him, almost on top of him. Edmund looked around. Hammocks were cramped two feet apart. Half were empty.

"I was in the wrong place at the wrong time."

The voice laughed. "You still are!" The man leaned over and extended his hand to Edmund. "I officially welcome you to Her Majesty's Royal Navy. Jon Galvin. Pleased to meet you."

A face appeared out of the shadows, and Jon looked no older than him. "Edmund Drake." They clasped hands.

Edmund tried to roll over, but the welts on his back made him cringe.

"Just stay down." Jon reached to the deck and grabbed a bottle. "I have olive oil. It'll take some of the sting out."

He rubbed it on Edmund's back. It stung at first then felt soothing.

Edmund finally asked, "Where are we?"

"Somewhere in the Atlantic, I presume. We never know where we're going or what we're doing. We just serve the ship."

"What do you do?"

"Keep the sails in one piece, clean the weapons, help the cook. We have to do a little bit of everything."

They talked for a while, and Jon didn't seem like the typical career seaman. He talked slowly, carefully choosing his words. He didn't appear rough and hardened by the sea. Finally, Edmund's curiosity got the better of him.

"There's no way you signed up for this. It's obvious you didn't volunteer for this abuse, so why are you here?"

Jon forced a laugh. He lay back in his hammock and placed his hands behind his head.

"My friends took me out the night before I was to be married. We hit a few pubs and really tied one on. Anyway, the press-gang came in and intimidated my so-called friends. They ended up running. I was too drunk to know what was going on, so they carried me out. They raided ten pubs or so that night and 'recruited' fifteen of us."

"Some friends you have."

"The press wanted them too, they get paid £1 for each recruit. The press thought it would be a cruel joke to sign me to a tour. It's been about ten months now. I still haven't been able to get in touch with my fiancée."

"Isn't she looking for you?"

"Are you kidding? How are they going to find me out here? She probably thinks I got cold feet and ran off."

"I don't get it. Since the end of the war, the docks are crawling with out-of-work sailors. Men are taking jobs for practically nothing."

"I'm one of the only ones that can read on board. They use me to translate Spanish and French maps and letters of marquess. They won't even let me leave the ship when we are at port for fear of desertion."

Edmund shut his eyes and started to doze off. Jon interrupted his sleep.

"You know, you better be careful. Morble doesn't seem too fond of you."

"What gave you that idea?" Edmund chuckled.

"A few months back, Morble had a cabin boy he didn't like. The boy was beaten every day. He even made the kid eat his own crap."

"What happened to him?" Edmund asked.

"He died, of course. His body was a rainbow of colors, flesh like jelly, and bones broken. They tried to bring Morble up on charges in London, but they were quickly dismissed."

Edmund's eyes rolled open. Now he had something else on his mind besides Sarah: survival.

"Where to begin?" Killingsworth asked, rubbing his hands.

Sarah stood in front of him. She smelled whiskey from his breath panting into her face. She took a deep breath and closed her eyes.

The dreaded wedding night had finally come. It was on her mind all day as the orchestra played. It was on her mind during the ceremony. It was on her mind at the reception outside the church. Hundreds of guests were chatting and laughing under the oaks and magnolias on the side of the lawn. Fine carriages were parked on one side of the lane. Smoke drifted in the air from the barbeque. Killingsworth held the bride's hand for most of the reception and gave her the proverbial peck on the cheek throughout. Guests lined up to offer congratulations, and then it was time to leave. She hoped it had tired him out. It didn't.

"Please. Not tonight."

He clamped his thick fingers on her breasts outside her gown and squeezed hard. Her body was trembling. His hands made their way inside, and he pinched her nipples between his forefinger and thumb.

"Please don't," she said, her body cringing.

"You wouldn't say no if I was your Edmund. Your clothes would be off already. It makes me sick to think of how fast they'd be off."

"I'm not feeling well." Her voice cracked. She felt hopelessly trapped.

"You're not going to deprive me. Not tonight."

He threw her on the bed. She crawled under the sheets. He swept them off her. He pushed the hem of her gown past her waist and shoved his hand to the cleft between her legs.

Killingsworth mounted her. His weight pushed down hard. She lay there, looked up at the ceiling. He thrust himself inside her. She stared at a painting on the wall—Knewt Gardens, the oak trees, magnolia, babbling brook. She tried to concentrate on it. She wished she was in the picture. Anywhere but here.

His thrusts became more assertive. She closed her eyes and clenched her fists. Finally, he was done. Tears ran down her cheek. Killingsworth wiped them with the back of his hand.

"Don't worry, my dear. You'll learn to like it. We have plenty of time. Till death do us part."

That night, Killingsworth exercised his rights as a husband two more times—roughly.

PART II

CHAPTER 9

THE HIGH SEAS

After nine months on the ship, Edmund was twenty pounds lighter. His face had a gray sunken appearance; his back was covered in purple blotches and scar tissue from random floggings he received. But he learned how to survive.

He sat on a crate in the corner of the ship. The sun was scorching, and he was dying of thirst. The fresh water supply didn't stay fresh very long and, within weeks, reeked and was a greenish color. He drank beer, which was rationed one gallon per day per crewmember.

Edmund poked fingers through his oatmeal, uncovering maggots and weevils wiggling in it. Shaking his head, he flicked them out and then devoured his food. He reached for a piece of beef and held it to his nose. It was rancid, so he threw it overboard, not wanting to get ill. He chugged more beer to kill the taste of the oatmeal.

Edmund made no angry comments, statements, or criticisms toward the captain or the ship. He wanted to blend in and hope Morble wouldn't notice him. Every day, he went about his monotonous jobs—swabbing the deck, cleaning the cannons, sewing the sails, tying the riggings.

Reaching into his vest, he pulled out the letter he had been writing to Sarah. When he heard footsteps coming toward him, he quickly shoved it back. He knew the letter by heart, trying to find the right words to describe the kidnapping and months spent at sea. He hoped someday to send it to her.

Chestus stood next to him with a sickened grin. As his grin turned into a smile, the gaps in his mouth were surrounded by yellow rotted teeth. He was a short portly man whose stomach stretched over his pants and was constantly sweating—not from physical activity but just from being overweight. He was Morble's eyes and ears among the crew for which he was rewarded the rank of bosun's mate. A position in which he would strike men with a rope or cane if he felt they weren't working hard enough.

"Drake, you need to clean the head before we pull into port."

As he approached, he kicked Edmund's bowl, and oatmeal sprayed the deck. Edmund showed no reaction.

"And clean that up!" Chestus yelled as he walked away.

Edmund slowly got up, grabbed some rags and an old brown leather hat that was creased in the front. It was covered in tar to repel water, as was his clothing.

The ship's head consisted of a plank with a hole at the end, which hung over and away from the ship, where men straddled to relieve themselves. Cleaning it was the most demeaning job on the ship, and Chestus assigned it to Edmund regularly

Looking around, half the crew was sick. Some were dying. Many had died. Lice, rats, and cockroaches swarmed the vessel; and typhoid and plague were becoming a concern for the crew. Many were weak from scurvy, losing their will to live.

There were two hundred men crammed on the two-hundred-foot-long HMS *Fitzgerald.* The four-hundred-ton frigate had been tailing Jack McGinnty since it left England. They sailed to Saint Lucia, Marinique, Saint Christopher, and Hispaniola. They missed him by two days in Tortuga.

He noticed Jon waddling toward him, covering his stomach.

"What's the matter with you?"

Jon bumped into him and steered him along the edge, maneuvering their backs to the rest of the crew. From under his shirt, Jon pulled out a piece of chicken, bread, and two limes.

"Here, take this," he said, handing it over. "Eat it quickly."

Edmund's eyes lit up. "Where did you get this?"

"I paid off the rations officer. I still have a little money hidden away."

Edmund filled his mouth with bread and, before swallowing, took a big bite from the piece of chicken.

"Slow down. You'll throw up."

Edmund mumbled, trying to swallow at the same time. He started coughing as his eyes watered.

Jon looked around to see if anyone was looking over. Edmund peeled the fruit and noticed Chestus coming back. He quickly shoved a lime in his mouth and tucked the rest of the food in his pants.

"What's going on here?" Chestus asked. His beady eyes squinted, trying to look around Jon at Edmund.

Jon turned his back to Chestus and walked away. Edmund froze.

"Didn't I give you orders before?" Then he turned and yelled to anyone that would listen, "We need to clean this ship before we get to Port Royal. We're picking up some supplies and a few new recruits to escort a slave ship to Charles Town."

Edmund started walking away.

"Of course, you won't be going ashore," Chestus said.

Edmund stopped. Then he continued toward the ship's stern.

That night, Edmund slept lightly in the close confines under a leaky forecastle. Each crewman had two feet of deck space to hang a hammock with men on either side. One-third of the crew slept at a time, with the others on watch or working topside.

The smell under decks was mostly foul as clothing was rarely changed. Jon came in and lunged into his hammock next to Edmund.

"We need to get out of here, we're not going to survive," Edmund whispered. "Morble doesn't want us to survive."

Jon turned toward him and spoke softer than Edmund. "We can't leave. If we're caught, it's desertion."

"You don't understand. We're just slowly dying here. All of us."

"What do you think we should do?"

Edmund placed his hands behind his head.

"What if we swim to shore tomorrow night when we arrive? They'll never waste time looking for us when they have to get that cargo to Charles Town. It'll take 'em days to get back here, and we could be somewhere else."

"I don't know. We have no money. I spent the last of what I had on our lunch. Besides, who would help us?"

"What about pirates? They must hate the British navy and would help. Maybe we could sail back with them."

Jon rose up and sat in his hammock. "Edmund, I think the sun is affecting your brain." His whispers were louder. "Why would they help us, and why the hell would they go back to England? They're a bunch of criminals and would kill us at the drop of a hat. Why don't we just ask Scarface McGinnty himself for a ride?"

Jon was not only Edmund's sole friend on board. He was also the only one on board that would even talk to him and had a way to make even the most desperate of times tolerable. To the crew, it was as if Edmund had the plague. There was a fear that anyone near him would anger Morble, and a seaman's life on board was harsh enough.

The next morning, the HMS *Fitzgerald* arrived at Port Royal. It was England's main base against piracy. Anything could be bought or sold, the only question was the price. The earthquake of 1692 had removed a large portion of the island, but it still thrived. It was also a great place to recruit for the navy but brought out some of the worst cutthroats on earth.

The bay was a narrow spit that arced from the land like an arm flung as a defense against the sun. The bay on the inside was crystal clear. The anchors ran straight down, scattering schools of colorful fish. The flukes were attracted by the lumps of coral from the chains and anchor fathoms below.

On shore, ships stood at the dock. Wharfs and warehouses lined the quays. Unloading the ships were slaves. Sweat glistened from their black skin. Female slaves worked alongside males, heaving sacks and rolling barrels. Some of the women moved slowly, one hand high to balance the great burdens, which they carried on their turbaned heads. Carriages transported people about town.

Blue lagoons were in the distance, and old slaves littered the beach. They lay like driftwood drying in the sun. Some were dead, and the others would be shortly.

Thirty sailors received pay and were allowed to go ashore. The rest of the crew had to wait. Sailors rarely received the wages they were due. The navy had a semiofficial policy, "Keep the pay, keep the man." This policy led to fewer desertions. Another form of pay was IOUs. These tickets issued by the government would be honored at a specified time in the future. Sailors in need of cash were forced to sell their tickets to loan sharks at a fraction of their value. Morble made extra money by supplying money for these tickets and cashing them in when he returned to England. Many sailors never received any pay at all.

Jon was one of the selected few picked for shore leave. Edmund felt good for him but was a little envious at the same time. Jon earned his leave by translating Spanish maps. He and Edmund were two of few crewmembers with an education.

Edmund stood on the starboard side and watched the sailors fill their rowboats and sail to shore. He saw the distant dunes on the shoreline and wished he was there. The guards surrounding the deck brought him back to reality. Any fantasies about escape were quickly diminished. They had orders to shoot anyone thinking about deserting.

When am I going to get off this ship?

He walked back to the bow and looked out to sea. The sun was hot, and the air heavy and moist. Sweat dripped from the tip of his nose onto the deck, but he felt at ease.

At least Morble and Chestus went ashore. I'll have some peace for a day.

Later that night, the ship set sail to escort the slave ship *Neptune III* and its cargo to Charles Town. Chestus and two other men quietly entered the sleeping quarters, which woke Edmund out of a light sleep. Jon Galvin was their target. One of the men covered Jon's mouth while the other two carried him off into the dark of the forecastle. Chestus started unbuckling Jon's belt.

"He's got a thin ass, but he'll have to do," Chestus said. "These men didn't get a chance to go ashore today. They have a built-up frustration, if you know what I mean."

"Please don't," Jon said as he struggled from the two men holding him.

"Unless, of course, you want to part with some of your pay. Tonight is going to cost you."

"I'm cleaned out. I had to pay Morble for letting me go ashore. I have nothing of value left."

"That's too bad then," Chestus said, laughing.

Edmund started to crawl from his hammock. He heard these things went on but had never witnessed them. He heard Jon being thrown on the deck and clothes being torn. He staggered to his feet and slowly crept behind them.

"Let him go," Edmund said. "If you have the urge, go take care of yourself in a corner."

"You have a claim on him, boy?" Chestus said, ripping the belt from Jon. "You can have what's left of him when we're done."

Jon tried to get up and run, but the two other men threw him back down. Edmund grabbed one of them by the hair and threw him back. Chestus whipped Edmund's cheek with the belt. When Chestus struck again, Edmund stepped back, avoiding contact, and ripped the belt out of Chestus's hands. He looped it over the crewman's head that was on top of Jon and crossed his hands. The crewman gagged. Edmund pulled harder as Chestus came down with his fist into the side of Edmund's face. Edmund retaliated by thrusting his foot into Chestus's stomach. It knocked the wind out of him, and he struggled for air.

One of the crewmen had awoken and shone a lantern on the group. Edmund pulled the belt tighter, and the crewman turned different shades of purple. Men woke and watched in horror. As he peered through the entrance, Morble saw the men in the dim light. He crept slowly down the steps.

"What have we here?"

Everyone except Edmund stopped what they were doing and froze. Edmund held the belt tight, and the crewman stopped moving. His eyes began to roll toward the back of his head.

"Let him go!" Morble screamed.

Edmund looked up and let go of the belt. The crewman fell forward and let out a choking sound as he hit the deck, gasping for air.

"What happened?" Morble asked as he walked toward Chestus.

"This man attacked us, sir," Chestus said as he was still bent over, breathing heavy. "We were talking to Galvin here, and he didn't like us disturbing his sleep."

"Not true," Edmund answered, trying to catch his breath.

Jon started to speak, but Morble silenced him with a wave of his hand. He was livid.

As he looked over the men, he motioned for Chestus and the other two to leave. They helped the man Edmund had choked up and made their way out. Morble looked at Edmund with a sheepish grin.

"Drake, we'll take care of you in the morning, I promise you that."

He turned and climbed the steps to the deck. Edmund turned to Jon. "Are you all right?"

"You shouldn't have helped. I would have survived that ordeal. They're going to kill you tomorrow."

Edmund helped him up. "I'll survive." He didn't sound convincing.

Jon thanked him fifty times and vowed no favor would be too big.

"Just go to sleep," Edmund said, lying back in his hammock. He thought about the repercussions of his actions all night.

The sun was bright early next morning. Edmund's wrists were tied together in the front of his body. Morble wanted to infuse his justice on the new recruits he picked up in Port Royal. Edmund was his victim. He assembled an audience of old and new crewmembers that lined up to watch and hoped to leave them with a strong and lasting impression. Flogging was treated as a formal ceremony, and the roll of drums added to the drama.

"Men, this is what happens when you are disloyal to the British Royal Navy. We will not tolerate disobedience."

Two men laid him down, tying his arms above his head to a mast. His two legs were tied to posts. When they tightened both ropes, Edmund was stretched prone along the deck, lying on his back. The drums beat again.

Morble grabbed a cat-o'-nine-tails with hooks attached. He looked over Edmund as if to decide where to strike first. A sickened smile came to his face, and he dipped his weapon in oil. He closed his eyes and struck. The whip singed Edmund's skin. His stomach bled instantaneously beneath his ribs as Edmund moaned. He tried to squirm, but the ropes were too tight to move.

Morble let out a cackle, raised his arm, and came down hard. Again, the sharp clamps bit down, ripping Edmund's skin. He squirmed in agony and nearly bit through his lower lip, muffling his cries. Blood leaked and trickled down his stomach onto the deck. Morble looked at Edmund as if to admire his work. He enjoyed this. Jon cringed next to the portside rail. Chestus smirked.

Morble again raised the whip over his head. His strike was interrupted by screaming from the lookout atop the mast.

"There's a ship!"

CHAPTER 10

AMBUSHED

Morble glanced up at the lookout who was pointing toward the coast of Tortuga.

"It's flying a French flag with a white one underneath," the lookout yelled. "Looks like a merchant ship!"

"It's in trouble," Morble mumbled and then barked out orders to deviate toward the ship. He yelled to the cargo commander of the *Neptune III* to continue toward Charles Town and that they would catch up shortly. The commander questioned his decision, citing Morble's unfamiliarity of the waters, but shook his head and stayed on the course.

The HMS *Fitzgerald* picked up a good tailwind and was approaching the ship off the mountainous side of the island.

Edmund was still tied to the mast. Blood oozed from his stomach, which continued to burn. Jon looked on as the men went to battle stations.

"What about him?" Chestus asked, pointing to Edmund.

"Leave him, we'll get to him later," Morble answered.

As the HMS *Fitzgerald* approached the French ship, Morble armed forty men for boarding. There were only a handful of men on the deck of the merchant ship. A few were waving their arms, but most were sitting on the deck wrapped in blankets.

The vessel looked like it had been in a battle. The deck was splintered, sails were torn, and the men looked in bad shape. The HMS *Fitzgerald* pulled alongside as men secured boarding pikes to attach the two ships together. The smell of tar filled the air.

One of the men from the merchant ship greeted Morble. He was short with scraggly black hair and whiskers.

"Sir, thank you for coming," he said with a thick French accent. "We were attacked by pirates a few days ago. My name is Gilgo."

"Where are the rest of your men?"

"Most of them rowed or swam to shore looking for help. What's left is here, trying to sew the sails and repair the ship."

"You are on the wrong side of the island for help. Nobody will be able to get to you for days. Who attacked you?"

"It was a pirate flag. It was the darkest of black and streaked with red. Maybe streaked with blood."

"McGinnty," Morble murmured to himself. "Why did your men stay on board?"

"We have to protect our stock."

Morble looked around and saw five crates. He waved his hands, and the men started checking them out.

"What are you doing?" Gilgo protested.

He walked over to stop them but was held back by Morble's men. Two other men took irons and broke open the crates. They were filled with gold doubloons. Morble ordered more men to board, this time with pistols and muskets pointing at the French sailors. They just sat and watched, with no desire to move. Gilgo shook his head.

"You have no right!" He was furious and shrugged his shoulders to loosen the grasp of the men holding him.

"We're taking these," Morble said.

"The hell you are."

Morble ran his hand through the coins and walked back to Gilgo.

"What would a merchant ship be doing with crates of gold coins?"

"It was from trade."

"Bullshit."

While the commotion was going on and everyone on the deck of the HMS *Fitzgerald* watching, Edmund saw Jon sneaking over.

"My stomach is burning."

Jon looked around for oil or ointment. "Just hold on, I'll find something."

"What's going on down there?" Edmund asked.

"I think Morble is about to lay claim to anything of value on that ship."

Edmund struggled to look up, but the ropes limited his sight.

Morble's men tried to move the crates, but they didn't budge.

"Are these nailed down?" Morble screamed, frustrated. He wanted to get the plunder quickly and catch up to the cargo ship. He looked around at the French and Spanish crew. They were wrapped in blankets and hadn't moved since he'd been on board. It was as if they were lifeless.

"Chestus, bring some sacks over here. We'll just empty out the crates."

Gilgo snarled at Morble, "France will hear about this."

"Who are you kidding? This is obviously stolen. The only question is from where or whom."

A scream came from the lookout atop the HMS *Fitzgerald.*

"Another ship is approaching!"

In the backdrop toward the stern of the HMS *Fitzgerald* were two large sails. The ship was a sloop, and the flag flying high atop the middle mast had a black background with a mixture of red and white lettering. Cross-shaped bones were mixed with two swords forming the letter *X.*

"C'mon, men, let's get this gold to our ship and get out of here." Then Morble walked up to Gilgo. "You'll be lucky if we don't burn this ship down with you on it."

He ordered the men holding boarding axes to cut down the ropes and sails. The men grabbed the sacks and poured the doubloons into them. Seven, eight were filled, and then one of the men stopped.

"Captain, you have to have a look at this."

Morble walked over to the crewman who was holding one of the coins. As Morble looked closer, he could see it was too rough and jerked it out of the man's hand.

"Rocks. Rocks painted gold." He was fuming and turned toward Gilgo.

The men sitting down threw off their blankets and emptied their pistols at Morble and his men. Gilgo grabbed a torch and lit the sails and deck. They were soaked in tar and ignited quickly. Morble jumped behind one of the crates. He checked his body, and somehow, it was left unscathed. After emptying their pistols, the merchant crew jumped overboard. Fire spread across the deck, and smoke formed a black mist as chaos ensued.

"Get me out of here!" Edmund screamed.

Jon looked around. He found a knife near one of the torn sails and grabbed it. The edge was dull as he carved the rope around Edmund's wrists. It didn't cut through, it only frayed the rope.

"Hurry!"

Jon threw it into the corner, and it ricocheted off the steps. Smoke filled the air, and shots sprayed both decks. He quickly ran to the captain's cabin and came out with a boarding axe. Edmund's eyes lit up.

"What are you going to do with that?"

"I'll have you free in no time. Try to widen your grip as far as you can."

Jon raised the axe over his shoulder and was about to strike.

"Don't wind up so much," Edmund said. "Shorten it up."

Jon came down and chopped at the rope with short thrusts, careful not to hit Edmund's wrists. On the third try, the rope split apart and dropped to the deck. He freed the ankles, and Edmund rubbed them, trying to get circulation flowing.

"Another ship is coming!" the lookout screamed.

Morble's men ran from the merchant ship back toward the HMS *Fitzgerald* as a ship approached from the north. It wasn't a sloop like the one closing in from the stern but a galleon. A very large galleon.

The sloop from the stern was angling in, getting its cannons into position. The *Fitzgerald* wasn't moving. It was still attached to the merchant vessel, and men were prying out the hooks as smoke and flames filled the air.

"Just blow it out of the water. We need to free up our guns!" Morble ordered.

The galleon was slowly approaching like a cat approaching its injured prey. The sloop behind them held its position but didn't fire. Drums were beaten to signal battle stations.

Edmund stayed out of the way. He just observed the chaos as men ran from side to side, from front to back. The merchant ship was covered with too much tar, and the flames intensified and spread out of control.

The sloop sailed into position and formed a *T* with the *Fitzgerald.* It could have fired at any time but waited.

The galleon was in the process of maneuvering to aim its guns at the front of the ship. Morble's guns were blocked from one side by the French ship and useless on the other.

A crack of thunder exploded as a cannonball splashed near the stern of the *Fitzgerald.* The crew was mesmerized by what they were seeing and froze in their positions. Most had never experienced battle as the war with Spain had ended.

Jon ran over to the side and heaved. Edmund ran over and held him up.

"C'mon, we have to take cover."

The galleon was carrying twenty guns on its broadside and well within firing range. It was in perfect position to cripple the ship. The black flag streaked in red flew from the center mast.

The two ships surrounded the HMS *Fitzgerald* and waited. The fire from the merchant ship spread to the HMS *Fitzgerald,* and a handful of men tried throwing buckets of water to douse the fire but to no avail.

Men from the galleon lined its deck, holding rifles, muskets, and cutlasses. They cursed and taunted Morble's crew, then they opened fire. The cannons also went off, splintering the deck with grapeshot. Metal pierced the wood all over the ship. Chips flew everywhere. Flesh was torn from skin, and just as quickly, men fell onto the deck. Morble took shrapnel to his shoulders, neck, and left arm, then fell and hugged the deck.

Edmund and Jon laid low, crouching behind the captain's cabin until grapeshot came from the other direction from the sloop, creating crossfire. They both dove through the step entrance, which led beneath the deck. Edmund peeked his head out to watch. Morble screamed to fire back, but crewmen hugged the deck, afraid to move. The few that did reach up to fire were littered with grapeshot.

The galleon shot grapeshot every fifteen seconds to keep the sailors at bay as it sailed in closer in a circular course as to always have its guns aimed at its prey.

The Spaniards and Frenchmen from the merchant ship swam to the galleon where they were retrieved and congratulated for a job well-done.

Firing ceased for a few minutes, but it seemed like hours to Edmund. He popped his head up to encounter men lying in agony on the blood-soaked deck. Half the crew was wiped out.

Thunder exploded again as six cannons went off, sending cannonballs connected by chains. They quickly destroyed the center mast, which toppled over and fell into the sea. A round of grapeshot filled the air and tore apart the remaining sails. The galleon closed in on collision course. Some of the men wanted to surrender; others grabbed pistols, muskets, and cutlasses.

Morble grabbed four pistols and barked out orders as blood soaked through his shirt. Fire from the merchant ship engulfed the HMS *Fitzgerald*. The side of the ship and its sails were completely inflamed.

The galleon collided with the *Fitzgerald*, jolting everyone on board. Pirates quickly filled the deck with eighty men carrying muskets, pistols, and swords.

Edmund quickly ran below, grabbed a large knife from a table, and ran topside but stopped at the opening. Smoke made sight impossible, depending on which way the wind was swirling at any given time. He proceeded to run next to the captain's cabin for cover.

Grappling hooks were quickly set in place by the pirates to connect the ship. They quickly boarded—yelling, screaming, and cursing to intimidate the sailors.

A free-for-all melee broke out, and confusion was everywhere. Pistol fires filled the air, swords clanged together or connected with limbs. Pirates and crewmen slipped all over the blood-splashed deck.

One of the pirates pulled out his pistol to shoot, but Edmund knocked it out of his hand. He grabbed his knife and raised it to his throat, staring into the man's eyes. He shoved him overboard as men ran everywhere. Most pistols had been emptied and now used as clubs. Cutlasses were also flailing as the pirates emptied onto the HMS *Fitzgerald*, outnumbering the British.

Edmund watched wide-eyed as the crew tried to surrender, but the pirates were aggressively attacking. Out of the corner of his eye, Edmund spotted Morble. A fit of rage came over him as he avoided two men entangled and ran toward him, holding the knife in his fist.

Morble stood on a barrel, his sword swinging wildly in one hand and a pistol held in the other. Morble glanced at Edmund. For a split second, they made eye contact. Then he looked at the pirates that surrounded him.

With the reinforcements from the pirate sloop arriving, the battle turned into a massacre. The crew quickly went down in defeat.

Edmund ran through the crowd toward Morble whose pistol fired into the chest of one of the pirates and swung at another. Edmund's ears were ringing as he sloshed his way along the blood-soaked deck. Pirates and crewmen littered the deck, most grotesquely disfigured.

Edmund stopped, turned the knife around, and clamped the blade between his thumb and curled side of his forefinger. He cocked it back over his shoulder and threw it at Morble.

The knife tumbled end over end and began to drop.

Gonna fall short.

He forced himself to follow it and took a single stride before the knife landed into Morble's thigh.

Morble twitched and cried out. His leg jumped upward, and he fell back off the barrel and onto the deck, losing his cutlass in the process. He grabbed the knife and yanked it out of his leg an instant before Edmund pushed his way through and smashed down onto his chest.

Morble grunted under the impact. Edmund struck him hard to the stomach. Then he swung again, connecting to his chin, watering Morble's eyes. Edmund's other arm stretched sideways and grabbed the wrist of the knife hand. Morble swung his free fist wildly, catching Edmund over his left eye, knocking him back. Blood trickled down his cheek.

Keeping the knife hand pressed tight against the deck, Edmund hunched down and pressed his left forearm against Morble's throat and pressed, choking him.

Morble bucked and writhed, shaking his head. He dug his chin into Edmund's forearm. He shoved himself upward with his right arm. He threw two more blows to Edmund's jaw, and Edmund felt Morble's body start to rise and tilt.

Starting to slide, he swung his leg over Morble's hips, but it was too late. Together they rolled. Morble came down on top of Edmund. Though he could barely breathe under his weight, he kept his grip on the knife hand and tried to grip Morble's neck with his free hand.

Morble threw two more blows to Edmund's head, but Edmund squeezed his neck as hard as he could. Morble's face was turning purple. He then swung his leg hard to Morble's waist, rolling him over, and struck him in the nose.

Edmund jumped off Morble and quickly spotted a cutlass embedded in a man's chest lying next to them.

He ran over and jerked it out. Morble tried to get up and run, but he fell backward over a fallen body.

Edmund pounced on him, sending two punches to his face. He raised the cutlass over his head, and Morble's eyes bulged out in sheer panic. As he lunged to strike, Edmund froze and looked up. He noticed pirates looking on with curious glances. The fighting had ceased. What started out with a deafening roar of explosions was now an eerie silence. Every one of Morble's men was either killed or captured. Half the ship was engulfed in flames. He looked back down at Morble. He raised the cutlass again as a loud clap of a thunder blast rang his ears.

A man held a blunderbuss high in the air. Smoke was rising out of it. A large hideous scar ran down his left cheek.

"Allow me to introduce myself. I'm Jack McGinnty!"

CHAPTER 11

DUEL

McGinnty took Morble's crew ashore on Tortuga and marched them down the beach, surrounded by pirates. The HMS *Fitzgerald* now lay at the bottom of the Atlantic. The pirates pilfered what they could before the flames covered the entire ship. Most of their plunder took the shape of weapons and ammunition. Morble and his crew were now prisoners of the very pirate they sought to capture.

They stopped in an open area, and McGinnty climbed onto a large rock, waving the men to come closer. He looked around. He wore a broad tan hat with a feather cockade attached, cutlass at his side, and four pistols dangling from a sash around his waist.

His men settled in the front. Morble's crew gathered to his right. Fifty survived the bloodbath, though many were injured. Right before he addressed the crowd, McGinnty gazed upon one of his own men slouching in the back.

"Carrigan, come forward!" McGinnty yelled.

A small thin man stepped forward cautiously. He looked around and slowly looked up at McGinnty.

"Carrigan, you left your post during the battle. You know the punishment. You swore allegiance to my ship."

"No, sir, I can explain."

"Silence!" McGinnty looked around at his men. "You all fought bravely. Well done, men."

A loud roar went up and some of the men pumped their fist. Carrigan looked down.

"And you," McGinnty said, pointing a blunderbuss at Carrigan's head. "You know the penalty for cowardice."

Everyone watched in horror. Edmund cringed, waiting for the gun to go off. McGinnty cocked the blunderbuss. There was a sort of sadness that appeared in his eyes. He lowered the gun.

"You're to be left here, you're no longer part of the crew." McGinnty then addressed his prisoners. "The rest of you, you're welcome to join our select group. You must obey our ways and be loyal to the ship you sail with! The only thing I can promise is you will be treated better than you were." He looked at Morble. "You will be treated fairer than the man that previously commanded you! If you choose not to join us, you will be left here until another ship comes by and picks you up. We'll leave supplies we don't need."

Morble cringed. Cuts and abrasions covered his body as he looked around at his men.

McGinnty continued, "Those of you wanting to join, step forward!"

With that said, half of the men shoved their way forward and moved up to the front of the line while the others watched. Edmund and Morble stayed back. McGinnty glanced over at them.

He jumped from the boulder and marched toward Morble. He walked with a commanding presence as his men jumped out of his way. He stopped in front of Morble, placed his hands on his hips.

"So you're Morble. The man commissioned to bring me in."

Morble gave him a surprised look but kept silent.

"News travels fast in the Caribbean. It was well-known you were after us. The thing is I waited for you everywhere. The slower we sailed, the slower you followed. It was a running joke how hard you were looking for us. We wanted you to find us."

He looked over at Edmund. In one swift motion, McGinnty grabbed him by the arm and shoved him toward Morble.

"You two," he shouted, "have unfinished business to take care of. You'll take care of it the way we pirates solve our disputes!"

Each man was led toward the water's edge. Pirates started hooting and hollering. Edmund looked nervously at the group, unsure what they had in mind. His legs were still wobbly after months at sea. It was as if his rubbery legs had a mind of their own, going off in every direction.

They were told to choose seconds as gentleman did. Jon acted as Edmund's second, and Chestus was chosen by Morble. Chestus had hidden below decks during the entire skirmish while the others fought bravely. The seconds were handed pistols by two pirates and inspected them. Chestus loaded powder inside the barrel and stuffed in the balls.

Jon tried to load his, but he was shaking so bad he dropped the ball into the sand. Edmund grabbed the pistol out of his hand and reached down to grab the ball. He had a calm look about him, but inside, he was very nervous as a light sheen of sweat appeared on his forehead. Jon started pacing back and forth, leaving his trail in the sand.

McGinnty walked over to Edmund, pulling him with one hand, and whispered, "I know you're scared, but remember this: take careful aim, do not rush your shot, and make it count." He patted Edmund's shoulder and walked away.

"Gentlemen, are you ready?" shouted McGinnty.

"Oh yeah," replied Morble.

"Ready," Edmund responded.

They walked to a spot marked on the beach. Pirates and sailors alike were curious and excited as to how this would turn out. They elbowed each other and nodded their heads. Murmurs filled the crowd.

The two combatants acknowledged each other with nods. Even though Edmund was much younger, he looked far more poised and confident. Morble's hand was slightly trembling as he brought the pistol vertically in front of his face. Edmund raised his pistol and turned, so the two were back-to-back.

McGinnty cleared his throat and addressed the two. "I shall first say the word *begin*. At that time, you will start pacing off the distance in time to my count. When you have completed ten paces, you will turn and fire. If you hesitate to fire, your pistols shall be knocked out of your hands by the two men holding the bars."

McGinnty pointed to men on each side holding a bar. They were located where they thought ten paces would take the two combatants. From their look, they had seen many duels in the past.

"If pistols don't decide this, swords will. Usually first blood drawn wins, but since you two are not part of us, it's going to be a fight to the death. Are you both ready?"

Morble and Edmund nodded simultaneously. The pirates roared in anticipation. Most were placing wagers on the outcome. The betting line favored Morble.

"Ready! Begin!"

Edmund moved one way, Morble the other.

"Three, four, five."

Edmund took long confident strides. He thought of all the shooting practice he did in London, but this was different. His opponent was going to fire back! He always thought it would be Cutler on the other end. Now it was Morble.

"Seven. Eight."

The sunlight glazed off the water into Edmund's face. Morble's trembling had expanded to his shoulders.

"Nine."

Edmund stared straight ahead. His tongue flicked up to lick a bead of sweat from his lip. It was the only outward sign of anxiety that must have been twisting inside his belly.

Steady, calm, aim, and fire!

"Ten."

Morble turned and flung his pistol hand out in front of him violently and fired. Edmund turned. A sharp pain caught his chest, which jolted him, but he remained standing. Smoke was rising from Morble's pistol as he stood there staring at Edmund.

Edmund's gun was cocked. His arm and pistol were one. He kept it aimed at Morble, but his finger froze. His arm started to tremble as he slowly squeezed.

A sudden pain struck his arm. The pirate holding the pipe had struck Edmund's forearm, sending a discharge off high in the air. Morble took a deep breath. Edmund dropped the pistol and grabbed his arm. McGinnty shook his head.

"This will be settled by the sword."

Chestus gave Morble a cutlass. Jon looked around for a sword. McGinnty threw his over, which landed in the sand by Edmund's feet.

Edmund, his arm still sore, picked it up. The cutlass was heavier than any of the swords he used in London or Bristol.

The pirates on the beach started roaring as Morble quickly lunged at Edmund and swung wildly. Edmund quickly blocked the blows as sparks flew from the clanging of the metal. Morble swung three quick blows, which were also deflected.

Just survive this onslaught.

Morble kept coming. Edmund moved side to side, sliding on the loose sand and rocks. He quickly found an opening and struck forward, piercing Morble's thigh—the same one that had been struck in battle earlier. Morble stopped and looked down at the tear in his pants as blood trickled out. He groaned and attacked, swinging harder. Edmund blocked the blows, barely hanging on to his cutlass as his grip weakened. Morble was tiring. Edmund switched hands and deflected a blow with the sword in his left arm and quickly grabbed Morble with his right hand, pushing him back. Morble lost his balance but swung wildly, grazing Edmund's shoulder. Edmund winced but grabbed his cutlass with two hands and swung with all the force he could muster.

The blade struck Morble's forehead and deflected off the bone. It skidded over his skin and tore through his right eye.

Screaming and clutching his face, he tumbled to the sand. He lay moaning, hands tight against the place where his eye used to be. Blood spurted through his fingers and littered the sand as crews from both ships watched in horror.

McGinnty motioned for the men to back off. "Leave him. Let's head back to the ship. That'll be my gift to Killingsworth."

Killingsworth!

Edmund looked up. He hadn't heard that name in over a year. The pirates kept staring. Edmund wobbled and then dropped to a knee. The front of his shirt covered in blood. He tried to stand but fell back into the sand.

CHAPTER 12

THE CODE

Edmund sat up on a bunk. He remembered the duel. Morble's shot had grazed his chest. He checked out his chest and noticed his shoulder sewn up. Then he remembered the blow he struck that caught Morble's face.

He looked around and heard moaning from the surrounding crewmen lying next to him. They had all suffered wounds during the battle. Edmund crawled out of his bunk and looked around. One had his head bandaged, but blood seeped through. Another had his stomach wrapped and was covered in sweat.

"Help me." A hand reached out to him.

Edmund grabbed it. "What do you want me to do?"

"My leg is killing me. I'm cramping up."

Edmund looked at his leg. It was gone. Just a stump covered in tar. Tears filled his eyes. Everyone in the area was moaning.

"Please! Just rub my leg."

Edmund backed off. He bumped into another man. His eyes were just staring into space. His skin was blue. Edmund started to gag. He ran to the door. A man entering the room stopped him and grabbed him by the shoulders. Edmund stared up at him.

"You had a lot of fire and passion out there."

Edmund tried to say something, but he just froze.

"I'm Doc," he said as his eyes pierced through Edmund. "You got a name, boy?"

"Edmund . . . Edmund Drake, sir." Sweat poured from his face.

Doc pointed at Edmund's chest. "Don't worry, it just got grazed."

"I remember swinging the cutlass but not anything after that."

"You don't remember what you did to that wretched captain? You damn near carved his face off. There was nothing left."

Edmund stared at the deck.

"How long have I been out? Where am I?"

"You're on *Lucifer's Ghost.* You were out almost half a day. I don't think it was from the wound. Didn't they feed you on that ship?"

"The pirate ship? McGinnty?"

"It's pretty much one and the same. We weren't going to leave you on that island with that crew."

Doc walked by and attended the casualties. He pulled a blanket over the face of one and shook his head. Others that were injured looked to him for hope.

"I'll never get used to this," he said, looking at Edmund. "Get me some water and a few rags."

Edmund grabbed a bucket and noticed the water was clear and fresh. Pots of water boiled on coals, and one pot was filled with tar. As he lifted the bucket, he winced in pain. He checked his shoulder but shrugged it off. He felt embarrassed to compare his injuries with the men that lay on the cots that surrounded him.

"I guess I should thank you for the stitchwork."

"It was nothing," Doc said as he wiped down the face of the man with the missing leg. "Just like sewing a sail."

Doc started to describe the ship and some of the crewmembers on board when a hand clamped on Edmund's shoulder and spun him around. The man yanked Edmund by his shirt.

"Next time you have a chance to kill someone, don't hesitate. It may be your ass that's lying in the sand if you do."

He was a rough, with scars all over his arms and tattoos all over his chest and back. Doc stepped in between the two of them.

"Meet Connor Beckham. He's our ship's gunner."

Beckham let go of Edmund and looked at the men. He shook hands with the ones that were conscious. The man missing a leg tried to lean up to greet him, but Beckham eased him back down and stroked his face.

"Take it easy, son. We'll get you better." He looked around. "I'm proud of you all. You're all heroes."

Beckham patted Doc who went back to work. He made his way back to Edmund.

"If you didn't kill off that bastard Morble, the captain surely would have."

Edmund took a deep breath as Beckham was a foot away. "He's dead?"

"Well, if he's not, he's sure close. Let me tell you where you stand. We're out at sea. We didn't see much sense in leaving you with what was left of that British crew. We left them on the island. I don't think you would have been appreciated much there anyway."

Edmund fidgeted. "Where are we?"

"We're outside Hispaniola. We have to make a few stops, and then we head to New Providence. That's our resting place."

While Doc tended to his patients, Beckham nodded to Edmund, and they walked out to the deck.

"We grabbed a few of the crewmembers of the British ship, swore them in, and now we have an expanded crew."

"Jon?"

"Your friend from the duel?"

Edmund nodded.

"He has a new purpose in life."

Edmund shuddered when he heard that.

They stranded him!

"His purpose is to serve this ship and crew, as yours will be too if you so choose."

Edmund felt relief and blurted out, "What if I choose not to?" He hadn't meant to say that. Beckham stopped and turned toward him.

"If you choose not to, we'll throw your ass overboard." He gave a serious look then burst out laughing. "If you choose not to, you'll be left off on the next available island, whether there are people on it or not." He continued to walk. "Of course, you will choose to stay."

Edmund saw Jon in the corner of the ship. He was trying to sew one of the sails but had trouble lining it up. He looked over, and a smile gripped his face as he waved.

"Your friend doesn't look like a seaman at all."

Edmund smiled. "You won't regret having him aboard."

"What about you?"

"Is it worth it?" Edmund asked, following Beckham. They stopped in front of the captain's cabin.

"Boy, you're in for the most exciting time of your life." Beckham knocked three times and entered. Edmund stood outside before Beckham gestured for him to follow.

Jack McGinnty was lying on a cot, eyes open, staring at the ceiling, a bottle of rum in his right hand.

Beckham cleared his throat. "I'm here with that kid from the duel, sir."

McGinnty rose on his elbows. "Come in."

Edmund didn't say a word. He walked into the cabin holding his breath. He felt sick as he couldn't take his eyes off the long red scar, which ran down his cheek. He had stubble on his face, but hair was missing where the scar traced. His fierce piercing eyes penetrated through Edmund.

"I take it you've heard of me."

Edmund nodded.

Scarface Jack McGinnty was fast becoming one of the most notorious pirates in the Caribbean. Edmund heard stories of his ruthlessness and torture. Morble and the first mate were always talking about running into him and what to expect when they did. Their mission was to find him, but they never did. Until now.

"Relax, boy, no one's going to harm you here. You fought bravely against Morble. You must have really despised him." McGinnty waited for a response, but Edmund stood frozen. "You don't look like the typical sailor in the Royal Navy, which means you're a criminal or you were kidnapped?"

Edmund looked away. A lump formed in his throat.

"I'm sure Mr. Beckham informed you of your options. You're welcome to stay."

Edmund nodded.

"He's not a talkative type, sir," Beckham interrupted.

"That's good, Mr. Beckham. The less opinions on this ship, the better."

McGinnty grabbed a Bible.

"I'm going to swear you in. You have no past here. Your life starts today and this day forward. We are self-governing, so when you're ready, place your left hand on the Bible and raise your right."

Edmund did so and looked up at McGinnty who grabbed documents.

"This is our pirate code. It is our rules, and we live by them. I'll read them to you, and you will swear allegiance."

Edmund nodded in agreement as McGinnty read.

"One, every crewmember has a vote in affairs of the moment. Each has equal title to fresh provisions or liquors at any time seized and may use them at their pleasure unless scarcity makes it necessary, for the good of all, to be rationed."

"Two, defrauding the value of a dollar in plate, jewels, or money is to be punished by marooning. If robbery between two individuals occurs, the guilty party will have his ears and nose slit and be sent ashore or marooned."

"Three, no playing dice or cards for money."

"Four, lights and candles are to be put out at eight o'clock. After that, anything done is to be done on the open deck."

"Five, keep your pistol and cutlass clean and fit for service."

"Six, no women on board the ship. If any are brought on board, the person responsible will be punished by death."

"Seven, if you desert your post or the ship, the punishment is death or marooning."

Edmund thought of Carrigan, the crewmember McGinnty singled out on the beach.

Was he killed or marooned?

"Eight, no striking another on board. All quarrels are to be ended on shore by pistols or swords."

"Nine, no man will talk of breaking up their way of living until each had a share of £1,000. If any man should lose a limb or become crippled in their service, he was to be awarded £800 out of the public stock. Lesser injuries pay proportionately."

"Ten, musicians rest on the Sabbath. The other six days and nights, no rest."

McGinnty looked at Edmund. He agreed and swore his allegiance. He then signed the final document. He noticed Jon's signature four names above his. He jaw dropped when also noticed Chestus had signed. He pointed to the name and looked up at McGinnty.

"He's a—" Edmund caught himself.

"I told you, no one has a past here. It's a fresh start . . . for everyone," McGinnty said.

Edmund handed him the signed document. McGinnty nodded and held out his hand.

"Good. Welcome aboard." Edmund stuck out his right hand, and they shook. Beckham poured three cups of rum, and they drank. The rum burned Edmund's throat as it went down.

CHAPTER 13

PIRATE LIFE

Edmund walked freely about the deck. In the days that passed, life on board *Lucifer's Ghost* was vastly different from of its predecessor. While the quarters were still cramped, there was more room for sleep and storage because the crew was split between two ships.

Lucifer's Ghost was a three-deck, three-mast galleon that was cut up and crafted for battle. They added room for extra cannons, which totaled forty-six. Its speed and maneuverability was good enough to outpace many of its counterparts. The weaponry exhibited looked intimidating and could even match a Royal Navy warship.

Hellspite held its own weaponry and was very useful in shallower water. The sloop was especially fast. It had a bowsprit almost as long as its hull and was built to exceed twelve knots if the winds were right. It held fourteen cannons and could load up a crew of seventy to chase down ships for *Lucifer's Ghost* to finish off. In lower depths, such as channels and sounds, it was the most efficient sloop in the Caribbean.

While exploring the deck, Edmund noticed every sailor had a purpose, and the operation ran smoothly. Eyes greeted him with glares everywhere he turned. Any conversation he had, pirates would lean over to eavesdrop.

"Who are they?" Edmund asked Doc.

"Vagabonds mostly," he replied.

Doc introduced him to most of the crew. One after another would step forward and offer a hand. As they shook, they would make comments like "You're the guy from the duel" or "I bet this is different from that navy ship."

Doc was well-liked among the crew, but in fact, he wasn't a real doctor. He was mostly responsible for notifying the captain of any sickness that arose and suggest appropriate actions. Most of the diseases came from decaying matter, spoiled food, rotting corpses, or other sick people.

He would tell Edmund, "Illnesses are an imbalance of the body, and to treat them, the body had to be placed back in balance."

If you had a fever, you received food and drugs that would cause the opposite effect.

"Keep your nerves and blood flowing freely."

He used olive oil for burns to keep wounds clean and butter for infections and rationed plenty of fruit for scurvy.

Gilgo was the quartermaster. A position elected by the crew. He was responsible for morale and maintaining law and order among the crew. He was also in charge of dividing up the plunder. He kept records and accounts of who received what. All food and liquor were divided equally, as was the treasures recovered. The captain and the quartermaster were the only exception as each of them received double shares. If a ship was captured, he boarded first with a crew to decide what or what not to take. One thing about Gilgo, he was not confrontational; and if you did something he didn't care for, you may find a knife in your back.

Thomas Moore was the boatswain. He was in charge of the ship's maintenance and supply storage. He also kept up the riggings, sails, and all weighing and dropping of anchors. Moore was a gruff old salt, older than most on the ship, and every other word that came out of his mouth was a curse. Edmund was assigned to work under Moore when he first came aboard. At first he was intimidating. Then as Edmund became used to his foul mouth, he just laughed off some of the comments he heard.

There were two main carpenters, but overall, many of the crew was handy in dealing with plugs and carpentry work.

Aside from Jon and Doc, Beckham was his favorite. He was the ship's master gunner, in charge of guns and ammunition and responsible for keeping the powder dry, preventing rust on the balls and weaponry. Beckham always complained to the crew that they weren't keeping up with cleaning their pistols and cutlasses. He cursed more than Thomas Moore.

"You fucking have to have them bloody damn ready as if we were going to goddamn battle right now!" he used to scream. But beneath his rough exterior, Edmund found a sensitive, well-respected man.

Outside of battle, the ship was a total democracy with even the smallest items voted on. It was their way of voicing discontent of the British monarchy that most had come from. While the majority of the crew was British, there were also Dutch, French, Spanish, Africans, and anyone else that would pledge allegiance to the ship.

The men were fearsome looking. Most were bearded and sunburnt, wearing a bizarre collection of clothing and hats. The sailors that swapped their lifestyles for piracy wore their navy trousers and shirts. They wore scarves around their heads or woolen caps. Every pirate had a tale as to what brought them here. Some were more farfetched than others.

The key in this system was the success of the crew in finding and confiscating plunder. If they weren't successful in pilfering other ships, dissension was sure to take place no matter who was running the ship. With plunder, food, and rum available in great quantities, life on board *Lucifer's Ghost* was grand.

Lucifer's Ghost was a few days away from New Providence. The headwinds were not nearly as strong as usual for that time of year. The crew started getting antsy, and the rum started flowing, led by McGinnty. It seemed the closer the ship sailed to New Providence, the more he drank. With the sun baking hard on the decks of the ship, the alcohol's effect doubled.

McGinnty grabbed his cutlass in one hand and mug of rum in the other. The fiddlers started playing, and McGinnty started singing seafaring songs. The rest of the crew joined him. Edmund saw Chestus on the other side of the ship, and the two exchanged glares. Chestus was cordial with the crew, telling tales of exaggerated bravado and seamanship on the HMS *Fitzgerald*. The stories were less bold when Edmund and Jon were around.

As Edmund clapped to a tune about neglected women, a man approached him. His eyes were wild and bulged out. His face covered in scars, shirt torn and faded, stiff with tar and salt. He grabbed Edmund who backed up a step, ready to strike.

"You c-carved up that b-bastard c-captain," he said. He spoke in short breaths and jerked his head. His hair flew in every direction. He avoided Edmund's face while he was addressing him. His grimace reflected the frustration of his speech.

Edmund nodded.

Finally, the man looked up at him and smiled. "I l-like that," he said and walked back to a secluded corner of the ship.

Edmund had a shocked look on his face when Beckham came up to him. He pointed to his head and twirled his forefinger. "That's Charles. To say he's a little bananas is an understatement. As you can hear, he's got a cursed tongue, but don't ever make fun of him, he'll cut you in a blink of an eye."

"I don't intend to. What happened to his face?" Edmund asked.

"A victim of smallpox when he was a kid. He's a bit of a loner, but he's someone you want on your side in a fight."

"I'll definitely watch what I say around him."

"He's kind of like most of the crew on this ship, outsiders on the mainland, but on board, we're all equals."

After the festivities, Edmund headed for his bunk, but sleep wouldn't come. He spent that night tossing and turning. The band members played later into the night than usual. On most nights, they stopped at eight o'clock, but on this night, it seemed a lot later. He stared at the ceiling and reflected on recent events. So much had happened. He lay there looking at the darkness and then started thinking about Sarah.

The next afternoon, Edmund and Jon heard the bells go off and raced for grub. They worked all morning on one of the sails that lay victim of weather and saltwater. New Providence was not only going to be a place to blow off steam but also a place for the ship to get much-needed repairs.

Doc was in charge of the food and cooked two meals a day without rationing. The pirates' diet consisted of salted meat and very little else—beef, pork, fish. But for this morning, the delicacy was turtle caught off the coast of Tortuga days before encountering the HMS *Fitzgerald.*

They pulled up buckets and placed them upside down to sit on. Beckham joined them.

"You two work up an appetite working on the sails?"

The two just nodded as their mouths were full, grease spilling down the sides. They dipped stale bread in the fat. Beckham was the man that led the turtle hunt on Tortuga.

"The green turtles are the ones you want. You find them mostly on small deserted islands. You have to use a handspike to turn them over. Once they're on their backs, they can't move. We captured about a hundred of the rascals."

Edmund nodded but kept eating, almost choking; the flesh was very sweet, and the fat delicious. Beckham continued, "When you eat nothing but turtle for three or four weeks, your limbs become weighed down with oil." He laughed. "You actually sweat out turtle oil."

They laughed. Edmund wiped his face with his sleeve as Gilgo walked up to them.

"I'm sorry to interrupt this little party of yours, but the captain wants to see Drake in his quarters."

"About what?" Edmund asked nervously.

"I don't know. I just follow orders," Gilgo said with a sheepish grin on his face.

Edmund wiped his hands and made his way to the door of the captain's cabin. There stood McGinnty with a pistol in his hand. He had heard stories aboard the naval ships of McGinnty's temper and treachery. Now he was to experience it firsthand.

Edmund walked in slowly, and McGinnty looked at him with a blank stare. He lifted his arm, pointing the gun at Edmund's chest. Edmund looked him in the eyes, not saying a word. McGinnty flicked his hand, and the barrel, which was in his hand, was now facing Edmund.

"Go ahead, take it. You'll need it."

Edmund carefully grabbed the gun from McGinnty's grip and looked it over.

"Why?"

"Just take care of it. Consider it a gift."

Before Edmund had a chance to thank him, McGinnty walked away.

McGinnty kept everyone in check and did most of the navigating himself. He was flawless in his use of maps and navigational instruments, such as quadrants and astrolabes, to determine latitudes.

Location was also determined by the height of the sun during a specific time of day. At noon, McGinnty would peer at the horizon through a slit in a specific area on a wooden beam. He then slid an adjustable crosspiece that reflected the sun's shadow up or down until the shadow aligned directly to the slit. Any mistake in reading or alignment could have cost them hundreds of miles off course. McGinnty had become a master of his craft. Speed could be determined by throwing a log overboard tied by rope and determining how much rope was used in a set time.

He commanded the loyalty of a band of men. Sailors turned pirates, their loyalties turned toward Jack McGinnty. He was well respected by his crew and always had a plan. No matter how tough the weather became or how low the supplies ran, everyone on board had confidence everything would work out.

As well as he was respected, he was also very aloof among the crew. No one knew him or much of his past. The scar, which stretched from his forehead to his lower cheek, was intimidating and downright scary. The wound caused the loss of half his eyesight in his left eye, and the scar tissue surrounding it left little or no eyebrow above it. He was a distant man, like something was always on his mind haunting him.

Was it the deaths he caused? The stolen ships, plunder, or chests of treasure? Was it the scar on his face?

New Providence was a day away when a vessel was discovered in the distance. The lookout made the style of ship to be Dutch, which was later confirmed by its flag, as *Lucifer's Ghost* sailed closer.

Gilgo readied the men for an attack. This would be a nice way to go into New Providence, with a ship and cargo in hand.

McGinnty saw Gilgo pumping up the men and hurried down, ordering everyone to report on the deck. As was the custom on most decisions, they would vote on what they wanted to do. Some 186 pirates gathered. Gilgo quickly wanted a vote for battle, but McGinnty interrupted him.

"Before we vote, let's look at the options," McGinnty said, signaling with his hands for the crew to quiet down. "We can sack the ship, steal its weapons and trivial merchandise." The crew roared. "Or we can go back to New Providence with less wealth." McGinnty smiled as the crew started laughing.

A vote was called for. Edmund and Jon were too new to vote, but it didn't matter. The vote was unanimous. McGinnty's intense stare went from man-to-man. Pleased murmurs swept the crew.

"Let's get a move on!"

False British Union flags were hoisted. The gun ports were quickly covered by canvas screen painted to look like the rest of the hull. Surprise was essential.

There were no other ships in the vicinity, and McGinnty knew the owners of the merchant ships were frugal with their money, which meant understaffed crews and little munitions. The owners were also against running away from any foreign sail they saw, figuring the delays would be costly. As they sailed closer, McGinnty saw the Dutch ship only had three guns on each broadside. It hadn't sailed away, and as the pirates started waving their hands to relax their opponents, some Dutch crewmembers waved back.

Edmund felt nervous and cottonmouthed. He was unsure of how the battle would play out. The last battle on Morble's ship, he didn't have time to be nervous, everything happened so fast.

He looked around and watched how the pirates prepared for battle. Each had their own idiosyncrasies. Beckham shut his eyes, perhaps envisioning the battle. Others were checking their weapons and psyching themselves up. Edmund saw Charles sharpening his blade and then would just stare at it. Jon was spewing over the side, but no one said a word. Edmund walked up to him.

"Let's watch each other's back."

Jon nodded in agreement as Edmund patted him on the back.

Men grabbed axes, checked their pistols and cutlasses. A few men grabbed hatchets and boarding hooks.

As the three ships closed in on each other, McGinnty ordered the British flag to be lowered and hoist their Jolly Roger. The flag was black with a red streak stretched across it. Most of the sailors had heard of Scarface Jack McGinnty and knew his flag well. The canvases covering the cannons on *Hellspite* and *Lucifer's Ghost* were removed. McGinnty gave the signal, and cannon shots were fired at the bow close enough to scare the merchant ship. Smoke filled the air, and the deck reeked of gunpowder.

The Dutch sailors scrambled about the deck as pirates aimed muskets at their Dutch counterparts. Edmund pointed his pistol at the crew, but Jon had spewed again before taking aim with his. Chestus walked by and whispered to Edmund, "Beware of stray shot."

Lucifer's Ghost pulled alongside the ship and used grappling hooks to steady the two ships together. The crew pulled up and boarded. Edmund had his pistol primed and his cutlass ready to strike as a chill raked his flesh. His knuckles were white from gripping his cutlass. He looked over at Jon, who was mortified, and gave him a nod. They leaped the gap between the ships, ready to fight, but there was no fight. The Dutch offered no resistance.

Before a shot was fired, the Dutch flag was lowered. McGinnty ordered the Dutch captain to board *Lucifer's Ghost.* Once on board, the Dutch captain handed over his sword in a traditional ceremony to signal his surrender. Once they had him in custody, the pirates raided the Dutch ship while the Dutch crew watched in angst. They were helpless.

The fear Edmund felt couldn't compare to the fear the Dutch felt as the pirates raided their ship. From the Dutch ship, the pirates took two guns, thirty barrels of gunpowder, all the weaponry, food, rum, sugar, personal effects, and £1,000 worth of gold and silver.

The crew's decision to attack proved to be a profitable one.

"Now what to do with the ship?"

McGinnty offered the crew of the Dutch ship a chance to join him. There were thirty-three in all, but they declined.

"So be it!"

The pirates collected donations of food, drink, and clothing then let the captain return to his ship. As a reward for his cooperation and the fact that the merchant ship was in rough condition, they unhooked it and let it set sail. Edmund heard stories from the crew that they usually captured the ship and sold it or just burned it down.

Gilgo gathered up the plunder and set about dividing it among the crew. Usually, the first pirates to board had first choice in what merchandise they wanted, and everything else was to be split up equitably.

Later on the way to New Providence, McGinnty caught up with Edmund who was alone leaning over the side. He walked over, offering a mug of ale. Edmund gulped it down and handed it back.

"I pictured a bloody battle," Edmund said, staring off to sea.

McGinnty chuckled.

"You see, merchants are underarmed and not trained in battle. Very rarely will they put up a resistance. They barely have enough crew to man their weapons. If they do fight us, they risk certain torture and mutilation once we destroyed their ship. Besides, most men aren't paid to fight."

Edmund looked at him in shock as he continued. "That's the intimidation factor. We want them to believe that what we'll do to them is a fate worse than death. If they believe that, they will put up very little resistance and surrender. We rarely have to fight."

McGinnty's reputation was the most intimidating weapon they had. He then turned to Edmund and looked him in the eyes.

"Always try and avoid battle when you can. We don't want any of our men killed or injured."

The success of *Lucifer's Ghost* was one of reputation. Ships surrendered what they had and put themselves at McGinnty's mercy rather than fight. Opposing ships feared for their lives when they were captured. When a ship was captured, McGinnty's men took everything from gold, silver, rum to the clothes off the victims' backs. They plundered guns, ammo, spices, silks, food, and the ships themselves.

Other than the occasional plunder of a strange vessel, pirate life mostly consisted of boredom. There wasn't a whole lot to do on the ship. The crew mostly took care of keeping *Lucifer's Ghost* in fighting shape and their weaponry intact. They practiced shooting of the main deck and kept their cutlasses and pistols from corroding from the saltwater and being on the lookout for "the big prize!"

Why was McGinnty's reputation so harsh? Was this a bunch of propaganda from the Royal Navy? Maybe there was more to his privateering days than what was heard.

A yell came from the lookout.

"New Providence is in sight!"

CHAPTER 14

NEW PROVIDENCE

With the island in sight, the men roared and pumped their fists in the air. Rum was brought out, and many a thirst was quenched in celebration of their arrival. Many changed from their ragged clothes to fine silks and leather caps.

The men had raved about the island. Some were even calling it heaven on earth. Edmund felt like he belonged to this diverse group of lost characters that were organized and led by McGinnty.

New Providence was a sixty-square-mile island located in the middle of the British Bahamas. The English had abandoned it however in 1704, proving too difficult to protect after numerous attacks by the Spanish and the French. After the War of Spanish Succession, it became a perfect sanctuary for pirates.

The location was well positioned between westbound shipping lanes carrying provisions from Europe and eastbound lanes taking gold and silver to Europe. The ships that sailed the routes became targets for the pirates of the Caribbean. The island traded their resources and money for the plundered goods supplied by pirates. It was a service industry for traders and smugglers. The pirates bartered there, which made the island a major player in the up-and-coming smuggling trade that had been created.

The island also supplied pirates with everything they needed. It was abundant in natural resources of food, water, timber, wild game, sugar, tobacco, and rum. In the backdrop were wooden huts, taverns, and white-painted houses all close together. Plantations were filled with sugarcane.

Lucifer's Ghost was too big and heavy to enter the harbor area, so it anchored outside the New Providence's barrier called Hog Island, which was located between its two entrances. The men, with the exception of the few left to watch *Lucifer's Ghost,* transferred to *Hellspite* and made for shore.

Edmund couldn't get over the excitement of the crew. Gilgo had split up the coins from the merchant ship, so each crewmember had plenty of money to enjoy the "fruits" of the island. Edmund jingled pieces of eight in his pockets. He hadn't had money since Bristol and was excited about New Providence after hearing so many of the stories from the crew. As the sloop approached the docks, McGinnty addressed the crew. "Men, you've earned this little reprieve. Enjoy the next few weeks until we sail again!"

He toasted to them, and a loud roar went up from the crew.

They unloaded, and many ran to shore. Edmund and Jon walked side by side, patting each other on the back. Edmund felt like he was drunk the way he swayed back and forth. The dock felt like it was rocking, but it hadn't moved. The effects of weeks at sea had loosened their legs. The sun scorched down on them.

"Isn't it strange the way things work out?" Jon asked.

"What are you talking about?"

"I mean, a month ago we were trapped on a navy vessel, then attacked by pirates, and now I feel I have more freedom than I've ever had."

"Jon, we're cut off from everyone we ever loved and cared for. You were engaged for Christ's sake."

"Edmund, I can't explain it. I feel like we own the seas," Jon said with a soft smile.

"You're just caught up with helping Gilgo do the books and records. As for me, I want to get back to Bristol. That's where my future is. Come on, before you get too sentimental, let's enjoy this paradise."

Jon did feel a sense of belonging using his skills to assist Gilgo in the accounting that the pirates had. Every ounce of plunder was accounted for.

They heard bells in the background ringing. That was the signal pirates had arrived. They walked past the beach, and smiles stretched their faces until they saw the heart of New Providence.

"This is it?" Jon whispered.

The other pirates were running around, screaming and looking for ways to spend their money. Jon looked at Edmund.

"It's nothing but shacks, tents, and small houses."

"What did you expect? Queen Square?" Edmund answered.

They both laughed and toured what each hut or dwelling had to offer. It was a dream haven where prostitutes, bartenders, and local merchants vied for the attention of all passing seamen. A pirate resort to blow off steam, where law and order was determined by which pirate captain was in town. Royal authority was thousands of miles away.

They walked into a shack that resembled a tavern and ordered a couple of mugs of ale. The bartender poured. He was excited to have a new ship of customers land on the island. Pirates were good for business, and he proceeded to tell the two newcomers about life on the island and all it had to offer. The two shook their heads and acted interested, but they were the same stories they had heard from the crew the last few weeks prior to arriving.

Other pirates started traipsing in and ordering rum, gin, and beer from the bartender. This was their heaven.

"So, Jon, you told me back on the *Fitzgerald* you were engaged before being pressed into service. How are you going to get back to her?"

"Gees, Edmund, I haven't the foggiest. You think these blokes are ever going back?"

Edmund took a chug from his ale and smiled. "I doubt it. What was her name?"

"Caroline. She's from an upscale family in Southampton. I wish she was here now."

"I feel the same way about Sarah. It's strange how fate plays tricks on us," Edmund said, downing his ale.

"It's true. I was a successful accountant, and now look at me. It's a completely different world. Imagine, this is considered heaven," Jon replied.

They laughed.

"I mean, it's a dump!"

Jon finished his ale, and they both ordered another round.

As nightfall arrived, Edmund was very drunk. Jon was trying to reason with him to go back to the ship. Edmund fell over on his barstool, laughing.

"What the hell is that noise?" he yelled to the bartender.

"Frogs and cicadas. I guess you don't have them where you're from," the bartender replied.

Edmund crawled back to his stool. "Cicadas?"

His words came out slurred.

Two women noticed him and came over.

"You two fellas want some company tonight?" said a dark-skinned woman with a thick Spanish accent. She slithered up to the bar. Her hair was stringy, skin was weathered from the hot Caribbean sun.

Another one followed her. She had light brown hair and was missing a tooth that surrounded rotting gums. She was plump with wrinkles around her eyes. She rubbed Edmund's arm and put her other arm around him.

"This one's mine," she said, helping him sit back on his stool. The dark-skinned woman gravitated toward Jon who winced when she touched him.

Edmund stumbled up and leaned against the bar.

"Sarah, is that you?" Edmund looked at her and stared in amazement. The woman looked at her friend and shrugged her shoulders.

"I'm whoever you want me to be, baby." As she smiled, the hole in her mouth was more prevalent. She leaned over and kissed Edmund on the cheek.

"Can you buy us a drink?"

"Sarah, I thought I'd never see you again," he slurred and ordered two rums for the women.

"Sarah's here to take care of you, darling." She rubbed his stomach.

Jon grabbed the dark-skinned woman's hand and pulled it away from his body.

"I have a fiancée." Then he turned to Edmund. "Don't do it. She's not Sarah."

Edmund turned and stumbled. The woman held him up and pulled him away from Jon.

"She is so. This is Sarah!" Edmund yelled loudly, prompting others to turn around and look at him.

"Follow me, honey. Let Sarah take care of you tonight."

Jon watched as the woman grabbed Edmund's arm and escorted him outside and down a path leading to a group of tents.

"Hey, wait up!" the dark-skinned woman yelled and turned to Jon. "You're a disappointment. You have no idea what you're gonna miss." She ran out toward the two and made their way to a small hut.

Once inside, they eased Edmund down on the bed, but at the last second, he fell and landed hard on the ground. The room was spinning. The plump girl sat next to him.

"Let Sarah help you out of your pants."

They both grabbed the legs of his pants and pulled them off.

"Isn't that better?"

Edmund's eyes were half shut, and he struggled to stay awake. The dark-skinned woman rummaged through his pants and found some coins. The gap-toothed woman stripped Edmund of the pouch he was carrying that hung down to his waist and threw it to her friend. She undressed and lay next to him.

"C'mon, baby, let me see what you've got. I want to take care of you."

He mumbled as she straddled him, but he was too soft for penetration. The dark-skinned woman emptied the contents of his pouch into a leather bag and nodded to her friend. She had a large smile on her face.

The one straddling Edmund rubbed his stomach and stroked him some more, but there was no sign of life coming from below his waist. He mumbled again as drool came from his mouth. She stood up, got dressed, and the two left the hut. As she was leaving, she heard a sudden sound behind them. Edmund was snoring.

"Where the hell am I?"

Edmund looked around. The hut was empty with the flaps from the entrance wide-open. He grabbed his pants and forced his legs inside. His head was pounding. He staggered over to where his shirt was and saw his pouch on the floor near the entrance.

"Damn!"

He walked over and picked it up. Edmund shook his head.

"Empty. All of it gone!"

He slipped his shirt on and slowly walked outside. The early-morning sunlight burned through his eyes. He walked toward the beach. A few bodies were passed out along the shore from the previous night's festivities.

Where's Jon? He looked around. *Probably back on the ship where I should have been.*

Edmund walked down the beach and noticed a few bodies sprawled out in the sand, casualties from the previous night's activities. He just wanted to get back to the ship and pass out. He was dizzy and having trouble keeping his balance, sliding in the sand.

On his way toward the docks, he stumbled on McGinnty lying nearby. Edmund stopped. He didn't know whether to take a detour around him or just walk by. He looked like he was asleep, so he forged ahead. As he walked by, he looked at McGinnty and noticed his mouth turned up at the corners as if he was almost smiling. His eyes were shut and his hands placed behind his head.

Edmund continued on until he noticed something next to McGinnty's right hand. It was a journal bound in leather. He froze, looked around, and noticed no one watching him. He bent over and carefully reached for it. He untied the lace surrounding it then read.

In June of 1708, he described a privateering mission off the coast of Madagascar. He turned a few pages toward the beginning. McGinnty described his apprenticeship under Captain Underwood on a ship called the *Dorabella.* Edmund looked up and remembered the *Lucinda.* He flipped the pages until he reached 1713, and there it was. He started reading about the battle off the coast of South America.

"Have a rough night, boy?"

Edmund nearly jumped out of his skin as he fumbled with the journal and hid it behind his back. He looked at McGinnty who was now leaning forward with his knees up and arms rested on them.

Edmund looked at him nervously.

"Oh yeah, a lot of fun." His face said otherwise.

"Your eyes are bloodshot, face is pale. Looks like you did have fun last night."

McGinnty looked out at sea as he continued. "Have a seat. You met some of the local women?"

"Ah . . . no. I mean a couple of them."

McGinnty laughed. "So spit it out, boy. Do you have any money left?"

Edmund was shocked. "Ah . . . nothing."

McGinnty let out a howl, slapping his knee.

"I guess we should have warned you, but it's always better if you experience the local women firsthand. They're a treacherous bunch they are. They take care of us, but don't ever trust 'em!"

"Well, I won't be experiencing anything for a while. They cleaned me out."

McGinnty clutched his shoulder. "Don't worry. There's more money on the way when we deal the cargo on the ship. We're going to Hispaniola in a few days to trade silks, cloth, and weapons to them. We'll get a fair price. Next time, be careful. The women can sniff out you plebes in a second. I can get you back your money. While we're in port, we're the law, but they're here to make a profit also. It's free trade here. Now if they stole from you, that's a different tune."

"Forget it. I couldn't describe them anyway. I was a wreck."

They both laughed.

"Here's something to get you through the next few days." He reached in his pouch and handed over ten pieces of eight. "The tavern owners will extend you credit. They know we're good for it."

"Thanks," Edmund said. He looked over the silver and placed it in his pouch.

"I had a son that would be about your age if he'd lived," McGinnty said.

"What happened to him?"

"The plague happened to him. I have another son who I haven't seen in years."

"I'm sorry to hear that." Edmund was surprised he was opening up to him.

"I guess you have to play the hand you're dealt."

Edmund started to walk away.

"Don't you have something of mine?" McGinnty asked.

Edmund stopped in his tracks and looked up. The journal slipped his mind. Embarrassed, he slowly handed it back to McGinnty.

"I'm sorry, I was just curious. I read a lot of Dampier and thought your log would be interesting."

"Ah, Dampier, quite the voyager."

McGinnty grabbed the journal and tied it back up.

"Were you always a pirate?"

McGinnty laughed and shook his head. He paused for a moment and gave Edmund a serious look.

"I started in the Royal Navy at the beginning of the war. Conditions were horrible, as you found out when you served. I'm not a regimented person that follows orders, so I quickly became a privateer. I made it up to ship's captain in 1705, or was it '06? We had a great time." He smiled, reminiscing. "We drove the French and Spanish crazy. We hit them from all sides. They didn't know if they were coming or going. We used to follow the little fish to lead us to the big fish. Oh, the plunder we took home. There was such a competition between us captains—who would take home the most. We were competitive but very respectful of each other."

"What happened with the *Lucinda*?" Edmund blurted out. The question just jumped right out of him.

McGinnty stared out to the water.

"The *Lucinda*?" He paused. "You probably heard rumors or myths."

Edmund looked at the sand. He wanted to walk away, but he hoped McGinnty would tell him about it. McGinnty reflected and then looked Edmund in the eyes, staring through them.

"Because we sacked a lot of ships and made a lot of money, I ended up reinvesting the profits into buying part ownership of four other ships split between three men.

"We found out about Spain's treasure fleets in the Pacific. They used the gold and silver mines in Mexico and traveled to Manila to buy silks, porcelain, and other Oriental treasures. They would sail back to Mexico, load up with as much plunder as they could carry, and bring it home. They loaded up these enormous Manila galleons. They were a floating fortress, maybe one thousand tons and loaded with weaponry.

"I presented this to the board, but they were afraid of losing a couple more ships and overruled me. When we were commissioned to go to Indonesia to attack French and Spanish ships there, we diverted to South America instead.

"I took two ships, the *Duke* and the *Duchess*, and we were stocked to the hilt. We carried 350 men, 62 guns between the two of them, and as much ammunition as we could hold. After months at sea, we ran into one ship. It was a Swedish merchant ship. They're as neutral as they come, and the men were up in arms about not attacking it. I was starting to lose control of the ship.

"Finally, off the coast of South America, we found a Manila galleon. It was slow and we had no problem catching it. We sailed alongside it for days, and finally, in a single formation, we attacked, blasting its sides. Cannonballs flew back and forth, often through people, mutilating them. The decks were covered in blood and mangled flesh. My sharpshooters picked off their officers when we came around for a second rally. They sent up their flags for surrender. Their captain was killed, but their quartermaster told us that two ships left Manila, and this was the smaller of the two. The other ship was the *Lucinda.*

"From the description they gave us, it was twice the size of anything we had and twice the arsenal. We brought the *Duke* to a nearby port to get fixed up. The French ship, the *Begonia,* was also in need of repairs, and we were going to use it to get close to the *Lucinda.* Five days later, the *Lucinda* was greeted by the *Duchess* and the *Begonia.* It was huge—one thousand tons, twin gun decks. We flew the Spanish flag on the *Begonia,* which headed straight for it with the *Duchess* in tow. I sailed the *Duke* about a mile behind.

"The *Begonia* was greeted with waves from their crew, and it sailed close enough for the crews to shake hands, and then we opened up with everything we had. There was so much smoke you couldn't see anything in two feet in front of you. They tried to respond but didn't get nearly the shots off we did. The *Begonia* sailed away, and the *Duchess* pounded their other side. They started to get their wits about them and fired back at the *Duchess.* We came by and hit them with our heavy artillery. It seemed like we didn't make a dent in it. We retreated and then went back. This time, we surrounded it. We must have fired three hundred cannonballs at it, fifty chained cannonballs, grapeshot. They hit the *Duchess* hard—it was completely splintered and the sails were gone. We retreated again. This time, it was just us and the *Begonia.* The *Duchess* and its crew were completely destroyed. We had to go at them again and not give them a chance to regroup. We emptied our guns on them and prepared to broadside the ship. The *Lucinda* was as strong as they come, and finally, what little of their crew that was left surrendered.

"I've never seen so much gold, silver, silks, copper, and a lifetime's supply. The question was how to bring it home. Our ships were crippled. The ship that held together the best was the *Lucinda.* We sailed to New Providence, fixed up the *Duke,* and came back with as much treasure as we could carry. Of course, we left a whole lot more in New Providence."

"So the rumors are true? I mean, about the *Lucinda* and the treasure?" Edmund interrupted.

"Many good men paid a price," McGinnty recalled.

"What happened when you got home?" Edmund asked.

McGinnty grimaced. "Alexander Killingsworth is what happened. Apparently, he bought out my three other partners by calling for payments on his South Sea Stock that went south. He had me arrested as soon as I arrived."

"Sounds like you could have retired."

"What might have been?" He rose from the sand. "It was my last conquest for England. I've had many since."

Edmund sat at the bar thinking of the past few days, weeks, even years. He thought of McGinnty and how much different his story was than the version told in England.

He lifted his mug and drank as the rum burned down his throat. He made a grimace, setting the mug down.

Nasty. Just plain nasty.

The pub was half filled, but most of the patrons were busy with women or about passed out. New Providence was growing fast. More pirates were coming by the month, each with their own set of laws and styles.

A glass smashed in the back room, interrupting Edmund's thoughts. He heard rumblings, and then the shriek of a woman's voice pierced his ears. Another glass smashed, and he heard the laughter of men. Edmund stood up and walked slowly to the back room. He turned around and checked out the few patrons that were in the place. They acted as if they didn't hear a sound. They just went about their business. He made his way to the storage room door. It sounded like there was a struggle taking place inside. He opened the door slowly, poking his head around it.

Gilgo, the quartermaster, was leaning over a woman that was facedown on the table, bent over at the waist. Her shirt was shredded, and black dress lifted above her waist. Gilgo clenched a knife between his teeth, his pants wrapped around his boots, ready to enter her. He tore the skirt from her hips. Gilgo's hands traveled up her thighs, and then he spread her legs apart. Chestus was on one side of him, encouraging him on. Wolf, a tall, thick brute who joined the ship from Port Royal, was on the other side. The girl groaned and tried to cover herself. She held her hand tightly around her thighs.

"Just the way I like 'em," Gilgo said, pointing to his men to grab her and hold her down. "She's a wildcat! Now move your hands away."

"No, please," she gasped.

"Move 'em or I'll kill you."

The two men went to each of her legs, grabbing them and spreading them wide. Gilgo grabbed her rear end and started to mount her. She screamed, but Wolf shoved his hand around her mouth. She bit hard. He yelled but held his ground and smacked her head with his free hand.

"Wolf, can't you keep her still?"

Gilgo threw her face down hard on the table.

Edmund threw his head to the sky.

I don't believe this.

Edmund walked up behind them, pulling out his blunderbuss with his right hand and adjusting a pistol into position with his left. He hit Chestus over the head with the butt of the blunderbuss, and he went down with a thud. Gilgo turned quickly and was greeted by a pistol pointing to his head and the blunderbuss pointing at his engorged penis.

"I bet my gun is more powerful than yours," he said as Gilgo was still inside his victim. The knife dropped from Gilgo's mouth.

Wolf pulled out a knife and moved around Gilgo. Edmund took the pistol away and greeted Wolf by indenting the barrel of his pistol on Wolf's forehead. Wolf was four inches taller and weighed a lot more than Edmund, but the pistol evened their physical differences.

"Back off!"

Wolf didn't move.

"Better tell him to back off, Gilgo."

"Back off, Wolf."

Wolf backed up and threw his knife down. Edmund looked at Gilgo and watched his limp member slip out of the woman.

"I told you my gun was more powerful," he said, smirking.

Chestus, lying on the floor, was slowly rolling around and grabbing his head. The woman pulled her dress down and stared at Edmund.

"You're all a bunch of animals!" she screamed in a thick Spanish accent.

She shoved Gilgo and barged her way past Edmund, storming out the door. Chestus stood up slowly as all three of them were now seething at Edmund.

Edmund kept the guns on them by rotating his aim back and forth to each.

"Are you going to shoot all of us?" Gilgo said, pulling up his pants and slowly backing his way to the door.

"No, but I can take down two of you." Edmund waved his pistol, pointing to the door. "Now get out!"

They moved slowly toward the door, not taking their eyes off him.

"Now!" he screamed and pointed his blunderbuss at Gilgo's head.

The three headed for the door, and Gilgo turned before he left.

"I won't forget this. You'll pay dearly. You're a dead man!"

They left, leaving Edmund in the room to contemplate his next move.

Well, I'm in deep shit now.

He put his guns away and waited. After a few minutes, he peered his head out and looked around. The three cutthroats were gone. He walked through the bar, which was empty except for two passed-out pirates in the corner and three men in the other laughing at stories.

Are they going to ambush me out here?

He walked to the front door. He saw the woman from the bar down by the pier and headed toward her.

"You shouldn't be out here," he said as he walked up.

"Let me be. You're all a bunch of savages!"

She wrapped her torn shirt around her chest and walked away.

"Hey, I saved you, I helped you out!" he said, hands swaying in the air.

"Don't give me that. You pirates are all the same. You probably wanted me for yourself. You have no rules and ruin this island every time you come."

"I'm not like that. I never even thought of that," Edmund pleaded.

She shoved him and walked away.

"Hey," he said as he staggered backward.
She just kept walking, picking up her pace.
"Don't I even get a thank you?"
She disappeared around the corner.

CHAPTER 15

HURRICANE OF *1715*

Lucifer's Ghost sailed back to Nassau Harbor after a successful supply run from the Leeward Islands. McGinnty traded rum, money, and tobacco for weapons and powder. He also acquired information regarding the whereabouts of the British and French navies patrolling the area.

McGinnty looked out to sea as the wind picked up and rain started falling. For the past fifteen years or so, he had spent more time at sea than on land. He could detect the slightest shifts in winds and waves. There was nothing slight about this shift. In the distance, a dark mass of black clouds hung over the ocean and was moving rapidly at them.

"It's coming straight at us," McGinnty said.

"We'll outrun it, sir," Beckham yelled, pointing toward New Providence in the distance, which looked like a small speck of land.

"I don't think so. It's moving too fast. We'll leave the sail up as long as we can."

McGinnty knew how to sail, and none of the men doubted him. He put forward the same swagger and determination against the storm approaching that he did when facing an enemy vessel.

As it approached, the weather turned ugly. The storm that approached was beyond anything they had ever seen. The rising waves crashed against the bow, and the men clung to anything they could hang on to. The first crack of thunder shook the ship, and a few seconds later, heavy squalls of rain began to fall. It was as if a dam burst. The sudden black sky was lit up by bolts of lightning. The seas rose to twenty- and thirty-foot waves, which broke in cascades of foam all around. The rigging flailed as the wind increased.

"Shorten the sails!" McGinnty yelled as he leaned over the quarterdeck. The words barely left his mouth when the ship was pummeled with a huge wave, sending the men reeling.

Edmund grunted in pain as he fell hard to the deck and struck the side of his face. The next wave spilled over the railing, delivering an ice-cold jolt to his face.

Pirates jumped, scurrying up the ratlines into the rigging, hurrying to roll up the canvas, manning the ropes to haul in the yards so there would be less sail to catch. This slowed the ship considerably as McGinnty barked out orders.

Beckham fought the wheel with one hand and tried to shield the water spraying in his face with the other.

"We need to get to the shelter of the islands," he yelled, but the wind snatched his words and only a few could hear him.

The wind was coming from the southeast. The crew battled tediously to take in sail, all hauling together. Jon's hat blew off his head and skidded over the rising waves.

Whitecaps filled the sea, and the air surrounding them was filled with mist and spray from the waves crashing against the ship. Flashes of lightning cracked through the sky. The storm never let up. It shoved them up and down, side to side. Waves were like cliffs looming over them and, one by one, would avalanche on top of them. Men hung on to a crest or mast or anything they could get their hands on. The tilt was so steep at times it seemed they may flip over end to end.

Edmund clung on to the cordage, unable to do anything. Waves broke over the ship and covered him. The crowded deck had now been empty as anything that wasn't tied down had disappeared. Full barrels and crates had been dislodged and tossed over the side as if they weighed nothing.

The strength of the wind and the waves bent the huge masts like bows, threatening to snap them in two or dislodge them from their footings. Lightning flashed the sky, wind screamed through the rigging, waves rolled over the deck.

The ship bucked and plunged as Edmund fought with others to furl sails made many times heavier with water—all being torn by the wind.

Their vision was limited, and no one could see or hear the cries of men being tossed into the ocean. The wind would shriek through the rigging like a banshee. Water smashed up against the ship, trying to tear men loose and throw them into the sea.

The ship was suddenly hit with a tremendous wave from the starboard side, which sent it sideways. Edmund clung for his life as his feet slipped from beneath him. Although the ship leaned heavily, the side never touched water. Very slowly, the ship began to right itself as if it were a cork.

A whitecapped curl crashed into the bow. Edmund crawled along the deck, pulling himself forward. The ship bobbed high amid the enormous swells. The boat was seesawing violently. The wind whistled fiercely in his ears. The boat plunged deep into a swell then soared high over the wave.

Beckham, feet wide apart, spun the wheel, bringing the great ship's bow face-to-face with the wind.

Below deck, a cannon broke free from its tackle and careened across the lower decks, crushing everyone and everything in its path. Waves broke over the deck, and water poured into the bedlam of crashing cannons and barrels of cargo below.

As the ship headed toward Hog Island, McGinnty screamed to throw the anchors overboard and hoped the great iron hooks held firm enough to keep them from being thrown into the beach until the storm subsided. As the anchors entered the water, the cables stiffened and, miraculously, pulled the ship to a halt a few hundred yards off the shores of Hog Island.

The storm went raging on, but gradually, its control of the ship began to slacken. The waves crashing against them became less powerful. The ship still pitched and plummeted but was riding the waves. The wind became less consistent until it was possible to see the men on the deck and hear their cries. Men worked below decks in a frenzy, emptying buckets of water that flooded the ship. It was all they could do to hang on and wait for the storm to pass.

After the storm passed, the deck looked like a war zone. There was splintered wood everywhere, strewn ropes all along the deck; but somehow, the ship held together and so did the crew. The men came down limping from the rigging, falling the last couple of feet to the deck. Jon was one of them, and he fell to one knee on the deck. He wiped the water from his face and brushed back his hair with his fingers. He looked up at Edmund with a smile on his face. It was a smile of relief.

Edmund checked out the ship as a light rain continued to fall. He was shivering, soaked to the skin, and exhausted as he stared at torn sails and broken spars. The men were exhausted and many injured.

As the storm flew by, McGinnty ordered stoves lit below decks to dry clothing. Some of the men fell into their hammocks, totally exhausted. Others threw back rum as the ship made its way toward port.

Later, McGinnty rang the ship's bell and called the men to attention.

"You men were outstanding today. If it weren't for you, this ship would have been destroyed."

A large cheer went up as men threw up their hands and patted one another. McGinnty continued, "Let's sample whatever entertainment this town has to offer. You deserve it."

The men cheered on and celebrations began. McGinnty had the respect from everyone on his crew and rewarded their loyalty. Most of the men had served under captains that gave nothing but beatings and curses. That was not McGinnty's style.

As they pulled into Nassau Harbor, reality struck on just how severe the storm was and how lucky they were to survive. Ships were scattered all over. Many had run aground, and some had even capsized. Many men in Nassau had just lost their livelihood. Many men in Nassau would turn to McGinnty for help.

The hurricane of 1715 whipped through New Providence and destroyed much of the island. Ships were dragged all over the harbor, and one of the masts on *Hellspite* broke in two. Water engulfed all the ships, and days were spent hauling water out of each of them. McGinnty's fleet now included two more sloops and four merchant vessels to add to *Lucifer's Ghost* and *Hellspite*. Beckham and Moore fixed the ships like surgeons, and men quickly replaced the sails that were torn apart.

Lucifer's Ghost encountered a few leaks below the waterline and needed constant pumping. The men who stayed on the ships during the storm were regarded as heroes, and the local pubs were crawling with thirsty pirates.

"We've had a lot worse," one of the barkeeps was heard to say. "That one didn't really hit us full bore."

Edmund and Jon strolled along the beach toward inside the mainland. Edmund wore new silk shirts courtesy of the Dutch merchant ship and leather boots bought from the locals. Money was to be spent. Jon wondered what to do with his money.

"Are there no banks on this island?"

"Maybe you should start one," Edmund answered.

They checked out a woman selling beads when, suddenly, footsteps fast approached them from behind. Edmund grabbed his cutlass and turned.

"I don't think you need that. At least not yet," a voice said.

It was the girl Gilgo tried to attack at the pub. She stopped and stared at Edmund. Her eyes were black as night, and her skin was smooth and covered with a dark tan. Her dark hair was long and flew in the soft breeze. The night he first saw her, her face was smudged in shadows, but now the sunlight brought a glow to her natural beauty. She caught Edmund by surprise. Jon was mesmerized by her beauty and froze.

"How are you doing?" Edmund stammered.

"I saw you walking down the road, and I wanted to thank you for the other night. You risked your life for me, and I treated you like garbage. I owe you—how you say—an apology. My name is Felina."

Her accent wasn't as thick as when she was yelling at him, and her voice was much softer.

"Well, I am a pirate. We're not all like those men, and the name is Edmund. This is Jon."

"Pleasure to meet you. You two don't seem like pirates."

"We just kind of fell into it. Why did those men attack you?" Edmund asked.

"Does it matter?" She looked him in the eyes and slightly shook her head. "Look, I was delivering dresses to some of the local women, and those savages thought I was a working girl."

"So you're not a prostitute?" Edmund asked. He winced as soon as the words left his lips. He wished he could take them back.

Jon's eyes bulged out, and he poked Edmund in the side with his elbow.

"Edmund!"

"Do not be so quick to judge," she answered. "You don't know what everyone's past is like, and no, I am not. I work as a seamstress and make enough to survive."

After exchanging pleasantries, she led Edmund and Jon down a small road and made their way out to the sugarcane fields. As they walked, Edmund learned New Providence had no government. The Spanish and French had raided it often during the war, and the local governors had fled. What were left were inland plantation owners and the local merchants at the harbor. Usually, pirates were the highest occupants on the island at any one time and governed the island as they saw fit.

Felina talked of how her mother used to be a prostitute, and her father was a Spanish sailor she never knew. They watched as slaves unloaded stacks of sugarcane and took them to the boiling rooms.

"Sugarcane has to be taken to the grinders as soon as possible, or it doesn't crystallize," she said.

They walked over to the boiling house. The workers ignored them as they kept up their busy pace. The large copper vats were heated by a huge blazing furnace and was where the sugar would crystallize.

"They carefully skim off waste molasses from the sugar, and that's what is used to make the rum you pirates worship," she said.

Edmund laughed. He had never seen how much work went into making rum.

"I thought you just grew it and puff, it's being poured in our mugs," Jon said.

The process went on all day and night. Some of the slaves that worked near the vats had horrific scars and burnt skin. In a hut off in the distance, sugar was packed and ready for transportation. Farther in the distance were large two-story plantation houses.

The day spent with Felina was very relaxing and insightful. When they walked through the sugarcane fields with Felina, it reminded him of walking through Myers Plantation with Sarah.

I wonder how she's doing. Is she still in Bristol?

Edmund learned about New Providence and the people that inhabited the island. She also told the two of a plague that was sweeping the island and one that was not confined to just the locals but pirates as well. The plague was syphilis. Felina's mother suffered from it and was quickly affecting her mind.

Later that night, Edmund asked Doc about the disease, and he said there was nothing he could do. The only cure or medicine for the disease was mercury, and the island was about out of that.

"Edmund, this is an island. It's not a city like London or even your Bristol. There's no medicine here."

"How many of the men are sick?" Edmund asked.

"More than we know, I'm afraid."

With the ships patched up and ready to set sail, most of the men were out of money and ready to look for plunder. McGinnty left no word as to when the men would set sail, and the crew was getting edgy waiting to get back to sea. They were drinking most nights, and factions were drawn between the men. Pirates from other ships created a rivalry, and tempers were short.

On a crowded night in one of the local taverns, Jon brought back four mugs of ale. As he passed the table, Chestus stuck out his foot, catching Jon's ankle. He fell forward, spilling ale all over the floor. Pirates laughed. Gilgo gave a friendly slap to Chestus's head.

"What a buffoon."

Jon picked himself up to his knees and slowly turned. Chestus was looking at Gilgo as he continued to laugh, oblivious to Jon who stood in front of him. His bloody hand held half a mug of ale, which he tossed at Chestus's face. The laughter stopped. Both Chestus and Gilgo glared at Jon. Ale dripped from Chestus's beard. Wolf came over and grabbed Jon from behind as Chestus struck him in the stomach, knocking the air out of him. Wolf threw him to the ground as Jon wheezed for air. Chestus pounced on him. Jon tried to ward off the blows as Chestus straddled his hips. Chestus swung wildly, connecting at the side of Jon's face. Another blow was set to strike when Edmund intercepted his red-stained fist before it landed and twisted it behind Chestus's back. Using his arm for leverage, Edmund forced him to his feet. Wolf went on the attack.

"Back off or I'll break it," Edmund said, lifting his arm higher and swinging Chestus between himself and Wolf. Chestus's eyes bulged out, his mouth wide as he fought to suck in air. Edmund kept the pressure tight.

Charles ran over and grabbed Wolf from behind and held him off. Jon staggered to his feet. His cheek was scratched and bloody. His nose bled as he licked the blood from his upper lip.

Gilgo walked up to Edmund. "You and me, Drake."

Edmund threw Chestus to the ground as Gilgo attacked him with his knee. Edmund felt it thrust up and slide between his thighs as he fell to a knee. Then Gilgo jumped at him. Edmund tumbled and bent, taking Gilgo over his hip, and threw him down, slamming on the wooden deck.

He got up quickly as Edmund swept a leg around, knocking him down again. Gilgo flew straight down on his back.

Chestus flexed his arm and moved to help Gilgo but was intercepted by Jon. Charles and Wolf wrestled on the ground in a stalemate. Jon landed two blows to Chestus's face before Jon was elbowed, smashing his nose. Jon went down face-first. Chestus grabbed his hair and drove his forehead down against the floor.

Gilgo crawled over, only to be greeted by Edmund's boot, which blasted against his chin. Edmund turned to help Jon as Gilgo sat up and drew his pistol and aimed it at Edmund.

A shot exploded as Edmund flinched, checking his chest. McGinnty had his hand raised, smoke escaping from his blunderbuss.

"Enough!" he yelled.

Chestus looked up and slammed Jon's face one last time before he climbed off him and stepped clear. As Charles and Wolf untangled, Edmund gave Charles a nod and dusted himself off.

Charles liked Edmund, who was one of the few men on the ship that spoke to him as an equal and didn't fear him. Most men thought he was too peculiar and were afraid of him. They made fun of his stutter but never to his face. Even as big as Wolf was, Charles's temper and sudden outbursts were more intimidating than Wolf's size.

As the six of them separated, order was restored, and they commenced to drinking the rest of the night, exchanging glares.

CHAPTER 16

THE TREASURE CAMP

During a hot, humid morning in late September, bells rang early. It was a signal to round up the crew. Messengers raced around frantically and told whoever they could to meet at where *Hellspite* was docked. Most of the men were hungover but, out of curiosity, still staggered to the docks to report for duty. A large crowd gathered anxiously, awaiting McGinnty to arrive.

"We must be heading out to sea," Edmund told a yawning Jon as they lurched toward the docks.

Finally, McGinnty appeared in the distance. A cutlass by his waist, three feathers sticking out of his hat. He was neatly dressed and had a glow in his eyes as he walked through the crowd of sailors until he reached *Hellspite*. He quickly lifted himself on board and stood above everyone else as he addressed his audience. "Men, it appears that God has been looking out for us. That hurricane that blasted through here a few months ago also hit the coasts of Cuba and Florida. I have received word that a Spanish treasure fleet, loaded with plunder, has either sunk or been destroyed."

The men looked at each other, eyebrows were raised. Edmund nudged Jon whose eyes were closed.

"I received information on the location of these ships, and I think it's high time we help the Spanish out in recovering their treasure."

Edmund had heard rumors of sunken treasure off the coast of Florida, and now McGinnty confirmed it. The men roared. They pounded their fists, hugged one another, as McGinnty waved his hand to continue.

"Men, this could be our biggest score yet. When I tell you the Spanish lost a fortune at the bottom of the coast of Florida, I can't even begin to estimate the value. It may well be over £500,000—maybe even a million."

Mouths hung open in shock of the mere thought of that much money. Men started moving around in chaos. McGinnty, with the help of Gilgo, barked out orders and got them organized.

"We shove off in three hours!" McGinnty yelled.

McGinnty was a great organizer and loaded up a crew of 160 men, *Lucifer's Ghost,* and two sloops. He detailed everything from the ship's supplies to its ammunition. He also knew if news traveled east to New Providence, then news also would have hit the major cities of the colonies. There could be a free-for-all of ships outside Florida. How many would be friendly and what kind of price was on their head had yet to be determined.

As they sailed to the Florida straits, they intercepted a Spanish mail boat on its way to Havana. McGinnty quickly hoisted pirate colors to intimidate them. Just like the Dutch merchant ship, their crew quickly surrendered without a shot being fired. McGinnty told them he wanted information and nothing else.

The Spaniards told him of two salvage camps six miles apart, and the southernmost camp was where a majority of the recovered plunder had been taken.

Lucifer's Ghost sailed its way up the deserted Florida coast, flying Spanish colors. He thought if the British saw it was a Spanish ship, they would not want to explain what they were doing in Spanish waters. If the Spanish spotted them, they could just say they were there for a diving expedition. McGinnty spoke fluent Spanish, so communication was not a problem.

Farther up the coast, amid the haze, they witnessed bits and pieces of ships. It was more eerie when bodies were seen washed up on the barrier island beaches north of Saint Lucia. A hull was visible in the shallow waters a few hundred yards away.

On the shore were signs of campfires and crosses marking the graves of those that hadn't survived the wreckages. *Lucifer's Ghost* continued onward.

At night, campfires of the Spanish salvage camps flickered red against a pitch-black shore. McGinnty ordered all lamps doused and boats prepared to launch. An early-morning attack was planned.

Before dawn, dinghies were taken to shore. Gilgo's squadron left first. When Edmund and Jon finally hit the beach, they were greeted by McGinnty and learned they were assigned to his regiment. Gilgo's men were already on their way to the camps. McGinnty divided the men into two squadrons of forty men and distanced one hundred yards apart to better surround the camp.

Each man was armed to the teeth. Edmund carried a cutlass, four pistols hung down around his waist, and two knives were placed in his boots. Each battalion also rolled small cannons. They marched through the woods loud and boisterous, almost wanting to be discovered. Drums beat in unison. Edmund was nervous. Jon was mortified as they marched in the middle battalion.

"Why are we so loud?" Jon asked. "They'll know we're coming and position themselves for an attack."

Edmund shrugged his shoulders; but McGinnty, who was three body lengths ahead, overheard the question and turned around. With a certain amount of bravado, he answered Jon's question.

"We want them to know we're coming. If they see how many people we have and our firepower, they'll surrender or flee for the hills."

The jungle was so dense in most places they couldn't see more than a few feet in any direction. Also, not a lot of sunlight made it down to the crew level. They trudged through deep, murky shadows. Edmund was drenched with sweat as they walked through the thick, humid air.

Mosquitoes landed at Edmund's neck. He slapped mosquitoes constantly. They hovered around his ears and tickled his skin whenever they landed. They especially liked Edmund's scabs. Some even bit right through his clothing.

As they continued their walk through the woods, musket balls suddenly splintered the trees surrounding them as smoke filled the air. The sounds of thunder scattered McGinnty's men as they took cover behind trees and rocks. Spaniards were rising out of the ground and not surrendering as McGinnty had anticipated.

Edmund dodged a bush and raced between two trees. A sword in his left hand and a pistol in his right, he crouched in the thick brush ready to attack. His throat tightened, smoke stung his eyes. A few feet away to his left, a man was lying dead with half his face shot off. McGinnty barked out orders, but no one could hear a word. The crew fired back as they ran from rock to rock, tree to tree. The Spaniards were hidden in the mist, which floated thickly about the woods. Two men fell to his right.

McGinnty led a wild leaping charge with a wall of men behind him as each man emptied his pistols. One of the Spaniards ran forward, and Edmund aimed his pistol and fired, hitting the attacker in the chest. The Spaniard doubled over and fell forward. Edmund threw that pistol to the ground, reached for another, and fired, hitting another Spaniard in the midsection, forcing him down, legs rubbery.

The noise was too great to hear anyone. In the smoke and confusion, screams and pain and rage filled the air, replacing the sound of the thunder of gunfire as pistols and rifles emptied. Musket balls and bloodstains splattered the trees.

Someone pushed Edmund from behind. He yelled until he realized it was Jon trying to get him to cover.

McGinnty took a musket ball, tearing just under his right shoulder as blood filled his armpit. Shots were still fired in unison and then abruptly halted.

Edmund faintly heard McGinnty scream, “Where’s Gilgo?”

After the pistol and rifle fire ceased, McGinnty’s men chased the Spaniards with cutlasses in hand. The Spaniards made a hasty retreat as they were severely outnumbered.

Edmund’s face was covered in dirt and leaves. He encountered one of the Spaniards on the ground, holding his stomach. He had been done in by a cutlass as blood surrounded his arms and trickled from his mouth. Edmund moved forward.

As the Spaniards exited past their camp, a large party led by Gilgo emerged from the woods in the distant mist behind them. Instantaneously, the sound of cocking pistols was heard. The Spaniards were cut off from both sides. Pistols from Gilgo’s squad covered each of them as they raised their hands in the air. From the middle of the mist, Wolf walked a man bound and gagged, holding a blunderbuss to his forehead. It was an admiral, perhaps the leader of the Spanish battalion.

McGinnty's scouts were right. The camp was guarded by sixty men. What was left of that group the pirates quickly dismissed without a fight. They had only two cannons, which were quickly sabotaged. Much of the treasure had already been sent back to Havana, but there was still quite a fortune buried in the sand. The Spaniards dug it up, and McGinnty's men took as much gold and silver as they could haul and headed back to celebrate on the ships. The Spaniards even helped load up the treasure just to get rid of them faster and hope their lives would be spared. McGinnty knew there was more to come but wanted to get out of there before Spanish reinforcements arrived. He also felt the Spaniards would do more diving, and they could raid them again in a month or two.

As the ships were loaded, Gilgo questioned what to do about the twenty or so Spaniards left.

"We should shoot them all. Let's make an example of them."

"No!" McGinnty responded. "We've got what we came here for, we're leaving."

"Shouldn't that be decided by the crew?" Gilgo questioned.

"This is an act of war, and it's my call. No vote shall take place."

Gilgo's squad wanted blood. Voices mumbled in the background as Gilgo looked around and backed off, throwing his cutlass down and walking away.

They loaded up the ship, and *Lucifer's Ghost* set sail to North Carolina to trade with the locals up there when Edmund noticed a ship in the distance. It wasn't unusual to see ships heading toward the Florida straits, but there was something unusual about this one. Edmund saw a British flag atop the highest mast, but there was another flag below it that caught his eye. It was the flag of the Virginia colony. He ran up to McGinnty, who was in the process of being sewn under his right shoulder by Doc. The two were talking of the considerable size of the haul when Edmund interrupted them.

"Sir, I spotted a Virginia flag in the distance," Edmund said.

McGinnty looked at him curiously. "Your point?"

"Sir, isn't Killingsworth the governor of Virginia?"

McGinnty smiled a sheepish grin.

Lucifer's Ghost sailed up to the colonial ship under the guise of British flags. *Hellspite* paralleled her course to prevent the ship from outsailing her if they tried. Sailors were unloading sacks and suddenly stopped when they noticed *Lucifer's Ghost* fast approaching, white water thrown briskly from the bow.

McGinnty kept most of the men below decks and wanted them just as armed as when they raided the Spanish camp. The cannons were set, and the crew was prepared for a bloodbath.

"Ahoy! How is your haul?" McGinnty screamed over, watching everyone on the ship stop what they were doing.

A man who looked like the captain screamed over, "We're doing pretty good. What are you doing in these waters?"

Hellspite was circling and now approaching the ship from the other side. The Virginia ship used native divers to fish for gold, and they were now coming up out of the water, trying to catch their breath. A large bell was used for them to breath underneath the water, but it was still dangerous to dive that deep in these waters.

McGinnty yelled over at their captain, "We're coming from the Spanish camps. We're doing what you're doing, trying to capitalize on someone else's misfortune."

The captain looked at him with a quizzical look. "We're all out here, ships from every country, every colony. What's your name, sir?"

McGinnty laughed. "Jack McGinnty. Perhaps you have heard of me."

Once that was said, men on the navy ship ran to grab their guns. The deck of *Lucifer's Ghost* filled with men ready to strike on McGinnty's orders. He held his hand up to signal to wait. Every gun was pointed at the crew of the navy ship.

Hellspite angled to aim its cannons at the ship's broadside.

"We can have a fight. I promise you it will not go well for you or your crew. You will feel our wrath," McGinnty yelled over. "If you surrender, I promise you full quarter. Those are my terms."

The crew of the ship surrendered. The pirates boarded and noticed the sacks of plunder. It was not nearly the size and amount that they had just purged from the Spanish, but it did add more to their total haul.

McGinnty looked over at the slaves and Indians used to dive for plunder. Many were paralyzed and agonized on the deck as a result from the pressure in the deep waters. He turned toward the captain.

"I should make you dive down there and gather up the gold."

He lined up the crew from the Virginia ship who were now covered by pistols. They were over a mile out from land. He ordered all small boats and dinghies thrown overboard.

McGinnty was told by the ship's captain that Killingsworth had heard about the Spanish fleet and quickly commissioned two sloops to sail to Florida and see what they could find. He loaded his ships with firearms and divers to find any sunken treasures. His excuse for being in the vicinity would be "They were there to hunt pirates!"

McGinnty made sure he was to receive nothing. The other Virginia ship was farther south, but McGinnty chose to ignore it and continue sailing north.

"Those are your rafts. It's up to you how you board them," he said, addressing the crew and pointing to the rafts thrown overboard. "Also, off with your clothes."

The men looked at each other as if he was crazy. McGinnty pointed his pistol high in the air and fired.

"Now!"

The men raced to get out of their clothes and piled them off to the side. Naked, they jumped into the water.

Half of McGinnty's men stayed on the Virginia ship, and the plunder was brought over to *Lucifer's Ghost.* The native divers stayed with McGinnty and the pirates until they sailed closer to shore where they would be dropped off.

They headed up the coast to Ocracoke Island, which was fast becoming a second home. Their total haul was 120,000 pieces of eight.

Piracy was illegal but tolerated in North Carolina. McGinnty had a good business relationship with North Carolina governor Charles Eden. They could exchange their plunder at cut-rate prices in the colony's few towns while Governor Eden turned a blind eye to it all. He needed the pirates' business to help the colony survive. Since it was such a small-scale operation, North Carolina was a perfect haven for pirates to hang out and lay low.

While there were no decent ports in North Carolina, small-scale merchants traded raw materials or unfinished products to other colonies since there was no transatlantic trade. McGinnty traded with the merchants and became a smuggler of their goods. He used money from the Spanish haul to buy navigational equipment and food for his ship. He also had scouts row into towns and buy high quantities of tobacco and cotton. He planned on sending one of his merchant ships back to England to sell his products to smugglers he had connections with.

Navigating the coast of the Carolinas was another story. The Outer Banks had stretches of shallow depths, Pamlico Sound had tricky currents, and Cape Hatteras had both.

"Navigating by the stars is easy," McGinnty was often heard to say. "You have to learn the tides, the currents, and winds, especially when navigating the Outer Banks in North Carolina. The Outer Banks are the trickiest waters in colonial waters."

On the way back to New Providence, vessels of all types filled the Florida straits "to fish for gold." With a crowd that large, it ruled out sacking any more salvage camps for a second time, and the crew voted to sail back to New Providence and divide their take.

Edmund nervously walked up the deck toward McGinnty, who was fiddling with a Davis quadrant and other navigational aids he bought in North Carolina and didn't notice Edmund as he approached. Finally, he looked up startled and fumbled the quadrant.

"Don't sneak up on me, Drake. That's not favorable to a long life."

Edmund froze and wanted to walk away as McGinnty continued to piece the quadrant together.

"You ever see one of these?" he asked. Not waiting for a response, he continued, "At noon, you line up this adjustable crosspiece that reflects the sun's shadows up or down until the shadow lines up directly through that slit in the wooden base over there."

Edmund acted like he was interested. Finally, he just blurted out, "Captain, since we made enough plunder in Florida, I was wondering, according to the articles or pirate code, are we free to go?"

McGinnty looked at Edmund who looked down toward the deck. "Why would you want to leave?"

Edmund hesitated, looked up at McGinnty.

"As much as I appreciate all you've done, my life is back there. I have unfinished business to take care of, or at least try to."

McGinnty laughed. "Drake, you're a pirate—and a damn good one I might add." He stared at Edmund and his look became serious.

"If you want to go home, who am I to stop you? How will you get there?"

Edmund was speechless. He hadn't thought that far ahead or even contemplated McGinnty's answer.

"I guess I'll find a ship and pay my way across."

McGinnty laughed again. "After being a pirate for all this time, now you are going to pay for a ride home. That's rich."

"Well, sir, I overheard you talking to Gilgo about sending a trade ship to England. What if I was part of that crew?"

He patted him on the shoulder and scratched his chin. "That's a possibility. I'll tell you what. When we get back to New Providence, we'll work out the details on when a ship will sail. We know some smugglers, er, connections that is, we can deal with. They'll be very interested in the tobacco and cotton we have. Once you get to England, you're free to do what you want."

"Galvin too?" Edmund asked

McGinnty shook his head.

"Damn, boy. Yeah, Galvin too."

Edmund felt a rush to his face. He was finally going home.

"Thank you, sir."

The words barely left his mouth as he quickly sprinted down the deck, almost knocking down Beckham and spilling rum down his shirt.

"Blasted bloody hell! What are ya doin'?" Beckham screamed as he stumbled backward. He spit out words Edmund never knew existed.

Edmund ignored him and screamed for Jon. He finally caught up to him on the front deck. He was sewing one of the torn sails.

"Jon, we're going home."

Jon stuck the needles in his mouth and tied the riggings together.

"What the hell are you talking about?" he mumbled.

"We're going home. To Bristol. To Southampton."

Jon spit out the needles. "Home?"

"Yeah, we're heading back. McGinnty's got one of the ships heading home after we get back to New Providence. We have enough money to get our lives back."

Jon's eyes became misty. "Caroline."

The two men hugged, smiles stretched across their faces. Now they could get back to the lives they lost.

CHAPTER 17

HOME TO BRISTOL

The sun beat down on the crew, and a slight breeze filled the air. Edmund felt a certain peace as they set sail for Portsmouth, where the ship would exchange its cargo for gold and supplies. As a reward for their service, loyalty, and successful conquests, McGinnty offered any crewmember a chance to return to England. He considered this trip to be their last mission for him. Once the mission was accomplished, half the crew would leave to return or restart their lives. Many of the crew had sailed with McGinnty for over two years. Most originally captured from naval fleets and, instead of being marooned on some deserted island in the Caribbean, chose piracy. Some were even thought by the British government to be killed by pirates.

To other members of McGinnty's crew, royal authority was unknown to them; and the majority, including McGinnty, chose to remain in New Providence. The men were glad to see McGinnty assigning Beckham the captaincy for the voyage to England. Beckham always treated each of them fair and commanded a great deal of respect. He was sailing home to see relatives, but his life was now in New Providence. He was a pirate through and through.

They prepared a merchant ship they confiscated from the Dutch and spent over a month preparing for the long voyage ahead. The ship was originally captured off the coast of Port Royal and needed plenty of work to make the journey. Guns were placed on board along with a month's worth of provisions. They wanted no ships they encountered to mistake them for pirates. They even had proper documentation signed by the governor of North Carolina himself, Charles Eden. The accommodation of his signature cost £50 but was worth the investment to keep the Royal Navy off their backs.

Edmund smiled when he thought of McGinnty. He was going to miss him and the experiences they shared. When McGinnty saw the ship off, he pulled Edmund aside before he boarded.

"I hope you find what you're looking for."

Edmund shook his hand. "I hope so too, sir."

"You know, Edmund, you're always welcome here. Just be careful when you get back. Bristol may not be the same town it was when you left."

Edmund thanked him for his help. Edmund wanted to say more, but McGinnty gave him a nod and walked away.

As Edmund stared across the Atlantic, his thoughts were interrupted as Jon walked up to him.

"Edmund, I really want to thank you. I can't believe we're going home," he said as he looked out over the water, a wide grin filling his cheeks.

He hadn't stopped smiling or talking about Caroline since he received the news.

"She always talked about raising kids. She wants five. We planned on living on a large estate and coast through life. That was of course before all this," he said, waving his arms. He showed off a ruby necklace he bought in Tortuga. "Check this out. Sorry. I guess I'm getting carried away."

Edmund smiled and patted him on the shoulder. "I don't mind at all. I wish you the best."

"I can't wait. You know what, Edmund?" he continued before Edmund could answer. "I think I'm going to miss New Providence. It was definitely an experience."

"Me too. I wish we had a chance to say good-bye to Felina. I think she really liked you."

"You think so? How come she didn't see us off? We waited there for over an hour."

"Yeah, until Beckham screamed for us to board."

During their time in New Providence, Felina and Edmund became closer, but she took a special interest in Jon. He always wore a wide grin on his face when she was around, and his face was beet red. She, in turn, liked his manners and gentleness. Edmund let it slip out that Jon was engaged, which disappointed her, but she still hung around the two of them more and more. She would cook meals and prepare fruit dishes after they worked down at the wharf or on the ships.

On their last night in New Providence, Felina prepared a large feast for Edmund and Jon. Tears filled her eyes as they all sat around quietly. They had done so much in the past few months that it was going to be a sad good-bye.

"I guess Felina was too upset to see us off," Edmund said. "I'm going to miss her. We had a nice time together."

They stared out at sea until Jon nervously asked, "Do you think everything will work out with you and Sarah?"

"I don't know. I can only hope for the best," Edmund answered. "It's been so long."

Edmund's head had been spinning since they arrived back in New Providence. The thought of seeing Sarah made him feel nervous and excited. He pictured the reunion with Sarah every night. They would hug each other endlessly and talk with each other. They would refurbish his father's house and raise kids. He knew why Jon was so excited, they shared the same dream.

In reality, however, how would Edmund be received in Bristol? Was he truly falsely charged with Cutler's death? Had Cutler died at all? He had to get to Dr. Graham to clear everything up. If anyone could get him out of this mess, it was the vicar of Bristol.

Among the crewmen going home was Chestus. McGinnty allowed him to travel for he was a pirate and was treated equally as the others. Edmund was bothered by him and kept an eye on him anytime he was near. Although the articles of piracy forbid any confrontation on the ship, Chestus was not one to be trusted. He would walk by Edmund and mutter under his breath, "Enjoy your freedom in Bristol while you can."

Then he would take his hand and imitate slitting his throat. Chestus never pushed Edmund too far for fear of being challenged to a duel. After seeing what happened to Morble, neither Chestus nor Gilgo wanted any part of that. When Wolf was around, they were always more brazen in their comments to Edmund and especially Jon, teasing him unmercifully.

Charles was always nearby and hung out with the two. He was uncomfortable around people, but after the altercation at the tavern, Jon and Edmund tried to include him in activities with the men. Charles was always a loner, and most of the crew feared him. He was considered a time bomb ready to explode. Even Wolf wanted no part of him although he was much bigger. His temper was volatile, but Edmund had a way of calming him down, which Charles respected.

The ship caught a northeasterly wind and left the coastline. In the distance, the lookout spotted British colors flying on a ship heading in their direction.

"We're fine," Beckham told Edmund. "We have papers signed by Governor Eden to transport cargo to England."

The ship kept a steady pace, and the British ship gained little by little. Jon nervously ran up to Edmund and Beckham.

"That ship is coming after us. It knows we're pirates."

"Calm down. We're perfectly legal being out here," Beckham assured him.

Edmund understood Jon's concern. They both experienced life under the British navy and didn't trust them at all.

"Jon, in all our days with the navy, we never raided one of our own," Edmund assured him.

"Oh shit," Beckham mumbled.

Edmund turned to him and then to what he was staring at. The British flag was coming down; and in its place, the blackest flag he'd ever seen, with white skull and crossbones, splashed across its center. The three of them stood motionless.

"Bloody pirates," Beckham said.

"Pirates!" echoed members of the crew.

"We're safe, right?" Jon asked. "I mean, we're one of them. We can tell them we're pirates."

"I don't think that's going to work," Beckham answered. "We're flying British colors, and we are, by all accounts, a merchant ship. Even our cargo is what a merchant ship should be carrying."

"Fly our Jolly Roger," Edmund said. "Then they'll know we're pirates too."

"I think it's too late for that," Beckham answered.

"Well, we can't outrun them," Edmund said.

Beckham looked around. "You fellas know what we're up against. If we run, it'll just make it that much worse when they catch us. We either stay and fight, or surrender."

Edmund shook his head in disbelief. As the ship sailed closer, pirates came out from hiding and swarmed the deck, yelling and cheering. Heavy guns came out from the hatches. A cannon shot went off and landed thirty yards from the ship's stern.

"We can't fight them, they have too much firepower," Edmund told Beckham. "And we're not surrendering. I've come too far not to get back home."

Beckham looked at him. "If you're offering advice, tell me now!"

"Head for the Outer Banks. Maybe we can beat them there."

"Are you bloody mad? We don't know those waters, and we'll be a sitting duck to a bunch of very pissed off pirates."

Edmund tried to remember everything McGinnty told him about the Outer Banks—the strong currents, shallow sandbars. It was treacherous but doable.

"Chances are, they don't know it either, and their ship is larger than ours. They won't stand a chance of getting through."

"What about us getting through? It's bloody suicide."

"I don't know if we'll get through, but it's our only chance."

Beckham steered the ship toward the coast of Carolina and the Outer Banks. The pirate ship started drafting them and made up a great deal of distance. Since they could not broadside yet, they could only fire two deck cannons at a time. From the screaming on their deck, it looked like they had too much fun trying to scare Beckham's crew and, with the exception of a few shots landing broadside, held back their fire.

"Mr. Beckham, can this ship move any faster!" Edmund yelled.

"The barnacles are so clustered on its keel they probably scrape the floor of the ocean."

"We need to start throwing cargo overboard," Edmund replied.

With that said, Beckham ordered chests, cannonballs, and chains tossed overboard.

Should we risk throwing the cannons overboard? Edmund thought. "Mr. Beckham, are you open to a suggestion?"

"You bloody well better have a plan."

As he responded, musket fire splintered the deck. They hit the ground hard, and Edmund looked to him.

"How much gunpowder do we have on board?"

He thought for a moment. "Not a hell of a lot, maybe enough to fire thirty or forty rounds."

"Get all the gunpowder that's on this ship and bring it to the back deck. Get some men to prepare to launch the rowboats. We'll need to steer this ship slightly into the wind."

Beckham looked at Edmund like he was crazy. He shook his head but gave the order. Barrels of gunpowder were brought up top. The pirate ship was now fifty yards behind and closing. They spilled powder all over the stern. Edmund took a torch to it, and smoke spurted everywhere on the deck. Charles grabbed long fuses and connected them to barrels of gunpowder and dynamite, which were transported to three rowboats. As a distraction, grenades made of stuffing gunpowder, musket ball, and bits of iron stuffed into empty rum bottles were lit with short fuses and thrown at the pirate ship.

The smoke drifted toward the pirate ships and covered their sight. They fired their cannons, but their visibility was severely compromised.

The fuses were lit and boats launched. They controlled them with rope and let out the line so the boats drifted closer toward the pirate ship.

Jon lowered a rope with a metal chain to measure the depths. "We're getting awfully low!"

"We can't afford to stall. Those are some pissed off pirates!" Beckham shouted.

Edmund screamed back at Beckham, "Look for white ripples, that's where the sandbars are. You need to stay away from them."

They made it to the entrance of the Outer Banks with the pirate ship dead on their trail. The merchant ship started slowing down and dragged against the bottom of the sea. The tides were going down, and they were sailing into treacherous waters.

"If their ship gets any closer, it'll be drafting us, and then we're through. We need to get to the Hatteras Inlet."

"I can get us there, but not through this coast if the tide is low," Beckham responded with a concerned look.

The ship jerked, and suddenly it scraped bottom but kept moving forward. Behind the smoke screen, the dynamite went off. It must have sent quite a jolt, and there was no way the pirates would be able to see the entrance to the inlet.

Beckham avoided the sandbars as they sailed through Hatteras Inlet. Suddenly they pulled ahead. As the smoke cleared, the crew cheered off in the distance, they could see the pirate ship was slowing down. It was too heavy to sail through the shallow depths of the inlet.

"It must have hit a sandbar, or the dynamite did some damage because it's not moving," Jon said.

Beckham pumped his fist and gave Edmund a hug that almost took his head off.

"Drake, you son of a bitch, you did it. You got us through."

The crew was pumped up, and the men came by and each slapped his shoulder. They were on their way back home again. They sailed up Pamlico Sound and then headed back out to the Atlantic.

Once out to sea, they picked up a good tailwind and continued their journey. At dusk, Edmund caught Beckham along the side of the ship taking deep breaths, eyes closed, with a hint of a smile on his face. He walked toward him, but Beckham quickly turned around. Embarrassed for a moment, he looked back to the sea.

"There's nothing better than the salt air the sea has to offer."

Edmund stood next to him, imitating his breathing. "It is relaxing."

Beckham backhanded Edmund's chest and pointed a finger at him. "That was real good work what you did back there. Me and the crew were quite impressed. I wish you were staying with us. Why, when McGinnty hears what you've done, he'll be forever in your debt. You show McGinnty loyalty, he shows it back tenfold."

Edmund looked at him. "You have a special fondness for him, don't you? How long have you been sailing with him?"

"Forever it seems," Beckham said, grabbing his chin, and looked in deep thought.

"I think we started in '04, or maybe it was '05. There was always something about him. He was always fair and good to us."

"What about the *Lucinda*?" Edmund asked. He had wanted to know the story behind it since he took up with the pirates.

"The *Lucinda*?" Beckham cringed and looked around. "That still haunts McGinnty. We lost quite a few men during that battle. We bludgeoned it from all sides. Three of our ships fired. When they finally surrendered, I've never seen so much gold. It would make your hair stand on end."

"So you all split it up?"

"We split up some, gave some to the wounded and deceased crew's families, and McGinnty hid a great deal of it. It was too much. We didn't want to get caught with it if we were attacked, and I don't think McGinnty wanted to hand over more than he needed to the government."

"And what ever became of the *Lucinda*?" Edmund asked.

Beckham laughed. "You don't know?"

Edmund shrugged his shoulders.

"You were sailing on the *Lucinda* for the last year or so."

"*Lucifer's Ghost*!"

"Aye."

When they finally arrived at the outskirts of England after months at sea, Beckham wanted no part of customs at port. He picked a section of shoreline where they weren't likely to get noticed outside of Portsmouth. He sailed them to a place behind a jut of land for shelter from the wind and rough seas. Located a couple hundred yards from shoreline, they dropped anchor. The area was secluded enough to keep even the most inquisitive at bay. Seven men at a time would stand watch. Beckham planned to sail the ship back to New Providence early spring to avoid hurricane season.

They rowed the small crafts straight onto the sand. They scraped along then stopped with a rough jolt. The men leapt off onto the beach. Most of them were home again.

Jon had grown up in Southampton, just outside Portsmouth, and knew the area well. If he heard any news about us being discovered offshore, he would hear about it and get word back to the ship. His family was wealthy. He arranged to get each crewmember on their way with whatever supplies they needed for their journey home. He first saw his brother as Edmund watched the two hug tightly. He told him to go get his parents and find Caroline. Most of the crewmembers would just try and get back to their families and resume a normal life.

A normal life was far from Edmund's mind. He had to find out about Sarah. He hoped she was not married to Killingsworth or anyone else for that matter. He had no idea what to expect after being kidnapped by Morble. It was like he didn't exist for the last three years.

Jon helped Edmund acquire a horse and a few supplies, then rode with him to the edges of Southampton. Saying good-bye would prove to be especially difficult. The two had shared prosperous and horrific times together and had a hard time when it was time to split up. After a long moment of silence, Jon grabbed Edmund.

"Please come with me. I want you to meet my parents and, of course, Caroline," Jon begged.

"No, I have to go. When you see Caroline, give her a kiss for me. You two have an awful lot of catching up to do," Edmund answered. "I have a lot of catching up to do back home."

"It'll work out with you and Sarah, I know it will."

Edmund mounted his steed. "Come see me."

"I don't get to Bristol much," Jon said as the two clasped hands.

"I don't know what's going to happen with my life in Bristol, but I wish you all the best."

"I guess I'll see you in another life, Edmund Drake."

CHAPTER 18

PURGATORY

1716, Williamsburg, Virginia

Sarah stood in the shadows in her dressing room. She hurt not from physical pain but from loneliness. Her body showed a loss of weight, and she was losing her will to live.

She clasped her hands over her breasts as if she could end the pain. Her head was held back and her eyes closed, but the pain did not go away. Despondent, she walked through the spacious bedroom to the second floor piazza where she shivered in the coolness of dusk while hunting for a shawl she needed to mend. The smell of chicken rose from the kitchen building, roasting for Saturday's dinner.

Tomorrow was Saturday!

Each day was like any another. Find something to do that would get you through the day. She gardened outside, but only when Killingsworth was not around. A wife of the lord governor was not supposed to do anything unladylike. She played the piano, which cleared her mind and was one of the few pleasures that relaxed her. Most of the time, she shut herself inside her room, isolated from everyone and everything.

Sarah found no one to confide in except the house slaves. Killingsworth had kept her on a short leash.

Sarah thought back on her wedding night of what might have been. Her father's wish was for her to marry wealth and to be taken care of. Killingsworth was the perfect husband, and he pushed her into the marriage. She didn't blame her father for what happened, and she had no mother to confide in since she was seven.

Her father would have been proud if he had seen the new buildings being built on the estate. The house was huge and impressive. Large pieces of mortar that lay under brick pillars supported the newly built rear piazza, which faced the river. They had hosted many parties with orchestras and large barbeques. The finest buggies and carriages filled the front lawn by the entrance. The plantation had its own pier and served as a factory onto itself. Many of the locals complained about Killingsworth using tax dollars on his governor's palace with its appointed dining rooms, carved marble mantelpieces, formal orchards, gardens, and entry gates. He openly transferred eighty-five thousand acres of public land to himself by trust and named the area after himself. He controlled all appointments of priests and high officials of the Anglican Church, the official religion of the colony. The legislature was at odds with him and petitioned the king to repeal some of Killingsworth's economic regulations and to remove him altogether.

She tried to keep her letters to her father upbeat. He had suffered a severe stroke, and his answering her letters was dictated and written by his assistants. Hearing from her father kept her going.

Yes, Father would be proud!

She should have known by her wedding night what the future had in store. The night when he threw her on the bed, shoving his hands inside her thighs, forcing himself inside her, hurting her. Since their wedding, there were no acts of tenderness, no soft caresses, but forceful entry.

The marriage was like that until her pregnancy. A miscarriage terminated the child, and after that, he barely touched her. He did not deprive himself as he had his way with many women in Williamsburg. Sarah accepted it and was thankful she didn't have to worry about his dirty hands on her. The few times he did approach her, usually in a drunken rage, she put up with it and prayed it would end soon.

Now leaning on the rail of the piazza, she heard voices from Killingsworth's plantation office, a small building where he would work when not in the city of Williamsburg.

Guests? We never have guests here this early.

One of the voices was that of her husband, but she could not recognize the other.

Killingsworth was enraged, and she heard furniture being thrown about.

"Our receipts are low. We may have to raise taxes even more."

"My lord, the legislature is trying to petition your removal. The planters are still up in arms over the Tobacco Act. They feel it's extortion."

"The inspectors are getting their cut, and so are you!"

The man he was yelling at tried to calm him down when she saw riders approaching. One was General Pitts, but she couldn't make out the others. They were greeted by slaves that grabbed and tied up the horses. Pitts entered as the other men waited outside.

Sarah ran downstairs and moved closer. She hid in the shadows, three feet from the open windows, and listened as Killingsworth dismissed the accountant and addressed Pitts. With so many enemies in the legislature, he met in secrecy at his plantation with military and economic advisors.

Killingsworth stuffed snuff into his nostrils.

"Congratulations on your promotion to general."

"Thank you, my lord."

There was a moment of an uncomfortable silence as Pitts fidgeted with his white gloves.

"What news have you heard from Florida?" Killingsworth asked.

"Sir, ah, I don't know how to tell you."

"Spit it out."

"We lost one of our treasure ships. The crew was picked up intact off the coast."

"What happened? Out with it!"

Pitts stared straight ahead. "It was an attack, sir. The ship surrendered."

"Who attacked them?"

"My lord, it was McGinnty."

Killingsworth pounded his fist on the desk. "I should have killed him while I had the chance. Blasted!"

Sarah pressed her sweating palms against the white siding. Sunlight through the festoons of Spanish moss laid a shifting pattern of shadow on her pale wasted face.

"Pirates, they're like a plague. They smuggle what profits we get, and our economy has turned fragile because of it," Killingsworth muttered.

"We have no help finding them from other colonies. They're useless," Pitts said.

"Precisely. If the pirate epidemic is wiped out, we can go ahead with expanding Virginia. We'll expand it right into North Carolina and that twit Eden."

"Governor Eden, sir?"

"I hate that bastard Eden. How he was selected governor of North Carolina is beyond me. He's in bed with pirates. He tolerates their attacks of the Chesapeake, and then I have to hear jokes at my expense."

"We've lost enormous amounts of revenue. When word gets around about McGinnty, it may only encourage more smuggling," Pitts mumbled.

"We need to protect our interests," Killingsworth declared. "We need to end this piracy plague which is clogging up our trade routes. We're not going to bow down to them and make deals like Eden. We're going to get the Royal Navy involved."

"Sir, you only have authority in Virginia waters, and the Royal Navy only answers to the admiralty in London," Pitts responded.

"Since there is no proper admiralty here in the colonies, we are the authority! The ships protect us. They'll take care of us."

"What if they refuse?"

"We'll pay them off with the taxes. Let the farmers see where their taxes are going when we hang a few of those pirates off the galleys!"

"My lord, that would take care of a lot of problems."

"Yes, the sooner we end this piracy epidemic, the sooner we continue trade overseas."

The antipiracy laws gave governors the power to hold trials within their own region. Legal loopholes were removed, and it became easier to condemn pirates on evidence that would be insufficient and inadmissible. Killingsworth had all the legal muscle to hunt down, convict, and execute pirates on his own authority. The pirate trials already held were highly publicized, and mass executions followed.

Killingsworth looked past Pitts to an old saber on the wall. He moistened the ball of his thumb and wiped off a speck of dust on the shiny blade.

"North Carolina is in dire straits due to the war on Indians, and if we stop the importation of tobacco into Virginia, they would have to ship their goods to Charles Town, which is much farther away. If we take care of the piracy problem and bankrupt North Carolina, we can incorporate North Carolina into Virginia. That would increase our own influence, and with expansion comes greater wealth."

"My lord, it sounds like you have everything in hand," Pitts said as he signaled to the guard at the door.

Suddenly the door opened and a man walked in. He wore a patch over his left eye, but it could not completely hide the hideous scar on his forehead. A small patch of hair was missing above what was left of his eyebrow.

"Captain Morble, what a sight it is to see you again. I heard you survived a pirate attack, but you lost one of my ships."

Morble looked nervous. "Sir, I'd like to be part of your war on piracy. I owe McGinnty, and I want to make sure he gets his due."

"You screwed it up on your last assignment. The pirate you were chasing got the drop on you. How is that possible?"

"I did my best, sir."

"Your best wasn't good enough."

"It will not happen again, my lord. That I can assure you."

"You have done plenty of dirty work for me." Killingsworth looked down. "I heard it was McGinnty that scarred you up."

"Actually, it was someone else. You remember Edmund Drake?"

Sarah thought she heard the name Edmund Drake.

It couldn't be.

Her face became flush. She wanted to get closer to the window, but then she would risk her cover.

"The name escapes me," Killingsworth answered.

"You sent him to my ship years ago. He's from Bristol."

Killingsworth tensed up. He became uncomfortable and started flexing his sword about.

"No, I don't remember him," he said unconvincingly.

"I'm at your service, sir, and would like to start as soon as possible to capture or kill McGinnty."

"Yes, of course. You better not screw it up this time." He turned to Pitts. "I want you to be my right-hand man in all of this, and remember, it is to be hush-hush."

"Of course, my lord."

Killingsworth walked them out to the foyer with sword in hand. He looked over the ten soldiers that accompanied General Pitts.

"Men, I wish you well," Killingsworth said as he drew his thumb back and forth on the blade. "You'll be performing a public service by killing off McGinnty and his pirates."

"Yes, sir."

"I'll be waiting for news of your success," Killingsworth called as the men marched out. Giving a pleased sigh, he started back to his office. After taking a few steps, he was distracted by a faint noise at the side of the house.

"What the devil are you doing there?"

Standing in the deep-afternoon shadow, Sarah clutched the side of her dress tight. Then she descended toward Killingsworth who was quite annoyed.

"Were you listening in on us?"

"Not intentionally, I was on my way to the fields."

"Dressed like that?"

She stared at him. He glanced down at his sword and swung it. It was a trait he acquired when he was irritated. She started to walk away before Killingsworth stopped her.

"What did you hear?"

"Just some complaining of pirates." Then she added, "They're all barbarians, why would I continue to listen?"

She continued toward the fields, taking two more steps, looked up, and caught her breath. Her pale forehead glistened with perspiration. She heard hoofbeats riding away from the plantation.

Is Edmund really alive?

CHAPTER 19

HOMECOMING

Edmund's odyssey north toward Bristol began through the backwoods. He rode along a grassy bridle path, which ran along the foot of the hills. Then the horse picked his way through the small paths through the thick woods until dark. Edmund had an abundance of feed and mixed it with molasses to give the horse extra energy.

Jon had given him enough rations for the trip and a thick blanket for the cool nights. Once dusk hit, he pulled up near a small clearing and patted the horse's neck and dismounted. With the bridle over his arm, he led the horse up a steep hill and picked a small clearing to build his fire and spread his blanket.

Edmund sat at the foot of the oak while his horse ate feed. Resting the back of his head against the tree and closing his eyes, his mind began to wander.

Would things have been different if only he had met Sarah that night? If only he escaped Killingsworth's men? If only he never went to school in London. If only he never went to Ben Cutler's? What if—if only, if.

What's done is done.

He opened his eyes and saw Sarah standing there, smiling at him. Her eyes were glassy as she looked at him wearing a crooked smile. He wanted to stand and hug her, but his legs were paralyzed. He put his hands over his eyes for a minute. When he moved them, she was gone. He dragged the blanket up to his cheek and shut his eyes. Sleep came quickly.

Edmund woke up to find sunlight shining down through the trees. He felt fine just lying there, listening to the birds' chirp and the soft breeze that rustled the leaves. His mouth was dry as sand, and he drank the last remnants of his canteen. He needed to find a stream or well for a refill. The sun felt warm, but not as scorching as New Providence. It was a comfortable heat.

He climbed to his feet, tucked in his pistol, and continued onward, riding through the thick limbs of trees and brush until the woods came to an end. Stopping at a farmhouse, he rode to a well and sank the dipper into it and drank. He filled his canteen when a voice came up from behind him.

"Who are you stranger and what do you want?"

He heard the cocking sound of a pistol. Edmund raised his hands slowly and turned.

"I'm on my way to Bristol, and I needed some water. I apologize for startling you. I'll be on my way."

Edmund was face-to-face with an older gentleman with a broad wrinkled face and white beard. He lowered his gun, and with that, Edmund slowly lowered his arms.

"We're not used to strangers around here. You're a might ways from Bristol. You should have taken the main roads, it would have saved you time."

Edmund didn't want to tell him why he was taking the back way and placed the dipper back into its bucket. The old man noticed Edmund's pistol fastened to his belt and gave a look of concern. Edmund looked at it and back at the old man.

"Don't worry. I just wanted water."

"You seem like a decent-enough fella. Come on in. I'll have the wife give you a basket of food for your journey."

It was as if the man hadn't seen anyone in months and welcomed Edmund's company. He asked him questions about the so-called outside world, but Edmund had no answers and just smiled.

The man loaded up a basket, and Edmund hadn't had food that good in years. He thanked them, and as he left, the old man gave Edmund directions that would take him to the outskirts of Bristol.

He mounted and was off again. Now he thought of different concerns such as how was he to be treated when he returned and did Killingsworth really accuse him of the murder of Ben Cutler. He needed to get to the vicarage. Dr. Graham would have the answers he needed.

Late in the evening, Edmund snuck into the vicarage after a quick stop at his home. He traveled two days, stopping in secluded areas. He was cautious on his return and didn't know how he was to be received.

Earlier in the day, when he arrived at his house, it looked much different than the last time he saw it. The years took a toll on it. Windows were broken as the stones that were thrown through them lay on the living room floor. Inside dust gathered throughout the house. He walked around.

It's been so long.

Anything of value had been stolen. It was desolate. He was exhausted but knew he couldn't stay there. He had to find out about his status.

The vicar walked into his study, pipe in hand. He sucked the match into his pipe a few times and puffed out some smoke. He enjoyed a good smoke and read before he turned in. He reached for a book on the shelf and skimmed through the pages then placed it back. He fingered a few more, then stopped abruptly, and looked up to where Edmund was standing.

"Is someone there?" he asked.

"'Tis a stranger paying his respects," Edmund answered.

A look of shock covered the vicar's face.

"Edmund? How? Why?" The vicar's eyes widened while he raced over and gave him a hug. Edmund squeezed hard, closing his eyes.

"It's you. It's really you. I . . . ," the vicar continued, choking on his words. "I thought you were dead."

"Only half dead," Edmund replied, trying to force a smile. "I've been to hell and back."

"We haven't heard from you in years. What happened to you? There's still a price on your head for the murder of Ben Cutler. We both know that's not true!"

"I was taken by a press-gang. Killingsworth wanted me to disappear. He set me up."

"I thought that was the case. We have to clear your name. Unfortunately, when Killingsworth left, he spread a lot of propaganda about the Cutler ordeal. He wanted you hanged."

Edmund stepped back and gazed at the vicar. "Sarah. Is Sarah here in Bristol?"

"Sarah—" The vicar stopped in midsentence.

"Sarah? What happened to Sarah? Where is she? I thought about her every day."

The vicar pulled back. He dropped his jaw and looked at Edmund, shaking his head. Edmund stared back and felt uncomfortable with the look in his eyes.

"She's in Virginia. She married Killingsworth."

Edmund went rigid. He couldn't speak. His face rubbed against the wall. Tears welled in his eyes. The vicar reached over and grabbed his shoulder.

"Edmund, she told me about the meeting you two were supposed to have, how you were going to run off together. You never showed up."

Edmund mumbled, his thoughts scattered. "Why would she marry him?"

"There's more to it than you think. Killingsworth was going to frame her father in a crooked stock deal. She had to go with him. Poor Bolden, he never knew. God rest his soul."

Edmund shook his head and then looked up. "Bolden's dead?"

"He had a stroke and never recovered. We buried him months ago."

"What did Sarah look like when she came back?"

"You know, we all thought that was odd. She never came home even when he was as sick as he was. She stayed in Virginia."

"She loved her father. She never would have missed that."

Edmund looked confused and wondered if Sarah was even the same person. Maybe she was sold on the life of wealth and etiquette Killingsworth had to offer.

The vicar interrupted Edmund's thoughts.

"Let's get you out of here. It's dangerous for you in these parts. The bounty on your head is very high. Does anyone know you're back?"

Edmund shook his head no.

The vicar looked out the window, there was no one out there. His wife was upstairs asleep, so they snuck off out back.

"Let's go to a place I know that will be secluded. It's located outside the city."

Edmund followed him.

"My god," the vicar then added. "You're bone thin. Let me get you some grub."

He loaded a basket with biscuits and fruit, and they left for the hills. Once off the main road, they followed a thin trail through the woods, which led them to a clearing where a small cottage stood. It was surrounded by trees and hard to see if you didn't know exactly where to find it. It was owned by a cousin of the vicar who had business in York to attend to.

"Edmund," the vicar said as he dismounted, "we have to clear you of those charges so you can get back to a normal life. There's a reward on your head for the murder of Ben Cutler, and people are funny when it comes to rewards. Don't trust anyone."

"I trust you, Dr. Graham," Edmund said, a slight smile appeared against his cheek.

"Well, almost anyone. You'll be safe here. I'll be back in the morning if you need anything."

Edmund tried to catch his breath and regain some composure.

"I just need a place to stay for the night."

"You stay here as long as you like. I'm going to snoop around tomorrow and find out what kind of evidence the prosecutor had on you. Maybe it's lost. It was over three years ago."

Edmund shook his head. "I'd never want to put you out or damage your reputation. I'll find somewhere—"

"Nonsense. No one even knows where this place is."

When the vicar left, Edmund sat back in a chair. He pulled out his pistol and tapped his knee with it. He soon fell fast asleep.

Edmund stayed there a few days. The vicar brought baskets of food his wife made but never told her they were for Edmund.

On a particularly foggy morning, Edmund rode out to the old oak tree at Myers Plantation. It brought back memories of Sarah and him, good memories that left him at peace. He was starting to accept she would only live in his memories now.

When he returned to the cottage, the door was left open. He cautiously pulled out his pistol. A few people from town had seen him in the fields at a distance, but did they recognize him? Was he followed? A twig broke behind him, and Edmund turned and aimed. The vicar was waiting for him with a concerned look on his face. Edmund took a deep breath and looked up to the sky.

"You scared the hell out of me."

Edmund noticed the vicar's expression didn't change, and the two of them walked inside.

"Are you all right, Dr. Graham?" Edmund asked.

"I have some terrible news for you. There are soldiers in Bristol. They have orders to look for you on charges of treason. Edmund, they torched your father's house."

"What?"

"They said you attacked a captain of the HMS *Fitzgerald* and deserted. They even have you on piracy."

Edmund was startled.

How do they know I'm here?

"There is a party of ten of them," the vicar continued. "They are asking questions around the city, and they are posting a reward."

"Chestus must have got word to him," Edmund muttered to himself.

"Edmund, they want to hang you for treason. Is the story true?" the vicar continued.

"It's a long story," Edmund said.

"Edmund, what have you got yourself involved in? Treason, piracy? This McGinnty, the story here is he's a brutal killer. He's plundered ship after ship, killing hundreds of men."

He proceeded to tell the vicar about his years on the *Fitzgerald* and how they were attacked by pirates, about McGinnty, and the year in New Providence. Edmund was disappointed but unapologetic.

He lifted his shirt above his ribcage and showed the vicar his back.

"These are souvenirs for my service to the Royal Navy."

The scars ran deep and were grotesque. The vicar stood aghast.

"Dr. Graham, it's not like what you've heard." Edmund paused. "Look at what they say about me. The men in charge tell the tales, and they tell them as they see fit. As for McGinnty, he's a fair man who was betrayed by England."

"What about what happened to that Spanish camp in Florida? Everyone was found dismembered and butchered in that camp. A British battalion found them, limbs everywhere. All evidence pointing to pirates."

Edmund looked stunned. "There was a battle, but he let the ones that surrendered live. It wasn't us."

Edmund's mind was racing. He thought back to the camp and the attack.

Did someone get there after we did?

The conversation switched to the congregation, and the vicar updated Edmund on his old friends and fellow parishioners. Phillip, his old friend from school, married a local girl, and his wife just gave birth to a daughter. Other than that, everything sounded the same. Edmund asked about Sarah's best friend, Nell.

"She's been long gone. No one has seen or heard from her in years." The vicar grabbed his pipe and sucked in a few puffs. Then he moved closer to Edmund and, in a soft slow voice, said, "I heard she may have been pregnant and disappeared."

As they shared wine and talked, Edmund realized he was an outsider now. He felt distant from the Bristol he grew up in. He didn't belong anymore.

As the vicar opened the door to leave, he turned and gave a stern look.

"Edmund, the government is looking to eliminate piracy once and for all. The news here is that pirates have been killing hundreds of innocent people, stealing fortunes, robbing merchant ships led by what they think is this lunatic captain. It's over. How did you ever survive? How did you escape?"

Edmund told him about sailing home, but when the vicar was told about New Providence, he offered more news of his own.

"We've heard quite a bit from the sailors that visited New Providence, that the place is thriving. England is up in arms about it, and they want a piece of the action," the vicar said.

"But England gave it up during the war. It was too hard to protect!" Edmund said.

"Yes, but now they're trying to get Woodes Rogers to clean it up. He is to be lord governor of the island, and his first order of duty is to end piracy period. The king is going to back him up with money and the Royal Navy to see that his job is carried out. He'll be sailing there next spring.

"Wasn't Rogers a pirate?"

"He was a privateer, one of the most famous privateers of our time. He's got the backing of the South Sea Stock Company.

Killingsworth is a big player in that company. They are running the Caribbean now."

"What is South Sea? Is that the company Killingsworth tried to frame Bolden with?"

"Yes, Killingsworth had a big part creating it. The agreement bought England's debt from the war, and now they're making money from Caribbean trade."

"I want to find out everything I can about it."

"That's easy. Everyone in England is buying it. Our economy is starting to thrive, and now ordinary people are buying stocks which were only a rich man's pleasure in years past."

"How is it making money?" Edmund asked.

"Trading in the Caribbean, of course."

"We've never heard of them. They can't be doing that good." *I need to find out more about that.* "I've got to warn the others."

"You can't go back there, it's too dangerous."

"Dr. Graham, I'm going to be shot or hanged if I stay here."

"But you're innocent."

"Who would believe that? It's my word against Killingsworth. They'll never let me live. I need to start a fresh life somewhere. Either New Providence or the colonies."

"Edmund, we must get you cleared of all charges. What kind of life would you lead overseas?"

"I don't know. I'm going to visit my father's grave in the morning, and then I'm gone. It's best for the both of us. It's only a matter of time before those soldiers get wind of me being here, and I've troubled you enough."

"You're still as stubborn as ever." The vicar gave him a hug. "Please be careful."

The next morning, Edmund strolled through Cedarhurst cemetery. It brought back memories of his childhood where he and friends would take on the French in make-believe battles. They used broomsticks as guns unless one of them could sneak out one of their father's unloaded rifles. They hid behind gravestones, ready for their sneak attacks, and then fired at the enemy as they crossed into English territories.

Cedarhurst was one of the oldest and largest cemeteries in Bristol. It was seventeen acres with hills and trees mixed in. The oldest gravestone with a date on it was Charles Hulse, who died in 1359. Anything older either didn't have a date on it or the date had faded. The woods surrounded three sides of the cemetery with the other side leading to the main road.

Edmund was always fascinated by the dates and names on each grave. It was another game they played as kids—who could find the oldest slab. Edmund walked up to two gravestones that were situated side by side. The one on the left read,

Daniel C. Drake
1674-1710
Beloved husband to Cassie
Beloved father to Edmund
May the Lord be with you always.

He stared at it, lowering his head. To the right was another grave that read,

Cassandra Johnson Drake
1679-1696
Wife of Daniel
Died in childbirth
Taken early in life
May the Lord bless your soul.

He reflected on growing up with his father, remembering the support and love he gave him. His mother lived only through the stories told by his father, which made her real. He felt he knew her, and she was always with him growing up.

It was early in the morning, and with the exception of an elderly gentleman a few rows up, the cemetery was deserted. Edmund knelt down at the foot of his father's grave, made the sign of the cross, and began to pray.

He also reflected on how the events that had transpired the last few years would be held in his father's eyes.

He would have helped me. He would have been there for me

Looking up, he noticed a man in the distance, by the edge of the woods.

Another visitor.

He lowered his head and continued to pray. When he finished, he repeated the sign of the cross and rose to his feet. He glanced quickly at the man by the woods who was now entertaining another person. This person was holding a musket and was listening intently to the other, shaking his head as if agreeing to everything he had heard.

After remembering the vicar describe the effort soldiers were taking to find him, Edmund grew increasingly uncomfortable. He started walking toward the back entrance. It was a small path that led through the woods and into the back roads toward town. He stopped. There were two more men near the path carrying muskets and checking their weaponry.

He turned left and saw three more. There was a lot of ground to cover at this cemetery, but how many men were here?

How did they find me?

Was I careless when I first arrived into town? I was out in the open, walking the streets, but that was before I found out I was wanted for murder—the murder of Ben Cutler. It's a good thing I saw the vicar first, or else I'd be swinging from a tree!

He felt his pistol inside his vest and checked the cutlass. They would be of little or no use against the muskets that surrounded him. He still had distance on his side, but they were inching closer.

Edmund made his way to the west side, picking up the pace, careful not to look back. A shot rang out, and chips flew off one of the gravestones to his right. Another shot whizzed by his head, and now he was in full sprint.

The west side was a newer area that had wealthier and bigger plots. Also, bigger tombstones to give him cover and stall for time to think.

He dodged around two graves and glanced quickly over his shoulder, seeing two men taking a knee and holding up their rifles at him. Up ahead, a group of men were getting into position. They hadn't noticed him yet, but Edmund was sure they heard the gunshots going off.

He headed right, pulling out his pistol. The higher tombs would give him better cover. He remembered as a kid a hiding place they used to use to hide from the fictitious French adversary. It had loosened screws on one of the larger plaques on the side of the tomb.

Would it still be loose? Am I too big?

The tomb and graves were so close together he would be well hidden as he made his way toward the hiding place.

Can I even find it? It's the only shot I got.

He raced toward the tomb. Looking behind, he saw no signs of anyone, but the voices were getting closer. On his right read,

Phillip Butler
1601-1652
Lord Squire of Francis Square
Beloved husband and father

Edmund grabbed the plaque from both sides. It was still loose, and he pulled it out. The inside of the vault looked a lot tighter than he had remembered, but there was no time now. He squirmed inside and placed the plaque in its original position, hoping it would hold. Crouching down, he waited.

"I thought I saw him in this area. He's got to be around here, we have all the entrances covered."

The voices outside sounded muffled and faded inside the tomb.

"He's got to be around here. He couldn't have just vanished, he's not a ghost."

"Don't use that word *ghost* around here," another voice answered louder and closer than the other. It sounded like it was right outside Phillip Butler's tomb. Edmund cocked his gun and aimed it at the plaque in case they noticed it loose or if it fell.

He aimed and waited. Finally, the voices were gone. He stayed in the tomb until nightfall.

Edmund made it to the rendezvous point in time. His journey back to Portsmouth included many detours and side roads, but he knew where and when Beckham was going to sail back to New Providence.

He saw the ship in the distance and set forth to swim to it. Instead, he found a small dinghy in the woods. It looked complete, and he dragged it to the water's edge and started rowing. As he paddled closer, the crew recognized him and started cheering him on. Before he boarded, he tried to digest everything that had happened at home. It was obvious he would never be welcome in Bristol again.

As the crew helped him over the ledge, he recognized most of the men that sailed with him from New Providence remained. Beckham barked out orders to lift anchors and set sail.

One of the first to greet him in a long line of pirates was Charles. He offered his hand, and Edmund shook it. Charles's eyes were as wild as ever, and as he started to speak, he broke into a high-pitched laugh. It was more of a cackle. Edmund nodded and tried to smile. He wasn't fazed by Charles's quirks and patted his side.

"Charles has something to tell you," Beckham broke in.

The pirates encouraged Charles to tell Edmund his news.

"We owe y-you for what h-happened back in the Outer B-banks."

Charles spoke slowly and finally Beckham became impatient.

"What he means is Charles saw Chestus in Portsmouth running his trap about how he escaped from McGinnty and his battle against pirates. You would think he was a conquering hero the way everyone bought him drinks. Anyway, Charles followed him to the authorities where he ratted you out. How you attacked Morble and deserted the Royal Navy. He even collected money as a reward for his betrayal to you and the rest of us."

"Damn it! I knew it was Chestus. I wish he was sailing with us right now."

"He w-won't be s-sailing with anyone," Charles said. "I p-paid a c-couple of p-prostitutes to bring him where I c-could meet with him alone."

"What happened?" Edmund asked.

Charles made a slitting-of-the-throat gesture with his forefinger. "He's where he b-belongs."

Then Charles reached for a small pouch hanging from his side and unhooked it and gave it to Edmund. It was full of guineas.

"What's this for?"

"It's the r-reward for information leading t-to your arrest," Charles answered.

Edmund handed it back. "Keep it. You earned it."

The crew cheered.

Edmund was eerily pleased by Charles's actions. Almost as if justifying his behavior.

Chestus got what was coming to him.

The rest of the crew came forward and patted Edmund on his shoulder. He heard "I never thought I'd see you again" or "I guess you missed your old buddies here."

Finally, he made his way back over to Beckham who was wearing a wide grin.

"What would you like me to do, Captain?" Edmund said.

"You, I want you to take care of this runt."

Edmund gave him a quizzical look and then turned around. His jaw dropped and was quickly replaced with a wide grin. Jon smiled back at him and grabbed his shoulders.

"How, what happened?" Edmund asked.

"I could say the same thing about you," Jon responded.

"I guess I wasn't as welcome in Bristol as I thought. What happened with Caroline? You were going to get married."

"The marriage thing didn't work out as planned."

"But you were so excited about it. You talked about her for two years!"

"I guess she wasn't as excited. She had other plans, like marry the local court jester down the road. They already have a kid. He may be older than when I was kidnapped."

"What?" Edmund laughed. "I'm so sorry." He tried hard to hold back his smile but couldn't. "Is there anything I can do?"

"No matter," he said and then glared out to sea. "You know what, Edmund? This is the only excitement I've ever known—being a pirate. I feel like I belong." He looked at Beckham. "So, Captain, if you'll have me, I'm here to serve."

"Of course, you little runt you," he said, laughing. "Welcome aboard."

The anchors were raised, and the ship pointed southwest in the direction of New Providence.

CHAPTER 20

RETURN TO NEW PROVIDENCE

"My eyes are deceiving me. Drake, I never thought I'd see you again!" McGinnty shouted as he spotted Edmund and Jon marching into the tavern. He was decorated with women on both arms and was quite drunk.

Edmund smiled when he saw him and was handed a mug of ale by one of the men.

The Shark Den was owned by McGinnty and filled with thirsty pirates tossing down rum and ale. Several crewmembers from *Lucifer's Ghost* shook Edmund's and Jon's hands while giving them pats on the back. Edmund was not only surprised at the crowd at the tavern, but since arriving from England, he also noticed there were more pirates than ever on the island. New homes and shops were being built all over.

McGinnty reached over one of the women and raised his mug, signaling them over. He proceeded to toast the two.

"Beck told me about your heroics at Ocracoke," he yelled. "The story spread like wildfire! Very commendable, I think you'll be a captain someday."

"Beckham is the true captain, sir. He led us out of there," Edmund replied.

"I offered Beck a ship, but he declined. It seems he likes working as my gunner."

"He's truly loyal to you, sir."

"I need loyal men around me. Killingsworth has put a price on my head that would make a man very rich. It seems he wasn't pleased with our plundering of his ship and the Spanish camp."

McGinnty delivered a mug to each of them. Edmund was well respected among the crew, and the reception he received proved that. Jon was also entertaining and likeable even though he was the farthest person to be considered a pirate. They chugged their ale.

"I guess things didn't work out with Sarah," McGinnty continued. "And you, Galvin. I'm in shock that you're back here. Don't tell me you like this lifestyle."

"Well, sir, it does kind of grow on you," Jon answered with a grin. Foam appeared on his upper lip.

"We both suffered the same destiny, the women we loved are married to someone else," Edmund said.

McGinnty slammed down his ale and signaled for another.

"There's plenty of women in the world, trust me on that." As the words left his lips, he hugged the two women on each side with a tight grip around their midsection. They, in turn, rubbed his shoulder and smiled. One kissed his cheek.

"So how was journey home? I thought I lost a good ship and a couple of average sailors," McGinnty said, laughing. The crew around him howled.

"Actually, besides being shot at, chased, sleeping in bushes, it went well," Edmund answered.

They all had a good laugh and chugged more ale.

"We've had much success since you've been away. We've hit many ships, and it seems they are getting smarter. As soon as they see us, they run."

The men laughed as McGinnty continued. "They try to run, but no ship can outrun *Hellspite*. It's the best of the lot."

"We had a pretty good sell with the tobacco and cotton in Portsmouth. Beckham is dividing it up on the ship," Jon said.

After a few rounds of drinking, Edmund brought McGinnty over to the corner to have a word with him. Gilgo saw the two of them wander off and followed close enough to listen in.

"Sir, I have heard the British want to send Woodes Rogers over here. They say the Caribbean is too out of hand, especially New Providence, and he's to clean it up."

"Rubbish, they probably found out how profitable it is here and want to get in on the action. Besides, we have our own problems over here. Killingsworth has pushed a new law rewarding a special bounty for my capture."

"There are rumors about offering any and all pirates a full pardon for any previous acts of piracy as long as we turn ourselves in. They want piracy ended once and for all."

McGinnty grabbed his chin and shook his head. "Rogers, of all people."

"Do you know him?"

"We were both privateers for England during the war. We had a rivalry and competed for prizes. We were both very good. We used to meet in Bristol once in a while and compare our plunder. In 1709, he hit it big in Ecuador, purging money. He stole jewelry from women and captured his greatest prize to date—the Manila galleon. It was worth about £150,000."

"He made £150,000?" Edmund looked in amazement, he couldn't fathom that much money existed.

"Not exactly. I remember those crooks at the East End Company seized it, charging that he breached their monopoly. They said the treasure was seized in their territory."

"What happened to it?"

"Well, they settled. Rogers received £50,000, the company received the rest. It took him awhile to collect it. I can't believe he's coming here."

"You know him, he'll pardon you."

"I won't be pardoned by Rogers. I have too much respect for him and too much stubborn pride to let him offer me a pardon."

"It sounds like he went through the same things you did. He'd understand."

"He never went through dealing with Killingsworth. No, you get the pardon. Maybe then you can get back to England and restart your life."

"Restart my life?"

Edmund never told McGinnty about being framed for the murder of Ben Cutler. He didn't think he'd feel any less of him and probably would understand after all his dealings with Killingsworth. He kept silent.

I'd be running from British soldiers and riding officers.

A ship in the distance was spotted heading eastbound. McGinnty liked attacking eastbound ships, especially Spanish ships. There was more gold and silver on board if the ships were returning home. The bells rang, and the men gathered at the wharf.

Instead of gathering all the men on the deck and voting, he yelled out his intentions to attack, which prompted loud roars of approval from the crew. Once again, they covered their gun ports with painted canvas, and the men took to their stations as they boarded the ships.

Hellspite, with McGinnty in command, led the way toward the lumbering merchant ship. Edmund and Jon manned the guns below. They had both become quite adept to firing the cannons. *Hellspite,* by itself, had more firepower than most merchant ships in the vicinity. *Lucifer's Ghost* trailed behind.

They hoisted the British Union flags and headed for the vessel in the distance, which kept a steady course, not attempting thus far to run.

Despite their success in capturing ships, it had been quite some time since capturing a prize worth much value. In the past, most ships—upon seeing McGinnty's Jolly Roger—quickly surrendered. The visitors would smile nervously, give them what they want, and hoped they would leave in peace without any ramifications. A huge sigh of relief was felt when the pirates left the ship.

Lately, the delegations had finally wised up. Foreign ships trusted no one and sailed away at the first sign of trouble. Any time *Lucifer's Ghost* was seen, the targeted ship would sail away. McGinnty had to use different strategies to capture his prey. Most of the time, he used the wind to his advantage and tracked them down with *Hellspite.* McGinnty bragged it was the fastest ship in the Caribbean and was like an annoying gnat to the ships it followed.

As *Hellspite* drew closer to the vessel, it looked bigger than the typical merchant ship with a Spanish flag waving and still held its course.

McGinnty thought about letting *Lucifer's Ghost* catch up but didn't want to slow up the progress *Hellspite* was making on its intended victim in case it suddenly turned and sailed away. It had the wind at its back.

McGinnty angled *Hellspite* to cut off the ship down the line. At 1,500 yards, some of the crew started waving to the vessel, hoping to relax them into a false sense of security. The foreign vessel did not appear to have many sailors aboard and started to steer away from *Hellspite.*

The actions of his counterpart enraged but also excited McGinnty.

"A ship finally offering some resistance."

With both ships heading northeast, McGinnty's angle drew greater wind assistance, and it was a matter of time before *Hellspite* caught its prey.

At five hundred yards, McGinnty ordered round shot to be fired. Round shot were balls held together by rods and aimed at the hull. Three shots exploded out. Two of them missed altogether. The third one hit the middle mast, completely knocking it over. The crew roared. Edmund and Jon readied their cannons for firing. Their guns held grapeshot, which would be McGinnty's next tactic. The other gunners that shot the round shot quickly reloaded their cannons, packing the powder in, pounding it down, and carrying over the heavy balls. *Hellspite* lowered its British Union flags, hoping the Spaniards would see McGinnty's black Jolly Roger flying and quickly surrender.

They sailed closer, getting to within four hundred yards. The Spanish ship had five gun ports on its broadside. McGinnty proceeded cautiously as the Spaniards had not yet hinted at surrendering. Their flag still waved in the breeze. He saw only fifteen crewmembers on the top deck.

Shaking his head, he muttered, "Are we at war with Spain? Why don't they just surrender?"

Most of the crew, with muskets in hand, watched from the side of the deck. They were ready with pistols, cutlasses, axes, swords, blunderbusses, and any weapon they could get their hands on. The crew was laughing, teasing the Spanish crew who were completely outnumbered but had still ignored the pirates.

Three cannons exploded from the Spanish ship, filling the air around *Hellspite* with grapeshot. Metal pierced the wood all over the ship. Chips flew everywhere. Skin was torn from flesh, and as quickly, men fell on the deck.

McGinnty took shrapnel to his shoulders, neck, and left arm. *Hellspite* retaliated with cannon blasts of its own, with grapeshot aimed back at the Spaniards. Smoke filled the decks of both ships. *Lucifer's Ghost*, coming up from the rear, aimed its guns at its opponent and fired.

When *Hellspite* finished its flurry of grapeshot, the Spanish vessel quickly filled its deck with eighty men carrying muskets, pistols, and swords. They were coming up from below their deck. Cannon fire commenced at both ships.

Edmund fired and stuffed his cannon with loose metal and readied it for another round.

Jon was lying facedown in the corner, covering his head with his hands. Edmund raced toward him, but before he could say anything, he heard another shell coming in very fast, very loud.

He gestured wildly. "Jon, get out of th—"

The shell burst. The wall flew apart in hundreds of pieces. Dirt and debris filled the lower deck. Edmund blinked and choked, conscious of pain in his chest. He was lying on the deck and didn't even remember throwing himself down.

The explosion must have done it. He started to feel about his chest and stomach to see if he'd been hit. Edmund looked for Jon but didn't see him anywhere. He struggled to get up and lurched down the short stretch of deck. The smoke was dissipating. Behind him, he heard men yelling, cursing, and crying.

McGinnty tried to organize the men straggling through the ship. Edmund's attention fixed on something lying at the deck's edge.

He passed his right hand back and forth in front of his eyes, as if he was swatting a fly. He wanted to deny the evidence of his senses. He couldn't. He began to run.

Next to the hole in the sidewall laid a man's left hand and half of his forearm. The cloth around the forearm was torn and scorched. He found one of the men sprawled on the embankment on the left side of the ship, bleeding to death.

Gunfire exploded from both sides as the ships sailed closer. Two cannon shots hit *Hellspite*, inflicting major damage to its broadside. Edmund saw Jon.

"Get up. We have to reload the cannons."

Wood chips were flying everywhere as another cannonball burst through the hull. They were thrown from their positions into the corner without getting a chance to reload. Edmund quickly got up, grabbed his cutlass and pistol, and ran topside. Jon looked on but was frozen with fear. Smoke made sight impossible as the two ships struck. Grappling hooks were quickly set in place by the pirates to connect with the Spanish ship. The pirates, led by McGinnty, boarded the enemy ship—yelling, screaming, and cursing to try and intimidate the enemy.

Edmund got to the top deck, found two grenades, and lit them. He threw the two as far as he could toward the back of the Spanish ship so as not to hit any of his own men. He looked at the Spanish ship, which was now covered in smoke, and tried to sift out who was the enemy and who was not.

A free-for-all melee broke out, confusion everywhere. Pistol fire filled the air, swords clanged together and then connected with limbs. Edmund aimed his pistol in the chest of a Spanish counterpart and fired. He drew his cutlass and attacked his enemy.

The deck was now filling up with blood as the pirates and Spaniards were now slipping all over the deck.

Lucifer's Ghost hooked to the Spanish ship from the other side, opposite *Hellspite.* The Spanish ship was now surrounded. Men boarded firing blunderbusses and pistols. With the reinforcements in tow and the deck starting to clear from smoke, the battle turned into a massacre. The Spanish quickly went down in defeat. What started out with a deafening roar of explosions was now an eerie silence.

Edmund's ears were ringing as he slipped around the blood-soaked deck. He walked sloshing his way along the deck, bodies were everywhere. Pirates and Spaniards littered the deck, most grotesquely disfigured.

McGinnty walked over, blood soaked through his shirt from grapeshot, as the smoke dissipated. He had a look of shock as he gazed at the number of men that had fallen. From behind him, a Spaniard slowly crawled to a pistol and aimed it at McGinnty. Edmund grabbed a boarding axe and ripped it through his skull before the shot went off. McGinnty turned and looked at the two, then gave a nod to Edmund.

Edmund walked up to another of the Spanish crewmembers who was barely breathing.

"Why didn't you surrender?" he asked, knowing his victim probably didn't understand him.

"Porque ta atacas?" he reiterated in Spanish.

The Spaniard looked at Edmund and, with all the strength he could muster, leaned up and spat at him. Edmund winced and held up his sword, ready to strike. He stared at the Spaniard with rage in his eyes and then stopped. He dropped his sword and walked away.

Back on *Lucifer's Ghost,* the crew was numb as to what happened. They had lost twenty-six men, and another forty-three were wounded, including McGinnty. After sifting through the bodies on the Spanish ship, McGinnty ordered his dead to be buried at sea while the Spanish ship was torched and sank.

Jon was trembling, face covered in powder. When Edmund found him down below, he was too embarrassed to look up at him.

"I guess I went belly up," Jon said. Then he looked up at Edmund. "I was just so goddamn scared when those cannonballs hit us." He shook his head as tears filled his eyes.

Edmund knelt down beside him. "We all were. You're not human unless you are."

Jon took a deep breath and tried to recompose himself. "I hope nobody saw what happened."

"Don't worry, Jon, I'd take you on my side anytime."

Later, Edmund walked into McGinnty's cabin to check up on him. The two had become close in the past months with each of them earning enormous respect from the other.

He found McGinnty with his shirt off and Doc sewing the holes in his arm and upper chest. Edmund stopped at the entrance when McGinnty noticed him.

"C'mon in."

Edmund looked into his eyes. They were lost, and gone was that look of confidence McGinnty always carried with him in leading his crew. It was the first time he saw despair and confusion in the man who had all the answers.

"I wanted to see if you're all right."

"Fine. Look at you, not a mark on you. I know you were in the heart of the fighting. Talk about luck!"

"I've got some minor cuts," Edmund said with a smile.

McGinnty reached for his stash of rum and poured a couple of mugs. He handed one to Edmund, who promptly raised his glass and drank.

"Hard to believe that turned out to be a battle."

Edmund shook his head. "It went by so fast."

There was an uncomfortable silence, which McGinnty then broke.

"Drake, I think the party's over."

"Come again?"

"A pirate's life is a short one. When Rogers takes over New Providence, we'll have run out of places to stay."

"You're Jack McGinnty, the most feared pirate in the Caribbean. How can you say that?"

"Take a look around you. We'll be the ones hunted."

"What about the rumors of a pardon?"

"You take it, you have a lot going for you."

"I have my past going against me."

The goods were transported to *Lucifer's Ghost* before setting the Spanish ship ablaze. Back on the deck, Gilgo was counting the plunder. It was not as anticipated. Silks, cotton, tobacco, and rice were on board. There was a small chest filled with gold doubloons but not enough to make the attack worthwhile.

"All that mayhem for this?"

Now the crew was facing a new problem. Plunder was becoming scarcer and harder to come by, which meant the growing number of crewmembers was receiving less and less.

They probably would have received £2,000 for the Spanish ship if it had not been destroyed by the battle. Instead, it was sacrificed to the sea.

CHAPTER 21

WOODES ROGERS

"There are warships on the horizon!"

It was late afternoon when they were spotted. Bells rang out as pirates sprung into action and gathered by the wharf.

Edmund was fighting in a duel with swords when the bells struck. The match was a friendly exhibition rather than a fight to the death. He had kept up his practice with the sword and became a legend in New Providence, often matched against some of the best pirates. He would dominate them as his reputation grew.

As the bells rang out, Edmund and his opponent stopped and shook hands, then gathered their things and went to see what the commotion was about. When they arrived at the wharf, they caught McGinnty looking through his telescope.

"They'll be here by nightfall, the latest! There are two warships and two sloops. There must be hundreds of men on board," McGinnty said, turning toward his men.

There had been plenty of rumors, and now it was official. Woodes Rogers had arrived in New Providence. McGinnty predicted that by nightfall, Rogers would have the entrances secured, preventing any type of escape. By morning, they would attack and take over the island.

The word of Rogers's arrival in New Providence was not sudden. London had known for some time how lucrative the island had become. Now England wanted control of this prosperity, and Rogers was the man to take on the assignment.

There were close to a thousand pirates on the island. Many of them were divided in their loyalties. Some were ready to sign the king's pardon and be resolved for all past acts of piracy. They were eager to get a fresh start. Others needed to escape.

"What are we going to do?" Beckham asked.

McGinnty ran his hands to his chin and looked back out toward the warships. In the days leading up to Rogers's arrival, New Providence had seen its population grow. Since pirates divided their wealth equally, each man had less money, and pirate captains were being more frugal with how many crewmembers they carried.

"I'll go to Eden, the governor of North Carolina, or Killingsworth himself before I let Rogers pardon me," McGinnty said.

Edmund ran into town and looked for Jon. Since his return from England, he had distanced himself from the people he knew. He moped around wondering where his future lie, often walking about by himself. Jon tried to pick him up and invite him to the pub or Felina would offer to cook a meal, but he would politely decline. Finally, when he found Jon by his hut, Edmund told him about Rogers on the way, and they were going to leave. Jon let Edmund know he had other plans.

"Felina and I are getting married."

"What? When did this happen? I knew you two were friendly but not like that."

"It's been going on for a while. We're in love, Edmund, and I want to spend the rest of my life with her."

Edmund offered his hand, and Jon shook it.

"Congratulations. I wish you two the best."

Jon reached in his vest and brought out an engagement ring. "I'm going to give her this. It was the one I gave to Caroline when we were engaged."

"What?" Edmund smiled. "Isn't that bad luck to give a used engagement ring?"

Jon shrugged his shoulders. "I never heard of that."

"Take care, my old friend. Enjoy the king's pardon, and may God be with you."

Edmund patted his shoulder and made his way back to the ship.

"Edmund, I'll see you in another life."

Edmund stopped. He recalled Jon saying that on the ship when they arrived in Portsmouth. He thought it ironic that after he said that to him, they met up again pretty quickly. He waved and left for the wharf.

Gilgo gathered ninety men at *Hellspite* as Edmund made his way to the pier. McGinnty barked out orders. It would be nightfall in less than two hours, about the time Rogers and his fleet would be arriving.

"Drake, that little escapade you did off the coast of Carolina just gave me an idea. Take six men and report to that Dutch prize we captured for further orders."

"That sloop you captured a few months ago? It's not fit for battle."

"It's perfect. We're going to sail it out near the western entrance. Load it with powder and double-load the cannons."

Edmund grabbed six men and a handful of smoke bombs, then went on board the Dutch ship. It was smaller than *Hellspite* and was filled with numerous holes and splinters spread throughout, a result of when it was confiscated. McGinnty tried to capture it peacefully, but the Dutch had other ideas. There was little or no plunder on board, and the only reward was the ship itself.

"Load it up with as many barrels of gunpowder as it will hold. Give me all the long fuses you can muster," Edmund screamed out. He looked the ship over and strategically concentrated most of the dynamite toward the bow of the ship.

As dusk approached, Edmund finished preparing the ship. It was never even given a name, and now it was to help them do battle against Rogers. Powder was spilled all over the deck. They soaked the sails in rum and other flammable materials. Anything else flammable was placed at the front of the ship. The ship was ready for battle.

Rogers arrived with two warships and two sloops. His first ship, *Rose*, weighed 350 tons and carried 36 guns. The other warship, *Delicia*, was 260 tons and also carried 36 guns. Altogether, Rogers brought 330 men to tame the British colony.

Rogers's ships arrived just before nightfall. Rogers secured both entrances to the New Providence harbor with warships, preventing any pirates from escaping. They anchored and, as McGinnty had predicted, were in no hurry to sail into New Providence harbor at night. It would be an early-morning assault.

With everything in place, McGinnty waited until late in the evening to move ahead with his plan. They sailed the two ships, *Hellspite* and the Dutch merchant vessel, toward the western entrance, making sure they sailed with the wind at their back, blowing toward two warships that were representing Rogers.

Edmund sailed the merchant ship toward the western entrance. They launched boats off the side filled with gunpowder and dynamite. Edmund looked back to *Hellspite*, which was preparing to set sail behind them. He set the course and tied rope around the wheel, keeping a steady course. Its target: the British warship closest to them.

They spilled more powder over the deck and lit it, causing smoke to fly everywhere. They followed the wind so the smoke would blow toward the British ship. Edmund connected long fuses to the barrels of gunpowder to use as a timing mechanism.

This is going to be close.

"Everything set up?" He asked one of the crewmen. The crewman answered with a nod.

"Long fuses in place?"

"Yes, sir."

"Light 'em and set off the smoke bombs," Edmund said to the men.

The two men looked nervous as each ran to the two sections of the boat where the dynamite and smoke bombs were placed. The smoke fizzed at first, and then smoke started spurting everywhere. They lit the fuses on the boats that were launched in the water next to the vessel. They launched one more small boat to escape on.

"Good job, men. Now take the boat back to *Hellspite*."

"What about you, sir?"

"I'll follow shortly."

McGinnty signaled to Edmund to set the Dutch ship ablaze and pulled up behind it to rescue the men rowing over. Edmund set the last fuse on fire and jumped into the water toward *Hellspite*. As he swam, he looked behind and saw the Dutch ship heading right for the British warship. McGinnty tucked *Hellspite* right behind it and followed. Edmund grabbed a rope from the side of *Hellspite* and climbed on board.

"All right, let's get this ship out of the way," McGinnty barked. "Turn us toward the side. Let's fire the starboard-side cannons. All of them."

With that said, the first mate rose up, and one by one cannons were exploding, rocking the ship.

"Again!"

Edmund watched as powder went off, creating smoke blowing toward the British ships. The Dutch ship was in flames as the rum-soaked sails were ablaze, creating a diversion.

"Where do you want us to go, Captain?" Edmund asked, checking his pistols and securing his cutlass.

McGinnty looked at him as a proud father would his son after doing something of notoriety. Then the glow stopped, and he remained silent.

"Sir?"

McGinnty's eyes moistened. He pulled out his pistol and pointed it toward Edmund.

"You're not coming on this one, Edmund." He pointed to the edge of the ship. "Jump!"

"What? You're not going to shoot me!" Edmund looked at him in shock.

McGinnty waved his arms, signaling Gilgo and Wolf to come over. "Get him off here!"

Edmund went for his pistols but was quickly intercepted by the two men who grabbed the guns from him. He struggled against the men, but Gilgo tied up his arms while Wolf collared him from behind.

"Jack, what are you doing? I've been loyal to you. I thought you were my friend!"

McGinnty signaled. Wolf lifted Edmund overboard feetfirst. As his body was about to follow, he reached for Gilgo and got a good grip on his shirt. Gilgo tried to get his balance but slipped and followed Edmund over the rail. The two of them splashed into the water as the ship was picking up speed for their getaway. Wolf looked at McGinnty who looked overboard to see if they were all right and safe enough away.

"Leave 'em, we need to go." Then he turned toward the crew and screamed, "Men, take your positions and buckle down!" McGinnty looked back at Edmund and stared.

"I'm sorry, Edmund, but I am your friend. That's why I'm doing it," he mumbled to himself. The other crewmembers looked in shock for a moment but then had to prepare for their encounter.

In the water, Edmund lunged after Gilgo, striking him on the side of his face. They each grabbed each other's clothing, trying to use it as leverage and pull the other under. Swings were taken wildly but finally stopped when they heard explosions. The dynamite from the Dutch ship was exploding.

Edmund shoved Gilgo aside and started to swim back to Nassau. In the background, smoke filled the night sky, and the British ships were confused. Cannons fired from both sides of the Dutch ship, adding to the chaos of what was taking place. The fire spread to the masts, which quickly fell. Men on the British ships were cutting their cables and getting their ships out of the way of the floating inferno that was coming at them. They raced to man their guns. The sounds of cannons were exploding from the warship and *Hellspite.*

In the blink of an eye, the Dutch ship finally exploded, the entire ship disappearing within a massive orange fireball. Thick black smoke rose from the water surface. Bits and pieces of the boat fell out of the sky and plopped into the water in raging flames, only to be snuffed out when they landed in the water.

Debris shot up all over the water, some landing a few feet from where Edmund was swimming. Smoke hovered all around them like a dense fog. Edmund couldn't see any of the ships.

As Edmund swam to shore, he heard an agonizing scream coming from behind. He swung his head toward it, but it was too dark to see as his eyes were out of sorts from the fires blazing in the foreground.

"Help me! I can't swim!"

Gilgo's head was barely bobbing in the water and then disappeared. Edmund swam back to him, listening for splashing to find his whereabouts.

Edmund swam toward the area Gilgo was last seen, took a deep breath, and dove underwater. Deep into the water, Edmund's head began to ache from the pressure as he reached for Gilgo. He pulled Gilgo's arm hard and fast, jerking him up, then kicked hard, breaking through the water's surface without a moment to spare. Gilgo was panic-stricken as they both gasped for air. Edmund struggled to keep Gilgo's nose and mouth above water.

"I can't swim."

"Just relax."

Edmund barely got the words out when Gilgo lunged and pushed down on his head. A couple of words were all Edmund could get out before his mouth was filled with saltwater, burning the back of his throat. Gilgo jumped on top of Edmund, clawing and scratching, not to attack him, but rather to use him as a float!

Gilgo's weight started to force Edmund underwater. He quickly gave Gilgo an uppercut and made his way around him. He threw his arm around Gilgo's neck and shoulder, taking him in a choke hold. The rest of Gilgo's body was held up by Edmund's hip as he sidestroked back to shore.

"I'm starting to cramp!" Gilgo yelled.

"I should let you drown!"

Edmund's lungs started to ache. He looked back at the chaotic scene behind him.

As the smoke finally dissolved, Edmund saw *Hellspite* still firing cannons from broadside to port and starboard. They sailed past the confused British ships and headed northwest, out to sea.

"I'll be dammed. They're going to make it!" Edmund said as he swam back to the beach.

When they reached the dry sand, Edmund dragged Gilgo out of the water, far enough along the sand away from the shoreline, and let him drop. He walked a few paces away and fell to the beach. He lay on his back and gasped for air. Every muscle in Edmund's body was aching. His breath soon began to come more easily.

"You better not tell anyone about this, I swear . . . ," Gilgo said, barely able to catch his breath.

"You're welcome," Edmund answered in a huff.

Edmund finally got up, brushed the sand off his clothes, and watched the rest of the fireworks that was taking place out by the island's entrance. *Hellspite* looked to be home free.

Edmund was in a state of shock as he walked the beach, stunned. He felt rage at being betrayed by McGinnty. Not the kind made from vengeance but one of disappointment. He watched Rogers sort out the debris and spend the rest of the night on the lookout for anyone else trying to do the same thing as McGinnty. It never came. The rest of the night was calm and uneventful.

He stayed with Felina and Jon that night. Jon sensed his disappointment and talked to him throughout the night.

The next morning, Edmund witnessed Woodes Rogers arriving ashore under the cover of navy guns surrounding the harbor from his warships and sloops. He used a cane to walk around, a result of a piece of wood flying through it during a battle from his privateering days. His left cheek was disfigured as a result of a musket ball striking it. Seven hundred pirates welcomed Rogers and the king's pardon.

Most of the pirates walked around in a daze. They were confused as to what exactly Rogers was going to do. Some pirates, upon hearing of Rogers's arrival, had already fled. Those that remained offered little resistance and accepted the king's pardon, which Rogers had the authority to grant. The pardon stated, "Swear allegiance to the king and all previous acts of piracy are absolved." The royal pardon left the pirates of New Providence divided.

Edmund found Jon, and they went to the pub to figure out their future. The rumors of a pardon appeared to be true, but what would become of the seven hundred or so pirates once they received it? They would, in all likelihood, remain in the same predicament that caused them to be pirates in the first place. There would be no jobs, and most of the money the men had made had been squandered. They made it quick, they spent it quick.

It appeared a pardon was a temporary solution. Most of the men were destined to turn to a life of crime, the only life they had known the past few years.

One job that Rogers did solicit was to hire crews to seek out and capture pirates that did not accept the pardon.

One of them, a pirate captain named Benjamin Hornigold, even joined Rogers and became a pirate hunter. His first assignment: Scarface Jack McGinnty!

Edmund and Jon sat quietly, drinking rum and trying to replay the previous night's events in their minds. Jon remembered very little, but to Edmund, it was like the entire night was replayed in his head—every little detail. He just kept shaking his head when finally Felina walked up to the two of them. She had an envelope in her hand and presented it to Edmund.

"McGinnty gave me this yesterday afternoon. He said if I saw you, to make sure you receive it. I would have given it to you last night, but you were too upset."

Edmund grabbed the envelope and opened it.

> Drake,
>
> Since you are reading this letter, I offer you my apologies, but at least, you're alive. I thought it best you take the pardon and start your life over. We are running out of places to hide, and the end is in sight. I have business to attend to with Eden, and then we're sailing to Madagascar. I'm going to start a new life there. I suggest you do the same. Take the pardon and start a new life.
>
> You have a lot to live for, so start living!
>
> Your friend,
> Jack McGinnty

Edmund read the letter twice, as if he was missing something. He shook his head and looked at Felina.

"What did it say?" she asked.

"The party's over."

CHAPTER 22

PIRATE PROCLAMATION

Woodes Rogers, in a short time, molded New Providence to his liking. He was going to rid the area of its infestation of pirates. Living in what was left of the governor's mansion, under the threat of mutinous pirates, he received the king's proclamation for ridding the colonies and Caribbean of pirates.

On the morning of September 5, 1718, Edmund watched as Rogers, escorted by troops, walked to the head of the harbor. It was there he read a memo to all that would listen.

"I have here a memo signed by King George and it may be of interest to you all," he shouted.

Many of the pirates that gathered around the pier heard rumblings about a pardon coming, and the mutiny Rogers envisioned never occurred. Life had been peaceful since his arrival. The crowd listened in earnest as Rogers continued, "We have thought fit to issue this, our Royal Proclamation. And we do hereby promise, and declare, that in case any of the said pirates shall, on or before the fifth of September in the year of our Lord 1718, surrender himself or themselves to one of our principal secretaries of state in Great Britain, or Ireland, or to any governor or deputy governor of any of our plantations beyond the sea, every such pirate or pirates so surrendering himself or themselves shall have our gracious pardon, of and for such, his or their piracy or piracies, by him or they committed before the fifth of January next ensuing."

The crowd rumbled, and each of the pirates in the crowd looked at one another.

"We do hereby strictly command and charge all our admirals, captains and other officers at sea, and all our governors and commanders to seize and take such pirates who shall refuse or neglect to surrender themselves accordingly. We do hereby further declare that in case any person or persons, on or after the sixth day of September 1718, shall discover or seize any one or more of the said pirates shall receive a reward."

Rogers looked around the crowd, which had tripled in size since he started his speech. All eyes were on him. He lowered the proclamation to his side and continued on, pacing the dock, "The rewards shall be as such: £100 will be offered for a pirate captain, £40 for a quartermaster or gunner, £20 per crewmember and . . ."

He paused, making sure he had their complete attention.

"And £200 for any crewmember turning in a ship's captain!"

The crowd turned to each other, and the rumblings were louder.

They're offering £200 to turn in a ship's captain!

Edmund's mind quickly thought of McGinnty.

Rogers nailed the proclamation to the dock entrance and walked away. Troops started nailing them up in other locations. It was official. There was now a profitable bounty on all pirates, especially captains.

In the days that followed, Rogers set up a small camp where pirates lined up along the shore to be sworn in for their loyalty to England. Each was pardoned for all acts of piracy.

Each day, the lines were shorter until you had to meet with Rogers individually in his headquarters at a refurbished Fort Nassau. Many of the pirates that did not receive the pardon were quickly caught, tried, and hanged.

Edmund hid. He wasn't sure if the crimes he was accused of in Bristol were known by Rogers and the authorities. He stayed with Jon and Felina in a hut outside the small town.

Jon had already received a pardon on the day of the official announcement with Felina by his side. His plan was to take Felina with him back to England after the winter broke. Edmund knew that until he was pardoned, he had to conceal his whereabouts from the soldiers patrolling the island or risk being hanged.

After weeks of hiding, and at Jon's urging, Edmund met with Woodes Rogers at his office in Fort Nassau. When he walked in, he noticed the office was empty and dusty. Maps and plans filled one desk, which had a cabinet next to it. The rest of the room was empty with the exception of three chairs.

Edmund paced around the room until Rogers entered escorted by two guards.

"You're late!" he said as he sat in the chair behind the desk. The two guards flanked him on each side.

Edmund looked confused. "I'm sorry, sir. I didn't think I had to be here at a certain time."

"No, you should have taken this pardon weeks ago. I know of no new pirates entering New Providence. Therefore, what were you waiting for?"

Edmund felt his face turning red and his mouth became dry. The question caught him off guard.

"I don't know, sir!"

"What you're telling me is you never wanted a pardon in the first place. You've run out of options, and you don't want to be hanged. So you're here until you can leave and resume a life of piracy once you've escaped this island." Rogers lit his pipe and sucked in a few puffs. Then he added, "Well, is this true? Speak up."

Edmund was starting to get angry but knew this was not the time.

"No, sir, I just wasn't sure if the offer was real." Edmund shut his eyes, knowing full well that his excuse was flimsy at best.

"Who did you sail under during your pirate escapades?"

"McGinnty, sir, and no, I'm not going back to the pirate ways, I just want to—"

"McGinnty?" Rogers interrupted. "You sailed with McGinnty? How did you miss his final escapade here? You must have been drunk to miss sailing with him that night."

"No, sir."

Edmund was agitated as Rogers continued, "Tell me you're not going to leave here and take up piracy again. You waited too long for this pardon I just don't believe you're serious."

Edmund looked Rogers in the eyes, his face was full red.

"I was kidnapped and forced into this life. I had little choice as to where I am."

"So you're telling me now that McGinnty kidnapped you and forced you into being a pirate. Is that the excuse you're telling me?"

"It wasn't McGinnty that kidnapped me, it was Morble! It was the Royal Navy."

Rogers stood up from his chair and walked over to Edmund.

"What's your name?"

"Edmund Drake."

Rogers paused and then walked back to his seat. He stared at the document with the king's pardon written on it. The room was silent.

"Drake? Any relation to Daniel Drake of Clifton?"

"He was my father."

Rogers looked up at him. "Sit down."

He looked at the two guards and waved his hand, gesturing them to leave. There was an uncomfortable silence until the guards had left the room.

"I know your father. I did business with him frequently during the war. He was a fair man, a good man. I heard he died some years back," he said with a curious look on his face as if to say, *What are you doing here?*

"He was shot and killed."

"I remember you as a child. You were his pride and joy, his reason for living when your mother died. He was very proud of you."

"I was proud of him."

Rogers stood up and pulled a pistol from his side.

"I also heard you killed Ben Cutler during a drunken rage. You need to go back to Bristol and stand trial."

"That's not true. I was set up by Alexander Killingsworth."

"Alexander Killingsworth, one of the most powerful men in all of England, set you up?"

"He was courting Sarah Bolden, and she was in love with me. She didn't want anything to do with him. We were going to leave and get married. He had me kidnapped and sent to sea," Edmund responded desperately.

"Come on."

"He found out about us. His press-gang brought me over to see him so he could pay me off for not seeing Sarah. I said no. That's when he had me sent away."

"That's not the story I heard."

"Why do you think I'm alive? Why was I in the Royal Navy? As a reward? If they wanted to find me, I was right there. Killingsworth never wanted me to return. He wanted me to disappear at sea so I wouldn't say anything back home."

Rogers ran his hands through his hair. "Daniel Drake was as honorable a man as I've ever met. The apple has fallen far from the tree."

He called in his guards.

"Take and lock him up. We're going to hold him for a while."

He looked at Edmund. "If what you say is true, I'm sure a jury will find you innocent."

"You know I won't get a fair trial. They'll kill me before it goes to trial."

"I can't rule on your guilt or innocence. I can only pardon you of piracy. We'll sail you back on the next available ship to England."

The guards grabbed him by each arm and escorted him to his cell.

Edmund was placed in a cell at Fort Nassau. The fort was empty with the exception of a few armed guards and a couple of prisoners. Most pirates fled the island or took the pardon. The few that remained were hanged or hiding.

There were very few cells at Fort Nassau, and the one Edmund had occupied was a small room with bars on the window. A small cot was located in the corner. It was built to hold small amounts of prisoners. Trials were quick, and sentencing was quicker.

After a week in his cell, Edmund pondered what remained of his future. He fell back in his cot with his forearm over his eyes, shielding the hot sun that pierced through the window. Executions had dwindled since Rogers's arrival, but Edmund thought about one more that would take place.

In New Providence, like England, execution day was treated like a holiday. The prisoners would be escorted by chains through the town. The enormous crowds would squeeze through the streets and cram their way as close as they could to see the victims during their last minutes. Before arriving at the gallows, the prisoners would drink rum and get drunk. The gallows were quickly built with one beam supported by two vertical beams and a raised platform held up by small posts with steps leading up to it. The posts were just sturdy enough to hold the condemned men, executioner, and a few priests.

Once on the platform, the prisoners would then be allowed to have a final word. Many would beg for mercy or pray to God for forgiveness before the executioner cinched the noose around their necks. Then a rope would be tied under their arms in the back, pinning their arms together. The priests said a prayer for them, and then the executioner kicked out the posts holding up the platform.

Edmund would cringe when he saw the victim's faces turning purple while their legs kicked about. Piss filled their crotch as the crowd went wild. After the pirates were hanged, they were displayed on the wharf for one week to send a message that piracy was not to be tolerated. Their faces were covered in tar to prevent decay. Was this a preview of what was to become of him?

He was startled back to reality when Rogers walked to the cell. Since a week had passed, Edmund thought his transfer to stand trial in England was near. Sleep was erratic, and time had passed slowly as Edmund awaited his future. The guards unlocked his cell, and Edmund was told to follow Rogers. As they walked down the hall, Edmund noticed Rogers was unarmed.

"Where are we going?"

Rogers remained silent. They kept walking until they reached the shoreline.

"I couldn't sleep at all last night, Drake. I kept thinking what if you're telling the truth? I did some checking, and what you say seems to check out. Also, your friend, Jon, came by every day to plead your case. You're lucky to have a friend like that. He seems to be the only one left from Morble's ship, and he verified everything you said. I don't know how he was ever a pirate, he appears to be the furthest thing from one."

"He's a good man," Edmund answered.

"I wondered why you would join the navy, and it made sense you were telling the truth."

"I am, sir."

"I owe your father my life. Back in the days before you were born, we were privateers working under Captain James Lawrence. We were both so green, which is probably why we hit it off right away." Rogers wore a distant smile as he stared out to sea.

"During our first voyage, I took a shot." He unbuttoned his shirt and pointed to a round scar on the side of his stomach. "I fell overboard. It was your father that jumped in and fished me out."

Edmund was shocked. "My father worked as a pirate?"

"Privateer. He left that line of work when he met your mother, but he made a lot of connections. That's where his smuggling—maybe I should say trade business—started."

Edmund shook his head in disbelief. "He never mentioned any of this to me."

"My connections with your dad helped me tremendously when I ran into trouble with the East India Trade Company. When we sacked the Manila galleon, the company said we invaded their waters. They were going to give us nothing. Your father helped influence the company to withhold their claim. He was a very influential man your father."

"I thought he just traded plunder brought to him from the ships coming into Bristol."

"That was just a front."

Edmund looked seriously at Rogers. "So why did you bring me here?"

"You're free, Drake. I can't give you the king's pardon because I don't want your name on any records here. I want you to disappear. If Killingsworth finds out you're alive, he will stop at nothing to kill you."

"Where should I go?"

"I'd like to say stay here, but it would be too dangerous. This place is growing, and we'll have more troops here in no time. Go to the colonies, start a new life. Maybe you could even go back to England, live in Scotland. I wish I could help you but I can't."

Edmund shook his hand.

"So you do believe me."

"Daniel Drake's son could never be a cold-blooded killer," Rogers said. "I also know Lord Killingsworth has a checkered past. Don't ever let him know you're alive. Let me know if you need a ship to board, I'll arrange something,"

Edmund turned to walk away before Rogers stopped him.

"I also know if it was me that sacked the *Lucinda* instead of McGinnty, I'd have the noose around my neck."

Edmund paused and looked at him. There was a strange look in Rogers's eyes.

"Sir? What do you mean?" Edmund asked.

"You haven't heard?" Rogers paused. "Of course, how could you. They caught McGinnty off the coast of North Carolina. He's been brought to stand trial in Virginia."

PART III

CHAPTER 23

SOUTH SEA STOCK COMPANY

The news of McGinnty's capture circulated through New Providence like wildfire. He was captured off the coast of North Carolina and credit was given to Lord Killingsworth's ranking officer, Captain Morble. Edmund thought there had to be more to it than the rumors that were spread. Morble would have never taken McGinnty. The trial was set in two weeks in Williamsburg, Virginia.

Killingsworth must have gone outside his jurisdiction to capture McGinnty.

He felt helpless, thinking he should have been on the ship with McGinnty and the crew. Sitting on the wharf, staring out to sea, he placed his head in his hands. No crew. No boat. No plan. It was useless to think about. It was all he could do to keep from being arrested, let alone help McGinnty. Frustrated, he looked up, and a smile stretched across his face. The answer was right in front of him. On one of the ships flew a flag waving below the British colors.

Edmund ran into the Shark Den. There were no soldiers in there, only ex-pirates. He recognized many of them, especially the ones that sailed at one time or another with McGinnty. They were now free men.

He walked nervously to the front and stood on the bar. Looking around, he watched many drinking and telling stories. He cleared his throat and waved his hands in the air.

"May I have your attention?"

No one looked over at him as much of the talk was loud and boisterous.

"May I have your attention please?" he repeated, this time shouting.

The men looked up. Some were irked and annoyed at being interrupted. Others looked at him with a sense of curiosity. Edmund continued, "As most of you heard, they caught McGinnty outside of North Carolina."

There were mumblings in the crowd, and a few people chuckled. Edmund was getting frustrated as he talked over the noise.

"We need to help him, and we don't have a minute to spare. They are going to hang him."

Before Edmund could finish, the crowd interrupted him.

"Why should we go? We're free men."

"We're going to risk our necks."

Another voice shouted, "If we get caught, we'll be hanged too," as some of the men looked around. "We could be hanged just for talking about this."

Edmund held his hands up and waved. "Please quiet down. Listen to me."

Laughter filled the room. A few waved Edmund away and resumed talking among themselves.

"Shut up all of ya!" a loud voice echoed from the back of the room, and a large man stood up. It was Beckham. "Let's hear what he has to say." Then he gave Edmund a nod.

Beckham was one of the first pirates to receive a pardon, but even before Rogers's arrival, he had retired from piracy. He now owned his own merchant vessel where he successfully traded goods throughout the Caribbean and Carolinas. It was McGinnty who helped him purchase his ship.

Edmund felt relieved to see a friendly face as the crowd quieted down.

"Look at you all. You're here because of McGinnty. Everything you have—your wealth, home, prosperity—is because of him. Now he's in trouble and you all go belly-up. I understand you're all free men, and I understand you not wanting to risk what you have. Just remember, when the well runs dry here, you'll be left with nothing."

The words came across as a threat, and some of the men stood up, pointing to Edmund.

"It's easy for you to say. I hear you never got a pardon. I could turn you in right now and pocket myself a quick £50."

Edmund jumped down the bar and pulled out his cutlass, pointing it at the man.

"You try it." He looked around. "Or anyone else that wants to risk their life for that blood money."

The man backed off and hunched back into his chair as Edmund's cutlass came within inches of the man's chest. Edmund stared down the man and continued, "As pirates, we helped each other. I know you've all been given a second chance. I'm asking that we give McGinnty a second chance."

Edmund looked around. None of the men could look him in the eye. He placed his cutlass back in its sheath by his side. He shook his head in disgust and started to walk out until a voice from the back stopped him in his tracks.

"I'm in," Beckham said as he stepped forward. A wide grin filled his face.

From the corner of the pub, a man seated alone stood up.

"Me t-too."

It was Charles. The day McGinnty escaped from New Providence, he had been on a drunken binge and missed the action. He had felt guilty ever since.

One by one, a few more followed suit, and then a voice from the back yelled out, "I'm in also, your captaincy, your lordship, governor, or whatever you call yourself these days."

Edmund looked up and smiled as Jon Galvin stepped forward.

"My old friend, where did you come from? Isn't Felina expecting?"

"I wasn't about to interrupt that great speech. As for Felina, I'll be back before the birth, so my time is limited. Let's get a move on!"

"Fair enough," Edmund responded, and they shook hands.

The crew laughed as more stepped forward. Edmund looked around. From what he could tell, all the men that volunteered were former crewmembers that had sailed with McGinnty.

"What's the plan?" Beckham asked.

"We need more men. We've got fifteen volunteers."

"We'll take my ship," Beckham said.

"Thanks, Beck, but we need something bigger and faster if we're going to pull this one off. I think I have just the ship."

He addressed the crowd one last time to see if he could persuade anyone else, but no one was listening. A loud clap of thunder erupted from the corner, which silenced the room. A man held a smoking gun pointing upward.

"You need volunteers, my men need work. Let's talk."

The man placed his pistol in a red sash that slung from his shoulders, which also harnessed three others. Edmund recognized the owner of the pistols as William Beale. He had dark beady eyes, a dark beard, and a rough complexion from years in the sun. He wore a broad-brimmed hat with a feather cockade and strands of hair flying in every direction.

"Don't trust him," Beckham whispered.

"I don't have a choice."

Reluctantly, Rogers had given Beale and his men the king's pardon, but their money was about out. He slowly made his way up to Edmund.

"It seems my men have squandered their money on drink and dames."

"How many men can you muster?"

"I can get you twenty by tomorrow, maybe a few more."

"What do you want in return?"

"My offer is this. We'll get your captain back. If you want me and my men, 80 percent of the plunder we take along the way is ours."

Beckham grabbed Edmund. "William Beale is scum."

Beale pulled out a pistol from beneath his vest. "Careful what you say, matey."

Beckham grabbed his cutlass. Edmund grabbed his forearm and held it down. Beale's men quickly surrounded the two.

"This is not the time," Edmund said to Beckham. Then turning to Beale, he said, "I accept your offer, but I call the shots."

"Aye, for now."

"Looks like we have an arrangement then."

Beale lifted his mug of rum toward Edmund in a salute and then chugged. He then turned and signaled his men to follow him outside.

Edmund turned as if to beat Beckham to the first word.

"Time is of the essence. Once we get there, we'll figure something out."

The next night, the Shark Den was alive, and one particular captain caught Edmund's eye. He walked over with Jon and two mugs of ale and pulled up a stool.

"We hear you're looking for sailors," Edmund said to the captain. "You're in luck, we're looking for work."

Jon slid a mug over to the captain who graciously accepted.

"We're always looking for hardworking men," the captain responded and toasted the two men and drank.

After conversing with him for four drinks, the captain told Edmund of his ship's schedule and bragged of their trade.

"We're hitting Port Royal, Charleston, Williamsburg, New York, and Boston. Then we head for home. We're the main ship in the South Sea Company."

It was the company's one trip a year. Edmund still couldn't fathom how one company could pay off all that debt that occurred during the War of Spanish Succession. The interest alone was overwhelming.

The captain and his officers were quite drunk. Now it was time to act. As they left the pub, Edmund's men jumped them from behind. Sacks were thrown over their heads, and they were ushered away.

Later that night, Edmund, Beale, and thirty volunteers rowed out to the South Sea's ship with the British captain and his officers in tow. The ship would dock by the northeast wharf for deliveries but would moor out in the harbor when finished, being easier to protect in case incorrigibles had any funny ideas of attacking or stealing the goods on board. Edmund held a pistol to the captain's back.

"Get us on board. Anything funny and the ship has one dead captain."

The men on board guarding the ship rushed to the side, unsure of what was happening.

"New recruits!" the captain yelled as the men were helped on board.

They were greeted warmly until pistols were drawn.

"Up anchor," the captain said quietly.

Edmund pushed the pistol into his back firmly. Beale raised his cutlass to strike one of the sailors. Edmund quickly reached out and deflected the strike.

"No blood if we can help it."

Beale snarled at Edmund. "Be careful, boy."

Edmund shook the captain. "Get that anchor up."

"Up anchor!" he yelled with more urgency in his voice. Then he turned slowly to Edmund. "We were supposed to be in Port Royal tomorrow."

"The schedule has changed," Edmund answered. "Wake up the rest of the men down below and get them up here."

Edmund watched as men gathered to pull up the anchor. He watched the men struggle with its weight and pulled out his cutlass.

"That will take too long. Cut the lines. Leave the anchors here."

The deck filled as pirates ushered the men topside. Only half the crew was on board while the rest furloughed in New Providence. Edmund ordered them to line up along the starboard side.

The thick anchor lines were cut. Men rushed up the ratlines to unfurl the sails. The helmsman brought the ship off the wind while others hauled the sails into place. Slowly the ship pulled out of the harbor, under the guns of Fort Nassau, and into the open Atlantic.

"We are now heading out," Edmund addressed the ship's crew. "The rest of you men, unless you have a bone to pick with England, jump!"

Jon walked over to Edmund as they watched most of the skeleton crew on the ship jumped overboard.

"Edmund, what are you planning? Just go in, unlock the jail cell, and have McGinnty walk right out?"

"I haven't gotten that far yet," Edmund responded. He looked Jon in the eyes. "I'm kind of surprised we got this far."

"Oh great, you mean you're taking us to the lion's den wearing herbs and spices?"

"We have to get there first. We have paperwork that will get us docked inside the harbor. We have a kidnapped captain that knows the water there. So we have a start."

They sailed north to Virginia. The rough part of Cape Hatteras was coming to an end. Edmund had successfully navigated the treacherous coast and sifted through the worst currents of the Carolinas. The hard part was over. They had a clean path to Chesapeake Bay.

Beale and his men ravaged the ship for plunder, but most of the wealth was to be picked up in Port Royal and Charles Town. Beale was getting frustrated.

As they sailed their way up the coast, Edmund and Jon busted a chest in the captain's cabin filled with gold and silver. More coins than they imagined being on board. Jon ran his fingers through it and turned to notice Beale at the doorway.

"Remember our agreement." Beale didn't wait for a response. He turned and walked away.

As they neared Chesapeake Bay, they learned through passing ships that McGinnty's trial was in two days, and Killingsworth was turning it into a circus. He wanted it known that Alexander Killingsworth had captured the notorious Scarface Jack McGinnty.

Edmund, Jon, and Beckham met in the captain's cabin and grilled the British captain for information about Williamsburg but only received threats of treason. They pulled out a rough map of Williamsburg harbor, and they went over plans to get the ship docked there. Beckham looked as if his mind was elsewhere.

"Beck, what is it? You look as though you haven't heard a word we've said."

"I think we may have a problem."

"Spit it out," Edmund asked.

"It's Beale and his men."

"What? Besides the fact that they're drunk and rowdy every night?"

"It's more than that. I hear some of the men whispering all the time, and when one of us walks by, they stop. I've heard Beale talk of splitting up the gold and plunder now. They're up to something. I told you we couldn't trust Beale."

"I have to admit, I didn't think there would be gold on board."

"We should have left Beale and his men to rot on New Providence."

"We need them. Besides, it's too late now, we're stuck with them."

"There's no incentive for them to stay, they can steal what's on board. It's probably more than they thought they'd get."

"Maybe we should get rid of the plunder before we sail into Williamsburg," Jon said. "Let's get it out of their minds."

"We need something to keep them at bay," Edmund added.

A knock came from the door, and Charles looked in.

"Am I interrupting s-s-something?"

"No," Edmund answered. "What is it?"

"I was just b-below d-deck, and if you think we're going to attack anyone anytime soon, you're m-mistaken."

"What's wrong?"

"Well, for s-starters, the c-cannons need c-cleaning. We need to grease the wheels, and the p-p-powder is damp. We c-couldn't get a flicker out of it."

Edmund looked at Charles who had been named gunner for the voyage. It was just an unofficial title. He had never held a position of importance before, and he took it seriously.

"Just clean what you can, and we'll pick up supplies somewhere." He turned to Beckham. "Maybe you can pick something up in Bath."

Later, as Edmund and Jon walked out on the main deck, they were discussing plans to navigate Williamsburg harbor and noticed Beale's men drinking and whispering. Beale walked down the waist of the ship. He gave a nod to members of his crew, and they looked at one another.

Out of the corner of his eye, Edmund watched Beale grab a blunderbuss and threw a couple of pistols to members of the crew. Two pirates jumped Edmund from behind and slammed his face to the deck. They clutched his hair and turned his head upward. Beale held a pistol to Jon's head. Beale's men outnumbered Edmund's volunteers and quickly covered each with a knife or a pistol. Beckham shrugged off two of the men that held him but was quickly stopped in his tracks by a knife held to his throat, then a blow to his stomach.

"I've been waiting for this day since we first left Nassau. Drake, you served your purpose. You are now officially relieved of duty!"

"You think you know these waters?" Edmund responded.

"I know enough to get us out of here and back home. We just had to sail this coast as to not be seen by the navy. You did your job, and you did it well."

With that, he chuckled.

"Let's keelhaul him," one of the pirates yelled out.

"Ever been keelhauled, Drake?" Beale asked. "We'll tear your shirt off and spread your arms out and drag you under the ship's bottom. Your stomach will scrape off the ship's barnacles."

Beale's men laughed. Two men tied a slipknot around Edmund's wrists.

"Maybe we'll just throw you overboard and let the British or the sharks fight over you. I may send your head to Killingsworth as a present!"

He walked over to Edmund and smiled, clutching his cheek.

"Beale, you're so gutless. Why don't we settle this like men?"

"I don't need to," he responded as he slid the noose over Edmund's head. He turned toward Jon. "Don't worry, I'll see to it that bitch back home is well satisfied!"

"Stop!" a voice screamed. It was Charles. In all the confusion, no one noticed him. Now all eyes were at full attention, staring at him. He held a bottle of rum in one hand and, in the other, a flaming brand. Beale's men clustered around him, about to overwhelm him, but the converging crowd reared back when he swung the flaming brand around. He emptied the bottle of rum through a grating that was directly above the powder hold. He smashed the glass down and held the burning brand over the gaps in the hatch.

"Any c-closer and I'll d-drop it. I'll take us all down to the b-bottom of the sea, gold and all. I swear it."

The men looked at one another, wondering whether to believe him.

"He'll do it, he's crazy," one of Beale's men yelled.

They all stepped back.

"He can't hold that flame forever," Beale said.

"I don't intend to. I'm going to drop it in one second if you don't release him and lower your weapons."

Beale looked at Edmund, then to his men.

"He's bluffing."

Charles raised his arm and started a downward motion.

"No!" Beale screamed. "All right, we'll do it your way. Cut him loose for now."

They cut the rope to Edmund's wrists. He rubbed them to take the sting out as he watched, all eyes still focused on Charles. He noticed Beale's shooting hand fidgeting against the side of his leg, tapping it, and then he raised his hand to fire. Edmund pushed his arm upward, and the shot missed its mark. Charles threw the torch into the powder hold, and panic and chaos ensued. Edmund reached into Beale's sash and came away with his cutlass. Pistols were fired and smoke filled the deck. After the pistols were emptied, the men engaged in hand-to-hand combat. Smoke rose from below, and half of Beale's men jumped into the water, waiting for the ship to blow.

Edmund struck at Beale's chest but, at the last second, was blocked by a forearm. Blood soaked his sleeve in seconds. Edmund charged at him as Beale reached in his vest for a pistol. As he grabbed it, Edmund struck again, and the pistol flew harmlessly into the water. Beale had his back to the edge of the ship and turned to look downward, then back at Edmund.

"Jump."

Beale didn't need to be told again and dove into the water. Beckham and a few other men pointed muskets at him as he swam away.

"Let him drown," Edmund said, and with that, they shouldered their arms. Others gathered water for the powder hole. Two of the volunteers lay dead on the deck alongside three of Beale's men. Edmund pounded his fist against the mast, then looked over to Charles who had a choke hold on one of Beale's men, causing his face to turn dark shade of purple. Edmund signaled to release him. The man's body fell limp to the deck.

"The ship should have been blown to bits," Edmund yelled over to Charles. "What happened? Not that I'm complaining, but why are we still alive?"

"I've been t-trying to tell you, Edmund," Charles said calmly. "The p-powder down below is damp. We n-need to get fresh supplies."

After the ordeal, Edmund sat in the main cabin, head in his hands, as footsteps startled him. He whirled around with a pistol in hand.

"It's you. You scared the shit out of me."

Beckham walked in and sat down beside Edmund.

"You have to get it together, Edmund. That scab out there got the drop on you. That can't happen. As a ship's captain, you have to be prepared for everything. Every nook and cranny has to be accounted for. You have to be one step ahead. If it wasn't for Charles, we'd be fish food at the bottom of the ocean."

Edmund didn't want to hear it. "I know I messed up trusting Beale. There's nothing I can do about it now."

"You have two good men dead, two men that relied on you."

"You don't think I feel bad about that. What's done is done. We have to get on with what we're here for, and that is try and save McGinnty."

"One thing about McGinnty, he could always sniff out a mutiny attempt. He wouldn't have let Beale get the drop on him."

"I'm not McGinnty."

"I know, but you have good instincts. You have to use them because Beale and his men are not finished. Not by a long shot. We should have shot them dead where they swam."

"Is that all, Mr. Beckham?" Edmund sounded more irritated.

"No. We need more men," Beckham said. "We may not even make it through port."

Edmund grabbed the king's orders and handed them to Beckham.

"We need to fix these up so no one questions us once we're in the harbor."

"He's right, Edmund. We need more recruits," Jon acknowledged as he entered.

"We'll never get McGinnty out. We just lost more than half our crew. Killingsworth will have as many soldiers as he can scrounge up, guarding him."

"We'll moor the ship outside the harbor. Jon and I will row in," Edmund said, then pointed to Beckham. "You take our plunder on board and sail it to North Carolina. Trade for as much gold as you can get your hands on. Hit up every smuggler we've ever done business with, and be fast. Time is of the essence. I'm counting on Killingsworth's ego to let everyone know it was him that captured McGinnty and maybe prolong the hanging to soak in all the attention it's bringing him."

CHAPTER 24

WILLIAMSBURG

Upon arriving at the harbor outside Williamsburg, the pirates learned not only about McGinnty's upcoming trial, but also there would be an execution to follow two days later. Killingsworth used McGinnty's capture to schedule political meetings and raise his own political status. All of the elite and state legislators would be there.

The plan was to have Beckham sail to North Carolina to trade as much rum and sugar to the local smugglers they knew in exchange for money and powder. Edmund and Jon would feel out the town to develop an escape plan.

They walked a narrow dirt road from the harbor to the city and witnessed a lively town in celebration of capturing one of its greatest foes. Williamsburg, normally populated with one thousand people, had nearly doubled in size with many curious onlookers packing the inns, boarding houses, and taverns.

The city was more an administrative center with a large government building in the center. Williamsburg had been the capital of Virginia for fifteen years, but still, it was relatively in its infancy. There were public houses packed and spaced out along the streets. The smell of fresh bread filled the air as they walked by the bakery. Dealers haggled for bargains on food and clothing along the way.

People everywhere tried to get a look at the prison, which housed Scarface Jack McGinnty, and want to watch him hang after the trial. His reputation for terrorism grew as Killingsworth poured gasoline on the fire.

"Check it out. They have a theater here," Jon said. He stopped to gaze, but Edmund grabbed his elbow and nudged him along.

A block up the road, they saw the courthouse where McGinnty's trial was to take place, and as Jon predicted, there were soldiers stationed at every corner in Williamsburg.

Edmund and Jon were lucky and paid well enough to find a room at one of the local inns, which doubled its original price because of the festivities.

They cleaned up and visited one of the local taverns. They were surprised to learn not all locals were in a celebratory mood. Some were drowning their misfortunes in ale and spirits. It seemed half the revenues they made were going to the king, and what little profits that remained were being smuggled by pirates. Virginia's economy was in a fragile state, and the consensus was McGinnty was to be made an example.

"We're not going to get any help here," Edmund told Jon as they downed their beer and walked out.

They discovered from the locals that McGinnty was in the Williamsburg jail. It was a tall brick building located on the outskirts of the city. He had a cell to himself while the rest of his captured pirates were crowded six deep.

With the trial two days away, local prosecutors tried to rationalize Killingsworth's overstepping his boundaries to capture McGinnty in North Carolina.

Killingsworth answered the charges by stating, "The Royal Navy answers to the admiralty in London. Since there is no proper admiralty here in the colonies, we are authorized. The ships protect us from piracy."

It was a poorly kept secret he had paid off the Royal Navy with high taxes from the farmers, many of which were unable to pay and forced to lose their land. McGinnty's hanging would be a nice feather in Killingsworth's cap and shows results of how their tax dollars were spent.

Edmund mapped out the harbor where the warships were moored. Jon mapped out the courtyard where the execution was to take place.

The day before the trial, a wrinkle they had not counted on occurred. Gilgo, Wolf, and Morble sailed *Hellspite* into Williamsburg harbor.

"What's Wolf doing here? He should have been captured with McGinnty," Jon observed. Edmund nodded in agreement.

They made their way to O'Reilly's Tavern. The place was frequented by smaller land-owning farmers, many of whom were behind on their taxes. Edmund tried to get a pulse on the mood and spirit of the Virginia locals. He needed an ally and quick.

"They blame piracy for their debts, but it's really the king's taxes that are holding them back," Edmund told Jon. "We need to find out who's in the most debt. They would be the ones most apt to help us."

The next day, McGinnty's men were found guilty of piracy and treason. They were sentenced to death by hanging on a date to be determined. Everyone knew when that date would be—the same day McGinnty would swing from the galleys. He was the one everyone was interested in. He was reason the city was crowded and festivals were taking place.

The barkeep at O'Reilly's Tavern turned out to be a most useful ally. He supplied names of hardworking farmers not able to keep up with the high taxes and demands of the tobacco industry.

Jed Snead had been a farmer all his life in Virginia. He was elected to represent all farmers in their dealings with Killingsworth. No one was respected more, and when his tobacco farm experienced a harsh winter, tax collectors were the first to greet him. Edmund thought Jed would be his best chance, maybe his only chance to get inside help from the locals.

Later that night, Edmund snuck into his plantation and greeted him at the barn. Jed was startled and shed light with a trembling lantern on Edmund's masked face. He looked down at Edmund's arm, which had a pistol pointing at him.

"What do you want from me?" Jed asked. A corner of his mouth twitched, and he took a deep breath.

"I need help freeing a friend, Jack McGinnty."

"You've come to the wrong place. He ain't a friend of ours. He steals our profits. After the king's taxes, we have nothing left to feed our families."

Jed stared nervously at the pistol pointed at him. Edmund looked down and moved the pistol into his belt. He removed the leather mask he was wearing. Sweat filled his forehead.

"Killingsworth is your enemy. He's the one that's stealing out of your pockets. He's taxing you to death, and you can bet your ass he's not suffering."

"We have our legislators petitioning to the Board of Trade in England to repeal some of his economic regulations. Maybe they can even remove him altogether."

Edmund shook his head. "You're just going to get him riled up, and then you don't know what he's capable of doing. Right now, he has total control of this colony."

"There's nothing else we can do."

"You're saying that now. What about the farmers with smaller lands and smaller profits? They're going under. They're months behind, and you will be too. He's stealing from all of you. He's already acquired thousands of acres of land that's been defaulted, and that amount is growing."

"How do you know that?"

"How many of your friends have left because of taxes. Killingsworth's land dealings are on record. Obviously, it's been kept from all of you."

"I've heard rumblings."

"Then help us, please." He held out a small sack. "Maybe this will help you change your mind."

Jed raised his eyebrows, grabbed the sack, and looked at the gold coins inside. "Pirates are not a popular sort in this here neck of the woods."

"There's more where that came from. I need men inside the courtyard to create a diversion."

"I couldn't get you any help. My people want to see him hanged," Jed responded.

"Your people should be protesting the king's taxes. Make them understand that. The gold I just gave you should help pay some of your debt."

"Suppose we don't help you," he said, handing back the sack.

"If you don't help us, keep the gold as an offer to make amends on your plundered goods. If you choose to help us, there's no going back. If you betray us, I swear we'll burn your fields, houses, and everything that you own. That's the offer."

Jed walked slowly away and brought his hand to his chin.

"I reckon there's no harm in listening. What do you want from us?"

CHAPTER 25

THE TRIAL

Edmund snuck through the courtroom. It was packed with people, and there were hundreds more outside as the crowds lined the streets, trying to get a glimpse of McGinnty. Edmund looked around; there was no one that looked familiar until he caught Gilgo in the corner near the prosecutor. Morble was also in the corner a few seats from Gilgo. He ducked in back of a couple large bodies as he listened to the judge's sentence.

Judge Thomas Poole led the proceedings and, with a jury paid off by Killingsworth, read the sentence.

"Jack McGinnty, you stand here convicted on two counts of piracy: one by the verdict of the jury and, the other, by your own confession. You took and rifled no less than thirteen vessels since you sailed from New Providence in 1714. Eleven more acts of piracy off the coast of North Carolina. Any other acts of piracy, you must expect to answer to them before God.

"To piracy, you have added a greater sin, which is murder. How many men have you killed of those that resisted you? The power of the sword was never committed to you by lawful authority. You were not empowered to use any force or fight anyone, and therefore, any of those fallen in action, in doing their duty for their king and country, were murdered, and their blood cries out for vengeance and justice against you.

"Death is the only punishment due murderers. As for the testimony of your conscience must convince you of the great many evils you have committed, by which you have highly offended God, and provoked most justly, his wrath and indignation against you. The only way of retaining true pardon and remission is by a true and unfeigned repentance and faith in Christ. Only that way can you hope for salvation.

"So now, in your final hours, if you will sincerely turn to him, he will receive you. Do not mistake the nature of repentance to be only a bare sorrow for your sins arising from the consideration of the evil and punishment they have brought upon you. Your sorrow must arise from the consideration of you having offended a gracious and merciful God.

"I shall not pretend to give you any direction as to the nature of repentance. I consider I speak to a person whose offenses have preceded not so much from his knowing, as his slighting and neglecting his duty. It is not proper for me to give advice on this subject.

"I have discharged my duty as a Christian by giving you the best counsel I could offer. Now I must do my duty as a judge. That you, Jack McGinnty, shall go from hence you came and from thence to the place of execution where you shall be hanged by the neck until you are dead.

"And may God have mercy on your soul."

The gavel came down and all rose. There was a scream in the back and deep sighs in the audience. McGinnty stared expressionless as two guards led him out.

Trotter never looked over toward him. Killingsworth smiled and nodded to the jury. The verdict was vindication for his actions against piracy.

Sensing a chance to improve his political status among the elite, Killingsworth held a ball that night to celebrate the conviction and upcoming execution of McGinnty. It had been planned for weeks as the outcome of the trial was never in doubt. Killingsworth had met with Poole before the trial began to make sure they were on the same page.

Edmund and Jon raced back to the harbor to check on Beckham's situation. There was no sign of him. As they walked slowly back to town, Edmund held his head down and kept quiet.

"What do we do next?" Jon asked.

"I'm going to the governor's ball tonight."

Jon laughed and shook his head. "I'm serious. We need to get Beckham back here. We need more gold. We need the farmers to come through. If anything goes wrong, we're in deep—"

"I am serious. I'm going to that ball tonight. I can find out more information on how to get McGinnty out."

Jon stopped and stared at Edmund, giving him a quizzical look.

"You're not joking. This isn't about McGinnty at all? This is about Sarah."

"No."

"Bullshit. You have everyone believing we're here to save McGinnty, and you're really here to see if you still have a chance with her."

Edmund grabbed Jon's arm, but he quickly shrugged it away.

"Jon, listen to me. That's not true."

"I don't want any part of it. You're risking everything if you go there. There are men's necks on the line. Men that trust you with everything they have."

Edmund stood motionless. He looked down at the ground. Jon placed his hands on his hips and paced about.

"We're here to save Jack. That's always been the plan," Edmund said. "I just can't stop thinking about her. I need to know what happened to her. I can't go back asking myself what if. I know you won't understand, nor do I expect you to."

"Damn it," Jon responded as he looked to the sky. "Well, we can't go dressed like this."

Edmund looked at Jon, and his eyes widened. "We? You don't have to go, this is my problem."

"Yes, I do. Look at you, what do you know about etiquette? We need to get clothing and take a crash course on aristocracy."

Edmund smiled. "So you're going to school me on it?"

"Without a doubt."

After a visit to the tailors, they were ready to attend the governor's ball that night. Edmund dressed in a silk waistcoat, silk coat worn over the vest, stockings with trousers worn over them, neckerchief, wig, and a cocked hat with trim. Jon followed suit. The two were dressed like country magistrates.

"Imagine if Beckham saw us like this?" Jon asked.

"Yeah, he'd probably shoot us."

They still had to address the problem of getting in at the governor's mansion. It was by invitation only. Edmund didn't worry about Killingsworth recognizing him. It had been five years, and he hoped the wig, hat, and clothing would be enough of a disguise.

The next obstacle was getting in the front door. Edmund snuck into the alley at dusk. When the soldiers disappeared up the road, he signaled for Jon to follow. They waited until a ritzy carriage appeared, slowly riding up the road.

As the carriage rode by, Edmund jumped up alongside the driver. Before the driver could react, Edmund pointed a pistol in his face. Jon jumped on from the other side.

"Keep driving."

The driver's eyes bulged out. He tried to speak, but no words came out. He held the harness with shaking hands. Two men seated in the back leaned forward.

"What is the meaning of this—"

Jon answered them with two pistols.

"Where to?" the driver finally blurted.

"Just up the road will be fine."

As they pulled to a stop, Jon held a gun on the driver as Edmund jumped down and moved toward the two passengers.

"You're going to get out slowly and cooperate. If you do that, there will be no trouble."

Edmund reached into the man's suit and pulled out a large invitation. He looked over to the other man. "I take it you have one of these too."

The man slowly reached into his jacket and pulled the large card out.

"Perfect. Now what to do with you three?"

They escorted the men deep into the woods where they were bound and gagged. In the requisitioned carriage, they rode to Killingsworth's.

As they arrived at the party, they handed over the stolen invitations to the guard that manned the high entry gates. As they walked in, the opulent estate was breathtaking—formal orchards lined the walkways, well-trimmed and colorful gardens, appointed dining rooms. The two were in awe as the crowd swelled around them while the orchestra played.

Even though it was still being built, Killingsworth used the party to show the mansion's splendor to the Virginia elite and aristocrats. It would also reinforce his authority in the Americas' oldest and richest colony.

The aroma of chicken, pork, and fresh bread filled the air. Edmund thought back to the party the vicar held for him years ago.

This is a lot more extravagant than that was.

"Well, we're here. What now?" Jon asked.

They looked around. The crowd was too big to notice anyone. Finally, they located Killingsworth standing by the orchestra, entertaining aristocrats. One of them was Judge Poole. A waltz was being played, and on the dance floor, Sarah glided, wearing a silk gown that floated against her thin body. Her partner smiled, holding her hand, and held his other hand firmly against her waist.

Edmund's entire body went rigid. It reminded him of when the two of them danced. He stared at her as if in a trance until Jon nudged him.

"Get it together."

Edmund jerked and looked around. "I need to see her."

"She is lovely. No wonder you're risking everything for her."

Edmund gave him an intimidating stare. "I'm going to be quick, and then we're out of here."

By the time they made their way toward the dance floor, she was gone. So was Killingsworth. Edmund looked around and caught a glimpse of her heading into the mansion.

"Wait here," he said to Jon.

"Be careful."

Edmund snuck inside but ducked quickly behind the stairwell as he saw two guards stationed in the hall.

A loud roar was heard outside as the orchestra finished a song to a large round of applause. He heard voices coming from down the hall. It was Sarah and Killingsworth engaged in an argument.

"And don't think I don't know about your visits to the whorehouse!"

"At least they know how to satisfy a man," Killingsworth declared.

"I'm going upstairs, I don't feel well," Sarah said as she stormed out.

Killingsworth intercepted her before she left the room. He grabbed her and pulled her hard, digging his fingers into her shoulders. He thrust his face into hers. She retreated in front of him as he spoke. "You are going upstairs, and you will fix yourself up. Then you will come down and act like the perfect hostess. Do you understand?"

His grip on her arms tightened until she let out a shriek. Then he threw her toward the stairs and followed her. He grabbed a vase off a small tripod stand and threw it over his shoulder, smashing against the wall. The guards came in, took one look at Killingsworth's nasty glare then the pieces of the vase all over the floor, and walked back out. His hand shot out, clamping her wrist.

"Let go of me or I'll scream. I'll make sure every one of our guests hear me."

He released her and stepped back. Sarah's defiance was unexpected, and it appeared to amuse him.

"Go ahead. No one will pay any attention. You needn't look so alarmed, my dear." His tone was soft and pleasant. "I won't injure you physically. I'd never so much as leave the smallest mark on you. It would be bad for appearances. After all, you are a lady. You're my lady."

In spite of herself, she began to cry. She tried to hold it back, but she couldn't control it.

"Get yourself fixed up and try and put on a pleasant facade for our guests."

She rubbed her eyes and walked past him. Killingsworth stopped smiling and allowed his true emotion—rage—to show itself. He walked back outside.

Edmund snuck into the next room and hid behind the door. As Sarah walked by, he grabbed her and covered her mouth with his hand.

"Shh, not a word."

He held his gun out in case Killingsworth came back. Sarah turned, and Edmund let go of his grip. She looked at him as if she didn't recognize him at first. Then her tearful eyes bulged out as if she had just seen a ghost.

"Edmund? Is it really you? Where, what . . . ?"

"Be quiet. Where's Killingsworth?"

"He went back out to the party."

Edmund slowly closed the door. He listened for the two guards in the hall to walk by. Nothing. He turned to Sarah and eyed her up and down. She'd changed a lot, but not in ways that made it hard for him to recognize. Her hair was still golden blond, same blue eyes, but her face was more defined, more mature, and more beautiful.

"Sarah, you look incredible."

He also thought she looked tired and thin. He lurched forward to hug her, but she staggered away and slumped against the door.

"What do you want?" she blurted.

"I came to see you."

"You bastard. After all this time, where have you been? When you didn't show up that night, I kept asking myself why. Did you just run off? Did something happen to you? Were you dead?"

"I was dead," Edmund interrupted. "Thinking of you was the only thing that kept me alive."

"All I know is you pulled a disappearing act. Not a day went by that I didn't wonder what made you do it. I believed in you and you left me. You don't do that to someone you said you were in love with. How could you?" She walked toward the back of the room. "Every time Alexander touched me, I cursed you."

"Killingsworth had me kidnapped, tortured—he took away my life. And you married him?"

"I had to marry him. He threatened my father. I had no choice. Damn you."

Edmund walked up to grab her, but she shoved his chest and turned away, hugging her head with both hands. Edmund placed his hand on her back.

"You better go, this place isn't safe for you."

Her eyes were puffy and red.

"I can't go, I've come too far."

He opened his arms. She stepped between them and buried her face into his chest, sobbing uncontrollably.

"It's just that I missed you. You hurt me so much."

"I'll never hurt you again," he whispered.

She squeezed him tight. He rubbed her hair, wishing the moment would never end. If only they escaped that night when they were to meet at Myers Plantation, how things would be different.

"How did Killingsworth threaten your father?" he finally asked, breaking the silence.

"He took him with that phony stock company, they invested heavily."

"South Sea?"

She nodded her head and pulled away. Tears welled hers eyes. "Their company consists of one ship, and it sails once a year."

"And we sacked it. There was a lot of plunder aboard but not enough to pay off the war debt."

"So you've heard of it?"

"The vicar gave me bits and pieces."

"How's he doing? My father always talks of him."

"Your father?"

"Yes," she said quizzically.

"When was the last time you heard from him?"

"I just got a letter recently. He wrote everyone was doing fine. He had a stroke a year ago and was sick for a while, but his assistant wrote letters for him."

Edmund looked to the ground and then looked away.

"What is it?" she asked.

"Sarah, I was back in Bristol. Your father died almost a year ago."

She was in shock and shook her head.

"No. You're lying."

"The vicar wondered why you weren't at the funeral or at least there to see him those last days."

She clamped her eyes shut as Edmund held her in his arms. He had longed for this moment for years, but not under these circumstances. His body pressed against hers.

"Killingsworth must have had the letters written to keep you here."

"The letters, they didn't sound right, but I thought that was due to my father's illness. Alexander played me the whole time."

"Sarah, I had to see you tonight. We're breaking out McGinnty."

"Edmund, take me with you!"

He squeezed her and kissed her cheek.

"It's too dangerous. I don't even think we're going to make it out of here, but I have to try."

"Why are you risking your life for him? He's a pirate."

"Sarah, I'm a pirate. It's a long story. I am what Killingsworth created."

"No, Edmund, you are a very special person, one that I always loved. Let's just go away together."

"Sarah, I promise I'll be back for you, and nothing will stop me this time."

"No, please take me with you."

He looked into her sad eyes. "When the execution takes place, go to the harbor. It'll be chaotic, but you'll find me at the last pier on the east end."

"I'm supposed to go with Alexander to the execution. He wants to bring me for appearance's sake."

"Then get away. Any way you can. Before McGinnty is to be executed, make up some kind of excuse and ride to the harbor."

They heard footsteps outside the room and quickly hid behind the china closet.

"I have to go. This isn't safe for either of us."

She kissed him and squeezed him tight. Edmund closed his eyes and held her just as firmly.

"Someone's coming," she said as she pulled away from his grip.

"Meet me tomorrow, please."

She barely hesitated. "All right."

She quickly gave directions to the first spot that came to mind and whirled away. Edmund hurried in the other direction.

After the ball, Jon left Edmund and stopped at O'Reilly's Tavern. He lifted a mug of ale to his lips and smiled a sheepish grin. The thought of crashing the governor's ball and getting away with it was too humorous. It was a far cry from the quiet and conservative life he led in Southampton.

Maybe we can actually free McGinnty.

His thoughts turned toward Felina and his promise to be there by the birth of their child. It would be close. She was supportive in his decision to help Edmund, but also she made him promise no more adventures after this. They were going to raise a family and move back to England.

A mug of ale slammed down on the bar, interrupting his daydream.

"Why, Jon Galvin, imagine my surprise when I saw you here—in Williamsburg."

Jon turned and saw Gilgo with a smirk on his face. Next to him was Wolf who reached over and patted him on the shoulder.

"Bet you're surprised to see us," Wolf said.

Jon's first thought was to run, but he knew it would be futile.

"Hi, fellas. It's been awhile."

"I thought I saw you"—Gilgo turned to Wolf—"and said, 'Could it be?' Then I asked myself, 'Why would Jon Galvin of all people be here in Virginia? I'm surprised you left that Spanish whore back in Nassau, but then again, you got what you wanted from her."

Jon chugged the rest of his beer. "Well, guys, it was nice seeing you, but I have to run."

"Not so fast," Gilgo said. "We've heard rumblings of pirates here in Williamsburg. I don't suppose you don't know anything about that."

Jon stood up but was quickly pressed back down on his stool.

"No, I don't. We were all pardoned."

"All of you? I know if you're here, Drake isn't far behind. Where is he?"

"I think I saw him awhile ago in Nassau."

Gilgo chuckled and turned away. He waved over a man in the corner who stood up and walked over to them. The man wore a large hat, which hung down the front of his face.

"I love reunions, Galvin, and you're going to love this one."

The man approached, but Jon couldn't recognize him. He watched Gilgo shake his hand, and then Gilgo pointed his finger toward Jon.

"You don't remember your old shipmate?" the man asked.

He took off his hat. His forehead was hideously disfigured. Jon felt his breath being taken away.

"Captain Morble, I thought you were—"

"Dead? Your friend is going to wish he was the one dead on that beach when I get through with him."

Jon tried to run, but Wolf grabbed him and threw him to the floor. Patrons looked up at the disturbance, and the barkeep walked over.

"No trouble here," Gilgo said with his arms held out. "It's just a friendly reunion of old shipmates." He turned toward Jon. "Don't be an idiot. If we wanted you dead, you think we would have come over here in front of all these people. We heard rumors from some of the farmers that pirates are here to free McGinnty. We know you're not leading the charge, so I say again. Where's Drake?"

Morble grabbed Jon by the shirt and hoisted him up. The skin on his forehead was wrinkled and leathery. His left eye was white with no pupil.

"WHERE IS HE? I want payback for what he did to me."

Morble's face was wild with terror, and his fist smashed Jon's nose. Gilgo quickly stepped in between the two.

"Everything's all right," Gilgo yelled to the crowd. Blood spurted from Jon's nostrils and ran down his lips and chin. He closed his fingers over his nose to stop the flow.

"Don't be a fool, Galvin. All we want is Drake. Of course, anybody else would be extra. You'll be free to go back to that wench in Nassau unless I get to her first."

"Go to hell."

A look of surprise came over Gilgo's face, and he laughed. He threw a fist into Jon's stomach, which doubled him over. Wolf lifted him back on the barstool as Jon gasped for air. Morble went to grab Jon's neck, but Gilgo held him back.

"What? You didn't think we knew about your Spanish whore. It made me sick watching you two all lovey-dovey in Nassau. Give us Drake or your bitch will be mine for the rest of what little time she has left. My friends and I will use her with such vigor you won't be able to recognize her."

"Tomorrow night."

Jon could barely get the words out as he sucked air into his lungs. "We're meeting tomorrow night."

"Where and what time? I can't wait to get reacquainted with my old friend," Gilgo said, then leaned over to Wolf. "At £50 a pirate, we could run up a nice little tab from Killingsworth."

Jon filled them in on the details about the old barn near Pine Creek. They were to meet at the old barn near Pine Creek and organize their plan for freeing McGinnty.

Gilgo pinched Jon's cheek and then gave it a soft pat.

"Very good. And now you can leave."

Jon dusted himself off and kept his eyes on the three of them as he walked out. Gilgo and Wolf laughed. Morble stared intensely.

When Jon made it back to the room, he found Edmund fast asleep. He crawled into bed and stared at the ceiling until dawn.

CHAPTER 26

PINE CREEK

The next morning, General Pitts was frantically organizing security for McGinnty's execution. He checked out the courtyard and was plotting points on a map of where he wanted his soldiers located. He had warned his men of the large crowd that was expected and received orders from Killingsworth not to let the crowd get out of hand.

"I want thirty men inside the courtyard, lined up along the gallows, to oversee the crowd," he told his lieutenant, pointing to the exact location on his map. "Place the sharpshooters along the rail up high. I want no foul ups." He stopped and watched two guards blocking one of the locals. The man had a panic-stricken look on his face. The guards threw him back and raised their muskets at the man's chest.

Pitts threw his map down and marched over.

"What the hell is going on here? Who the hell are you?"

"Jed Snead, sir. I'm a farmer. My place is just outside Pine Creek. I've looked all over for you. I need to speak to you."

"What is it? I'm busy," Pitts said, looking him up and down. "Make it quick."

He picked up his map as Jed spoke, "Sir, the farmers of this state have been threatened. Pirates have infiltrated Williamsburg."

Pitts looked up. His eyes were at attention, and his interest peaked. He waved the soldiers to back off and approached Jed.

"Pirates you say? I haven't seen or heard of any here."

"Have you heard the name Edmund Drake?"

"Drake? The name escapes me."

Where have I heard the name Edmund Drake?

He remembered hearing something about that name at Killingsworth's plantation house. Killingsworth and Captain Morble were discussing something about him, but what? Pitts's thoughts were interrupted as Jed went on.

"He has threatened the farmers of Williamsburg unless we help him free McGinnty. I was wondering if you could ask Lord Killingsworth for help."

"You mean Drake is going to try and free McGinnty? How is he going to do that? We have guards and soldiers everywhere."

"I don't know. I'm meeting him tonight. I need Lord Killingsworth's protection."

"Hmm. Let's take care of this business ourselves. Where are you meeting him?"

"We're meeting tonight at an old deserted barn near my place at Pine Creek. It's surrounded by woods except for a small clearing in the front."

"Pine Creek you say? If we can gather them all there, we could have the barn surrounded and trap them. Maybe we can leave Lord Killingsworth out of this. He has enough on his mind. We can take care of this little matter ourselves."

Edmund walked outside the tiny burned-out church. It was well hidden in the woods and could be reached only by following a long and winding path near Killingsworth's plantation. As Edmund waited, he became increasingly certain that Sarah wouldn't show. The church was a perfect spot for a meeting as it was surrounded by woods on three sides. The fourth side offered a breathtaking view of the marsh. As he pushed away the last overhanging branches, a horse whickered. Underbrush stirred. Sarah appeared at the edge of the marsh to his left.

Screened by some trees, she quickly jerked around.

"I didn't even think how dangerous it was for you to come," Edmund said.

"I just told the house servants I wanted to ride by myself for a while. They know Alexander can be insufferable. Besides, he's heavily involved with McGinnty and all the politicians in town."

Her hair was tied back, and the sun reflected off her blue eyes.

"You look better than ever."

"You too," she said.

Edmund's heart started racing. Sarah leaned up against his arm. Edmund looked down at her. Their faces were drawn together, and he noticed her eyes darting up and down. He could smell the warm scent of her breath.

"I've waited so long to be with you," he said.

"Me too," she whispered.

Sarah turned herself sideway and slipped her arm around Edmund's back. They both leaned toward each other and put their arms around one another and kissed. They kissed. Sarah's lips felt dry and cracked, but it was the best kiss ever.

She loosened her grip on him and pulled away. She still remained close as she stared into his eyes. Edmund stared back. Smiling softly, she leaned toward him again. Her lips barely touched his when she pulled them away and started to laugh.

"I must be dreaming," she said as tears rolled down her cheek.

Edmund opened his mouth but couldn't talk. His head was spinning until he finally managed to say, "Same here."

They went inside and lay on a rough mattress of hay. He caressed her soft skin while she stroked his hair. Edmund peeled off Sarah's layers of clothing. She took off his shirt as they rolled into each other's arms.

Her hands roamed his backside against scars received compliments of the British Royal Navy. She was timid about touching them at first.

Edmund grabbed her buttocks with his hand. His fingertips slipped into her crease, and she slowly swung her leg over him. She rolled him on his back and came down on top of him. Edmund ran his hands up and down her back and rump. She eased herself down, taking him in slowly and deeply. Her mouth was on his, and she thrust up and down on him. Sweat dripped off her nose and onto Edmund's face. She was breathing hard. Edmund took her breasts in his hand and squeezed them. She moaned and arched her back. Edmund thrust upward and erupted inside of her.

For a long time, they lay next to each other—staring at the sky, panting for air, and dripping with sweat. Edmund took hold of her hand and closed his eyes.

This is the way it should be. The way it was meant to be.

He had almost given up all hope of them being together. The hot wind seemed to cool their bodies, and soon they fell asleep.

When Edmund awoke, Sarah was sprawled on top of him, asleep and breathing slowly. He felt her breath on his chest. Edmund smiled and caressed her hair. He gently jostled her shoulder. Her head moved, and she let out a soft moan.

"I thought I was dreaming," she said with a smile.

"I don't think I can move."

Edmund watched Sarah as she put on her clothes. Her hands were trembling.

As the night approached, Edmund met Jed in the barn. With McGinnty's execution scheduled for noon the next day, all plans had to be precise. They sat down at a makeshift desk, which they assembled for the quick meeting.

"Now we wait."

Jed looked around conspicuously. Edmund fumbled with his blunderbuss, which he treated like a gavel, and noticed Jed fidgeting.

"You seem nervous, Jed."

"I'm all right, just a little antsy."

"Everything will work out," Edmund assured him.

The fact was Edmund hoped everything would work out. Beckham and the other men arrived from North Carolina that afternoon and had unloaded the cannons. They were to plant them around the city later that night. Charles spent the afternoon scouting out a fast ship, and he would take a few men to confiscate it in the morning. The men were stretched thin and, on this night, would go without sleep.

Jed continued to pace back and forth. "I'm going to go for a walk, grab some air."

Edmund looked at him for moment. "Not too long, the men will be here soon."

Jed looked back and walked hastily toward the barn door. As he went to grab it, the barn door burst open. Gilgo and his men stormed in, shoving Jed backward. They surrounded Edmund, who raised a lantern from his desk and pointed the blunderbuss at Gilgo.

"Is that any way to treat an old shipmate? Put the gun down, Drake. I want you alive."

Edmund stayed steady on his target.

"Gilgo, what are you doing here?"

"Haven't you heard? I now hunt pirates for a living, and I might add I'm quite successful at it."

"You turned McGinnty in, didn't you?"

"He was almost as easy to capture as you."

"When you left New Providence, you met with Killingsworth before meeting them at Ocracoke. You set him up. The only way McGinnty would have been caught was if he was betrayed by someone he trusted. You were there feeding information to Killingsworth all along." Edmund cocked the blunderbuss.

Gilgo nodded in agreement. "When you knocked me off the ship, it delayed the process, but everything worked out as planned. The governor paid me well for his capture. Now let's not have any trouble. Hand over the gun."

"Not before I take you out."

"I'm surprised at you, Drake. You're really taken by this pirate life. I thought you would just disappear and go back to England. Wait a minute—you can't go back to England, can you? As much as I'd like to take credit for that, meet the man that is responsible, your old captain."

Captain Morble stepped out from the shadows. He wore a grin that stretched from ear to ear.

"We finally meet again." He whipped out a pistol and a cutlass.

Pitts was waiting for Jed to slip outside the barn. As soon as he was safe, Jed would fire a shot that would signal Pitts and his men to attack. Pitts left an opening outside the rear entrance so Jed and any farmers trapped inside could escape. Every other path of escape was closed off. He watched a group of twenty pirates walk in. When Pitts was satisfied that all was showing up, he waited.

He was excited. To suppress a pirate uprising, this could be the nice little feather in his cap. It would go a long way in Killingsworth's eyes, and he would get the recognition and status of being one of the leading generals in the colonies. Killingsworth had recently lost confidence in him because of his failures at stopping the local bootlegging and smuggling epidemic that had ramped down the east coast. Now he was going to prove him wrong. Fifty soldiers surrounded the barn, ready to strike. If the pirates didn't surrender, they would pick them off one by one as they tried to escape.

Edmund raised his hands. One was holding the lantern; and the other, a blunderbuss. He pulled the trigger, and the explosion jolted Gilgo and his men. With the other hand, he threw the lantern against the side of the barn. It smashed over a pile of hay, which was quickly engulfed in flames. Gilgo held a pistol to Edmund.

"No, he's mine!" screamed Morble.

Outside the barn, a loud piercing whistle went off. Wolf checked a small window.

"There's men all around us."

"Must be Drake's men," Gilgo said, then turned to Edmund. "So it's a fight you want."

"Surrender in the king's name," yelled a voice outside the barn.

Wolf laughed. "That's a good one." He cocked his pistol and fired into the woods. His shot was answered with a heavy round of fire from the woods. Wolf yelped and tripped over himself as a ball crashed against his skull.

Meanwhile, the fire inside was out of hand. The far sidewall was going up, and smoke filled the room, making it hard to breathe. The room was well lit, but smoke limited their vision.

Gunshots were fired at the barn, and Edmund slipped back and pulled a scarf over his face to avoid breathing in smoke. Gilgo and Morble raced to the opening to look out but couldn't see anything.

"Drake, are those your men? Tell them to halt or we'll kill you."

"My men aren't here."

Edmund pulled out a packet of powder and ripped off an opening with his teeth. He poured the powder into the barrel. He followed the powder with a ball and jammed it down.

Gilgo's men were racing around, trying to find windows to get into position to shoot. The fire was now out of control. Both sides exchanged gunfire. The fog inside was too thick, and breathing was now a major concern.

"Make a run for it," Gilgo yelled. "There's only a few of them out there."

Edmund grabbed Gilgo. He brought down the blunderbuss, and it cracked against Gilgo's head. Gilgo dropped to his knees then fell forward, his face hitting the ground with a thud.

"C'mon, we have to leave now," Jed said, grabbing Edmund's elbow.

Edmund placed his blunderbuss down and bent over to pick up Gilgo. He sensed a presence right behind him. Turning, he saw a shadow. The shadow swung an object. Edmund quickly ducked as Morble's cutlass whooshed by the side of his head. Edmund reached into his boot and pulled out a knife. He quickly thrust the blade into Morble's thigh. He pulled it out and thrust again into Morble's groin. Blood pooled around the ground beneath them. Morble dropped his cutlass as Edmund thrust the knife upward as hard as he could. He drove the point through Morble's neck. The blade punched deep into the skin. Blood ran hot down the blade and covered Edmund's hands. He looked like he was wearing a crimson glove.

Morble contorted in agony. He gulped his last breath of air and slumped into Edmund's arms.

"Grab Gilgo," Edmund yelled to Jed, and Edmund threw the bloody corpse of Captain Morble over his back and followed Jed out the back.

As they left, they heard the agonizing screams of Gilgo's men being picked off by the soldiers.

Jed led Edmund to a shack where everyone was to meet. It was located in the woods half a mile from the ambush of Gilgo's men. As they walked through the door, Beckham greeted them with a relieved look on his face. Everyone cheered.

"We're not done yet. Not by a long shot," Edmund said and then turned to Beckham. "Cannons in place?"

"Aye, but one problem. We saw some of Beale's men in town."

"Was Beale with them?"

"We didn't see him."

"Jon, did you and Charles get a ship?"

Jon laughed. "You're not going to believe this, but we got *Hellspite* back. It was practically deserted tonight."

"That's because everyone that was usually on board was after us, including him."

He shoved Gilgo forward. Gilgo was semiconscious and stumbled, taking two steps before falling onto the floor, sending up a billow of dust.

"What are you going to do with him?" Jon asked.

"Make an example out of him. We're going to show what happens to traitors. There's another piece of meat outside."

Gilgo screamed and stumbled toward the door. Charles tackled him.

"Gag him."

Charles took a sash and wrapped it around Gilgo's mouth. He squeezed it tight.

"Jed, tomorrow you'll lead McGinnty and his men to Beck's ship. It'll be docked up river. By the way, I can't thank you enough. You did nice work tonight."

"I still don't give a hoot for McGinnty, but I care for Killingsworth less."

Edmund turned toward Jon. "After our visit to the prison, you need to get Sarah to Beck's ship also. It'll be safer than *Hellspite.* Charles, have *Hellspite* loaded up and ready to sail. The pier is the diversion. We'll all meet at Ocracoke as soon as we can."

CHAPTER 27

LAST RITES

During the morning of McGinnty's execution, Edmund dressed in a vicar's garb and nervously walked to the jail cell with Jon at his side. They both garnered wigs, and Edmund kept a pistol hidden in his robes to help him ease his nerves. Killingsworth had appointed all Anglican priests in Virginia, so Edmund used the notion McGinnty was Catholic and, therefore, needed a Catholic priest. The wardrobe wasn't much different, and Edmund used their newly acquired gold to make a donation for the apparel.

"Halt," one of the guards ordered. There were two at the main entrance, and others positioned around the small brick building.

"We are to deliver a service to the prisoner," Edmund announced.

The two guards looked at each other. "Wait here," one said, and one went inside.

Edmund knew they were taking a chance visiting the prison, but he had to tell McGinnty of their plans. The timing and execution of their plan had to be precise.

A jailor came out and looked the two over.

"What are you doing?" the jailor asked.

"Last rites. I am to address the prisoner, and he's to repent his sins," Edmund quickly answered.

"And what about him?" he asked, pointing to Jon.

"He is here to assist me."

The jailor shrugged. "You look a little young to be a parson, and I've never seen you in these parts."

"McGinnty's not Anglican. He deserves prayer from someone of his own faith. With all due respect, none of the others wanted to be here. Since I'm the newest, I was assigned."

"All right, you follow me," he said to Edmund. They walked inside the main corridor, and the jailor turned to Jon. "You wait here, only one visitor at a time."

The jailor escorted Edmund down the hall. Empty cells were to their right as McGinnty's men were taken to the galleys already. Killingsworth wanted McGinnty paraded through the streets separately. The jail was as quiet as a morgue.

The last cell held a prisoner lying in a large pile of dirty hay. A rat whisked by his feet.

"Up on your feet, show some respect to the reverend," the jailor yelled as he led Edmund to the jail door. McGinnty lurched to his feet. He had shackles on his hands and ankles. A small chair stood just outside of the bars.

Edmund placed his Bible on it and stepped up to the jailor. "I'm about to conduct a service. I'd like to be alone with the prisoner."

"It's not safe, he's a tricky devil," the jailor replied in a shocked tone.

Edmund turned and looked at the jailor. "I'll be the judge of that. He's locked in a cell. What harm could he do me? Please leave us so I can attempt to free the soul of this heathen."

The guard looked surprised. He shook his head and walked away as Edmund started his service.

"Lift up your heart. Let us pray. Maybe the Lord will have mercy on your soul."

McGinnty clasped his hands as though in prayer. Edmund looked over to make sure the guard was out of range.

"So you want to hear my sins, do you?" McGinnty asked. "Sorry I couldn't offer you better accommodations."

"Sir, it was Gilgo that set you up. He sold you out to Killingsworth."

"They ambushed us right outside of Bath. They killed half the men."

"We have him now. We're going to make an example out of traitors."

"Maybe he can hang alongside the rest of us."

"We're going to get you out." And he whispered the plans to McGinnty. Edmund looked at the shackles surrounding McGinnty's wrists and ankles. "Those present a dilemma."

McGinnty pointed down the hall. "The keys are down the hall, if we can get them." Edmund saw a set of keys dangling high near a lantern, suspended on the wall near the corridor entrance.

"They'll probably keep the same shackles on you when they take you to the courtyard."

"You can't just steal them. They'd search all over with you as a main suspect."

Edmund noticed candles under the lantern. "What if we make a copy? Help me stall for time."

Edmund walked down the hall and grabbed the keys and tucked them under his robe. He met the jailor in the main hallway to escort him out of the prison.

"You're a good man, Father. He's not worth your time. He's a hopeless case."

Jon nodded solemnly. "It's the hopeless that are in most need of prayer."

Edmund hit his hand against his forehead.

"My Bible. I forgot my Bible. Could you be so kind?" Then he whispered, "I can't bear seeing him again."

The guard walked back as Edmund grabbed a candle off the wall and spilled hot wax on the bottom of an unlit candleholder to soften the leftover wax already on it. He indented the keys quickly, blowing on the wax to harden it. In the background, he could hear the jailor and McGinnty arguing. The jail cell door closed, and the jailor's footsteps came toward him. He quickly placed the keys on the wall and the wax indentation under his robe. The keys had small pieces of wax stuck to them.

"What have we here?"

The voice came from behind. Edmund froze. The wax holder was slipping beneath his robe.

"Parson!"

Edmund slowly turned. Sweat filled his forehead. Killingsworth approached, hands clasped behind his back.

"You mean me, sir? I'm a priest."

Killingsworth's icy stare penetrated Edmund who returned an icy stare of his own.

"Who are you, and what are you doing here?"

The jailor walked back and came to a halt when he saw Killingsworth.

"Last rites, my lord. He gave the prisoner last rites," the jailor stammered, handing the Bible to Edmund. Killingsworth quickly grabbed it.

"Go find General Pitts. I need him immediately."

"But the parson?"

"I'm sure he can find his own way out."

The jailor nodded and quickly left. It was now Killingsworth and Edmund.

"I don't give last rites to murderers," Killingsworth said.

"It's one of my duties, sir," Edmund replied. A drop of sweat fell from his nose.

"Well, it's not a duty I'd relish. It's bad enough with the stench of this place."

"Our duties are not always made easy. If that is all, I must be going."

Edmund started to walk away.

"Stop!"

Edmund froze in his tracks. He rubbed his robe and traced the pistol with his hands.

"You forgot something. What kind of parson would you be without this?" Killingsworth said, handing over the Bible.

"Priest, sir."

"Good day."

Killingsworth disappeared around the corner, and Edmund could hear his footsteps until they came to a silence. Edmund peeked around the corner to observe Killingsworth in front of McGinnty's cell.

"Ah, McGinnty, I hope you're enjoying my accommodations for your last few hours on this earth. I have to admit, I'm enjoying the attention I'm receiving, being the one responsible for your capture as well as the scar on your face."

McGinnty stood motionless against the back wall of his cell as Killingsworth continued, "We never did find the *Lucinda*'s treasure. I guess we never will. There will be no bargaining. This time, you will not escape."

"This time?"

"What did you think? You just walked out of Newgate with ease? I arranged that. Of course, it turned out to be a waste. We never located your treasure, and you never led us to it. What a shame. All of this could have been avoided if you had just dealt with me. Why?"

McGinnty moved closer, holding his hands against the bars. "Maybe I just don't like you. The people of Virginia will come to know just what you are."

"What I am is the man to bring down the notorious pirate Jack McGinnty."

"What about my men? We were in North Carolina. Eden was going to offer my men a pardon. You have no jurisdiction there. Your soldiers butchered them."

Killingsworth rubbed his chin and leaned back. Edmund jerked back to stay out of sight.

"You're a fool. You and your men are ruthless pirates. You have no rights. As far as Eden, we know of no pardons to you or your men, and he has no jurisdiction here. I am the law here."

"Someday, the tide will turn against you," McGinnty said as he shook the cell.

"I gave you a fair trial, and you were found guilty. Soon you will dangle from a rope with a broken neck, choking on your vomit, and I will be drinking wine and celebrating."

"You know, you should have waited one more day to ambush us. We were on our way to pick up the treasure. It is more wealth than you've ever seen, and now it will die with me. You'll never get your hands on it."

Killingsworth took out his sword and slammed it against the bars on the cell as McGinnty flew backward.

Edmund pulled his pistol out from under his robe and cocked it. He had waited for this moment for six years. He took two steps from the corner then seemed to reconsider.

"Don't do it," a voice said from behind.

Edmund held still and grimaced. Footsteps came from his back side until they were beside him. He slowly turned.

"Are you out of your mind?" Jon asked as he pulled him back, safely hidden from Killingsworth.

Edmund let out a breath of relief. “What are you doing here?”

“Never mind me. I saw Killingsworth come in here and the jailor leaving in a hurry. I thought something happened to you. I got here just in time. Put that pistol away. If you shoot him, everything we’ve worked for would be wasted. There are soldiers everywhere, and it’s just you and me here. We have everything in place, stay the course.”

CHAPTER 28

MCGINNTY'S EXECUTION

A packed house waited for the procession to begin. The courtyard looked like a minifortress as three sides were surrounded by a large brick wall, which prevented anyone from saving the condemned. Soldiers were positioned strategically throughout the area with most of them concentrated at the open entrance.

The galleys were built quickly and placed in the middle of the courtyard—an area usually reserved for speeches and meetings. This day would serve as a reminder to everyone of Lord Killingsworth's domain.

McGinnty was marched down the streets and arrived to a hostile crowd, his hands and ankles in shackles, as soldiers parted the crowd.

"Hang 'em high!"

"String him up!"

Fruits and tomatoes were thrown in his direction as he made his way to the stockade. Some hit the guards, which resulted in angry stares.

Killingsworth had spread tales of rape, pillage, and murder, which fueled an uproar throughout Williamsburg. The crowd wanted a glimpse of the famous pirate Jack McGinnty.

Edmund searched the crowd. He remained in his vicar's garb although it was hot and humid, pistol by his side underneath the robe.

He worried about the slight breeze, which would affect their escape when they reached the water—if they reached the water.

The courtyard was wall-to-wall with people and tough to maneuver through. It was just what he anticipated. His men were in place, scattered throughout the crowd. Jed's men also surrounded the inside walls. Jed gave a nod to Edmund and waited for the signal.

As they walked up the steps to the galley, McGinnty stopped and stared at the hangman's noose. He saw each of his crewmembers lined up side-by-side with nooses around their necks.

"A lovely day for an execution," the guard said as he nudged McGinnty forward.

Killingsworth watched from atop the main courtyard building with Sarah by his side. He had his own sanctuary up there where he watched many a pirate swing from the hangman's noose. Watching with him were local magistrates and squires, including Judge Poole. They were all drinking wine.

The executioner turned McGinnty toward the crowd and slipped the noose around his neck.

Edmund forced his way up to the front. Finally, he made eye contact with McGinnty. His right hand covered the side of his face as he mouthed, "Stall."

"Any last requests?" the executioner asked. Last requests were always given to the condemned as a last chance to ask forgiveness.

McGinnty paused and stared at the crowd, which suddenly became silent. They waited for him to say something. Would he repent his sins? Would he tell the whereabouts of his famous treasure?

Judge Poole turned toward Killingsworth. "This should be good."

"I would like a glass of wine," McGinnty announced.

The executioner looked quizzical and gestured to one of the guards who left and went inside the building.

Edmund noticed his men twitching. He looked to Jed. He looked to the soldiers. Also to Killingsworth with Sarah behind him. Jon was in place to the side of the galley. He was to make sure to unlock the shackles and lead McGinnty out. Would the key fit?

A soldier came out moments later carrying a chalice.

The executioner reached behind McGinnty then unlocked the chains on his wrists. McGinnty rubbed his wrists as the chalice was handed to him. He smelled the wine, then raised the cup high, and turned to the men lined up alongside.

"A toast to my crew whose loyalty I shall miss." He turned toward the crowd. "To the people of Virginia who know nothing about loyalty." He brought the chalice to his lips and stopped. Then he raised it high in the air again and turned toward the top of the courtyard building where he spotted Killingsworth.

"And to you, I'll see you in hell!" He drank.

"Not anytime soon I'm afraid," Killingsworth muttered and then gave the go-ahead.

The executioner stepped back and threw a hood over McGinnty's head. He jerked McGinnty's arms behind and tied his arms on the elbows. The rope was thrown over the hood and secured tightly around McGinnty's neck. Sarah stood up and excused herself.

"I'm sorry, I can't watch this."

Killingsworth turned red and reached for her as Judge Trotter laughed.

"Let her go. She probably doesn't have the stomach for this anyway."

"No, she's going to watch."

Edmund waited for Sarah to leave. Sweat stung his eyes.

Get out of here.

The executioner headed for the lever and paused. Killingsworth jerked Sarah back into her seat. He then looked down at the condemned and gave the nod.

There's no time left. Now or never.

As the executioner pulled, Edmund gritted his teeth, pulled the pistol from under his robe, and fired. The executioner stumbled backward, grabbing his shoulder. Men lit the smoke bombs from all sides and threw them into the crowd.

Cannon fire from the outskirts of town blasted the buildings as men and women screamed, running into each other, looking for cover. Walls crumbled, and brick flew everywhere. The soldiers, not knowing who to shoot at, looked for orders.

A musket came at Edmund. The muzzle rose toward him. Edmund grimaced, waiting to be hit by the blast, but a clap of thunder came from behind him and knocked the soldier off his feet. Jon looked at his pistol as smoke was rising from the barrel.

"Get McGinnty!"

Jon pulled out his key and raced to the galley. There was so much smoke that visibility was next to impossible. Smoke bombs landed all around.

Someone grabbed Edmund from behind and knocked off his wig. Edmund landed an elbow to the man's jaw and ran to the platform. He picked up the executioner's sword and swung through the ropes above the heads of each of the condemned men, then cut through the ropes that bound their hands.

Jon shoved the keys in McGinnty's shackles and freed him. Jon was quickly tackled by one of the guards and wrestled to the ground. McGinnty lifted the soldier off Jon and threw him off the galley stage. A free-for-all broke out. The soldiers didn't know who to shoot at.

Edmund made it to the wall below Killingsworth. The smoke had started to subside.

Killingsworth shouted from the top building but could not be heard in all the screaming. He wanted a large crowd to witness his triumph, but now chaos had ensued. People were running into each other. Sarah ran to the stairs.

The soldiers tried to guard all exits, but the crowd ran around frantically, bumping into them and each other. The smoke started to clear, and guards were grabbing anyone they could. There were too many people.

Edmund hesitated for a second and thought about going after Killingsworth. He looked up at the top of the courtyard building, but his vision was still obstructed by smoke. He started to run and looked back again. He wanted to make sure Sarah was gone. He didn't see her as the soldiers regained their vision.

Jon grabbed him. "We have to leave now!"

Edmund started to run but noticed Killingsworth pointing at him through the haze.

"Drake!" Killingsworth screamed but could not be heard among the crowd's noise.

"Now!" Jon yelled, shaking Edmund. "We have to get to the ship now."

Edmund moved toward Killingsworth, but Jon threw him toward the entrance and they started to run. He kept looking back when a guard grabbed him. Edmund struck him with the butt end of his cutlass, sending him to the ground.

"Where's McGinnty?"

"I don't know."

"Go to the harbor. Tell Charles to get *Hellspite* in motion."

"What about you?"

"If I'm not there when you're ready to leave, go without me."

Edmund looked for Sarah, but there was no way to find her. There were too many people.

"Please be at the pier."

As the courtyard cleared, Killingsworth made it down to the stockade. Cannon fire ceased as men and women ran past the gates. All the pirates that were condemned to death in the galleys were gone except for McGinnty. He dangled loosely from the rope. His body was limp.

"Get to the pier," Killingsworth shouted to the soldiers. "Cut off all escape routes!" As he looked up at the body, a smirk came to his face. He reached up to pull off the sack covering his head and gave it a yank. He jerked backward.

"That blasted bloody bastard!" he screamed.

It was Gilgo swinging on the rope. His tongue fell limply from his mouth as his eyes bulged out of their sockets.

Killingsworth looked up. "The harbor. Sarah."

He quickly grabbed one of his mounted soldiers and threw him off his horse. He yelled at two other guards that looked confused, "Follow me."

When Edmund and Jon arrived at Williamsburg harbor, they were greeted by Captain Morble's dead carcass suspended from the gallows. It hung the way McGinnty's body was supposed to dangle after his hanging. Dried brown blood caked the front of his shirt. Tar covered his face and body to slow the decomposition.

Meanwhile, soldiers grabbed anyone they could get their hands on. Even women were being held up as the chaos ensued.

"Let's hurry," Edmund yelled, and they sprinted to the pier.

Two soldiers ran after them, and Edmund pulled out his one pistol remaining and a cutlass. Jon was empty-handed.

"Where's Charles?"

"I don't see him," Jon answered. "Over there." He pointed to men waving their arms from *Hellspite* two docks away. The ship was heading out, and a third sail was launched.

"Go," Edmund yelled. "Get on the ship and get moving. Don't wait for me. I've got to find Sarah."

The soldiers came up to Edmund as Jon took off. He swung his cutlass and knocked one of the soldiers off balance, landing him in the water. The second stared at Edmund with a frightful look in his eyes. He nervously grabbed his sword and lunged. Edmund deflected it with ease and aimed his pistol at the man's chest, then signaled him over to the dock's edge. The soldier lurched backward.

"Jump."

The soldier dropped his sword and hurled himself into the water. *Hellspite* was sailing away and supplied cover as shooting began.

Edmund looked for Sarah and then started to scream her name. He turned and saw her two piers away, waving her arms. He also saw Killingsworth dismounting and running in her direction. Edmund sprinted after them.

As Sarah made her way toward Edmund, she was jerked from behind.

"Trying to relive the old days? Well, this is one reunion you're not going to make."

A look of shock came across her face as Killingsworth looked up and saw a blunderbuss pointed at his face. He quickly grabbed Sarah to shield him as Edmund fired.

Killingsworth fell back, grabbing his shoulder. Sarah peeled off him and ran to Edmund as they raced toward the dock. Killingsworth, from the ground, aimed his pistol and fired. A ball whizzed by Edmund's head and rang off a wooden pole.

They arrived at the dock's edge and turned around.

"We have to jump."

He grabbed her by the hand and entered the water. They swam underwater to where they thought *Hellspite* would be. Sarah fell behind, so Edmund grabbed her by the arm and pulled her forward. His air was running out, and his chest felt like it was going to explode. Edmund and Sarah popped their heads out of the water and gave a quick look around. Soldiers ran to the edge of the dock and aimed their muskets at them.

Killingsworth rammed into the soldier about to shoot.

"You idiot! That's my wife out there."

They continued to swim. Edmund was kicking like a madman. Sarah started windmilling her arms, slapping the water. There were shouts and shots being fired behind them. Edmund couldn't make out anything but the sound of splashing. Sarah's head was up, blinking the water out of her eyes.

"C'mon, just a little longer."

The crew on *Hellspite* was cheering them on, and one of them threw a rope toward them. Edmund's lungs were burning. Sarah started coughing as Edmund grabbed her arm and guided her to the rope. Edmund wrapped his arms around her, protecting her, and held the rope tight. The crew yanked them to the edge, and Edmund shoved Sarah on board.

A hand stuck out, and Edmund grabbed it. He looked up and saw the hand helping him belonged to Beale. With a sly grin, Beale crashed his other hand against Edmund's chin, sending him to the deck. Beale ordered full sail and to fire the cannons. Grapeshot scattered the soldiers on the wharf.

Hellspite headed down the James River toward the Atlantic Ocean. It fired chained cannonballs at the masts of the navy ships docked in the harbor. Most were left unoccupied or with small crews so most available soldiers could attend and provide security at the execution.

Edmund looked around. Charles lay motionless in the corner, blood matted against his hair. Jon looked over, shaking his head. The crew was large. Beale must have recruited heavily while in Williamsburg. Many faces Edmund didn't recognize. He did recognize the five men from Beale's crew that swore allegiance to him.

Soldiers lined the shoreline with muskets from both sides as *Hellspite* sailed down the narrows. A blizzard of shot began to sweep the deck. Edmund crawled over to Sarah, grabbing her. He threw her below decks and hugged the floor. Splinters sprang up all around as volleys of musket balls ricocheted off the deck as the crew kept low. The opening of the narrows was now in sight. Beale grabbed a telescope and looked ahead. The ship started drifting toward the shoreline. Beale yelled at the helmsman, but he wasn't there. Below the wheel was a body covered in blood. There was no cover for anyone that steered the ship.

"Galvin, grab the wheel and get us out of here," Beale yelled.

"I'll do it," Edmund replied. He started to crawl over.

Beale grabbed his shirt and wrestled him down. "I said him. I give the orders now."

"He's never steered before."

As the words left his mouth, gunfire tore through the sails and mast. Jon raced to the wheel and navigated the ship back toward the middle of the river. He knelt on one knee and used one arm to steer, staying as low as possible.

In the distance, a ship carrying three masts was sailing toward them. It was small because of the distance, but with its flag waving, there was no mistake it was a British warship.

Beale looked over at Edmund, screaming over the shots that resumed firing from the shoreline.

"What kind of weapons do we have?"

"They didn't leave us with much," Edmund shouted back. "Most of the cannons were left outside the city to blast the courtyard walls."

"Fire a few rounds of grapeshot."

Cannons exploded, and shrapnel filled the banks and scattered the soldiers positioned on the banks, halting their fire.

Hellspite was closing in on the mouth of the harbor as the warship closed in. The crew looked on, waiting for orders.

"Winds are from the southwest," Edmund yelled to Jon. "It's in our face now and at their back. We have to get out to the Chesapeake before they cut us off."

Six rounds fired from the warship splashed fifty feet in front of them.

"We're faster than them," Edmund said.

Six more rounds were fired, splashing dangerously close. Edmund looked at the ship and the forty guns blasting simultaneously at them. He saw their captain ranting and barking out orders.

The ship was rocked as a cannonball blew through the side of the ship. *Hellspite* made it to the mouth of the narrows, and the men cranked the sails to the starboard side. The helmsman spun the wheel hard, and the ship turned northeast bound to the Atlantic. The warship kept its angle on them and was cutting them off.

Hellspite fired back as another ball blew through its side, destroying one of the cannons and the men that were manning it.

They picked up speed, but the galleon kept its angle. Edmund raced below decks and saw the two large holes surrounded by pieces of wood dangling.

"Throw the cannons overboard! We need to get faster, throw them."

The men looked at him like he was crazy. Another cannonball blew a hole in the side, this one dangerously close to the waterline. Edmund ran and grabbed a cannon, but it would not budge. The rest of the men teamed up and struggled to push it through one of the holes. It finally tipped over the side and splashed into the ocean.

"Let's fire 'em and dump 'em," Edmund yelled.

Hellspite picked up speed, and the warship started to lose its angle. They were safe from the galleon's side guns, but the guns on top of the deck were being maneuvered and aimed at them.

This is going to be close.

The galleon was now directly behind *Hellspite*, trying to draft it, but it was too heavy and falling behind.

As a last-ditch attempt to slow *Hellspite*, the galleon peppered rounds of grapeshot that tore up the deck. Everyone jumped for cover. Splinters tore through Edmund's shin as he crawled behind a barrel, which leaked rum. He looked up and saw Jon hug the wheel.

Edmund rose up but was quickly hugging the deck as more shots peppered the deck, but they were pulling away.

Minutes seemed like hours as the cannons still went off, but nothing was reaching the deck. *Hellspite* was finally out of firing range.

"We're gonna make it," Edmund yelled.

He poked his head up, and now the warship was getting smaller.

"We made it. Jon, we made it!"

Edmund looked around as bodies slowly rose from the deck. Pirates checked themselves for cuts and abrasions. Different types of metal were embedded in the wood all over the ship. Sails were torn, and several bodies lay motionless. Jon hugged the wheel, his head held down.

Edmund sprinted over and wrapped his arm around him. "We made it. Nice job grabbing the—Jon?"

Edmund looked down and saw blood spurting from Jon's neck. He quickly lowered him onto the deck and tried to place his hand against Jon's neck but stopped. There was a thin piece of metal embedded in his throat. He hesitated pulling it out for fear of blood gushing even faster. Blood from other cuts started to seep through his shirt. He grabbed Jon's head and cradled it. Jon looked up at Edmund, his eyes were lost as he tried to speak. Each shallow whistling breath sounded like it may be his last. His hand gripped Edmund's sleeve and tried to pull him closer. Edmund bent down and leaned in. Blood gurgled out the side of Jon's mouth. His words were hoarse and raspy.

"Felin . . ."

"Don't say anything," Edmund said, taking off his shirt.

Beale raced over. Edmund turned to him. "We have to get that out. When I grab it, cover the wound with this."

"He's dead, leave him," Beale said.

"Please, we can save him."

Jon looked at Edmund. His eyes were lifeless. Edmund closed his eyes and turned his head skyward. He tried to cover the wound but was careful not to move the sharp object embedded in Jon's throat.

"We need to go back. He needs a doctor."

"No. I told you he is dead."

Beale pulled his pistol out of his sash and fired, blowing a hole in Jon's stomach.

Edmund screamed and surged at Beale, tackling him on the deck. The men pounced on the pile and pried the two apart.

"You better think this through," Beale said, catching his breath. "I know you want to kill me so bad you can taste it. But think about your beloved below decks."

Men surrounded Edmund with pistols pointed at him. He thought of Sarah down below and backed off. From the corner of his eye, Charles elbowed the man watching him and ran at Beale. He was in full sprint when Edmund dove and tackled him. Charles kept coming and beat him over the side of his head with his fist, determined to get up. Edmund held on with everything he had, clasping his hands around Charles's back.

"It's not the time. Please, Charles, you'll only get us killed."

Charles let up.

"Wise move," Beale said and lurched to his feet.

“Believe me, I want him dead more than anything, but now is not the time,” Edmund whispered.

“Tie Drake up,” Beale ordered. He walked toward the steps to go below deck.

Sarah.

Edmund jumped up, but pistols were pointed at his face. Two men grabbed him. Beale pointed at Charles.

“Kill him. Hang him for that incident above the powder room.”

“No,” Edmund argued. “What about the South Sea ship? I can get you there, but Charles is the only one who knows where to meet McGinnty.

“You’re lying. He’s illiterate.”

“I’m telling you. We lose him, we lose the location.” Edmund’s eyes stared intently.

Beale laughed and shook his head.

“All right, I’ll buy it. If this is a trick or you’re stalling for time, that bitch down there will be used with such vigor by every man on board she’ll wish she were dead.”

Beale looked at the men holding Edmund. They tied his hands behind his back and gave the rope a rough tug. Edmund winced as they knotted the rope. When they were secure, Beale walked over and thrust his fist into Edmund’s stomach. He let out a moan and fell forward, doubling over, wheezing for air.

“That’s for throwing me off the ship.”

With his other hand, he swung his fist, still carrying the pistol, and pounded Edmund’s head. His knees crashed to the floor, and he rolled on his back. Blood trickled out from his forehead.

“That’s because I just don’t like you.”

When Edmund opened his eyes, a gray murky light appeared through the porthole of the cabin. It was the captain’s cabin where he was laid out. The same cabin he watched McGinnty rule for years, now it was ruled by Beale.

Ropes were tied around his wrists and ankles. Though his head was aching something fierce, he raised it off the hammock to look around.

Sarah was on the cot in the corner. She was wide-awake and gazed back at him with weary, sad eyes. Her arms were lashed against her sides, her feet bound together. Her head rested on Beale’s lap.

"Good morning. I've spared your miserable life, so I expect you to cooperate."

"You hurt her and I swear—"

"You'll do nothing. You're in no position to do anything but shut up and listen."

With his left hand, Beale stroked Sarah's hair. The knife in his right rested on her belly while he stared back at Edmund. Then he raised it and gave it a twirl in the air.

"What do you want?" Edmund asked.

Sarah's eyes darted back and forth between Edmund and Beale, who traced his knife along her chest.

"The men actually wanted to vote on what to do with her. I don't think you'd like the choices. Two of them nearly came to blows. You see, Edmund, that's why we don't allow women on board. The men lose focus."

"Please let her go. You don't need her here."

"This is where we stand. I would have killed you without thinking twice, but I want the plunder on the South Sea ship. We made a deal. I expect you to honor that."

"They took it to the Carolinas," Edmund blurted out. He couldn't tell Beale the truth. There was very little gold left after Edmund paid off Jed and his men for saving McGinnty. That bit of information would result in a death sentence.

"Good. Now I want to know where Beckham and McGinnty are," Beale said. "I want you to lead us to them and work out a deal to give me my plunder. You help me and you go free."

"What guarantee do we have you'll let us go?"

"None. It's the chance you have to take. You're in no position to bargain. Trust me, the men are starving for this lovely woman."

Sarah jerked up, but Beale yanked her hair so her head dropped back on his lap. Her eyes blinked and watered as tears rolled down her face. Her chin trembled. He laughed and reached down, rubbing Sarah's breast.

"I suppose I have no choice."

"No, you don't."

"Well, we're wasting time," Edmund responded.

"What?" Beale said with a grin.

"We need to point these sails toward Ocracoke."

The trip to Ocracoke took longer due to the escape route. Once out of Chesapeake Bay, the ship headed northeast as far as New Jersey in case any other ships were tracking them. When they felt it safe, they headed south.

During all the chaos, they lost only two: Jon and the helmsman. Injuries were to be expected, yet none were serious.

Beale let Edmund and Sarah roam around the deck freely once they sailed far enough at sea. They made sure they stuck together and ignored the crude remarks made by the crew.

Throughout the trip, Edmund couldn't get the vision out of his head of Jon lying on the deck, looking at him and knowing there was nothing he could do. His eyes turning lifeless, almost pleading for help.

"I'll see you in another life, my friend," he said, staring out toward the ocean. He stared at the sea until his thoughts were interrupted by a tug on the shoulder.

"I'm sorry about your friend. What are we going to do?" Sarah asked.

"What am I going to tell Felina? She's going to have his kid."

Sarah went to wrap her arms around him but held back. Edmund sensed the crew's wanting eyes piercing her back. Throughout the trip, they tried to be invisible. They stayed in the corner of the ship, avoiding most of the crew. Being the only woman on board, she was hard not to notice. Greed was the only reason she was left unscathed. The anticipation of plunder from the South Sea ship kept them safe, so far. At least they were free to move about unlike Charles. His wrists and ankles were shackled, and he was kept in a forecastle down below.

When it was time to enter Pamlico Sound, Edmund navigated them through the sandbars and currents. He purposely anchored between two large sandbars, which were only visible at low tide and made for a difficult escape route. Chances were Edmund would never be on that ship again.

CHAPTER 29

OCRACOKE ISLAND

The campfire burned bright as Beale's men surrounded the flame. Mugs of rum were toasted. Rabbits impaled on a stick roasted over the fire. One of the pirates piled loose meat on a stick and flung it at another, who quickly shoved it into his mouth, grease spilled down his chin. Beale's men were drinking heavily, all the while making eyes at Sarah. Edmund sat next to her in a tent made hastily from excess sails. Flaps opened.

No ship was seen, and Beale was antsy. He wanted plunder from the South Sea ship, and it had been hours since they arrived on shore and still no sign of Beckham, McGinnty, or any of their crew. Time was not Edmund's ally.

"Where is Beckham?" Beale yelled as he stormed toward Edmund's tent. "They should be here by now. You promised us plunder if we came."

"He could be in Bath. Maybe they're trading the ship's supplies. Maybe they've been captured."

"I sure hope not for your sake. This all seems like a trick to stall. Maybe you weren't meeting them at all."

Sarah watched nervously as Edmund stood and approached Beale.

"You'll get the plunder."

One of the men walked up to Beale.

"They're probably long gone," he said in a high scratchy voice. His hair was wild and gray, face filled with stubble. "They left us with nothing." His pale eyes fixed on Sarah. "Well, almost nothing." A sheepish grin filled his face, and as he smiled, brown teeth with wide gaps became visible.

Edmund didn't recognize him as one of the men from Nassau. Beale must have recruited him from Williamsburg.

The night stretched into dawn. Edmund could not sleep as he heard pirates outside the tent. He lay next to Sarah who was curled up and shivering.

It's been three days since the rescue. Something must have happened.

Edmund overheard Beale order his men to get him and Sarah out of their tent. Edmund rolled over and quickly woke her up to warn her as two men barged in and grabbed them. Sarah was jerked from the ground as the pirate fondled her breast as he brought her outside. Edmund went to her aid but was intercepted by a cutlass and a pistol. The two were thrown outside in front of Beale who was addressing his men. All eyes were on Sarah who ended up next to the fire.

She leaned over and sat nervously on the trunk of a fallen tree. A cool breeze stirred across her arms as she wrapped them against her waist. Beale's men looked at her. A wanting look. Edmund followed close to her.

"Where are they?" Sarah whispered.

"They could be anywhere. We just need to keep waiting, nothing else we can do. Just bide our time."

They stood near Charles whose hands were chained and legs tied with rope.

"We'll take everything on *Hellspite* and make our way back to Nassau," Beale ordered. As he spoke, bits of food flowed out of his mouth, which muffled his voice. He was seething.

"What about her?" a pirate asked. "She may be the most valuable cargo you have."

Beale raised his hand to his chin.

"The wife of Killingsworth? We could get plenty for her after we have our way with her, of course."

Charles had stood up. The men around him jumped up nervously.

"He's chained for God's sake. Sit him back down," Beale barked out.

Two of the men cautiously approached Charles whose eyes burned with rage. Beale lost his patience and stormed over. He grabbed Charles's vest, hooked a leg behind him, swept his legs forward, and shoved him down. Charles's back hit the ground. Beale stomped on his belly with his boot. Charles's breath whooshed out of him as he rolled onto his side, coughing and wheezing.

Beale walked back to Sarah. His upper lip twitched as he eased into a slight grin. His right hand reached out and caressed loose strands of her hair. Sarah stared back with frightened eyes.

All eyes were on Beale and Sarah, oblivious to Charles as he slowly made his way to his feet. Edmund noticed the pistols dangling loosely on the sashes of the men beside him.

Charles, his two hands together, reached and pulled out a cutlass from the man standing next to him. He swung it wildly and sliced an arm of one of the pirates. With another wild swing, he decapitated another. The head flew from the man's neck, tumbling into the sand. Blood spouted from the stump of his neck. Charles pulled out a pistol from the headless man's body, which was still standing; but an explosion went off, leaving him paralyzed. He fell to his knees as another shot caught his side. He grunted and landed on his back.

"Charles!"

Edmund grabbed Sarah as two pirates moved in. Edmund smashed a fist in the mouth of one as the other pulled out his pistol. Edmund kicked it out of his hand and, at the same time, pulled a pistol from under the man's vest. He slammed his hand forward and took dead aim at Beale's face. Beale's eyes bulged out, and his body froze. Edmund squeezed the trigger.

Click.

He squeezed it again.

Click.

The men mobbed Edmund as the butt of a pistol caught him over the side of his head. He was surrounded by crouched and kneeling bodies as he was rolled onto his side, hands covering his head. He gasped and grunted as blows came down on him. A loud blast echoed in the beach. Smoke rose from Beale's pistol.

"You bastard, you want to see what happens when you fuck with me? Have the pretty young lady come over here," Beale ordered, and he turned toward Edmund. "Where's that cocky arrogance now?"

Edmund's head was spinning. Blood spilled from above his eye. He tried to stagger to his feet but fell backward into the sand. Pistols surrounded him.

The pirates shoved Sarah over to him. Beale grabbed her by the arms.

"What are you going to do for me to save his life?"

"Please, don't hurt us. Just let us go," she blurted.

Edmund tried to scream, but his words came out slurred. He scrambled to rush to her aid, but his legs didn't work.

"String him up!"

"No!" she cried.

Pirates lunged at Edmund and raised him off the ground. He twisted and jerked. Two pirates tied his hands behind his back. One of the pirates hurled a coil of rope over a thick branch and grabbed it when it came back around. They covered Edmund's neck with the noose and pulled the slack out. It choked him as it was pulled, lifting him to his toes. He moved his feet to keep his balance and make the noose as taught as possible. Two pirates grabbed the other side of the rope and pulled. Edmund rose up in the air, feet dangling. He felt the strain of the rope burn against his neck.

"Not yet," Beale yelled and lunged at Sarah. He threw her to the ground by Edmund's feet. Beale grabbed a lock of Edmund's hair and looked him in the eye.

"You may want to watch this, boy."

Beale smiled and lowered himself onto Sarah. She squirmed and kicked as groping hands fondled her. Her mouth opened to scream, but Beale's hand slapped across it. She bit into his hand and flung herself away, but Beale slammed her flat on the ground. He clutched her throat, holding her down, while he pushed himself up and straddled her hips. He yanked at the neck of her dress and tugged it down. She bucked with pain and screamed as his rough hand squeezed her breast. His other hand jerked at her undergarments. The ground was wet under her buttocks, and he slid his right hand between her thighs and moved it upward. She was trembling. She let out an assault with a flurry of wild punches, most blocked by Beale who pulled out a knife. He held it to her face as the pirates surrounding them laughed. He twirled it above her face.

"Move and you're dead."

He pinned down both her arms, leaned heavily on her, and shoved his knees between her legs to force them apart. His mouth was on hers, mashing her lips. The rest of the crew cheered wildly, raising their mugs and patting each other's back sides.

Beale plunged the knife into the ground by her face. He lowered his pants and forced himself into her.

Two of Beale's men interrupted the festivities as they raced through the woods, gasping for air.

"The merchant ship—it's docked just beyond the ridge."

Beale looked around nervously, drawing his pistol, as he crawled off Sarah. He looked at Edmund who stood on his toes, trying to loosen the tension of the rope. The laughter among the pirates ceased. Edmund struggled with his balance.

"Beckham," Beale called out. "McGinnty!"

The pirates pulled out pistols and cutlasses, ready to strike. Beale's head turned like it was on a swivel. He reached for his knife, eyes wide. The pirate with the wild gray hair grabbed Sarah and held a knife to her cheek. She covered her breasts with the top of her dress.

"Did you see anyone on board?" Beale nervously asked the two men.

"I couldn't tell, sir. It was too dark."

"Take two men and one of the boats. Try and get as close as you can and see if they're on board." Beale looked around and yelled toward the woods, "We have Drake. I'll gladly put a ball through his head if you don't signal your men to come out!"

Nothing.

A shimmery orange glow of light pierced through the woods. If McGinnty's men were on this island, Beale's crew was sitting ducks with the blaze of fire scorching from the beach on the other side of the island.

"Cut him down," he said, pointing to Edmund.

A cutlass tore through the rope, and Edmund stumbled backward but kept his balance. His senses were slowly coming back to him. Beale held a pistol to his head.

"McGinnty? Show yourself if you want Drake alive."

Beale shoved Edmund forward, and they headed toward the light. The pirate with the wild hair escorted Sarah behind them. They moved cautiously through the woods, stopping often to check around and listen. The only noise was the shrieks and squeals of crickets and other wildlife in the thick brush, along with the sigh of leaves stirred by a soft breeze. The woods were a thick jungle. Edmund stepped aside from a thick trunk. The tree looked normal with its branches starting about ten feet up and with large leaves.

The body dangling was a little higher up. Sarah shrieked. At first, he saw the bottom half of a man dangling directly above him. He was up so high Edmund could barely see his face. Torn clothing fluttered in the breeze. The skin was wrinkled and leathery.

Beale laughed and said to Edmund, "That'll be you very soon."

They made their way past the body as the murky light grew brighter. They made their way to a clearing at the edge of the woods, which led to a small beach. A large cracking bonfire lit the beach. In a clump of trees at the edge of the clearing, Beale held up his arm and his men halted.

The men looked around, deathly silent, trying to hear any slight hint of sound. Edmund worked at loosening the ropes behind his back. He rubbed his hands together, trying to stretch the ropes but burning his wrists in the process.

A twig broke next to him that sounded like a footstep. Nothing. Just crickets singing. Beale signaled to one of the men to guard Edmund and proceeded cautiously as the light from the fire grew brighter.

Beale crouched down as he saw McGinnty's men finish loading a rowboat and dragging it through the water, out to the sound.

Edmund strained his eyes, but all he could make out was shades of dark gray and a lot of black.

"Good, they don't know we're here," Beale said.

A pistol flung out and pressed against Beale's head.

"I wouldn't be so sure of that."

Beale flinched as the rest of his crew aimed at the shadow of the figure. Beale froze. The arm attached poked out from the shadows and, with his free hand, pulled Beale closer as if to use him as a shield from the crew.

"You better tell them to back off or your brains will be splattered all over the beach!" McGinnty ordered.

"Was this supposed to be some sort of trap?" Beale asked.

"Yes, and guess who got caught in it?"

"Shoot the girl and Drake."

McGinnty put a choke hold on Beale and dragged him backward to the beach.

"You men shoot them and you have a dead captain. Look around you. There's a musket on every one of you."

Edmund saw muskets sticking out of the bushes and trees.

McGinnty squeezed Beale's neck a little tighter and stumbled toward the fire, all the time facing Beale's men who appeared too nervous to follow. They remained in the shadows at the edge of the clearing, trying to get cover from the trees and brush.

"How many men do you have?" Beale shouted so his men could hear his question. "I only see a handful of muskets. You don't have enough men."

"Maybe I picked up a few along the way."

Beale's men lurched forward, and Edmund found himself and Sarah at the back of the group. Out of the corner of his eye, he noticed the man guarding him, holding a gun at his head, splitting his attention between McGinnty and himself. His arm drooped slightly. He carried two pistols in a sash dangling by each side and another pistol tucked away in the front of his pants.

The man holding Sarah loosened the grip of his knife hand, eyes on McGinnty.

"I guess we have what you'd call a stalemate. So you'll have to hear me out," McGinnty shouted to the men. He dragged Beale to a large chest next to the fire, which had decreased in size but still bright enough to watch the two men. They were so close together they looked like one person.

"You're in no position to bargain," yelled the man next to Edmund.

"I have all the plunder. I'd say that puts me in a great position to bargain," McGinnty answered. "I'm counting on greed to let my friends go. I want to make you an offer."

"Don't trust him!" Beale yelled out. "He'll never make a move as long as we have Drake. He saved you, McGinnty, so you and I have nothing to talk about."

McGinnty let out a howl. "You have it all wrong, Beale. I'm not making any deals with you. I'm counting on the greed of your crew to choose a new captain." McGinnty lifted his right leg onto the top of the crate. "I have a proposition to make," he yelled to the crew. "I say we vote for a new captain, divide the plunder, and get out of here. By the way, gentlemen, there is a time limit on the discussion. As you can see, we are shoving off shortly."

"How do we know what kind of plunder you have in that crate?"

"Who mentioned anything about the South Sea ship? I'm talking about real treasure. I'm talking about the *Lucinda*."

"I thought it was just a myth. Where is it buried?"

McGinnty looked around. "Some of it is right under me. Some, right out there."

He pointed to the bay. Dinghies lined the waters far enough away from the shoreline and close enough to *Hellspite* whose sails were being lowered.

"I hope you will forgive me. We had to take our ship back."

Beale's eyes widened. "This is a trick of some sorts."

Edmund was shocked. He heard the *Lucinda* treasure was buried at Ocracoke, but he never believed it. McGinnty kicked open the hinge and lifted the top open with his foot. Gold glowed off the moonlight.

"You men let them go, and this is yours along with the South Sea ship. We won't need that anymore. I'd say it's a pretty good deal, one that I would take."

"Why don't we just go ahead and take it? We outnumber them," voices yelled.

"We have cannons aimed at the beach. Do you really want to test the aim of my gunners?" McGinnty fired back.

The men looked around. They started to talk among themselves. Then they crept forward. Edmund looked at the muskets from the bushes as the dawn was breaking on the beach. One he saw was clearly aimed at the beach where the men were, but he saw no one holding it. The gun was planted in a tree. He carefully looked at others. All planted. He lunged forward, positioning himself next to the man guarding Sarah. The ropes finally fell free. The man guarding him jerked his arm and then squinted at the muskets in the woods.

"What the—"

Edmund ducked and pulled his wrist down with his right hand. A gun blast slammed his eardrum as the man guarding Sarah fell to the ground in agony, holding his hip. With his free hand, Edmund grabbed the pistol from the sash, thumbed back the hammer, and fired. The ball punched the center of the man's chest. Mouth hung open, his eyes bulged.

Beale's men turned and returned gunfire toward the woods, shooting at anything, emptying their guns. Some dove in the sand. Some ran.

Edmund grabbed the remaining pistols. The man that had Sarah squirmed on the ground as she walked over him.

"Get down!"

Balls sprayed off the bark of the trees surrounding them.

McGinnty let go of Beale and pulled something from the chest. Beale fell to a knee as McGinnty reached back into the fire and threw something into the crowd. As McGinnty released it, Beale shot an elbow to his stomach, which discharged McGinnty's pistol.

An explosion filled the beach as the grenade McGinnty threw went off. Men screamed in pain, others limped into the woods.

Edmund grabbed some of the loose muskets from the bushes.

I hope they're loaded.

He blasted one of the pirates on the beach taking aim at McGinnty and knocked him down face-first into the sand. What was left of the rest of them quickly raised their hands.

Beale reached into his boot and pulled out a knife. He slashed downward and thrust it into McGinnty's thigh.

McGinnty grimaced, uttering a low cry. Blood ran down his leg into his boot. Beale got up and ran toward the woods. He looked over his back shoulder as McGinnty was bent over, falling into the sand. A smirk came across his face. It was quickly erased when Edmund intercepted him at the path with a pistol aimed at his face.

The two stared at each other until Edmund rammed the muzzle against his mouth, shattering the front teeth. He shoved hard, forcing Beale's head backward.

"This is for Jon."

His forefinger snapped the trigger. An explosion thundered in the air. Bone and skin sprayed from the exit wound, filling the air with a glittering red.

Edmund gazed at the smoke rising from the pistol.

"Sarah."

He ran back and slid to the ground next to her.

"You all right?"

She just gave him a blank stare. His eyes went shiny with tears. He eased a hand on her shoulder and wrapped his arms around her. She flinched and looked at him with wide eyes.

"It's all right," he said, caressing her back.

She hugged him tightly. She buried her face in his chest and shook with small sobs.

"I'm sorry, Sarah," Edmund whispered. "I'm so sorry."

She wrapped her arms around his back and pulled him tightly against her. For a long time, they stood motionless, holding each other. Edmund listened to her quiet breathing. He felt her warm breath on his skin. Her eyelids tickled his neck when she blinked. Her heart was pounding fast. He could feel it against his chest.

She pulled away and rubbed her eyes. He grabbed her hand and made their way toward McGinnty. Men were sprawled on the beach. One grabbed his pistol, but Edmund quickly aimed his at the man.

"Drop it!"

McGinnty pulled out two pistols. Blood was streaming from his leg as he limped forward.

"You all right?" Edmund asked.

"Yeah. Gather up their guns before they realize there's no one in the woods."

McGinnty handed Sarah a pistol. She grabbed it carefully as if it was going to explode if she made a sudden movement.

"If they get up, shoot them."

A small boat rowed to shore. As it hit sand, Beckham jumped out and ran to McGinnty.

"Everything is loaded up and ready to go."

"Take this last chest."

"What about them?"

"Let them go. They can sail the South Sea ship."

Beckham looked at him in disbelief. Edmund also cringed when he heard that.

As they moved closer to the chest, Edmund saw it was filled with fine silk and pieces of eight, gold doubloons, and watches. It was also filled with fuses. Short fuses that disappeared inside the plunder.

"Let's just say it was an insurance policy," McGinnty said. "In case things didn't go as planned.

"Charles! We have to check on Charles," Sarah said.

"We left him on the other beach. I'll go get him," Edmund started to run off but stopped and turned toward Sarah.

"Are you sure you're all right?"

"I'll be fine. I promise."

Edmund scampered through the woods, his pistol cocked and ready. In the darkness of the woods, he looked like one of Beale's men escaping. When he reached the other beach, he was an open target.

He slowed down, carefully looking for any movement from the woods, and finally, he saw Charles by the water's edge. He was still breathing, a quick constant pace, as Edmund grabbed a bottle of rum and knelt beside him.

"We'll get you through."

Charles looked up, barely able to open his eyes.

Edmund cut Charles's bloody shirt and noticed a hole in his side and upper left arm. He grabbed rum and poured it into the wound, which jolted Charles, widening his eyes.

"Sorry."

His wet hair slung to Charles's forehead. His face was sweaty. Edmund took off his shirt and dried it. He cut the shirt into strips and pressed a rag against the wound to his side.

"Rum," Charles whispered.

Edmund placed the rim of the flask to Charles's lips, and he drank. With the strips from the shirt, he made a tourniquet to wrap around Charles's shoulder and used the muzzle of an empty pistol he found lying nearby to twist it tight.

"Hang in there, Charles. We'll get you to the ship in no time."

Edmund lifted him up and threw him over his shoulder. He started back but stopped abruptly. Four sails were heading toward the Ocracoke inlet. They were flying British colors.

"Ships are coming," Edmund yelled through the clearing. He looked around and stopped in his tracks. Sarah was gone. Everyone was gone. A boat was rowing out to *Hellspite.*

"She's been taken to *Hellspite,*" McGinnty said, walking forward. "I think it's best if we get a move on."

"Beale's men?"

"They're rowing their asses off back to the South Sea ship. Let's get Charles on the ship."

They eased Charles onto the canoe and made their way to *Hellspite.* The ship was anchored north of the dangerous sandbars, which forced them to head north up Pamlico Sound. They would exit at the Hatteras Inlet and out to sea.

The naval ships were growing larger at sea and picking up speed. A man-of-war sailed with a sloop by its side.

McGinnty ordered everyone on board *Hellspite.* Crates of gold and plunder were loaded up on the deck.

As Beale's men made their way to the merchant ship, McGinnty heard screaming from the ship.

"They must have found the plunder."

"You really left it on there?" Edmund asked.

"Whatever scraps were left. They did after all help save my life, as you did. I owe you a debt of gratitude."

"Why did you let them escape? You know we'll run into them again."

"I didn't let them escape. Ships are coming for them as we speak. They should arrive in an hour or so. They can't escape through the mainland because I paid off Eden to make sure his troops are guarding it."

"What if they follow us?"

McGinnty laughed. "We left that ship in no condition to sail any great distance. They'll be pumping water out of it for hours. Maybe the British will accuse them of stealing it and all its plunder on board."

Edmund shook his head. "I still don't think we'll go blameless for this. What now?"

"We head back to the islands. I don't think Killingsworth has given up on us."

Edmund and McGinnty watched through a telescope as a light wind carried them slowly up the sound. The South Sea ship was trapped in a sandbar as the navy's smaller sloop headed toward them. The larger warship waited outside Ocracoke inlet while the smaller sloop maneuvered its way through. Beale's men opened fire and scattered their deck with grapeshot. The sloop had the advantage of maneuverability and arranged a broadside on the vessel.

The naval vessel opened up another broadside, quickly loading their cannons. Blood filled the deck as the sloop pulled up next to the South Sea ship. Men started jumping in the water, but the navy sailors picked them off with their muskets. Finally, the sailors boarded and finished the onslaught.

Sarah approached the two.

"We need to get Charles to a doctor or he'll bleed to death."

Edmund looked at McGinnty.

"We need to find a port that's safe. Maybe we can stop in Charleston. That's the closest place I can think of with decent doctors."

"We'll go there or Nassau," McGinnty replied. "Whichever way we can avoid that man-of-war behind us." He looked over at Sarah. "You must be the famous Sarah. I've been hearing stories about you since I've known the lad."

Her face turned blush. Edmund stretched his arm around her.

"Isn't she something?"

"She's lovely. You two have a fine future ahead of you, if we get out of here alive."

Sarah's eyes shot open as Edmund quickly squeezed her.

Early evening, Edmund checked in on Sarah. Beckham told him she was still asleep and tucked away in the captain's cabin.

As Edmund slowly opened the door, Sarah rolled over and looked at him.

"I hope I didn't wake you. How are you feeling?"

"I'm fine," she said. "Better than I have in a long, long time."

He believed her. Although she was exceedingly pale, her eyes were clearer than when they first came aboard. She pushed at her unbound hair with embarrassment.

"I must look frightful."

"You look incredible."

"Please, my clothes are torn and tattered."

"Sarah, the only thing that matters is that you're here."

He longed to put his arms around her. Images of their meetings at Knewt Gardens swept through his mind.

"I'd like to walk outside."

"You should be resting. You've been through so much."

"I'm all right, really." She rose off the cot and grabbed Edmund's hand.

They walked outside, on the deck, to stares and glances. Edmund smiled and placed his arm around her.

"Just ignore them. They haven't seen a pretty woman in a while."

"How's Charles doing?"

"He's hanging in there, but Beck says the wounds are pretty deep."

She listened while Edmund recalled Charles's transformation from when he first met him.

"I swear the guy was creepy. He just kept to himself, and the only thing that put a smile on his face is when we were in a battle. He just had no friends. He grew up alone, and when Jon and I showed him some attention, he became a changed man."

He stared out at sea and became quiet.

"Edmund, are you all right?"

"I was just thinking about Jon. I'm really going to miss him. He made it bearable. He used to smuggle so much food to me it probably saved my life. There was so much scurvy on board. I used to just shake my head at some of the things he did. Poor guy. He really didn't belong. He was kidnapped from a life that suited him. I wish so hard he could have had his life back. His normal life back home." Edmund shook his head. "He was just a great guy."

They gazed at the sunset, which glistened off the water causing a bright yellow streak that appeared aimed at the ship. Her arms were folded across her breasts, her hands clasping her forearms.

"Sarah?"

His soft anxious voice interrupted her reflection. She turned to him.

"You had a fearful look on your face. What were you thinking?"

"I was thinking about Alexander. What do you suppose he'll do about my leaving?"

"I'm sure he'll try and find us. Don't worry, I'm not going to let him get close to us."

Edmund said the words, but without much conviction. He wanted to believe them, but he knew deep down that Killingsworth would stop at nothing to find them.

Sarah started to nod, and Edmund grabbed her.

"Let's get you back inside."

He escorted her back into the cabin and laid her down on the cot.

"Edmund, are you certain you want to risk all this for me?"

"Are you out of your mind? I'd risk anything for you. Don't you know that?"

She pressed her left hand to his lips. "I know you would," she said with a smile, her eyes slowly closing.

Edmund couldn't sleep and gazed at the skyline. For the first time in weeks, there wasn't someplace he had to be or something he had to do. Time stood still.

He stared at the sea until his thoughts were interrupted by a hand clutching his shoulder.

"Are you all right, Edmund?"

McGinnty kept his hand on Edmund's shoulder. Edmund just stared straight ahead and nodded as McGinnty continued, "I'm sorry about Charles. He was one tough son of a bitch."

"He spent his whole life as an outcast, and now he was finally fitting in."

"How's Sarah doing?"

"She's out cold in the cabin. The last few days have been overwhelming."

"She's a fine woman. Maybe now things will settle down for you two."

"We both know that's not going to happen. Be real. I've taken her from the lion's den to the lion's mouth. I didn't want her involved in this kind of life. I hope to get her back to England, she can stay with relatives there."

"I'm sure you've talked this over with her, and that's what she wants."

"Jack, this is no life for her."

"Open your eyes, Edmund. She just risked everything to be with you. That's what she wants."

"What do we do?"

McGinnty laughed. "You'll think of something, you always do."

Edmund leaned back against the rail. The warm ocean breeze felt refreshing, and mist from the waves felt cool.

"We have to get everyone back to Nassau. Do you think their pardons are still good?"

"I don't know anymore," he patted Edmund's back. "By the way, I never thanked you for what you did."

Edmund smiled. "You would have done the same."

"I doubt I would have pulled it off. I'm just sorry about Jon. It seems we traded one life for another, and I'm responsible."

"We all knew the risks, and no one wavered. I just don't know what I'm going to tell Felina."

There was a silence between the two men until McGinnty gave Edmund a quizzical look.

"Out with it, boy. I've known you too long not to know there's something else bothering you."

"Not bothering me, but I always wondered why you took such an interest in me all these years. You always seemed to go out of your way to help me."

McGinnty laughed. "I guess you reminded me of myself when I was your age—full of piss and vinegar but no direction."

CHAPTER 30

NOTORIOUS

Three longboats rowed toward shore. A white flag flopped from the bow of the lead. McGinnty had his leg raised high in the front of the first boat as it scraped up on the beach and jolted to a sudden halt. Edmund and Sarah sat behind him. Rogers and his troops lined the beach to greet them, muskets raised. The locals gathered behind the troops, watching nervously.

Piracy had all but ended in New Providence, but the economy slowed to a crawl. Tensions between pirate sympathizers and Rogers had divided the island. Twelve pirates swung from the harbor, and now the most infamous pirate of them all had landed at Nassau. McGinnty hopped off and landed in the sand. Rogers approached, followed by his troops.

"We come with a flag of truce!" McGinnty declared.

Rogers's men surrounded McGinnty as two more boats grounded ashore.

"Lower your weapons," Rogers shouted.

McGinnty strode toward Rogers. They stared at each other, neither one flinching.

"Your legend is growing all over the Caribbean," Rogers said. "Rumor has it you've plundered the east coast, raising havoc. Other rumors have you hanged. Obviously, the latter is not the case."

"I can't control what people believe or say."

Rogers looked at Edmund who slung Charles over his shoulder and made his way out of the boat.

"Edmund Drake, you just couldn't stay away," Rogers said and signaled for a stretcher.

"This man needs help," Edmund said. "He has a pardon. We need to take him to Doc."

"Look," McGinnty blurted out, "we've got information from merchant vessels outside of Charles Town that Spain is sending troops this way. As a gesture of truce, we brought guns and ammunition."

"What are they sending?"

"I don't know, but whatever it is, it's more than what you have to defend this place. Many of my men have pardons signed by you. I came here to drop them off or, if they choose to leave, pack their belongings. We'll be gone in a day or so."

Before Rogers could respond, screaming interrupted them. A woman ran frantically down the beach, losing her footing in the sand, a small baby clutched against her breast. She dodged her way through the troops and raced toward the shoreline.

"Jon! Jon!"

Felina looked around. Edmund lowered his head and took a deep breath. A couple of men took Charles and started taking him up the beach.

"Jon!" she belted out.

Rogers leaned into McGinnty. "She's been waiting at the pier every day for him to show. She's had a rough go of it lately with the recent passing of her mom."

McGinnty shook his head. Felina searched the boats. Her voice sounded tight, her eyes frantic. Finally, she saw a familiar face and wore a nervous smile.

"Edmund, it's been so long. I thought something happened. It's so good to see you. This is my baby. Our baby, Jon and I."

The words rushed from her mouth, and she could not hold back her excitement. She looked at the three boats that were washed up on the water's edge. Then she looked out toward *Hellspite.* Rogers and McGinnty both watched in silence.

"Where's Jon? I want to show him our baby."

Edmund stared down at the sand. She ran past him, looking to see if any other boats were departing *Hellspite.* She turned back to Edmund, a confused look showed on her face.

"Did he stay on the ship?"

Edmund slowly shook his head, unable to look at her.

"Did he go back to England? Did he leave me?"

"No, he didn't leave you," Edmund said in a low whisper. Felina's smile faded. Tears welled her eyes.

"Something's happened to him. We have to find him."

She started running toward the boats. Edmund followed.

"Felina!" Edmund yelled.

Still running, she glanced over her shoulder and stopped. She faced Edmund and walked backward toward the water. As Edmund caught up to her, he moved closer and clutched her shoulders.

"He didn't make it," he whispered.

Felina shrugged her shoulders and pulled away. "I don't believe you. It's a lie!"

Bursting into tears, she whirled past him toward the water and screamed at the ship. Edmund followed, but she just looked past him. She started to stumble, and Edmund grabbed the baby as she fell. She lay on her side, mouth open, her body trembling. She covered her face with both hands as the tears leaked between her fingers. Edmund stared at the baby, Jon's own flesh and blood. How proud he would have been if only . . .

Sarah walked over, and Edmund handed the baby to her. He knelt down, and Felina wrapped her arms around him and sobbed. Her face was buried in his chest.

Rogers looked down and signaled McGinnty's men off the boats.

"Jack, let's take this somewhere else."

McGinnty nodded in agreement.

Rogers walked over to Edmund. "Why don't you come with us? Your name seems to be bandied about these days."

Edmund looked up at Rogers and nodded. He pulled away from Felina, brushing her hair with his fingers. Sarah quickly stepped over and put her arm around her, giving her a tight squeeze.

"I'll be right back," Edmund said, stroking her hair.

McGinnty and Edmund followed Rogers to Fort Nassau.

"We have a lot of work to do here. We took care of piracy, but since the war with Spain, we've been under constant threat of attack. We could use your help."

"Why are we at war with Spain?" Edmund interrupted.

"Well, we received word last March about it. Spain wants control of the Bahamas and Carolinas for its empire. At least they don't have France teaming up with them this time."

"So much for six years of peace," McGinnty said.

"We had word Spain was sending a fleet of four thousand troops," Rogers added. "But luckily, one of their fortresses in Pensacola was captured, so they diverted. They would have stormed right through this island."

"How many men do you have?" McGinnty asked.

"One hundred soldiers plus five hundred militia, along with the *Delicia*, a sloop, and a fifty-gun fort. I thought we could count on pirates-turned-privateers, but they are after Spanish ships with plunder. There's no money in it for them to stay."

"I thought you had more men. You should take cover at one of the local islands. They'll destroy this place."

"I'm not leaving. I could use your help."

McGinnty laughed then looked at Rogers. "You're serious. You're bloody serious."

"You're damn right I'm serious. Do you know what I've sacrificed? King George has all but forgotten about us. Since the defeat of the pirates, it's business as usual for him. There haven't been more than two naval ships in the harbor, and we're getting no production from this colony. I'm personally in debt £20,000 already. My supplies have been cut off for nonpayment. Back home, I'm up to my neck in bills, and my wife has all but left me. If Spain destroys this place, everything I've done is for nothing."

"So the reason I'm not being strung up by my neck is that you need my help."

"Jack, you're free to go anytime. I won't stop you. I owe you that much."

When Rogers said that, it caught Edmund's attention. He gave a curious look to Rogers and then McGinnty.

"Woodes, I'm not welcome here or anywhere in the Caribbean," McGinnty said. "I'm heading to Madagascar. At least I'll find peace there."

"You don't know that. The most dangerous cutthroats known to man live in Madagascar. If it's freedom you want, King George has extended pardons to pirates since the war with Spain broke out. He needs privateers. You're perfect."

"I'm through with King George, England, and everything it stands for. Killingsworth will stop at nothing to see me dead." McGinnty paused. "Look, I'll ask my men, but come sunup, I'm gone."

"Killingsworth has no jurisdiction here," Rogers said and closed his eyes. "Jack, remember that time outside Jamaica years ago, during our privateering days?"

"Yes, I remember it well," McGinnty answered.

Rogers turned to Edmund.

"Do you know how he became the notorious Jack McGinnty?"

Edmund shook his head and looked at McGinnty who sat down, rolling his eyes.

"The Spanish navy bombarded English-owned islands in the Caribbean. They burned houses, stole whatever they could get their hands on. People on the islands waited for reinforcements, but they never came.

"So the governor of Nevis, a wealthy planter, hires McGinnty and me to sail to Jamaica to pick up troops and ammunition. Also, to bring back any information we could get our hands on about the next Spanish or French attack.

"On the way back, McGinnty captured two French sloops and a brigantine. The governor is so elated he gave him his first commission, and he recruited a raucous crew of 540 men. Their job was to wreak havoc on the enemy by any means possible. McGinnty developed quite a reputation. As fearful as the enemy was of him, the crews that he sailed with found him fair and open-minded. As you can attest to, his crews are the most loyal in the Caribbean."

Edmund nodded in agreement as Rogers continued, "This created a competition between us. I went after French and Spanish ships while McGinnty led sneak attacks on French towns, and as the townspeople would flee, he would take whatever he could. Between the two of us, we collected quite a small fleet.

"We received a hero's welcome in Nevis, but the governor was still nervous. He expected retaliation from the French anytime soon.

"After my ship led an attack on Saint Martin, the French ambushed us, and we were trapped just inside the harbor. They manned the fort at Marigot, and three warships were outside the harbor. There was no escape.

"As the French troops were celebrating their victory and in no hurry to attack, McGinnty waited for nightfall and the tide to go out. They swam out to one of the French ships, took out their daggers, and each assigned a man. They had to strike before their crew could ring the bell or fire their cannon to warn the mainland. When the ship was captured, he sailed it toward the other two ships and fired. The French were caught off guard. We made our move and escaped."

"We got lucky," McGinnty clarified, bored with the conversation.

"You could have taken your plunder and moved on, but you helped us. I just wanted to say thank you."

McGinnty stared at Rogers and shook his head. "I bet that really hurt to say."

"More than you know. But, Jack, I need your help again."

"What can you offer me that will make me stay? I have all the money I need. I have a fast ship. I have a place to go."

"I thought maybe you'd stay to defend the island you helped build."

"I'm sorry, Woodes. I wish you luck."

McGinnty turned to leave but stopped.

"It's hard to imagine how our lives have turned out. We were both privateer captains. We're the only two to sack a Manila galleon. But I'm wanted for piracy, and you're a hero."

Rogers sat down and placed his head in his hands.

"I don't feel like one."

"I'll round up the men at the Shark Den. The ones that stay, I trust, will never have to look over their shoulders. You'll take care of them?"

"Of course," Rogers replied.

McGinnty nodded.

"We'll leave you what we can spare as far as guns and ammunition."

"Jack, you're really going to leave?" Edmund asked.

"We've overstayed our welcome in the Caribbean, we need to find a safer haven."

"This place will get destroyed. The only chance to save New Providence is for us to stay and protect this place. They need our help."

"We're not welcome here. The next time I'm caught, they'll parade me around the streets of London, Williamsburg, Paris, or wherever. You don't think I've thought about being paraded to the gallows, being spit at, cursed at, dangling by a noose, wetting myself. I will not be captured again."

"It doesn't have to be that way," Edmund responded.

"I thought you of all people would come with me. You could make a new life with Sarah."

"Of course I want a new life with Sarah. Of course I've thought about that, but running is not the answer."

McGinnty shook his head and started to walk away. "I'm sorry then."

Edmund ran up to him and grabbed his shoulder. McGinnty gave a fierce stare at Edmund's hand, then at Edmund. Edmund eased his hand away.

"This was our home. We built this place, and now you're going to let the Spanish take it over?"

"We have everything we need on *Hellspite*. We have more money than we can spend in a lifetime. Why risk it?"

"Everything we've done here will be wasted. The Spanish will burn this island to the ground. You made this island what it is. Take the privateer's commission. You can start a new life. If England knows you've fought for this island, Killingsworth can't touch you."

Rogers nodded in agreement.

"He won't touch you on this island while I'm governor. That I promise."

"I don't see Killingsworth ever not tracking me down," McGinnty grimaced. "I'll fight, but once the Spanish are gone, so am I."

Edmund found Sarah back at the beach, and they walked to Doc's to check on Charles.

"How is she doing?" Edmund asked.

"She's devastated. She lost the man she loves."

Edmund wrapped his arm around her. "I'll do whatever I can for her. I owe Jon that much."

"I know what it's like to lose someone you love."

Edmund stopped and stared at her.

"But I found him again."

When they arrived, Doc greeted them with warm hugs. Charles lay on a table, lanterns lit overhead.

"He's feverish and the shoulder looks bad. The ball appears to be embedded pretty deep. We also have to remove the ball from his side."

"Is he going to make it?"

"I don't know. He may lose his arm."

"No," Edmund protested. Doc gave him a scathing look.

"If you want to diagnose him, be my guest."

Edmund wiped his lips with the back of his hand. "No, of course not, but don't take his arm."

"He's lost half of it already, and he's still breathing."

Doc reached into his bag and pulled out a syringe.

"What's that for?" Edmund asked.

"I'm going to give him opium. I need him unconscious for a while."

He grabbed a scalpel and clamps and dug into Charles's side.

"Get that light on here," he yelled at Edmund who was holding a lantern.

The ball wasn't as deep as Doc first suspected, and he pulled it out with a clamp, dropping it into a pan. Edmund turned away and saw Sarah start gagging. Edmund reached over and pulled her aside as Doc sewed up Charles's side. She stopped him.

"I'm all right." She grabbed a wet rag and wiped Doc's face.

The arm was trickier. Doc worked on it but struggled to find the ball. It was embedded deep in the shoulder socket. Edmund looked up on the table next to Charles and noticed the saw.

Please don't take his arm.

"There's some food on the table inside. You two look like you haven't eaten in days."

Sarah took him up on his offer and went in the kitchen. Edmund looked at the shoulder being wiped off and started to walk away.

"She seems to be quite a woman."

Edmund smiled and watched Doc drop a second ball into the pan. Charles started waking up.

"Hold him down. I have to cauterize the wound."

At once, Edmund's hands gripped Charles's shoulders. Charles twisted his head, he saw Doc heating a cauterized iron in a brazier of coals. He screamed. Edmund poured rum into his open mouth. He jerked and squirmed until he finally passed out.

After Doc sewed the second wound, he washed the blood from his hands and escorted Edmund to the living room.

"What now?"

"We wait for the fever to break."

"How long will that take?"

"Days, weeks, maybe never."

They waited in the living room, and after eating, Sarah read aloud by the fire. Edmund had trouble keeping his eyes open, and they would spring wide-open and then drift shut again.

Later that night, the Shark Den welcomed McGinnty's crew, and rum flowed freely. Arguments erupted about women and drink, about New Providence, the Spanish, and Jack McGinnty.

Edmund took Sarah inside as two women gave Edmund a hug and a kiss on the cheek. She frowned and leaned close to him, whispering, "Who are they? Are they what I think they are?"

Edmund blushed. "Just some of the locals, I barely know them."

One of the pirates pointed to the wall of shame. The wall was covered with wanted posters of some of the most famous pirates in the Caribbean. The likes of Benjamin Hornigold, Charles Vane, Jack Rackham, Blackbeard, Jack McGinnty, and at the bottom, Edmund Drake.

Edmund walked over, eyes wide. He looked at the portrait of himself in disbelief. The article was signed by Alexander Killingsworth, and the reward was £150.

"You're almost worth as much as a captain," Beckham declared.

Edmund leaned into Sarah. "Probably more if they knew about you," he whispered.

He grabbed his rum and was about to escort Sarah outside when McGinnty burst through the door. He signaled his men over, and they quickly surrounded him.

"I know some of you are going to stay. You've chosen Nassau to be your home, and you left that home to save me. I'll always be eternally grateful. As you may have heard, the Spanish fleet is preparing an attack. I know I promised you we are leaving for Madagascar first thing in the morning. Those plans have changed. We are leaving first thing in the morning for the Leeward Islands to pick up more weapons. We are going to stay and fight."

Rumblings went through the crowd. The men were divided down the middle of those that were going to stay in New Providence and those that were leaving for Madagascar. McGinnty held up his hands and continued, "I can't order you men to fight. You've done more than enough already, and there is no money involved. It's not like we're capturing a ship. We're defending our home."

A roar was heard, and fists were pumped as McGinnty nodded toward the men. A sense of pride filled his face. The men would fight one last battle as a crew.

McGinnty brushed into Edmund on the way out.

"You need to get *Lucifer's Ghost* into fighting shape. It's been hidden on the other side of the island for too long. It's probably going to take a lot of patchwork, so take a large group of men with you."

"Yes, sir, and thanks. Everyone on this island thanks you."

McGinnty grimaced and walked away.

Edmund clutched Sarah's elbow, and they walked down the beach to check on Felina.

"What have I gotten you into?"

"I'm fine. The past few weeks have been a blur," she responded, shaking her head.

Edmund stopped and put his arms around her. He kissed her cheek and squeezed her tight. Images of their meetings at Myers Plantation swept his mind—images from long ago.

The next morning, McGinnty loaded up *Hellspite*. Forty men joined him as Edmund and Beckham watched. There was no one else around. McGinnty left hundreds of muskets bought from the Leeward Islands earlier and six cannons to place on the *Delicia*. His job now was to bring back more and try to bribe another ship or two to help.

When they finished packing, McGinnty walked over.

"I say we just take the ship to Madagascar and start all over," he said, half joking.

"I may take you up on it," Edmund responded.

McGinnty turned to Beckham. "Do your best to fix up *Lucifer's Ghost*, we're going to need her."

"Yes, sir."

The men boarded and waved as they sailed toward the ocean. Edmund watched *Hellspite* get smaller as it sailed away. When it finally disappeared, it was time to prepare.

Lucifer's Ghost was still where they left it. It was anchored close to the cove but laid low in the water. Edmund, Beckham, and a couple of men rowed a longboat up to her. As they tread closer, he noticed the ship was severely damaged. Months of idleness led to ravenous sea worms thriving on the wood, resulting in rotting and major leakage. The seams on the hull were opened up. The sails ripped and shredded.

"Beck, we can't sail this. Look at her—we can't even get it out of the cove."

"We have our work cut out for us, I'll give you that. We need to sail her to have a fighting chance against the Spanish. Well, you and I can't fix her by ourselves, and we're wasting time staring."

They returned to Nassau and recruited slaves from the plantations, soldiers, pirates, and any able body they could get their hands on to pump water from the ship.

They sailed *Lucifer's Ghost* to the shoreline to careen for leaks and general maintenance. They began the laborious task by off-loading as many heavy items as they could. Cannons, kegs of powder, and probably useless cannonballs were hoisted out of the hold and lugged ashore. Men scurried up trees and placed pulleys on the sturdiest of branches. Ropes were slung through the pulleys and attached to the top of the mast to tilt the ship on its side.

The bottom was worse than expected. It was severely worm-eaten. Barnacles built up, and seams between the planks gradually opened, contorting the vessel. The men pounded hammers to sheer off the engraved encrustations on the bottom. They opened the seams to pack fibers and reinforce them with tar.

They nailed wood into the holes, and as a precaution, Edmund ordered men to wrap the ship in very thick ropes to hold it together. They patched triple-thick layers with scraps of leftover sails. He hoped she had one more battle left.

After three days of nonstop patchwork and constant pumping, *Lucifer's Ghost* limped back into Nassau harbor and hovered off the west end of Hog Island. The ship needed five weeks to repair the damage and was a mere shell of itself. Edmund thought that by being moored in the harbor, it would create a scarecrow effect and thwart a Spanish attack. However, if the Spanish came too close, they would realize it as more an ornament with few guns and little mobility.

As strategy was being planned for the island's defense, a sloop was spotted in the distance headed for Nassau. Bells rang as they would for any visiting ship during a time of war. Edmund escorted Sarah to the wharf to check on all the commotion.

"You think it's Spanish?" Edmund asked Rogers who was looking out through a telescope. "Maybe it's giving us a warning."

"Or terms for surrender," Rogers answered.

Behind the lead sloop, the Spanish fleet appeared on the horizon. Three large frigates led the way. A brigantine and seven more sloops followed. Rogers estimated there were 1,000 to 1,500 troops in tow.

He handed the telescope to Edmund. He held it to his eye and quickly pulled back.

"They're flying a bloody red flag."

"What does that mean?" Sarah asked.

Edmund just stared at her, unable to spit the words out.

"It means," Rogers interrupted, "there will be no quarter unless immediate surrender."

CHAPTER 31

SPANISH INVASION

Beckham gazed at Nassau Harbor. He aimed his telescope at the mainland and then the eastern entrance. His head jerked back and forth like it was on a swivel. Edmund tried to follow what he was looking at, but they were too far out. *Lucifer's Ghost* was anchored at the western entrance of Hog Island accompanied by Beckham's merchant ship tied alongside.

"How are we looking?" Edmund asked.

"Well, Rogers and his men are manning the fort. Snipers are set up along the eastern shore, and the *Delicia* is smack-dab in the middle of the harbor, protecting the mainland."

"How about the scarecrows we set up?"

"They look real enough from this distance. I just hope the Spanish think they're real and that we have hundreds more men than we actually have."

"It looks like everyone and everything is in place."

"Imagine soldiers, pirates, and slaves fighting for the same cause."

"To protect Nassau. I just wish we were in there with them. I feel useless out here."

"Edmund, Rogers said it was important to protect the west entrance, that's why he gave you command of *Lucifer's Ghost.* We have to bottleneck them through the east. At least till McGinnty gets back with more men and weapons."

"I guess. I'm just glad they don't know how crippled this ship is."

Lucifer's Ghost was a mere shell of itself. Rogers counted on its size and reputation to intimidate the Spanish into avoiding a confrontation and take the eastern channel. The shallow depth's narrow crossing would make it almost impossible for their bigger ships to invade. Only the sloops would be able to sail through.

The Spanish had landed days earlier and laid camp on the back side of Hog Island. Upon arrival, the townspeople cleared out and fled to the fields and woods. Sarah left with Felina and her child to a hut positioned beyond the sugar fields. Their first attack was a weak effort when they tried to cross the channel in small boats, but sharpshooters waited in anticipation and successfully drove them back.

Beckham paced the deck and threw his hands in the air.

"Why don't they just attack and get it over with? Or better yet, just leave? Instead, they just keep us waiting." He kicked a bucket and water sprayed the deck.

"There's your answer," Edmund said, pointing to the east. Eight sloops were heading toward the harbor. Edmund and Beckham approached the rail and saw the ships sail in two rows.

For what felt like hours, they watched in silence until the sloops sailed close enough and let out a barrage of cannon fire at the town, but their main target was the *Delicia.* Guns fired from Fort Nassau fell short and splashed away from the sloops. The *Delicia* tried to stay within the cannon fire of Fort Nassau.

Edmund watched ships exchange cannon blasts. The fort fired cannon shots, but their targets were too far away to be accurate.

"We can't just sit and watch this," Edmund yelled over to Beckham.

"We have to protect the west entrance."

Edmund knew he was responsible to detain the larger Spanish warships from gaining access to the western entrance, but he was growing impatient watching the Spanish attack Nassau. He screamed over at his crew.

"Load the sails! Let's sail around and attack them from the north."

"We have our orders to stay put," Beckham responded.

"We're doing no good staying here. They'll get pummeled. At least if we help them, they'll have half a chance."

"What about the west entrance?"

"You guard it, we're going in."

Beckham looked around. He saw crewmembers untying his ship. "We're not staying here by ourselves." He ran to the side where his ship was starting to drift from *Lucifer's Ghost* and jumped. "Load the sails! We're going into battle!"

They didn't have time to weigh anchor, so Edmund cut the anchor lines with an axe, and *Lucifer's Ghost* readied itself for battle.

Please, old girl, just have one more battle in you.

Beckham's ship paralleled *Lucifer's Ghost* at first then pulled ahead. Edmund was frustrated with the speed of his ship. He hoped the hasty patchwork they applied would hold.

"We're crawling. We'll never be able to help out like this."

Beckham's ship closed in on the Spanish sloops, but it was built more for cargo than battle. They supplied extra cannons on board, but a one-on-one altercation would be futile. They held their position and waited for *Lucifer's Ghost* to catch up.

With the cannons ready to fire, each of Edmund's crew had their own prebattle ritual. Some prayed, eyes closed, lips moving silently. Some prayed out loud and called on God to watch over them. Others told jokes, showing complete indifference, but it was just an act. Deep inside, everyone's fear was the same; but once the battle started, terror, exultation, even excitement would rush through their blood. He just hoped he had enough men to reload and fire after the first assault. Another concern was most of the men were British soldiers supplied by Rogers. Men not experienced in naval battle. He hoped they could reload the cannons as quickly as the Spanish.

Lucifer's Ghost was still too far out. They watched as Spanish sloops sailed in a line and broadsided the *Delicia*, which couldn't reload fast enough to return fire. Guns from the fort fired but had little effect because of the distance of the ships. Beckham's ship fired erratically.

From the east, a sloop was spotted. The crew cheered as it surprised the Spanish warships at the east entrance with a broadside as it passed them on its way into the harbor. The Spanish fired back as clouds of smoke filled the skies. Edmund watched the battle, and a smirk came to his face. He shook his head.

"McGinnty."

The eight Spanish sloops already established in the harbor split up, and four headed toward McGinnty. *Hellspite* looked like it held more men, and Edmund noticed more cannons on the deck, which caused it to sail lower in the water.

"Let's cut 'em off!"

Hellspite tried to tack out way wide and get the wind for an approach but failed to outangle the Spanish ships. Edmund angled *Lucifer's Ghost* to intercept the line of sloops headed toward McGinnty. Once close enough, he shouted out orders to fire. He needed to take out one ship at a time. The men on the deck emptied their muskets. Cannons exploded, filling the air with clouds of smoke.

The Spanish returned fire on *Lucifer's Ghost,* and cannonballs missed the ship, spraying geysers all around the bow. A second wave of cannons exploded between the two ships simultaneously. Cannonballs caught *Lucifer's Ghost* this time and blew apart the starboard wall and damaged the hull.

Edmund felt a ball flicker his shirt, another shot dropped one of the men. Water poured in as creeks and crevices in the ship failed to hold. He hit the floor at the sound of another round from Spanish cannons. Grapeshot blew apart the deck. Thousands of pieces of metal hissed throughout the deck. Cannonballs exploded from both ships. More shells burst, and the deck was covered with thousands of splinters.

The attack left the crewmen on the deck unable to reload. Men were shouting, others lay on the deck bleeding. Another was struck in the middle of the back and staggered down.

The *Delicia* sailed to join *Hellspite* as it swung around coming from the outskirts. Four Spanish sloops followed. McGinnty used every trick of wind he could muster to get an advantage on the ships. The Spanish turned around to meet McGinnty. They had double the firepower, better sailing ships, and a more seasoned crew.

McGinnty used the wind to parallel the Spanish. The *Delicia* paralleled on the other side and readied for a broadside. Sharpshooters from both vessels tried to pick each other off. Pistols were being fired and reloaded in a minute's time.

Men below decks feverishly loaded and reloaded cannons. They bombarded each other, shredding sails and riggings.

Edmund watched in disbelief. Then as if coming to his senses, he barked out orders to fire. *Lucifer's Ghost* joined the other two ships and surrounded two Spanish ships, catching them in crossfire. It unnerved the Spanish crew. The Spanish looked lost, confused, frightened. Everywhere, the Spanish were shouting, trying to organize their crew. For several moments, none of them shot at the ships surrounding them. By the time they figured they better, *Hellspite, Lucifer's Ghost,* and *Delicia* were bombarding them with shells.

Edmund passed his right hand back and forth in front of his face as choking smoke stung his eyes. He could barely see any of the ships fighting through the musk. Shrieks of pain came from the Spanish ships. The shrieking didn't stop.

Two other Spanish sloops were maneuvering to aim its guns at *Lucifer's Ghost.*

"Hard to starboard!" Edmund yelled, but there was no one manning the wheel. A body lay underneath.

Cannonballs landed at the bow of the ship as geysers shot up out of the water around the ship. A shell blew a huge hole through the center of *Lucifer's Ghost,* rocking it as water gushed in, debris falling everywhere. Edmund barked out orders, but confused looks were the response he received.

Edmund remembered the grenades. Slipping on the bloody deck, he ran to the powder hold and grabbed a boxful. The ship was rocking between cannon blasts it was receiving and those it was handing out. He sprinted back. Chaos ensued. His much-bigger ship was being pounded from all sides by the Spanish sloops.

He grabbed a lantern from the stairwell and threw it on one of the fallen sails. It was immediately engulfed in flames. He lit the grenades and, one by one, tossed them onto the decks of the Spanish sloops, which now surrounded them and were joined by a third.

Guns fired from both sides. The Spanish were faster in reloading their guns and firing. Edmund felt a stinging pain in his stomach. Specks of blood spilled through his shirt. He thought he had been shot, but it was splinters scratching him from the cannons and grapeshot spraying the deck. The sails were torn apart, and the main mast came down, landing hard in the water. One of the Spanish sloops was bearing down on them and rammed the starboard side of *Lucifer's Ghost.* Edmund leaned on the edge and threw a grenade, which exploded on the middle of the sloop's deck. At the same time, a cannonball rocked the ship and sent Edmund over the rail. He reached for the edge but missed and dropped headfirst into the water.

While underwater, musket balls whizzed by Edmund's body. He kicked hard and fast to get under *Lucifer's Ghost* so as not to get picked off by Spanish snipers. His fingers met the sharp barnacles and slimy wood. He walked his hands along the hull and kicked harder. His air was running out. He found the port side and swam to the surface. When his head broke through the water, he sucked in hard, trying to catch his breath, while he gave a quick look around. He was shielded from the Spanish sloop. Another ship was farther away, but it had its hands full, fending off McGinnty.

Edmund watched as *Hellspite* gained the windward side. Normally used for a defense against attacks, McGinnty used the windward side for offense. The Spanish landed a couple of prime shots to the ship's side, several more into the sails and riggings. Edmund winced while he watched, but then it was all McGinnty. He orchestrated the ship and crew like a maestro. He yelled out instructions with rapid gestures while he stood defiantly on the deck, holding on to the center mast, one leg up. Sharpshooters atop the rigging flooded the Spanish ships with musket balls. Cannons pounded each of the Spanish sloops they passed, and the wind blew the smoke from the cannons toward the enemy. The Spanish had no visibility.

The wind caused the ships to tilt. *Hellspite* started to roll with the wind and, on the downward roll, blasted the exposed hull of the Spanish sloops, spreading destruction along the gun ports. When the ship rolled upward, their cannons fired chain shot and grapeshot, destroying the mast, sails, and rigging. McGinnty was masterful in synchronizing the fire. He pumped his fist. He enjoyed it.

Longboats landed in the water thirty yards from Edmund. They were being thrown from *Lucifer's Ghost*, and men followed them into the water as the ship was now on fire and sinking. Sails went up in an inferno, and black smoke provided a screen from the Spanish sloops.

One of the men was drowning by the bow, so Edmund swam over to him. He lifted his head out of the water but couldn't tell if the man was alive or dead. Edmund squeezed his eyes shut, clearing the water from his eyes, and wrapped his arm around the man's chest. He used his hip to lift him above the waterline and sidestroked to one of the longboats, where he was grabbed by his arms and hoisted on board. Men quickly pressed their hands to his stomach. He showed no sign of movement until he shook and coughed up water. Edmund took a deep breath and pressed himself into the boat. He looked at the battle taking place, but there was too much smoke and haze to see who had the upper hand. He also saw *Lucifer's Ghost* dead in the water. But all he could do was watch.

Two of the Spanish sloops were destroyed as their crewmen dove into the water, trying to swim to their other sloops. Soldiers from the *Delicia* picked them off one by one. *Hellspite* followed another sloop, ready to board it. Grappling hooks and pistols were waving, but the Spanish ships sailed north and did not engage. McGinnty maneuvered his sails and prepared for another attack. It never came. The Spanish did not stay around. They turned around and headed past Hog Island and out to sea.

The *Delicia* anchored outside Hog Island to make sure the Spanish weren't coming back. Edmund watched from the longboats as men roared and pumped their fists. Cannons went off in celebration as the ships returned to port.

During the row to shore, Edmund tried to digest what just occurred. *Lucifer's Ghost* was destroyed. The battle seemed to replay in his mind. The long-drawn-out battle was just a blur.

Beckham's ship pounded Spanish troops on Hog Island with fire, and the few Spanish troops that survived were taken prisoner. *Lucifer's Ghost* rapidly filled with water and slowly made its way toward the bottom of the sound. Edmund and the crew continued their long row to the mainland.

Edmund and his men dragged the longboat ashore. He looked up and saw McGinnty jumping off *Hellspite* onto the wharf. He waved over. Rogers and his men raced over from the fort. Beckham's ship docked on the far side.

"You came back just in time," Edmund said to McGinnty.

"We learned from passing seamen the Spanish were almost here. We bought as many weapons as we could and rounded up more men. By the way," he said, pointing to Rogers, "we found out your credit is no good."

"It hasn't been good for a while," Rogers answered with a smirk.

"They outnumbered us. Why did they leave?" Edmund asked.

"They saw the black Jolly Roger," Beckham boasted as he approached.

"Why would they stay?" McGinnty countered. "Why risk a struggle over this place when they can't maintain it? It's not worth losing men or ships. They're just looking for easy British targets to destroy. They thought they had one here, but our response proved otherwise."

McGinnty looked and saw the last remains of *Lucifer's Ghost.* The hull and mast were the only parts of the ship that remained above water, but it was only a matter of time before all traces were gone. He shook his head.

"There'll never be another one like her."

"I lost your ship," Edmund muttered.

"You did good out there. That old ship had no business being in the water, and you still put up a great battle. I always said you'd make a good captain."

"I lost men."

Edmund was mortified. He knew how a bloody attack could haunt a man, how the *Lucinda* haunted McGinnty. He felt a hand grip his shoulder.

"I've lost men also. Maybe we both need to forgive ourselves and move on."

As Nassau celebrated its stand against Spain, British troops, pirates, and ex-pirates alike drank rum, shared hugs, and swapped stories about the battle.

Local women danced toward the nearest men, rows of candles were lit, wax dripping on the ground. A couple holding hands disappeared under a nearby tent.

Beckham, red faced, patted one of the girls on the rump. She quickly turned and threw her arms around him and planted kisses on his cheek.

Edmund stepped close to Sarah, and they worked their way through the crowd. He took hold of her hand as they watched the festivities.

Suddenly an explosion of cheers, whistles, and shouts erupted in the crowd. Two men were wrestling on the ground. The man on top straddled the other's hips and swung wildly. The man below had his arms raised, blocking blows.

Sarah took hold of Edmund's sleeve and started pulling him away.

"This party is getting out of hand."

"Hang on," Edmund replied.

He walked behind the man on top and wrapped his arms around his waist, pulling him off.

"C'mon, guys, we won for God's sake."

Cheers and whistles followed Edmund.

"You tell 'em, Drake," a man yelled, raising both his hands, a mug of ale in each.

Edmund lunged back to Sarah who was clinging to his arm.

"Let's get out of here."

Pats on the back followed him through the crowd. He grabbed her hand and led her toward the wharf.

When they finally pulled away from the noise, the docks were clear. A few boats were tied to it including *Hellspite* at the far end.

"Edmund, we should take Mr. Beckham's offer."

Edmund hesitated. His feeling of contentment had dissipated, and tenseness set in.

"I don't know. Going back to England, we'll be on the run from Killingsworth for the rest of out lives."

"You don't think he'll find us if we stay here?"

"I don't know. Maybe I'm just fooling myself thinking we'll ever be free of him. If we stay here, he'd have to search the whole island to find us. If we go back, he'll have troops everywhere."

"People could sell us out here also. It's amazing what a little gold will do to people. We should go. We have family that would protect us."

As they made their way alongside *Hellspite,* Sarah nudged Edmund and pointed to the ship's stern. McGinnty stood alone, leaning over the edge, staring out toward the water.

Edmund gave her a questioning look.

"Go ahead," she said.

"You won't get jealous?" he said with a sheepish grin.

She gave him a playful slap and pushed him toward the ship. He climbed aboard and lifted her up alongside. McGinnty stared out, ignoring the two as they crept up behind him.

Edmund looked out and saw the object of his trancelike state. *Lucifer's Ghost* was nearly sunk. It leaned heavily on the bow, two-thirds of it underwater. He placed his hand on McGinnty's shoulder and handed him a mug of rum he carried with him from the celebration.

McGinnty sipped it and immediately looked more relaxed.

"To think that ship used to be the *Lucinda*—the unsinkable *Lucinda.* I think of how foolish I was to attack such a ship."

"You won though."

"It was an ego-driven suicide mission. I lost many a good man. I was young and foolish. Now I'm serving my penance."

A yell from behind startled Edmund, but McGinnty never flinched.

"I finally found you. I looked all over, but it figures you'd be here."

Beckham climbed aboard, spilling rum on his shirt as he almost fell on the deck.

"What is it, Beck?" McGinnty asked.

"I think I'm getting too old for this," he answered, trying to catch his breath. "You should be out there celebrating with us. It's amazing. Everyone is talking about you. No one has ever seen anything like it."

"I'll be there shortly," McGinnty said.

Beckham raised his thick eyebrows, grinning. "It's hard to believe. Pirates and soldiers are celebrating as one. A couple of months ago, they would have hanged us."

"One minute we're fighting Spain, the next minute we're at peace. The same thing with France. It just doesn't make any sense," McGinnty said.

"I almost forgot. Rogers wanted me to give this to you. He feels you will need it."

Beckham walked over toward McGinnty. He handed him a scroll. Confused faces looked on.

McGinnty unraveled the document. He shook his head and rolled it back up.

"What is it?" Edmund asked.

"A pardon."

Edmund grabbed him by his arms. "You're free to go back. You have your life back. You can go back to your wife, be with your son, you have wealth for the rest of your life."

Sarah smiled and kissed him on the cheek. "Everything will work out for you."

McGinnty's eyes were glossy. "My boy, it's been almost nine years. My wife has probably remarried."

"Jack, you'll never have to look over your shoulder again."

"Nine years of my life being chased, cursed at, shot at, and now everything's all right."

McGinnty looked at the scroll again and gave a small chuckle. "That bastard, he even commissioned me as a pirate hunter. How strange is that?"

"It doesn't matter. You have your life back. Come back to the celebration. Everyone would want to see you there."

McGinnty stared down at the deck. "You go. I'll be there in a little bit."

"I won't argue with you on that, sir," Beckham said. "My mug needs a refill."

Beckham led them off the ship, and they eased Sarah into the wharf. Edmund threw his leg over and paused. He looked back at McGinnty who pulled out his pardon and stared at it in a trancelike state. Finally, he crumpled the page and went to throw it overboard but stopped. He looked at it again and stuffed it into his pocket, staring out to sea.

CHAPTER 32

HUNTED

Edmund watched Rogers walk through the fields. Stalks were high and thick. Uncut cane stood higher than the men cutting it. The sun scorched down on them as Edmund sucked on sugarcane.

"You're easy to find," Rogers said. "That's not a good thing."

"What's the problem?" Edmund asked.

Rogers wiped the sweat on his forehead with the back of his hand.

"You've become a problem. A big problem. General Pitts sailed into port this morning from Virginia. Word is out about your escapades." Rogers ran his hand through his hair. "You shot a governor. You kidnapped his wife?"

"It's not what you think. She came willingly."

"It doesn't matter what I think. The fact is soldiers are here for you. McGinnty too. When McGinnty bought weapons at the Leeward Islands, he paid with gold doubloons, Spanish gold doubloons recouped from the *Lucinda.* Gold fever has now struck the Caribbean, and people will stop at nothing to find it."

Edmund threw the cane down in frustration.

"Who would have told?"

"Does it matter? It could have been soldiers, pirates, or locals. Maybe even one of your crewmates. Money tests loyalties. My advice is to leave. If you stay here, it's only a matter of time before you're found."

Edmund looked up, jaw open, and shook his head.

"I better let Jack know. It doesn't seem right. We fought for England, and now they're coming after us."

"You're pirates, your time has come. Tell him the privateer commission is good here, but I'd be concerned when leaving."

Rogers escorted Edmund under a palm tree and stood in the shade under the wide-spread fronds.

Edmund pointed to the slaves working in the fields. They cut, bound, and pitched bundles into wagons. Sweat glistened from their black skin. "What's to become of them? They helped defend this place. They should be free."

"It doesn't work like that."

"You and I both know this island would have been burned to the ground if the Spanish had their way."

"What do I tell the plantation owners? They paid for them. They are property. I know they helped save this island, but they're property."

"Let 'em go. Let 'em go with McGinnty. They'll be equals on his ship."

"Ah yes, McGinnty. Somehow it always boils down to McGinnty."

"If they sail with him, they'll be free."

"Free? Do you know the price tag on McGinnty's head? It gets more expensive every day. It's so high now that he's not even safe here."

"What about his pardon? The pardon you signed."

"It's good for piracy, and I'll honor it while he's on this island. Killingsworth may have other trumped-up charges on him."

"Everyone is loyal to him."

"Everyone has a price. Money does funny things to people."

"Not us."

"Don't be so naive."

Edmund nodded. "And the slaves?"

"I'm not going to argue with you. If some of them happen to escape or run off, I promise I won't look very hard for them. Just let them know what's in store if they choose to leave."

Edmund ran into the Shark Den and found McGinnty who was sharing rum and three female companions with Beckham.

"Pitts is here," he yelled, catching his breath.

McGinnty could barely make out what he was saying. Beckham pushed the girl next to him aside and looked up.

"Who?"

"Pitts. They must have gotten wind Sarah and I were here."

McGinnty stood up, furious. "Someone sold you out?"

"I don't know, but we have to leave."

"Killingsworth will never rest until he finds you. Granted he wants me dead, but you took away Sarah. The price on your head is far greater than mine. Come with me to Madagascar, he'll never go that far."

"England is our home. We're going to give it a try."

McGinnty noticed the sincerity in Edmund's expression.

"What else is on your mind?"

"It's Charles. He passed away this morning."

"I'm sorry to hear about that. He was a good man."

"He saved us back at Virginia. I wish we could have saved him. Doc said the infection took over, and he couldn't wake up. He's really broken up about it. He said if he was a real doctor, he probably could have saved him."

"Nonsense. Doc has helped hundreds of men over the years."

Edmund handed McGinnty a piece of paper.

"Charles's pardon?"

"I didn't know what to do with it. Maybe we can bury it with him. He was actually proud of that."

McGinnty stuffed the pamphlet in his shirt and patted Edmund's shoulder. Beckham scratched his chin with his fingers.

"My ship is three quarters filled with cargo. Maybe we can set sail early tomorrow and get you out of here."

Edmund eyes widened. "Beck, I don't know what to say."

"You'll say thanks. We'll load up tonight. They'll probably check every incoming and outgoing ship, so we'll meet you at the eastern end of the island."

McGinnty downed the rest of his rum.

"It's settled. I'll call together the men. When you leave in the morning, we'll sail with you as far as we can. Maybe you'll change your mind about Madagascar before we split up."

Edmund laughed. "Stranger things have happened."

Later that evening, Edmund walked outside of Felina's hut as Sarah wrapped an arm around his back and rubbed it gently. They finished saying good-bye and tried to convince Felina to come with them to meet Jon's family. If that didn't work out, Beckham offered to help support her and claim she was his niece.

"No," she declined. "This is the only home I've ever known, and this is where little Jon will grow up."

"If you ever change your mind, take the first ship out of here," Edmund said.

Edmund left her Jon's share of the money. Since his life was taken, he received a substantial amount in accordance to the articles of the pirate code.

After an emotional farewell, the couple left to pack.

"What are you thinking?" she asked.

"Just about everything we've been through. Everything I've put you through—the pirates, the Spanish, sailing, Ocracoke. I wanted everything perfect for us. I wanted us to have a great life together, and here we are, on the run."

She pushed her forefingers to his lips and smiled.

"This is perfect, we're together."

He leaned over to kiss her.

"Well, isn't that just so sweet?" a voice called.

Edmund looked up and saw a soldier and one of the locals ahead. They stopped in the path ahead of them. He didn't recognize the local, but from the way he was dressed, Edmund figured he was an ex-pirate. Since they arrived from Ocracoke, tensions had risen between McGinnty's crew and locals that were hard-pressed to find money.

"You have a nice little price on your head, Drake. Why don't you come quietly with us so no one gets hurt?" the pirate said, reaching behind his back. He pulled out a six-inch blade. In his other hand, he held a club. His wide grin exposed gaps between his teeth.

"Don't do this. We all fought together against the Spanish."

"And look what we got for it," the pirate said. "Nothing."

"Why don't you sail with McGinnty? Everyone has had success with him."

They both laughed. "He's the next to go."

The soldier worked his way to Sarah and grabbed her arm. Edmund reached for the knife in his belt, but it was too late. The pirate hurled himself down on him and knocked the breath out of him, trapping his right hand against his belly. With his left hand, Edmund caught hold of the man's wrist before he could bash his head in with the club. The pirate's other hand clutched Edmund's face and jerked it sideways.

Edmund rammed a knee up, and the top of his thigh punched between his legs. A second blow scooted him farther up Edmund's body, and with a third blow, he twisted and flung him off.

The pirate still clutched the club, so Edmund kept a tight grip on his wrist and tumbled on top of him, perching on his chest.

Suddenly Edmund let go and took a blow to the face but punched him in the face with a right and a left.

The soldier let go of Sarah and held a pistol to Edmund's head.

"Run, Sarah!"

She looked at him and took off toward the wharf. In the soldier's brief hesitation of whether to run after Sarah, Edmund shoved his foot forward, snapping the soldier's knee and causing his gun to go off. Sarah immediately froze and ran back.

"No!" Edmund screamed.

The soldier held his knee and screamed in agony. The pirate, bleeding from his eye, grabbed his knife and rushed Edmund, grabbing him in a headlock with one hand and holding the knife to his throat with the other.

"Move and you're dead."

Soldiers ran toward them after hearing the commotion. Sarah slipped behind a tree.

"What's going on here?" one of the soldiers yelled.

"We caught Edmund Drake. He shot Lord Killingsworth, and there's quite a bounty on his head."

The other soldier lurched to his feet, unable to put any weight on his left leg.

They signaled Edmund to move ahead, but he struggled to stand still until he was sure Sarah was gone.

Sarah dashed through the woods, dodged a bush, raced through a gap between two trees. She shortened her strides on a downslope, her feet crunching twigs.

Then her foot slipped on a damp rock. Her leg flew up, and she slammed on the ground and skidded. When she stopped, she lay sprawled. Facing the treetops, her chest expanded, sucking air into her lungs. She jumped up and continued on.

Sarah stopped behind a tree and scanned the woods. It was too dark to see anything except a murky glow from the moonlight. She heard voices in the distance, but nothing close.

Looking around, she noticed a space between an old tree trunk and the ground. She bent over and peered into the opening. It could hide her if she squirmed to the back, but if they saw it, she'd be trapped.

Keep going.

She shoved away from the trunk and broke into a run. She dashed as fast as she could, dodging trees and underbrush. Finally, winded and aching, she ducked behind a large bush. She bent over and gripped her sweaty knees, gasping for air. As she leaned back, her legs trembled. Her head fell back, and she closed her eyes, her chest heaving but not as fast.

Sweat dribbled down her face, stinging her eyes. She moved ahead then was grabbed from behind. A hand covered her mouth, and another wrapped around her waist as she was jerked backward.

She squirmed and kicked as he hauled alongside the bush away from the path.

"Shh. Keep still."

She couldn't make out anything but a dark shadow above her. She could feel the man's breath on her neck.

"It's me, McGinnty."

Her eyes widened as the grip on her mouth loosened.

"They have Edmund, we have to—"

"Shh, I know. I overheard some of the locals. They sold him out. When I arrived at Felina's, they were already there. I was lucky enough to follow you through the woods."

"I didn't hear you."

"I've learned to move quietly about. It's a great ally to have in my profession."

"We have to find Edmund. They'll hang him for sure."

"We'll take care of that. First, we have to get you out of here. They have troops all over looking for you two."

"What about you? They're hunting you too."

"As long as I'm on this island, I'll be all right."

They slowly made their way up, and McGinnty led her down a path that led deeper into the woods.

"I'm going to find Beckham. He'll take you to Pirates Cove on the east end of the island."

"Is it safe there?"

"The locals used to hide there when the Spanish invaded here in the early 1700s. There are plenty of hidden caverns and caves there. The trick is getting you from here to Beckham's ship."

They snuck through the woods and toward the back of town. McGinnty saw a man staggering about, ready to fall. The result of too much rum. He ran up to him and helped him toward a secluded area.

"What are you doing?" Sarah asked.

"He's going to help us get you out."

He helped her pull up the man's shirt, and she slipped on his trousers and buttoned them up.

"Tie your hair back, and we need to find you a hat."

Sarah finished dressing and held out her hands. "What do you think?"

"We have one problem," McGinnty said. "You're busting out of your shirt."

He took off his own shirt and cut away the bottom into one long strip.

"Use this and flatten your chest."

She gave him a surprised look.

Edmund opened his eyes. He pushed himself to his hands and knees, but any kind of movement made his body hurt like hell. He touched his face to feel his right cheek twice its normal size. His hair felt crispy in some places, and when he ran his hand through it, specks of dried blood appeared on his fingers.

On his knees, he kept still and let his eyes explore the room. There were no windows aside from a small one on the door. The room was empty except for a filthy blanket and a pile of hay next to it. He leaned up and sat back. He wanted to vomit.

Sarah!

He jumped up and stuck his face as far as he could through the small window and screamed. His head throbbed, ribs ached.

"Hey, take it easy over there," a man said in a thick French accent. The voice came from the room next to him.

To his left, two guards stood, ignoring him. To his right, he located a shadow moving.

"Who's there?"

"You should lie down. Looks like they had a lot of fun with you last night. We saw them drag you in."

"We? Who's we? Sarah, are you in there?"

"Sarah? If she were in here, she'd grant a condemned man his final wish, no?"

Edmund took a deep breath. The room was spinning.

"Who's in there with you?"

"My friend Pierre. My name is Jean Du Buc. How's your head, my friend?"

"Sore as hell."

"It'll pass. If you received the same sentence as us, it'll pass tomorrow."

Edmund grabbed the door. He felt it move a little and tried jerking it open.

"You're wasting your time. Besides, where are you going to go? Soldiers are everywhere."

In frustration, Edmund pounded the door with his fist. He stood for a moment. "Where are we?"

"You don't know?" The Frenchman laughed. "You're being held prisoner in Fort Nassau. They must have beaten you pretty bad last night."

A high-pitched shriek came from the Frenchman's room and then sobbing.

"What's going on over there?" Edmund asked.

"It's my friend Pierre. He's worried about them stretching his neck tomorrow. I told him not to fear. He'll end up pissing himself, and his tongue will swell," Jean said. He sounded amused. "He'll dangle in front of all those people."

"Shut up!" a voice yelled. "Just shut up!"

Edmund walked around the room. His head started to clear up, and he lifted the blanket and dust floated off it to the ground.

"What's your name?" Jean asked.

"Edmund. Edmund Drake."

"Well, Edmund Drake, what are you in here for? Myself, I have been accused of piracy. My friend Pierre, the same."

The sobbing became louder.

"Sorry to hear that."

"Why do you get a cell to yourself, Edmund Drake? Are you special, Edmund Drake?"

Footsteps approached from down the hall. The guards quickly sprung to attention, and Edmund heard orders for them to open his cell.

That has to be Rogers getting me out of here. Thank God.

He heard the guard fumble with the keys by the door and finally fit one in it, and the door flew open.

Edmund's look of anticipation and hope quickly turned to disappointment as General Pitts stormed inside. He grabbed Edmund's jaw with his hand and threw him against the wall.

"Where is she?"

He slammed him again.

"Don't make me ask you a second time."

Edmund's jaw was shut tight as Pitts's fingers dug in deep.

"Go to hell," he managed to mutter.

Pitts took his knee into Edmund's stomach, doubling him over, and he flopped to the ground.

"It's going to go hard on you."

Edmund coughed as Pitts leaned over him, grabbing a lock of hair and lifting his head up. "We'll find her. If we have to search every crevice on this island, we'll find her. Then we're taking you both back to Virginia. His lordship is especially anxious to see you again. This time, there will be no escape."

Later that afternoon, McGinnty approached Fort Nassau. Soldiers held rifles aimed at his chest.

"I'm here to see Rogers."

The guards held their position; but McGinnty, in defiance, marched past them. Guards positioned themselves around him, and finally two stood in front of the entrance.

McGinnty stopped and waved his arms.

"Will someone please let him know I'm here?"

"What's all the commotion out here?" Rogers said as he opened the door. He waved his arms, and the soldiers stepped aside.

They walked up the steps to the top of Fort Nassau. It overlooked the Atlantic Ocean.

McGinnty followed Rogers into his office but stopped short once inside. General Pitts looked up at him.

"McGinnty?" he said, pulling out a pistol. "God has smiled on me."

McGinnty reached for his pistol, but Pitts took aim at McGinnty's chest. McGinnty froze.

"Stop!" Rogers ordered. "He's a privateer, he works for me."

"He's a killer and wanted for piracy in Virginia."

"I have complete authority to pardon any crimes for piracy. I've commissioned him a privateer under the king's name. He fought for this island. Unless you are charging him with any crimes besides piracy, he's a free man."

"You pardoned the likes of him? I'm sorry, sir, but I have orders to take him with me."

"You have no authority here, and unless you want to go against the king's orders, I suggest you lower your weapon."

"You're making a big mistake." Pitts lowered his weapon and leaned closer to McGinnty. Their two faces inches apart. "Your friend won't be so lucky he walked out. We'll gut him like a pig and hang his parts all over Williamsburg." McGinnty didn't take the bait and walked past Pitts to Rogers. Pitts was infuriated. He looked at McGinnty. "Enjoy your freedom now. When his lordship gets here, he'll finish the job he started in Virginia."

As Pitts left the room, he again screamed at Rogers, "A big mistake."

Rogers took a deep breath and lowered his body into a chair.

"What are you doing here?"

"I want to offer my condolences about one of your men. Charles, I believe, his name was."

McGinnty reached into his shirt and pulled out Charles's pardon. He stared at it and threw it on the desk. "Yes, he was a free man. He paid with his life saving me."

"Sorry to hear that." Rogers paused then shook his head. "Jack, what are you doing here?"

McGinnty grabbed a flask of rum without asking and poured.

"I want Edmund Drake pardoned for everything he has been accused of."

Rogers looked at McGinnty. He grabbed a reward pamphlet with Edmund's name on it and held it in front of McGinnty's face. The orders were signed by Lord Killingsworth.

"I can clear him of his crimes of piracy. I can't clear him of attempted murder of a lord governor, kidnapping a governor's wife, and the old charge of murder back in Bristol."

McGinnty chugged the rum and wiped his lips with the back of his sleeve.

"C'mon, you and I both know he's innocent. You've dealt with Killingsworth. You know what scum he is."

"Jack, I just can't pardon that. Edmund is lucky Killingsworth only suffered a flesh wound. When they find Sarah, they'll take them back and hang him. I wish there was something I could do, but I can't."

"Let him go. Release him. Give him his life back."

"Just like that, let him go. I'm in enough trouble saving your ass. Killingsworth will take that as far as he can. You know he'll come after you. You just don't escape his wrath and live happily ever after. And if you're under the delusion of breaking Edmund out, forget it. Pitts has this place surrounded with every man he's got. He has two ships guarding the sea escapes. They're expecting a breakout. They want a breakout for an excuse to knock off every ex-pirate on this island."

"That's the thanks we get. Edmund fought hard for this island, and for what? To be taken back to Virginia and put on display at Williamsburg harbor."

"It would be a huge feather in Pitts's cap to bring back Edmund. Even bigger when he finds Killingsworth's wife."

McGinnty looked out the window toward the wharf and saw gallows being built.

"We have to get him out of his cell for any chance of escape. While he's locked up in here, he's untouchable."

"You don't get it. Edmund is still a wanted man. I just told you the crimes he's accused of. Hell, if I was doing my job, he'd been swinging already. He'd probably be better off hanging here than what I expect they'll do to his body in Virginia."

McGinnty paused. He gazed over at Charles's pardon in bewilderment. "What did you say?"

"I said if I was doing my job, he'd be hanged already. He's still considered a pirate."

McGinnty watched beams hammered together and boards being sawed. Rogers walked up next to him and watched the construction.

"Who are the gallows for?" McGinnty asked.

"A couple of French pirates. You don't know them."

McGinnty picked up Charles's pardon. He rubbed his fingers to his chin.

"When are those pirates being executed?"

"Tomorrow afternoon. With the amount of pirates and ex-pirates on this island, it should cause quite a stir. I'm just lucky French pirates aren't as popular on this island, so any riots will be at a minimum."

"What if there was a way to free Edmund with no risk to you?"

Rogers rolled his eyes. "I don't see a way, but if there was, I'd help you. Don't tell me you have a plan."

"Well, it's so farfetched it just may work. The key is to get Edmund out of his cell before Pitts takes him back to Virginia."

"You think they're just going to let him walk out of here just like that?"

"Yes, and if you'll help us, you'll be the one escorting him out. There's one way out of here, you just said it."

"Jack, one thing. I help you, and you leave this island for good."

McGinnty gave a stern look

"It's nothing personal but you represent piracy, and I've worked too hard to rid the island of it. You're a hero to them, and we can't have that."

McGinnty pulled out his pardon, the pardon Rogers signed for him, and threw it on his desk.

"I'll be gone in two days. Let's give him his life back."

CHAPTER 33

THE DEATH OF EDMUND DRAKE

Rogers, alongside Pitts, led three prisoners outside their cells to the gallows. Six soldiers escorted them. Two Frenchmen, Jean Du Buc and Pierre Pinoche, were first. They were found guilty of piracy and sentenced to hang. Since the defensive stand versus Spain, their sentence was never carried out until today. Edmund Drake followed.

Earlier, when the announcement of Edmund's execution was made, Pitts became infuriated. He followed Rogers around all morning and argued to delay the execution until they found Sarah.

"It's imperative Drake be taken back to Virginia to stand before Lord Killingsworth."

Rogers returned a stern look and bit his lower lip.

"If I put it off or let him go, every pirate will return to their old ways, and I've worked too hard to clean this place up. I need to make an example out of him."

"You haven't even tried him."

"He's been tried and convicted already. Justice moves swiftly down here, unlike what I've heard in Virginia."

Pitts gave him a keen stare. "We demand his body."

"You'll get the body after it hangs for a week at the head of the harbor. I need to make an example out of him, showing we don't condone piracy on this island."

Edmund listened from his cell as the two men argued and tried to make deals over his dead body. He was shackled at the wrists. Pitts was in a state of frenzy.

"What about protection from McGinnty? You realize Drake saved McGinnty from hanging. I'm sure McGinnty will be apt to return the favor. He'll cause some kind of uprising when the execution takes place. You'll need our protection."

"Maybe my men are more competent than Lord Killingsworth's. Besides, I've hanged worse than Edmund Drake."

Pitt's eyes widened, his nostrils flared up.

"Lord Killingsworth is going to have a field day with you if you don't stop this."

The prisoners found out about the sentencing days before, but word spread throughout Nassau like a plague about Edmund. Rogers finally agreed and let Pitts station his men around the harbor and gallows to prevent any disruption. Soldiers were stationed around the harbor, and extra men stationed around the gallows to prevent any disruption.

At four, Edmund and the two Frenchmen were marched in front of a raucous crowd to the gallows. The gallows stood next to the docks. One wooden beam held up by two vertical beams and a raised platform, with a few steps leading up to it. Short stout posts that could be yanked supported the platform, which had to be sturdy enough to hold Edmund, the two Frenchmen, the executioner, and the priest.

During the entire walk, Du Buc talked about what to expect.

"Your tongue's going to pop out. You'll piss yourself."

His words were slurred, the result of drinking a gallon of beer and numerous shots of rum.

Once on the platform, Edmund looked out to the crowd. People celebrated hangings like a holiday, and many tried to cram their way to the front. But soldiers were everywhere, forcing them back.

There was no sign of McGinnty or any of his men. He watched the harbor looking for *Hellspite.*

Was Hellspite *on its way?*

Ships were seen in the distance, jockeying for position to get a good look at the festivities. Two British warships protected the harbor area from any rescue attempts.

On the roofs of buildings, snipers watched the crowd with great intensity. Snipers were also located at each corner. Escape was impossible.

The priest assigned to the execution first approached Du Buc. With his thick French accent and slurred words from the alcohol, he confessed to piracy and a host of other sins including murder, stealing, and adultery.

"And to you, my English captors, I damn you straight to hell!"

The crowd went wild with hoots and howls.

One man shouted, "String up the bastard now."

Another yelled, "I want to see him rot in hell."

Someone else said, "I hope you suffer for a long time, you piece of shit."

The noise was horrific. Rogers walked onto the platform and waved his arms.

"Please be quiet! Silence!"

The crowd simmered down. Despite the priest's plea, Du Buc insisted on dying a Roman Catholic.

Next up was Pinoche who became hysterical when the priest walked up. He stood there trembling. Sweat poured down his face.

"Please, I'll do anything. Don't hang me. Not here, not now." He finally threw up. The priest tried to solicit a confession, but Pinoche begged for mercy.

"You can't do this. Please, I have a family."

Rogers walked up to the priest. "Enough." The priest nodded. With his right hand, he blessed Pinoche and moved on to Edmund.

"My son, is there anything you would like to confess?"

Edmund answered him with silence. The priest asked again and again to repent his sins. He just stared straight ahead, finding Pitts and giving him a cryptic glance. He looked into the crowd, which was mostly local and seemed divided in their views. Half knew or sailed with Edmund and wanted him free. The other half opposed everything piracy stood for and wanted to watch a hanging. It was also this half that was getting frustrated with Edmund's silence.

"Admit what you done, you bastard!" someone yelled.

More shouts and curses erupted from the crowd. Edmund spotted Beckham in the second row. His eyes bulged out in disbelief, tears running down his cheeks.

Other crewmen were gone. The people unknown to him were shouting obscenities at him and drinking excessively. Rogers again waved his arms, and the priest read a few passages, which Edmund ignored. When the priest finished, he blessed Edmund and walked away.

The executioner tied each of the condemned men's arms in the back, pinning their elbows together. He moved each under their noose and onto a block. He tightened the rope around their necks and backed away.

Each of the condemned was allowed a last word. Jean Du Buc cursed at the crowd and promised "vengeance to you all."

The crowd was riled, and fruits and vegetables were thrown at Du Buc, landing on the platform. Rogers restored order once again.

Pinoche pleaded for one last chance. His voice was low and rapid.

"Holy Mary, Mother of God. I beg for your forgiveness, I have sinned . . ."

His knees were shaking, which made the block he stood on wobble.

When it was Edmund's turn, the crowd listened for him to repent his sins. He said nothing and shook his head.

Rogers walked up to each and uttered, "May the Lord have mercy on your souls."

He paused at Edmund and stared at the rope. He outstretched his hand and jostled the rope securely around Edmund's neck and tightened the slack. He pulled back and signaled to proceed.

The executioner first walked behind Du Buc and kicked out the block. People flinched, then shouts and cheers erupted. Du Buc fell six inches, snapping the rope tight. His feet swung wildly, eyes bulging out, until he rocked slowly back and forth. The crowd, almost in unison, let out one big sigh.

Next was Pinoche. He was breathing heavily when the executioner kicked out the block. Pinoche's legs danced like he was running in place. The rope dug into the soft flesh of his throat. His tongue fell out of his mouth, and his neck elongated until his last breath.

Du Buc's face was already a shade of purple. His body started jerking and then nothing. In seconds, he hung limp, his neck stretched twice the size it had been before.

Edmund took a deep breath and stood motionless. Sweat poured down his face and onto the rope as the executioner approached. He developed an unbearable itch in the middle of his back. It could have been perspiration rolling down. He had a strong urge to urinate.

Just breath, keep as still as possible.

He looked up and spotted McGinnty. He sidestepped through the crowd until he reached the cleared area of steps, then ran toward the right corner of the gallows, cutlass in hand. Pitts did a double take and ran after him. He screamed out orders to stop him. Two soldiers tackled McGinnty and wrestled him to the ground. McGinnty pushed himself to his hands and knees and lunged forward only to be intercepted by Pitts, who aimed his pistol at his chest.

"Give me the excuse."

His eyes swept up and down McGinnty. Looking disgusted, he shook his head.

Rogers screamed for order, but the crowd was edgy and started turning into a swaying mob. Soldiers armed with pikes and swords lashed out to keep the crowd at bay, impeding screeching, and fights broke out. Two people were pummeling a local merchant by the side of the gallows.

"I know you're behind this somehow," Pitts yelled to McGinnty. "This time, it's not going to work."

Then he shouted orders to his soldiers to form a straight line, backs to the gallows. They started pushing the crowd back.

People were shoved and bumped into. A lady was trying to kick the shins of a soldier who was holding her off with one arm. Another rode the back of a soldier. People were falling over each other. A man was clinging to a soldier's leg. The noise was horrific. Children were dodging soldiers and yelling. One by one, soldiers pried men apart from each other.

"I'll arrest all of you in the king's name!" Pitts yelled. "Lieutenant, get those men." He pointed to a spot where two men were punching Beckham. The men saw troops approaching and scurried away. Beckham sat up, feeling his jaw.

The platform started shaking. Edmund planted his legs farther apart to distribute his weight more evenly. By doing so, the noose tightened around his neck. He held his breath, let air out slowly, and inhaled. Sweat stung his eyes. McGinnty's words rang in his ears.

"Trust me . . . Trust me."

The executioner saw the ruckus in the crowd and froze. He looked at Rogers who gave a nod, but the executioner still hadn't moved.

Rogers shook his head, walked over, and kicked the block out himself. Edmund dropped. The rope pulled tight. His body dangled, trying hard not to struggle, until finally there was no movement. Pee covered his crotch.

A hush fell over the crowd as they tried to look past the soldiers at Edmund's body. His head slumped to the side. His eyes bulged out. The soldiers continued to push the crowd back.

McGinnty kneed the soldier standing next to him in the groin, causing him to double over. He ran toward the steps of the gallows. Pitts pulled out a pistol and fired. The ball splintered off a beam as Pitts pulled out another pistol. McGinnty ran toward Edmund's body but was tackled by Rogers who pulled a gun to his head.

"It's over."

Two guards grabbed McGinnty and led him away. The crowd watched in utter silence and then began to disperse. The executioner cut down the bodies and laid them on the platform. Doc ran up the steps and knelt next to Edmund. He placed two fingers on Edmund's neck and shook his head.

"It's done."

CHAPTER 34

NEW BEGINNINGS

As dusk approached, McGinnty waded in the water toward Edmund's body, carrying a sack over his back. The first of three tides was set to wash over Edmund's body.

The moon was almost full, and the stars were out.

That's one extremely bright moon, McGinnty thought.

The moon made a silvery path on the water. There was no other light in sight. None from the boats on the water or the docks on the shore. There was a small glow from the lanterns at the entrance of the wharf.

After the execution, McGinnty had been tied up and brought to the same cell that held Edmund. Rogers ordered his release after the execution, much to the dismay of General Pitts, and McGinnty ran down to the gallows.

He watched as the bodies were carried off and brought down the dock. Each was to be tied to a post away from the shoreline so three tides would wash over the bodies—a tradition in all executions. After three tides, they would be hanged where they could be best seen over the harbor to discourage piracy.

McGinnty took a deep breath and glided softly through the water. The water made the sack light. He trembled as if he was freezing, but the water wasn't cold at all. The closer he swam to the body, the more nervous he felt. He let out a small shiver.

He saw Edmund's head stuck out above the surface. His eyes were closed, lips were purple, and the water came up to his chin.

"My dear boy, what have they done to you?" McGinnty whispered. He looked at the other two pirates whose eyes were open and back at Edmund.

Edmund's eyes sprung open. "Get me out of here, I'm cramping up."

"Shh, there are soldiers at the entrance of the dock."

"My body's numb. I'm waterlogged," he murmured.

McGinnty hung the edge of the sack on a nail next to Edmund. He pulled out a knife and cut the ropes.

"Hang in there. I'll have you free in a second."

"I didn't think the vest would hold up."

"I didn't think so either. But it was that or let Killingsworth have you."

Once the ropes were cut from Edmund, he sank. McGinnty grabbed him with both hands and jerked him upward, and he burst to the surface. Water spilled from his mouth. His eyes rolled upward, only the whites showing. He shoved him to the post.

"Just hang on."

"I feel like my neck is broken."

He pulled the limp body and shoved it against the post.

"We have to get you out of these clothes."

McGinnty used the pole for leverage, but Edmund's clothes stuck to him like an extra layer of skin. McGinnty jerked and pulled until the shirt came free. Under Edmund's shirt, he wore a leather vest with three hooks sewn into his collar. McGinnty reached for his knife and cut the vest off. He reached for the sack and propped it next to Edmund.

"I hope this works."

He slit it open, and a corpse appeared. Edmund cringed when he saw Charles's body. He was discolored and stiff. They struggled to switch clothes.

Edmund was too weak. He had trouble staying afloat. Finally, he gave up and wore nothing. He stared at Charles and shook his head.

"I'm sorry, Charles. Please forgive me." Edmund gently patted his cheek.

McGinnty finished placing the clothes on Charles and grabbed Edmund.

"We're not done yet. We have to hope Charles's body bloats and swells beyond recognition, at least for the few moments before they apply the tar on his face."

"I'm lucky we're the same size."

McGinnty wrapped rope around Charles's body and tied him to the post in place of Edmund.

"Let's get out of here. Can you swim?"

"I think so."

They eased out from the dock and out to the sound. McGinnty used a breaststroke, but Edmund started wavering. He swung his arms and sank beneath the surface. McGinnty swam back. He swept the water with his right hand until he found Edmund's head. He reached lower, grabbing his shoulders, and jerked him till he burst through the surface. Edmund gasped for air.

"Let's try this again," McGinnty said and turned Edmund on his back. He threw one arm around his chest and placed him on his hip. He used his other arm to sidestroke out into the harbor.

"You're going to be fine. Sarah is waiting for you at the cove."

Edmund forced a grin.

They made it to a nearby fishing boat where McGinnty's men were waiting. McGinnty pulled Edmund's limp body to the stern of the boat. A couple of men jumped in and helped lift Edmund over the rail. Another from the boat grabbed beneath Edmund's armpits. The boat wobbled as they lifted Edmund. McGinnty released his hold and pushed Edmund's rear end. His legs flew upward, and he dropped onto the boat.

Breathing heavily, McGinnty pushed himself onto the boat and was quickly grabbed by one of the men who gave him a quick pull forward. He sprawled onto the deck and stood over Edmund, shivering. He briskly rubbed his hands together for warmth, but it didn't seem to help much. The boat moved along silently except for the murmurs of water lapping the hull.

A couple of warm blankets were thrown on Edmund as McGinnty rubbed his legs. A weak smile came to his face—a tired smile, a smile of relief.

McGinnty slouched back and looked at Edmund.

"I must say, when you pissed yourself, that was a fine touch."

Edmund smirked and coughed up some water.

"Not my finest hour I can assure you."

McGinnty patted him on the leg and waited for the ship to sail and transfer the men to *Hellspite*, which was now fully stocked, and sail it to the cove.

They weighed anchor and sailed to the eastern corner of the island to meet up with Sarah and Beckham.

Early next morning, a nervous Connor Beckham waited as *Hellspite* arrived at the rendezvous point at the cove. Longboats were rowed toward the shore, and he watched McGinnty at the forefront of the first boat.

He spent a sleepless night, waiting for the crew to meet up with them. He thought of Sarah who slept through the night. He didn't have the heart to tell her what he witnessed. He would leave that for McGinnty.

The vision of Edmund's body dangling from the gallows stayed in his mind and guilt that nothing could be done. McGinnty failed in his attempt to rescue him, and when the riot broke out, it was all Beckham could do to get out of there in one piece and sail to the cove.

Might as well get it over with.

He walked over to wake Sarah up. She greeted him with a soft smile and then gave him a questioning look.

"I'm the one that just woke up, but forgive me for saying you look like you didn't sleep a wink."

"I didn't. I just wanted to tell you McGinnty is sailing in. They should be landing as we speak."

"Edmund!"

She quickly jumped up and rushed toward the beach. Beckham shook his head and lurched forward. He ran his hands through his hair and staggered behind her. He watched her at the shoreline, waving her arms at the men rowing toward them.

"Poor girl," he muttered. "Leave the bad news for McGinnty to tell."

Beckham had carried out his orders to have his ship loaded with cargo acquired from Port Royal and Leogane. He would have much explaining to do back home if customs found a chest of gold coins from the *Lucinda*, so he bought goods with his share.

As the boats landed and scratched along the sand, Sarah greeted them at the water's edge. Beckham turned his head and walked back to camp. He would wake his men that were scattered along the beach in tents and have them ready to sail then he paused.

There's no need to rush back now with Edmund gone.

He lay on his blanket and stared at the sky. He wasn't ready to deal with McGinnty yet.

What happened with McGinnty yesterday! He always comes through but not this time. Is he going to tell her about Edmund?

He started to doze.

"Get up, Beck!"

McGinnty greeted him with a warmhearted smile and then gave him a questioning look. Beckham stayed put.

"C'mon, we have a long voyage planned and new quests to conquer."

Beckham was annoyed but kept silent. McGinnty fell to one knee next to him and gave him a pat.

"Beck, everything is all right. Everything turned out all right."

He lifted himself to his elbows. "How can you say that? How can you be so smug when one of our friends just died?"

"That's because no one has died," a voice said, walking behind McGinnty.

Beckham squinted, but the sun blocked his view. A shadow walked toward them. His mouth opened wide. "It's a ghost! I saw you yesterday. You were hanged. You're dead!"

Edmund smiled with Sarah wrapped around him.

"Almost dead. About as close as you can get."

"I'm sorry, Beck. I didn't know you would show up," McGinnty said. "I thought you were going to be here waiting for us. We didn't have time to fill you in."

"I saw him. Doc said he was dead." He closed his eyes and looked upward. "Doc."

"He was in on it, but the key was Rogers."

"How?"

Edmund looked at McGinnty. "Why don't you tell him? It was your plan."

McGinnty smiled. "Rogers couldn't let Edmund go back to Virginia, so he convicted him for piracy. We felt if Pitts and his men see Edmund hanged, that means he won't exist anymore. Rogers bought into the plan, literally."

"You bribed him," Beckham asked.

McGinnty nodded.

"How much?" Edmund asked.

"More than you're worth, Drake," McGinnty answered with a smirk. "More than you're worth."

"How did you pull off the hanging?"

"That was the tricky part. First, we fit a vest tightly around Edmund's waist with three hooks attached at the collar. If the executioner managed to touch them, we were sunk. Second, we had to have Rogers in on it and nonchalantly place the rope around them."

"The worst part for me was when the block was kicked out. I thought for sure it wouldn't hold," Edmund said. "That was the longest six inches in my life."

"Pitts was expecting us to break him out, and we created such a diversion. They concentrated more on us than the actual hanging. They saw Edmund hang but never had a chance to view it up close."

"Then you had Doc declare him dead. But won't they come looking for you when they find your body missing?"

"It's not missing," Edmund said, facing the sand. "We tied Charles to the post."

"Charles?" Beckham gave a sign of the cross.

"We knew we'd get a late high tide, so we switched the bodies that night. Poor Drake here was completely waterlogged."

"Will they recognize him?"

"No. After the third tide, which occurs late tomorrow night, Rogers is going to have his men tar the body to preserve it. No one will be able to tell the difference between Charles and Edmund."

Beckham placed both hands on his head. "You can't make this up!"

The two ships were packed and ready. Both were joined at the side by two grappling hooks with *Hellspite* aimed at Madagascar and Beckham's ship pointed toward England. Edmund was talking to Sarah and Beckham when he spotted McGinnty gazing over some maps, probably of the South African coastline.

McGinnty looked up, startled. Then he shook his head, walking over, and jumped on board. McGinnty joined Beckham's crew for the final time.

"It's not too late to come with me," he said with a wide grin. "I'll make you my quartermaster."

Edmund smiled, and the two clasped hands.

"Sounds tempting, but we're going to take our chances back in England. Sarah and I are going to be married."

McGinnty laughed. "I'm not a bit surprised. Maybe a little surprised at you going back to England."

"We're going to try and slip back into society. She has relatives up north, and maybe we start a new life there."

McGinnty's outstretched arms brought the couple together.

"One last toast," he said as Beckham walked over with mugs of rum.

"What should we toast?" Beckham asked.

"New beginnings," McGinnty answered.

"Yes, a new beginning," Edmund repeated with a smile.

They clanged their mugs and drank, and a sense of sadness came over Edmund. He knew he would never see his friend again. His smile faded, and he looked at McGinnty.

"I don't know what to say," Edmund said. "I mean, I guess this is good-bye. We've been through so much all these years."

"I still remember when you first came onto my ship. You were a lost sea dog. You've come a long way as a crewman, as a person, as a friend."

"I don't know how to thank you."

They embraced. McGinnty reached into his vest and handed over Charles's pardon.

"In case there are any problems at customs, but never lose sight of who you are."

Edmund nodded. "I wish you the best."

"There's a new life awaiting you," McGinnty said and turned toward Sarah. "For the both of you."

"Don't worry, I'll take care of him." Sarah hugged him and kissed him on the cheek. "Thanks for everything."

Beckham walked up.

"It's been an honor and a pleasure, sir."

"Beck, get them home safely. That's my final order."

Beckham reached over and grabbed McGinnty's hand.

"Good luck to you, sir. You're the best I ever sailed with."

"You too. Mr. Beckham, you will be sorely missed. Godspeed."

McGinnty jumped over the rail and onto *Hellspite*, barking out orders. Men unhooked the two ships, and they slowly drifted apart.

Edmund watched with Sarah wrapped around him as *Hellspite* became smaller and smaller.

After three tides, Charles's body was bloated and pasty. They carried him to the pier and tarred his face to preserve it—a custom only awarded to the most ardent of pirates. His body was fitted with an iron giblet that lay open on the ground. They squeezed Charles's body in and hammered the cage shut. He was then hung at the head of the harbor for all to see. He served as a warning for all those that chose the pirate way of life.

EPILOGUE

The vicar held out a small velvet box. "You may need this. I confiscated it from your house when the troops were raiding it. It belonged to your mother."

Edmund opened it up. "Her wedding ring. In all the commotion, I completely forgot about a ring."

"I figured you might. Everything was so rushed."

They stared atop Crescent Hill and watched a breathtaking view across several miles of fields and marsh. An early-morning sun shone through a small cover of clouds and beat down on the back of Edmund's neck. A slight breeze tossed the long grass and surrounding flower beds.

"What do you think will happen to us?" Edmund asked.

The vicar paused and grabbed Edmund's shoulders. "There's no telling. I do think everything will work itself out in due time. I mean, you had no idea how upset we were when we heard your body was quartered and hung all over Williamsburg as a trophy."

"Poor Charles. They thought he was me and hung him in front of the harbor. I'm sorry for putting you through that."

"You did what needed to be done. I hope Killingsworth doesn't look as hard for Sarah. I think he's spreading rumors she was killed by McGinnty and his pirates." The vicar shook his head. "To think you were held captive by that cutthroat makes me shudder."

Edmund smiled. He wanted to explain the vicar was wrong about McGinnty, but who would understand? To England, he would always be a rogue.

"I feel bad for Woodes Rogers. Word is he's being relieved of his governorship. He's a good man. I just hope Killingsworth wasn't the reason. I hate the feeling he got away with everything."

"Edmund, what do you want? Revenge? You have Sarah back. Enjoy what you have and this day forward. He'll get his."

Edmund shrugged. "You're right, as always."

"Word is he's under investigation for his involvement in the South Sea Company. You may not know this, but pirates captured the company's ship. It was probably that rogue McGinnty."

Edmund shook his head as if he didn't know what the vicar was talking about.

"Anyway, when news got back here, the stock plummeted. Now there are questions about how legitimate the company really is. People have lost thousands on it. Killingsworth will have his hands full trying to explain his involvement in a crooked company."

"Yeah, but it would have been nice to take him out while I had the chance," Edmund muttered.

The vicar shook his head.

"Hey, this is a happy occasion. Let's get this ceremony going."

Edmund looked over at Sarah. She looked lovely in her orange and white silk dress. Now was the moment Edmund waited for his whole life.

"And now you may kiss the bride."

After the pronouncement, the vicar exhaled in a way that carried the fumes of brandy, which brought Edmund out of his daze. Mrs. Graham pressed her palms together like a delighted child. She had watched the ceremony with great interest even though it had been ages since she'd seen Sarah and Edmund.

Edmund's embrace of Sarah was tight, and when he finally pulled away from her lips, he wore a wide grin.

Edmund scarcely heard a word of the vicar reading the prayer book during the ceremony. Even though the garden was empty—except for Sarah, the vicar, Mrs. Graham, and him—he was still nervous. When they had to kneel, Sarah had to give him a gentle nudge. He knew the ceremony was sacred and important, but his heart was beating too fast for concentration. In a couple of hours, he would be leaving the land of his childhood and start a new life in a country he hadn't seen in years. The prospect was terrifying until the moment he gazed into her eyes, so full of love and reassurance.

She placed her arms around him. He felt her strength flood into him. With Sarah by his side, he could suffer the worst of what the country had to offer. He could hide all his fears and build a fine future for the both of them.

Kissing her, he made that silent vow.

The vicar leaned in and kissed Sarah's cheek.

"I know everything will work out for you two. I just wish you weren't leaving. God how I wish everything could be as it was."

Edmund wrapped his arm around Sarah as Mrs. Graham kissed her on the cheek.

"Oh, I do wish you both Godspeed and much happiness. A long life too," she added as tears welled her eyes. She gave a big hug to Sarah.

The vicar stepped up to Edmund and extended his hand. "Take care of yourself, especially the first few months. Don't trust anyone you don't know."

Their clasp was firm and long. They embraced.

"Thanks for everything. I'm going to miss you," Edmund said.

"You keep in touch. Of course, I know you won't be able to do it right away. Other things occupy a man who's just married."

"I'm sure counting on that."

They both laughed. Sarah finished embracing Mrs. Graham one final time. She wiped away a tear and said teasingly, "That sounds wicked."

Edmund grabbed both of Sarah's hands.

"Happy?" he asked.

She sighed. "Blissfully. I never thought we'd reach this moment."

They loaded up the carriage, and Edmund lifted Sarah on board. The vicar's eyes turned misty.

"Where will you go?"

Sarah smiled and turned toward Edmund.

"Madagascar."

LaVergne, TN USA
03 November 2010
203354LV00005B/24/P

9 781450 023337